# SEMPITERNAL

# SEMPITERNAL

By Yashodhara Singh

PARTRIDGE

A Penguin Random House Company

**To order additional copies of this book, contact**
Partridge India
000 800 10062 62
orders.india@partridgepublishing.com

www.partridgepublishing.com/india

# CONTENTS

# ACKNOWLEDGEMENTS

A book can never reach its completion, without the undeterred assistance, guidance and help of a handful, without whom the project would remain a dream. There is a vision that is dear to each writer, that can begin by putting pen to paper; but, to make that vision a reality, there are angels sent for that extra special sparkle. That is who you all are for me..that extra special sparkle.

To begin with, I thank all of you readers who have made my journey as a writer as exciting as the books I create for you, books which you can enjoy, to be passed on as nurturers of emotions that personalize our very beings.

A bouquet of thank you to my mother, Mrs. Mita Poddar; who showers affection despite all my whims and eccentricities. She is the guiding force into making me stronger than I was yesterday. A heart of gold, a creative mind, a soul that never tires… I adore and admire you.

My father (Wg.Cdr.DD Poddar), my brother (Lt.Cdr. Debashish Poddar)…I honour your memory with a smile and a tear, knowing you watch over me and mine. My work is your legacy, as I progress over time… to be passed on to all those, who hope to believe in the goodness of man.

Mitsy Playmates, owned by Mrs. Mita Poddar, is a one-of-a-kind, one-woman-run business, that has her creating cloth dolls that cannot be found or replicated anywhere in the world. She was kind enough to design a whole new doll line called the 'Sempiternal Collection of Mitsy Playmates', for which I am grateful.

A heartfelt thank you to Navtej Singh, who just like in 'Braids-The Beginning' furnished pictures of Rajasthan taken by him, to be used as collages for 'Sempiternal'. I cannot thank you enough, for making the visual treats available, for my books.

Heartfelt thanks to Puneet Kochhar & Bobby Sood, founders and directors of Studio One, the famous menswear brand that ranges from ethnic to formal and semi-formal western wear. A special thanks to Geeta Joshi for all the assistance she provided as well.

Many thanks to Vidushi Sanguri and her brand Buckchoo.com, that designs and customises real gemstone jewellery certified by the international gem lab. Her pieces are as exquisite as the mesmerizing lady she herself is.

My sister, Sharmishta Basu, owner of B&G Salon, one of the best salons in Agra, an almond-eyed deer who never ceases to amaze me with her imagination and creativity. You are one of my best friends since I can remember. Thank you for the cover author pic original and the shoots that followed thereafter.

A big thank you to the team at Om Studio, led by the owner- Ranjit Bhuiyan. Rajkumar helped in finalizing the cover of this book, as well as sorted out all the collages at the end to my idea of perfection.

The timeless Indian beauties, Krishna Basu (my grandmother), Mita Poddar(my mother), Aditi Mazumdar Dhar, Devopriya Bhelki Miller (my aunt), Vidushi Sanguri, Smita Rai and Naina Dolly....your grace could weave melodious tunes, floating through time.

An eternal thank you to my children - Vikramaditya and Vasundhara, who, at such an early age have understood their mother's needs to follow her heart. They are the compassionate and large-hearted jewels I adorn my motherhood with. May you have a chance to follow your hearts too one day.

Last but not the least, I thank the inspiration to all my books, Raja. You make me believe in me when I falter at the choicest of moments. What we have, we know. You have encompassed my entire being and given me all I needed to write unendingly. I thank you for letting me live my dream, my passion...as you are indeed my dream, my passion...forever.

Many thanks to my soulmate for designing the cover, helping me decide the title of the book, and writing the poem exclusively, to enrich the text content of the pages in Sempiternal. You bring out the best in me, as ever. Thank you for being my reason to smile as I rest at nights, assured the next day brings a better, brighter hope.

# PREFACE

Many of us have attempted to define what true love is. Everyone has their own rendition, of which even fewer have actually experienced how it feels. There is a constant requirement of consistent deliberation, when one expects an emotion as fragile as love, to grow into unconditional companionship.

Howsoever one may attempt to manipulate timings, circumstances; love will come to only those, who aren't searching to be acknowledged. The canvas of life has colours which can only be filled, if one knows what would suit the painting best.

The spectrum of choice is something only the one who holds the brush, namely us, has the right to choose from. It is imperative, that each stroke will guide us to the chosen path of destiny, that awaits us all.

The process of creating the journey, is far more quintessential than the destination, for that defines who we have chosen to become. The highest order that can be asked of any of us, is whether we have it in us, to love at least one other human unconditionally.

It is a gift most of us choose to be frugal with, for to trust would imply to remove our armour, making us prone to reason why true love is rare to find. Once it is found, there are yet several reasons why it could walk out of one's life, as smoothly as it had waltzed in.

Nurturing what one has, treasuring it at every moment, is the only way to keep it alive. Sempiternal was never planned, just like meeting the love of my life once again, wasn't either. It is said that surprises in life often come as a pleasant breeze meant to be taken in, like a breath of fresh air.

'Braids-The Beginning' was about the life of the Prataps, the Chands, the Cottons and the Anands; the myriad of ways in which they acted, or reacted to situations that presented themselves; how their lives kept getting more entwined, over time.

Sempiternal is the sequel to Braids-The Beginning, that focusses on the lives of the next generation; whether they hold the flame of honour, tradition, love, respect; or whether they choose to let life take them wherever they had to go in limbo, remains to be seen.

Each character has emotions that justify his or her actions, at that point of time. There are more than one truths in every situation, more so when the lives of several are involved. Needless to say, that the web of deception doesn't always have an evil twist to it.

It is our perception that sees what we wish to believe. Letting yourself sway repeatedly is the repetition of an error, which skews our points of view. Holding it against one is as bad as the one who attempted to deceive.

There are heroes in real life, resting within us. The characters in Sempiternal have proven that the same person is capable of emotions, varying from good to questionable. The scale to measure such acts depended on who the characters were dealing with.

A good husband could be an inconsiderate boss. A manipulative woman could be a doting mother too. The word 'Sempiternal' in itself implies perennial, everlasting, never-ending. True love is Sempiternal for those who are willing to welcome it in their lives, treasure and nurture it while it's there. Love travels through time, space, and yes… generations as well.

One could fall in love with anyone the heart might fancy. The real challenge is to allow yourself to experience it, rather than fearing the 'what if' of a heartbreak. The act of the plunge in itself though is a feeling worthy of an experience, to be carried forth into the lesson of a lifetime.

India is a land where majorities of the people pride in the women who are classic, timeless beauties. Bassi, the village from where one such nomad Suhani's story originated, is one of many such villages, where beauty is not just visible on the outside; but the humility, simplicity and natural enigma of being a woman, is enhanced over time.

Walk into this journey of the Sempiternal…take away a bit of the flavour of India. There is a lot to learn from everyone and everything in this book, that I present to you under the genre of 'Human Relationships'.

To begin with, here is what I got from my soulmate, as a complete surprise. The poem you are about to read, is what he wrote in less than five minutes. It may not be a masterpiece for some, but it is straight from the heart and means the world to me. I had to include it to honour our love.

Enjoy and happy reading!
Love and stay blessed,
Yashodhara Singh

# SEMPITERNAL

Some memories are imprinted in the mind,
others carried in the heart;
while time's vagaries override the mind,
what's carried within is never torn apart.
Sometimes the milestones of one's life,
seems past and forever gone;
But to the lilting joys that their memories give,
one is but always inextricably drawn.
The feelings within are repressed and throttled,
with the unrelenting passage of time;
The music of repudiated love though remains,
forever a dulcet and melodious chime.
Time moves slow for those who wait,
and rather quick for those who fear;
But for me time stopped still the moment,
I knew I was in love with you my dear.
I failed to unshackle myself from primeval binds,
and braced the vice grip of tradition;
And condemned myself and you my love,
to a lifetime of emotional perdition.
Years went by and so did I,
in an interminable and meaningless pursuit of bliss;
I tried endlessly to find worth and motivation,
but something was a touch amiss.
The revolving door of time and people,
transformed the panorama just a bit;
Distracting the heart from its intimate contents,
till emotions took another brutal hit.
Never the eternal optimist… I was certain,
love needed banishment from the mind;
With every relationship I did comprehend,
there was to be a barter in the grind.

Picking up the pieces of a broken life,
I was at the crossroads yet again;
Realizing how cruel the world could be,
never to trust anyone, and just follow my grain.
The whack of Providence did me good,
for it provoked an earnest search within;
That is when I realized, time had been imprudently lost,
but eternity was just about to begin.
Not knowing what the future held in store,
I collected myself to start anew;
Though I had lost almost everything I held dear,
I still had a vivid recollection of you.
Intending to live out my tenure on earth,
hopelessly damned as a washout of a man;
I never knew the Lord up there was busy,
brewing another enigmatic plan.
Sometimes I wondered where you were,
and whether you were happy and warm;
Though I was sure that you would have won over,
all those around you with your charm.
Informed that you were taken care of,
and secure in your happy life;
I thanked the Lord that he had,
graciously saved you from any strife.
I was blessed for a moment though,
with a transient meeting among some friends;
We talked, spoke, exchanged pleasantries,
but had no freedom to make amends.
Having lost the chance to know even where you were,
a thought I did not lament;
I held that moment close to my heart,
it was eternity's tiny but prized fragment.
Fate though willed otherwise,
and we too were destined to speak about our pain;
And this time we realized somewhere down the line,
our roads were going to cross again.

We've built our little fortress of togetherness steadily,
it is not a castle in the air;
What the future may hold for us,
we don't know and really don't care.
Proud of the purity of our bond,
we stand together on the world stage;
Your deep love gives me strength,
loving you deeply gives me courage.
Unmindful of the twist and turns,
that the journey of our life may take;
I promise you this time,
you shall never be left behind in the wake.
Having lost and then found you in this cruel world,
I shall never let go of you now;
And for the manner in which you kept our love alive in your heart,
I respectively bow.
We earnestly strive to realize our shared hopes,
standing side by side;
Our love is not an impetuous passion,
it's a commandment by which we abide.
So come with me and follow your dreams,
as we tread our endearing path;
And touch with joy and happiness,
the lives of all we come across in the swath.
You are impermeable testimony,
of a glorious flame that burnt eternal;
That while suffering is ephemeral,
true love is a deep-seated emotion…Sempiternal!
Love for keeps…Raja

# CHARACTERS

## IN DELHI

### THE PRATAPS

➢ ARJUN PRATAP: Owner of the Dare To Dream or DTD Gallery (a photo gallery that displays theme-based pictures on a periodic basis) in Delhi; Suhani's husband and father to A.J and Dan.

➢ SUHANI PRATAP: Owner of Maya's Reality (an exclusively-handcrafted silver jewellery line) in Delhi; Arjun's wife and mother to Ajju and Dhanush.

➢ A.J, AJJU, or ARJUN CHAND: Suhani's eldest and Arjun Pratap's step son.

➢ DAN or DHANUSH PRATAP: Arjun and Suhani's offspring ; A.J's younger brother.

### THE ANANDS

➢ SAN or SANGHARSH ANAND: Arjun Pratap's best friend; co-owner of Anand Creations (a well-established apparel house) in Delhi.

➢ NAL or NALINI ANAND: Sangharsh's wife and co-owner of Anand Creations.

➢ ANDY or NANDISH ANAND: One of the twin offsprings of Nalini and Sangharsh; works in DTD gallery as an assistant photographer under the keen eye of Arjun Pratap.

➢ ANNIE or SARVANI ANAND: One of the twin offsprings of Nalini and Sangharsh; Head Designer at Anand Creations.

## THE COTTONS

➢ RAMONA RAI COTTON: Arjun Pratap's ex-wife; ex-owner of DTD gallery; mother to Mia and Diana Cotton.

➢ MIA COTTON or ARADHANA: Elder daughter of Ramona; Diana's elder sister.

➢ DIANA COTTON or JIYA: Mia's younger, half-sister; daughter of Gerard Cotton and Isabella.

# OTHERS IN DELHI

➢ MR. GUHA: Manager at DTD gallery; Bantu's uncle.
➢ BANTU or BRIJESH KUMAR: Mr. Guha's nephew; employee at DTD gallery.
➢ MOHAN: Chauffeur of the Prataps.
➢ DR. KRISHNAN: a doctor at Lilavati Hospital detailed to look after Ramona.
➢ GURU: The doorman at Swarn Niwas (the residence of the Prataps).
➢ SHANTI: the faithful maid of the Prataps.
➢ MR. PATIL: Dr. Shekhawat's lawyer.
➢ MR. SAHU: Ramona's lawyer.
➢ MR.YADAV: Arjun Pratap's lawyer.

# IN BASSI, RAJASTHAN

## THE CHANDS

➢ CHAUDHARY AKASH CHAND: *Chaudhary* of the villages of Bassi and Nagri; Bindiya's husband and father to Vansh and Leenata.
➢ BINDI or CHAUDHRAIN BINDIYA CHAND: *Chaudhrain* of the villages of Bassi and Nagri; Akash's wife and mother to Vansh and Leenata.
➢ VANSH CHAND: Elder son of Akash and Bindiya; also known as *Chote Thakur*; Leenata's elder brother.
➢ LEENATA CHAND or LEENA: daughter of Akash and Bindiya; Principal at Gurukul (the village school); Vansh's younger sister.

## THE SHEKHAWATS

➢ DR. SHEKHAWAT: renowned, large-hearted, lonely, wealthy doctor at Jaipur.
➢ ABHI or ABHIMANYU SHEKHAWAT: the doctor's only son ; assistant to Suhani Pratap at Maya's Reality.

# OTHERS IN BASSI, RAJASTHAN

- ➤ TARA: Giriraj's wife; mother to Viren and Malika.
- ➤ GIRIRAJ: Tara's husband; father to Viren and Malika.
- ➤ VIREN: Offspring of Giriraj and Tara; Malika's elder brother.
- ➤ MALIKA: Offspring of Giriraj and Tara ; Viren's younger sister.
- ➤ RATI SINGH RANA: an orphan at Bassi, Dhara's elder sister; a common village belle with an uncommon destiny.
- ➤ DHARA SINGH RANA: Rati's younger sister.
- ➤ SURAJ: The jeep driver at the Bassi Wildlife Sanctuary.
- ➤ GOPAL *CHACHA*: The owner of the sole block printing house in the area of Bassi, as well as surrounding it.
- ➤ VIJAY: Gopal *Chacha*'s son.

# IN JAIPUR, RAJASTHAN

- ➤ JAI PRAKASH: the man who sold fresh livestock to villagers.
- ➤ NEERAJ: Akash Chand's cousin' one of the *Panchayat*(village council) members.
- ➤ RAKIB CHAND: The man at Dr. Shekhawat's hospital in-charge of sanctioning loans to the needy.

# ABROAD

- ➤ GERARD COTTON: A rich Englishman who died in a mystery-laced road accident with his mistress; father to Mia and Diana.
- ➤ ISABELLA JONES: The nurse who was hired to take care of Ramona many years ago; mother to Diana; died in a car crash with Gerard.

# CHAPTER ONE

The uniqueness of a city is not just the places it offers for visitors to pick curios from, or fast-food joints from where a quick bite can satiate the rumbling belly. The people of the city participate in giving a city its character as well. Delhi, as a metro is divided into the New and the Old.

The more people that settled around its outskirts, the wider Delhi expanded. Large-hearted and temperamental as she is, the city has many galleries to flaunt. Call them the outlet for the artist who wants to express through a chosen art form, if you may.

DTD or the Dare to Dream gallery at Chanakyapuri was one of the landmarks of the area. The outside was exactly the same as before, except the paint had to be redone annually due to the harsh weather.

The expansion of the gallery was done to accommodate the growing staff, along with the labyrinth of picture displays, tastefully accentuated by concealed lighting. Arjun Pratap liked to keep the colour coordination simple. His two sons A.J. or Ajju, and Dhanush or Dan, loved experimenting with them.

What evolved was something that looked artistic with laser streams of paranoid flavour. "The bi-annual report is not bad, but we could do better" Arjun said, taking off his glasses after his long, hard look at the file that maintained daily reports of his gallery.

"Agree with you on both the points, *Baasa*. But there seems to be a rut. Plus, the competition is paralytic at times. An average of a gallery every five kilometers? Come on!" A.J., the second-in -command to Arjun, added.

They both looked at the 'Hunter' - Dhanush; A.J.'s younger brother, who was also the one in charge of scouting ideas for display at DTD. "I'm burnt out. I think I need a break, Dad. Nothing appeals to me anymore. It's like I got brain flu!" Dhanush said, annoyed at his own admittance.

"*Baasa* not Dad, please Dhanush. You know how our mother keeps reminding you of that. Now listen. You have ten days to come up with an idea that's going to be different, new and appealing enough for the funds and customers to keep coming. Your break can wait. DTD's business can't" reprimanded A.J.

Arjun Chand was known as A.J. to friends, Ajju to his parents and some family members. He was tired of being his father's mouthpiece, when it came to Dhanush. Their father never spoke a harsh word to either, that bordered anything beyond stern.

Dan wasn't afraid of his elder brother, but respected him nonetheless, immensely. He was the one who would rescue him from innumerable situations, some of which their parents were oblivious to, till date.

The Manager of DTD, Mr. Guha, barged into the conference room, before Dan could commit to the deadline, or otherwise. "Sorry to disturb, gentlemen, but Mr. Pratap must see this!" he blurted, hastily switching on the LCD screen into life.

The sports channel was telecasting budding equestrians, of which one was familiar to all of them. "Nandish Anand handles his horse, like it was an extension of himself. A definite champion in the making…" the broadcaster was still singing praises, when Dan snatched the remote from Mr. Guha's hand and turned the box off.

"Are you aware we are in a meeting that was called to discuss the future of DTD, of which you also are a part, Mr. Guha?" asked Dan, defiantly glaring at the man. "Yes, but.." "Unless there is anything pertaining to the gallery, refrain from disturbing our meetings in the future! Understand?"

Mr. Guha looked at Arjun helplessly, who dismissed him with a nod and a smile. Apologizing, the embarrassed fellow left the room, with Dan still fuming at his stupidity. "Before you say anything else *Betaji*, I asked Mr. Guha to keep me updated on Nandish's equestrian accomplishments"

"He is your cousin and friend too, you know. Besides, you must listen to a thing in its entirety before reacting. Do you understand?" asked Arjun, smiling all the time. Dhanush nodded, offered to apologize to Mr. Guha and left the room immediately.

"You spoil him, *Baasa*" A.J. said, watching his brother leave with adept swiftness. "Your mother has the same opinion. You and Dhanush are a lot alike, Ajju. The only difference I see is that you can control your anger, whereas it is the other way around with him!"

Laughing at his father's wise insight, A.J. said, "I think I'll stay with him for a few days and see if I can get him out of his present state. Women and wine are all he is into nowadays"

"He used to be so sharp earlier. This blunt Dhanush better be just a phase" A.J. said, sounding a little worried. The meeting was over, after both went through a pile of facts and figures.

A.J. caught up with Dan for a quick debrief, before they got back to their respective adjoining cabins. "Hey, little brother! Why the long face?" asked A.J., trying to sound as friendly as possible.

Looking at him, Dan replied, "No need to assume there isn't any pressure on me. I am out of ideas and churning new ones is just not happening. I don't even know where to begin, *bhai*!"

"Begin with yourself. You have let yourself go off late. Partying till late in the night, not to mention drinking to a point that just might put an alcoholic to shame, is not going to leave much room for any creativity" A.J. said.

"I like my life. The parties, the attention money can buy, all of it! Why should I put my nose to the wheel like you and Dad, I mean *Baasa*, do? We have accumulated enough for three generations after us!"

"At the rate you are squandering it, along with the dwindling status of DTD; it would be a miracle to see the money lasting just our lifetime alone!" The friendly debate between the two continued, all the way to their respective offices.

Wringing his hands together, Dhanush started to get his raw material out. Personally made slides, short clips, photographs. Blank! He had to come up with something to make his father proud.

His mother was getting on his nerves, which was nothing new. *Baasa* was the universal pacifier, trying to calm both mother and son down. A.J. was very conscientious about his 'big brother' role. Deep in thought, a black-zipped bag caught Dhanush's eye.

Not remembering having noticed it before, he dusted it down and tried to open it. Just his luck. The zip was rusted. "Mr. Guha, could you send Bantu in here, please?" Dhanush asked, giving Bantu precisely a minute before he sped in, without knocking.

If there was anyone who followed Dhanush blindly, it was Bantu, Mr. Guha's nephew. "What can I do for you, Sir?" he asked, over-enthusiastically. "Find out what this is, from the old inventory list. I want it back, opened within the hour. Go!"

Bantu sped off like a greyhound eager to win a race, leaving Dan right where he was before the black bag-blank! He knew, will power and determination was required of him, to break out of this paranoid phase.

Dhanush promised himself to mend his ways, bit by bit. This was a trait he acquired from his mother. What had to be accomplished through actions, would be highlighted with very few words.

"Ready for lunch?" A.J. peeped in, pleasantly surprised at Dan surrounded by what he called 'raw materials to invoke ideas'. "Dad's not coming?" "No, *Baasa* isn't coming. He's still a little upset about not being able to watch Andy on T.V."

"He is trying to get a CD through his contacts to present to Sangharsh *Chachu*!" answered A.J. Chuckling, Dhanush said, "Nalini *Chachi* will be more eager to see it, than him. *Chachu* is constantly on Andy's case, like *Maasa* is on mine" "That is because they love enough to care!" A.J. justified.

"Excuse me Sirs" Bantu said, clearing his throat. "I did as you ordered, Sir. The inventory list shows the black bag is not to be opened without your father's permission. I have fixed the zip with a little wax though" he narrated, mighty pleased at his accomplished mission.

"What could be so important that we need *Baasa*'s permission? Here, show it to me" "Wait Dhanush. We must take it to him before opening it. This could be important" "*Bhai,* if it were so important, it would be kept safely, not covered in a layer of dust, under a pile of unwanted items!"

"A rule is a rule, Dhanush. Bring the bag and come to my office" A.J. interrupted. "Bantu, tell Mr. Guha we three have a working lunch today. Order our usuals. Thank you" Bantu raced off for his next mission, intending to achieve it in record time.

The trio team of DTD sat in Arjun's office, as he began to show them slide after slide. Memories began to mirror the expressions of the father of the two, while A.J. remained stone-faced.

He didn't want to remember his biological father, his step-brother's namesake-Dhanush Chand, *Chaudhary* of the *Raika*s. As far as he was concerned, Arjun was his father, the one and only. "Is that *Maasa*?" Dhanush asked, amazed at how beautiful his mother looked in those pictures.

"It is said that a good photographer captures a piece of the muse's soul for the moment, offering a frozen piece of memory in return. A.J. does it too, like an artist should. And, to answer your question, *Betaji*...yes, that's your mother" Arjun said, changing to the next slide.

"And this is Dhanush Chand, *Chaudhary* of the *Raika*s. He was Ajju's biological father" Arjun carried on, swept with the flow of seeping memories, which hold the hands of time still. "My mother is sitting with your father!" said Dan, feeling a bout of heavy nausea at the thought.

"My father is sitting in front of me. In front of us" Flattered, Arjun patted A.J.'s shoulder. "So he is. I'm just showing pictures. Dhanush, you needn't take it to heart. Everyone has a past, you know."

"What is important is to accept them as a complete package, not just the parts that appeal most" Embarrassed at his statement, Dhanush smiled slowly. The next moment, his smile faded with the same suddenness.

Jumping up, he yelled, "Stay here both of you. Be back in a flash!" He ran to his workstation, picked a few items and balanced all the way back. "Have a look at these. I've been watching them since morning"

"Somehow it looked incomplete. Now, it all makes sense!" Frowning at the other two not having a clue as to what he was talking about, Dhanush sat down to explain. "I have a few slides on Rajasthan."

"But they are merely of cities like Udaipur and Jaipur. You have pictures of a village. If I go to the same village now, I bet it is going to be very different from how it used to be" Arjun knew what his son was getting at, but A.J. was as clueless as before.

"I think I have found the next theme for DTD! Listen to this. There will be a crisscross of the old meeting the new. You have pictures that are at least two decades old. Mine are a month old..tops. What do you think?"

The beaming smiles of both his father and brother, exuberant with pride and pleasure, reaffirmed his brilliance as the 'Hunter'. "Good! We have to get Andy on board with A.J. if we have to leave for this village. What's it called again?"

"Bassi" Arjun said. "Strange name" said Dan, frowning again. "On the contrary, *beta*. It's the locally-brewed version of *Basti*, which in Hindi means 'a small village'. The village was small when I saw it the first time"

"Ever since about half a decade ago, it has thrived and grown like all of you children" Arjun said with a sense of pride, giving away his love and magnetic pull towards Rajasthan's tiny village, twenty kilometers from Chittorgarh.

"Nandish's whereabouts will be known to us by this evening. We're going to the Anands for dinner. Once you know when he's back, plan your itinerary accordingly" Both sons nodded in agreement.

Every one of the Prataps loved going to the Anand villa, since they could remember. Sangharsh's sense of humour complimented Nalini's culinary skills, making them perfect hosts for a fun-filled evening.

A.J. got along well with Sarvani Anand well; or Annie as she was affectionately called. The other Anand twin, Nandish or Andy, was Dhanush's bosom pal. Although Dan was the youngest, he still managed to somehow bully Andy time and again.

The sun shied away from the cold concrete, watching A.J. in his burnt orange Ford Eco Sport and Dan in his yellow Humvee, roll out of the driveway, onwards towards home. "I can never understand why Dhanush never wants to come with us" complained Arjun.

"It is his way of declaring independence. You do know he is constantly trying to impress you?" A.J said, eyes glued to the road. "Woohoo!" came Dan's shrill voice over blazing rap music, as he zipped past them, waving.

Arjun smiled resplendently about both his sons. They were a contradiction within a contradiction; alike and different, both at the same time. A.J. was simpler in comparison to the street-smart Dan.

Dan always slowed down his vehicle before entering Swarn Villa, knowing how his mother detested his speeding. "Hello boys! How was your day?" Suhani greeted them at the door, smiling at her husband, a bit aged, but handsome nonetheless.

"I had a breakthrough idea, *Maasa*! You won't believe it, but…" "*Bas, bas!* We'll talk on the way to Anand villa. We're late already. And a forewarning beforehand. No shop talk at their place!" declared Suhani, after cutting her enthusiastic younger offspring down to size.

She didn't mean to snub her youngest so, but that is how Dhanush felt. A.J. didn't like this quality of their mother either. She was always in a rush; as if on a timer all the time. Their father was far more relaxed, understanding.

Arjun took the lead, while driving the family in his raven black Mercedes Benz, on the way to the Anands, coaxing Dhanush to narrate his idea. "He isn't called the 'Hunter' just like that, you know!" he said, glancing at his beautiful wife.

"Well done, Dhanush! Now if only you remember to be equally responsible in life, in general" Dhanush winced looking out of the window, not wanting to show his wounded pride. There was a clear undercurrent of tension that seemed to be cropping out of nowhere. Arjun had to speak to Suhani to take it easy on the boy.

He chose to do so, on their return from Anand Villa, when they would be alone. For now, he was looking forward to meeting his old friend and *rakhi* sister, Sangharsh and Nalini, who were the only company he really enjoyed.

Other than his wife's, of course. She may be hard on the outside at times, but her intentions were always as soft and gentle as he found out she really was over time.

# CHAPTER TWO

The Anand villa was just like it was meant to be. *Anand* literally denotes 'happiness'. There was always someone laughing, generally elated with life. There was no dearth of problems in daily life, nonetheless.

The Anands had, despite this, mastered the art of counting their blessings in the face of each and every calamity. The bungalow was a few minutes away from Swarn Niwas, the Pratap's residence.

The traffic slowed the Prataps down a bit, but the moment they saw the lights that bordered Anand villa, their moods brightened almost immediately!

"Hey and hi!" came Sangharsh's special greeting for his childhood friend. "Hi and hey!" came Arjun's prompt reply, followed by a hug.

"Getting more and more beautiful by the day, Suhani!" flirted Sangharsh casually, glancing at his best friend's wife, the elusive charm of the *Banjara*s of Rajasthan, still shining in her heavily-kohled eyes.

Laughing at his flirtatious nature, she walked in to be greeted by Nalini at the door. "Another one of my designs I see! You do it thorough justice, *behan*!" remarked Nalini, watching Suhani.

Suhani was draped in her marbled, malachite - green chiffon sari. *Mukkaish* work studded all nine yards of Suhani's *sari*; a pair of silver *jhumka*s in her tiny ears adding charm to her over- abundant elegance.

A stark contrast to the divine diva, Nalini was in a pair of jeans and a pink polka-dotted peasant blouse, with simple, yet feminine peep – toed sandals.

She looked like a college student with her hair pulled back, at the nape of her neck in a fishtail. "You're getting younger by the day, Nalini *behan*!"

Arjun complimented her, gaining a smile at the genuineness of it. "How come we don't get any compliments, *dost*?" enquired Sangharsh.

His look at Arjun to second him fell through as his friend stated, "Because we don't need it to pump our already super-inflated egos!"

"*Namaste, Chachu-Chachi*! Hello, Arjun *Bhaiya*! Hi, Dhanush!"

Sweet Sarvani, or Annie as she was known to one and all, walked in beaming, on seeing her closest relatives.

Absent-minded that she was, her reading glasses were still perched on her nose.

You still have your glasses on, *padhaku*!" commented Dan, calling her by the nickname he had reserved especially for her, courtesy her being always tucked in some corner, reading a book.

"Stayed away from trouble off late, *ladhaku*?!" came Annie's prompt reply, for Dan could hardly stay out of trouble since she could recall.

"Where is Andy?" enquired A.J., looking over the Anands to see if his room lights were on.

"He is fast asleep. He came back late last night, getting up only to put a few morsels in. Now, he is just lazing! Why don't you go wake him up, Ajju?" Nalini said, walking into the living room with her prized family.

The living room of the Anands was spacious, that catered to making guests feel both comfortable, as well as welcome; to chit-chat over a few drinks and snacks, before dinner was to be served.

A.J. walked right in to Andy's room, at the far end of the corridor. "Hello, sleepy head! Wake up!"

Andy barely opened his eyes, red and drowsy, that he went back to sleep, affirming the same with a gentle snore.

"Alright. Have it your way then. I'm leaving this room. Five minutes is all that is being given to you hereon, to get yourself together and come out. If you don't, Dan is coming in next. And you know how generous he is, with his level of tolerance!"

A.J. walked out smiling to himself, right to where the party was. Dan was a big bully when it came to Andy, although Andy was elder to him.

The last time Dan woke Andy up, it was awful to say the least. Suffice it to say, it was funnier to watch than to experience.

Andy was wrapped by Dan in his own blanket, before being rolled on the floor that was previously wetted sufficiently, with half a bucketful of water.

The Anands had a beautiful patio, with a barbecue and a bar on the side. They entertained only close friends and family there; the Prataps being a bit of both.

The boundaries of Anand Villa were smothered with wisteria in shades of lavender, lilac and white. Sangharsh was explaining the nature of the creeper, to the ones admiring it.

"It needs to be kept under control, but is a show-off in mid - spring" "Its colour in autumn, is what strikes me as best, to be honest" added Nalini, furthering her comment by saying, "Sangharsh is my wisteria; to be controlled and quite the show-off!"

A.J. and Annie always got along, since day one. Initially, she was always a whining toddler, but the attraction between them was reserved silence; something both their siblings could use.

A.J. walked into the group, where everyone was debating the current statement. "Did you manage to wake up Rip Van Winkle?" asked Sangharsh.

"I think so. He should be out in five" replied A.J., winking at Dan, who understood he was used as a threat again.

Andy was out in precisely five minutes, as predicted by A.J., with a sleepy, boyish grin. "All dressed for the pajama party?!" Dan asked, slapping his back in the usual friendly manner.

"Came back late last night, *dost*. Hi everyone!" he replied, sounding just about alive. "Listen, I need you to be a little more awake than you are right now. I have to talk to you about work" whispered Dan, unfortunately within his mother's earshot.

"I would probably begin to cartwheel out of joy, the day you begin to actually listen to me, rather than hearing. I thought it was clear no one was to talk shop!" Suhani scolded stern enough for everyone to screech halt their respective conversations.

"I have to, if the itinerary needs to be made on time." pleaded Dhanush, embarrassed at being spoken to in a harsh tone by her, in the presence of all who mattered.

"You can do it tomorrow, Dhanush. One day will not make that much of a difference" Suhani persisted. "Yes it will, *Maasa*. Not for you maybe, but to DTD for sure"

Arjun was watching the argument that was gaining momentum as it escalated, knowing he would have to be the pacifier to both once again.

He and A.J. were constantly tossing coins wondering whose turn it would be next to be the moderator, for the clashes between mother and son were increasing by the day.

It was beginning to get cumbersome for both, but love is what kept them going. A.J. stepped on red-hot coals this time.

"I will call him tomorrow and finalize all the plans. Andy, stay in town for now. We leave for Rajasthan this weekend, so be prepared. Your presence is required"

"Dan will explain the rest when you come to work at DTD tomorrow" Andy worked with A.J. at DTD. Along with Dan the Hunter, the trio was magnificent in their work, under the continuous guidance of Arjun's expertise.

Just like A.J. had picked photography from Arjun at an early age; Andy had inherited the natural talent of Nalini's ability, to beautify simple pictures as well.

The two were passionate about making DTD a gallery, where their pictures spoke to those who came to see them.

Before Suhani could voice displeasure over the disobedience of both her sons, Sangharsh intervened.

"Wait a minute! Did you say you guys are off to Rajasthan? Then you must be going to Bassi too! Count me in. I haven't been there in a long time"

"Excuse me. We have buyers coming from the Philippines this weekend. Who will be with me when they come to visit Anand Creations?" Nalini said, irritated at her husband for taking a decision, without consulting her.

"I'm always with you, *jaaneman!*" replied her husband affectionately, pulling her cheeks the way he used to when they were younger.

The dinner was elaborate to say the least. Everyone's favourites were made in small portions.

Suhani avoided *laal maans* now, as against Arjun, who still pounced on it every time he got the chance.

The coffee after dinner was always the best time for small talk. Sangharsh loved the flavoured *hookah* he got as a birthday gift from Nalini.

The only other person, who was allowed to share it, was Arjun. Sipping her coffee, Suhani casually mentioned, "It's nice to see you both are still crazy about each other"

Smiling Nalini replied, "Arjun has stolen a hundred glances already. You should talk!" "We don't express how we feel in public though. He is very reserved that way"

"And you?" "How can I? I am a woman!" "True. But times are changing, Suhani" "Not for me. *Saheb* loves me, as I him. But, I fear routine might strangle what we have"

"Nalini, it becomes tiring to keep the novelty alive in a relationship, especially if the onus falls on one partner's shoulder alone"

At that moment, Nalini began to feel like something was not right. She motioned to Sangharsh to drag his conversation with Arjun a bit longer.

"Are you saying you two are falling out of love then, *behan*?" Nalini asked, wanting to stick to Suhani's line of thought.

"Never! I will love him till the day I breathe my last. It's just that we are so busy with our lives that we barely talk. He is busy with DTD and Maya's Reality keeps me on my toes. By the end of the day, exhaustion takes over emotion"

"And then?" Nalini asked, confusing her old friend. "And then what? We sleep off in each other's arms"

A slow smile made the unknown known to Suhani, who caught on fast.

"I must be thankful for the blessing of being his *Beendni*. To start the day with him. To be able to touch his feet after he puts *sindoor* on my forehead after our daily prayers"

Hugging Nalini, she said, "*Behan*, thank you for putting things into perspective" They clasped each other's' hands and shed silent tears.

"What's going on with our women?" enquired Arjun, watching them smile and cry together. "That is how women bond, I guess!" replied Sangharsh.

"Beats me how they can dual emote. We men have a hard time sticking to one emotion long enough before it becomes a drag!" joined in Dhanush.

Ruffling his hair like their father did to him even now, A.J. added, "Emotions come to those who have hearts. You are a regular heart-breaker, little brother!"

It was time to leave the recuperative residence of the Anands. Sluggishly, the party moved to the car and promised to stay in touch as usual.

"*Bhaiya*, you forgot your mobile!" yelled Annie, running towards A.J. He pulled her cheeks to thank her and she squealed.

"When are you going to stop doing that?" "Never, bird-brain! Even after your Prince Charming comes, I will have sole rights to pull your cheeks!"

Annie blushed at the indirect mention of her Prince, who was anything but. Abhimanyu Shekhawat, assistant to Suhani at Maya's Reality was the king of her heart.

Ananya Mishra, Suhani's assistant prior to Abhimanyu, was long gone now. Abhi was a real asset who Suhani banked on heavily to run her firm, smooth as silk.

The moment the Prataps reached home, the boys split to their respective rooms. They had a common balcony where they could meet at night, mostly to share a smoke.

Neither of the two dared to do so in front of their parents, more out of *ankhon ka sharam* than anything else. It would be quite thoroughly disrespectful towards the elders, as their upbringing had taught them.

They never thought of it as double standards, since they knew the rules of their home to abide by. "You have to go easy on the boy" Arjun began to run his fingers through Suhani's long hair, after she came and sat beside him on their bed.

Knowing he meant their younger son Dhanush, she began. "I love him enough to know someone has to check that boy before it's too late. If I left it to you, he would be completely, instead of partially spoilt by now!"

"Point taken. You do realize Braids, scolding him in front of everyone is not the solution" "I don't have your patience, *Saheb*. He probably hates me for being the strict parent!"

Pulling her closer Arjun spoke gently, "Nobody hates you, darling. Least of all our children. You are the centre of our universe, *Beendni*. Don't you know that by now?" "Yes I do, *Saheb*. I will speak to him in the morning" she said, turning over to open her book to read.

Taking the book from her hand, Arjun kissed her softly, "*Beendni*, your husband wishes to shower love on you tonight. Will you not oblige him?" Desire shot through them both, as their bodies began to express what words no longer could, out of extreme passion and ardent love.

Elsewhere under the same roof, two brothers were talking calmly about their common topic- the gallery. Taking a break from it, A.J. said, "*Yaar* Dan…you are testy when it comes to *Maasa*"

"When you knew she would not like you to talk shop, why did you speak to Andy about the trip to Rajasthan?" Shrugging his shoulders casually, Dhanush answered, "I have developed a thick skin when it comes to her. She says, it bounces off"

"If I had to show a bruise every time she said something to me, I would have marks all over!" Watching him laugh, A.J. frowned. "That is not funny. She means no harm. *Baasa* takes it easy because *Maasa* is strict with us"

"Us? You mean me, A.J.! You are the chosen one, their blue-eyed boy. I am the black sheep. That is the truth. And with those wise words from my not-so-wise mouth which is about to yawn; let's call it a day!"

Lying on his bed, A.J. began to worry for the first time about his brother. These tiny tiffs between *Maasa* and Dhanush had to stop before they become catastrophic, he thought to himself.

He knew he would have to talk to both his parents about this, before Dhanush would ride away into a tangent. At twenty-five, A.J. had observed his parents, up close and personal. The love they shared, was not very far away from the respect they had, for each other.

He silently wished he too would meet someone, someday, who was worthy enough for his love. Dhanush was blessed with instant sleep, a habit that got him up and about early morning on a daily basis, despite frequent late nights.

He had the most vivid imagination of them all. His dreams were laden with ideas, that piggy-backed on materials, seeping in from his conscious brain. He dreamt of Rajasthan that night, for the first time.

What was so romantic about the place, he could not fathom. He knew he had to brush up on his *Marwari* before they reached Bassi, making a mental note of the same. He hadn't been to Bassi in over a decade, the only person who visited the village being Arjun, his father.

He would watch his father coax his mother into going to Bassi, but she would decline every time. He never understood it, considering her roots were in that area. "Come with us to Bassi this weekend, Braids" Arjun said, sipping his chilled orange juice at the breakfast table the next day.

"You know what my answer is going to be, and yet you ask each time?" she replied gently. "I hope you will this time. I miss you when I'm there. Feels incomplete" Dhanush gate-crashed into the conversation.

"Yes, *Maasa*. Come with us. I'll be busy with A.J. and Andy. Dad, I mean *Baasa* and you can spend time with our relatives from the village. Besides, you are the only one who can control me!"

Melting at her son chatting merrily with her after a long time, Suhani gave in. "Fine. But I have conditions" Murmuring, Dan said, "Now why doesn't that surprise me!" "We take both Ajju's Eco Sport, as well as your Humvee. I am not sitting when Dhanush drives his monster truck!"

"And, I am driving Ajju's SUV for a little while as well!" All three men gaped at each other. "You'll drive, *Maasa*? But you don't know how to!" Suhani walked up to the counter against the corner wall and pulled out a card from her purse.

"I just got my Driver's License! I have been practicing on the side, knowing if I would have told you three, you would never agree!" "You sneaky vixen!" Arjun pulled Suhani's arm, making their boys chuckle along with their mother.

"Done to all three conditions!" he said. It was a happy moment as the sun shone on Swarn Niwas that day. Every one of them went to their respective jobs, pleased with the incident at the breakfast table that morning.

"Proud of you for reaching out like that" A.J. patted Dan who grinned, "Lack of booze is making me voice out my feminine side, I think!" Suhani waved to the three men in her life as they left for DTD, slipping into her Mercedes.

Her chauffeur, Mohan, looked in the rear view to check if she wished to drive to work. Shaking her head, she motioned to him to drive her to Maya's Reality instead. The volume of traffic of the working class, along with the lack of practice to gain confidence to drive, took over her will to do so.

While deep in thought, Suhani failed to notice Mohan's mobile vibrating next to him on his seat. He kept on disconnecting the call, trying to focus on the mad rush outside the car. He couldn't possibly take the call of the pesky, persistent caller, until he had dropped *Memsahib* to her destination.

"Yes. I'm here" he said, calling the number back, the moment he saw Mrs. Pratap step inside Maya's Reality. "The next time I call you, better pick up by the first ring!" came a harsh, bugged voice.

"She was sitting right behind me! How could I?" "How do I expect you to think when you're brainless? Now listen very carefully…" The seed of viciousness was being methodically placed by the caller.

The Mercedes was moving back to the Pratap residence, like the hands of a clock, that was about to rewind as well. Not even a clairvoyant could have predicted how soon a thorn, in - extractable, was about to be planted into two healthy, happy families.

# CHAPTER THREE

The approach to Bassi was nostalgia personified. Bits and pieces of *Rajasthani* architecture were kneaded into modern houses, struggling to keep their individuality intact. The great white wall jogging along with the road had marble slabs resting on it, perhaps shielding themselves from the desert heat.

A bold black arrow was painted on the white wall, that was pointing to precisely nowhere. An old lady was walking by with a tin can, for milk mayhap, dressed in a white *salwar* suit, which wasn't the typical outfit of the area.

A bit ahead, the mystery of the bold arrow was solved as a minutely-carved door that was richly painted, had a holy shrine peeping through it. The moment they parked their SUVs outside the *Chaudhary haveli*, a lady in a cardinal- red *ghaghra choli* crossed them; a reminder of the fact that the new had not forgotten the old ways.

"*Khammaosa aap sabko*!(Welcome everyone!) *Chaudhary Saheb* will join you shortly. He has gone horse-riding with his son. Please come in. The *Chaudhrain* is expecting you!" said a man dressed in a *dhoti-kurta* with a crisp, apple-green *pagdi*.

"If it weren't for your moustache, I would think you were Neeraj *Bhaisa*!" Arjun said, taking off his sunglasses, grinning at the tribal fellow. "How have you been, *Saheb*? It has been a while!" "So it has. Where is your firework *Chaudhrain*? Has she mellowed down, or..?"

Laughing Neeraj led them in. "She feels left out nowadays, on occasions such as these horse-riding escapades, that the father and son go on often." "*Aawo, Bhaisa. Kaisi ho*, Suhani? (Come, brother. How're you Suhani?)"

"My, my! The boys have grown into young men, I see! Sangharsh *Bhaisa*, *Khammaosa*!" chirped Bindiya merrily, taking turns to greet each one of the visitors warmly. "You must be tired after the long drive"

"Why don't you rest in the rooms that have been prepared for you? By evening, both men will be back and the sun will be kind to us" Agreeing to her sane advice, everyone had their *thandai*, ate a few *samosas*, and retired to their rooms for a quick siesta.

A.J. woke up first to the loud argument between two males. "I won and you can't handle it!" "I let you win! If you noticed, I slowed down at the bend, otherwise your horse might have galloped off the road!"

"*Baasa*, you are a sore loser!" "*Betaji*, I was merely pointing out the truth!" "Enough both of you! You'll wake up our guests. They have been resting for a while and should be awake by now"

"It will shame me if they wake up to you two bickering. Vansh, go inside and freshen up. Your sister is back from Gurukul and has been enquiring about you. And *Chaudhary Saheb*, kindly follow me!" Bindiya ended with a dollop of sarcasm.

"Man, I thought our family was dysfunctional!" Dhanush remarked, smiling at A.J. who couldn't agree more. The whole lot of city folk gathered at the courtyard, trickling out with their turtle walk and yawns.

"Arjun!" "Akash!" Both embraced each other with genuine affection. "Ajju and Dhanush look like staunch *Rajputs*! Nandish, you look just like your father. Sangharsh *Bhaisa*, you haven't aged a day since I last saw you! Suhani *behan*, *Khammaosa*!"

Pausing, Akash enquired, "Where's Nalini *Behan*?", looking over Sangharsh's shoulder. "Someone has to hold the fort, *dost*! Nalini and Sarvani are back in Delhi doing just that!" Sangharsh replied.

"Where is Leenata? Is she still handling Gurukul? Arjun asked, seating himself on a plush *baithak* in the centre courtyard. "My daughter does me proud, Arjun. She has not only taken over Gurukul, but is also training a few others to teach our village's children"

"There is a school in the city where the children give an admission exam and continue their studies, if they and their families wish to, for free!" Akash boasted, his smile giving way to parental pride.

"I cannot take all the credit, *Baasa*. Malika works as hard as I do to teach the children of our village. In fact, she is still there as we speak!" That was the first time Dhanush saw her.

She was a tall, hazel-eyed vision, covered from top to toe in a traditional *ghaghra choli* with her head uncovered, looking like a rainbow in *leheriya* print. She gave him a cursory glance too, for she was used to being gaped at, by tourists and city folk.

The men of Bassi did not dare look at her for she was not only the *Chaudhary*'s daughter, but also the sister of the much-feared Vansh. The tray Leenata was carrying, landed on its destination at the wooden centre table, accessible to all guests.

She went to sit next to Suhani, who she liked instantaneously. "*Pranam, Chachiji* " "*Jeete raho, beti* (Live long, daughter!)" Suhani secretly wanted a daughter, which she was reminded of the moment she saw Leenata.

"You look just like your mother when she was your age. Including the dimples! *Sambhaal kar rakho inhe* (Keep her carefully), Bindiya. She is beautiful!" Bindiya melted on seeing her daughter being praised so.

"I am glad you all came to visit us. Any particular agenda that you had in mind, Arjun *Bhaisa*?" she said, wanting to sound more enthusiastic than she actually was. "Work and pleasure both, to be honest" A.J. spoke, wiping the layer of *bel sherbet* with his sleeve off the sides of his mouth.

"Use a handkerchief, Ajju! That's bad manners!" Suhani reprimanded A.J. Not minding it one bit, he spoke to Akash about their requirements, for the gallery. "Consider it done. Vansh will show you the village, while your father and I catch up tomorrow"

"Bindi, take Suhani to our craft shops first. I'm sure she would love to see what our craftsmen have been up to. Sangharsh *Bhaisa*, you're free to be wherever you want" "In that case, I'll escort the ladies to the craft shops"

"That settles it then. All three parties leave early morning. Lunch will be served, wherever you are. The whole village after all, is our home. *Bitiya*.." Akash turned to his offspring. "Is it possible for you to take a day off from Gurukul?"

"My apologies, *Baasa*. You know I cannot leave Malika to handle the entire school and staff training, all by herself" Leenata replied softly. "All work and no play, makes Jack a dull boy!" blurted Dhanush, wanting her second glance on him.

"Be that as it may, my preferred adage is- work is worship!" she answered back, in the very same coin. Everyone present burst out laughing at the gentle retort, which was followed by a pleasant evening.

The dinner was a variety of vegetarian as well as non-vegetarian dishes; spicy, piping-hot, all in the curry form. Suhani had to have the *laal maans*, marinated to her special taste, that was made especially for her and Arjun.

She was flattered her village relatives remembered what she liked. The meal ended with the famous sweet milk rice dessert *Phirni*, which Arjun had to his heart's content. "*Bas karo Saheb*! (Enough already, *Saheb*!)" Suhani scolded him affectionately.

"I have to watch your sugar intake at this age!" she added. "There is no life without sugar, *Beendni*. See how sweet my life has been since you married me!" The men sat down for their *hookah*s. The women sat separately for their *paan supari*s. Both indulged, nay splurged in small talk!

Dan and A.J. escaped stealthily to their room for their after-meal smoke. "So, how do you like the place so far?" A.J. asked him, puffing on his cigarette. "Not bad. Except that girl has a sharp tongue." Dan replied.

"You mean Leenata? I like her. Don't you?!" "She's alright. A bit snobbish perhaps" Their boyish talk was interrupted just after they stubbed their smokes. "*Bhaiya*, *Baasa* is calling you"

It was Leenata, addressing the elder of the two brothers. "She's talking to you" said Dhanush calmly, disliking to be remotely associated as Leenata's brother. "She is talking to us both." whispered A.J. "*Aap chalo, hum aate hain* (You go on ahead. We'll join you shortly)" he told her, smiling back.

"What's your problem if she calls you *Bhaiya*?" he asked Dan, punching him gently. "I didn't like it and I have no idea why!" Dan replied, walking with his brother, back to the courtyard.

"You called, *Chachaji*?" A.J. enquired, sitting in the coir chair before Akash and his father. While the three spoke, Dan slinked away to where Leenata was. She was supervising the dishes being done.

"What does your name mean?" he asked her, as she jumped. "What?" "Leenata. What does it mean?" "Why should I tell you?" "Because I want to know!" "And why do you want to know?"

"Listen, girls in the city would swoon if I spoke to them for more than a minute, leave alone ask them what their names meant!" "Well, I'm not of the city. And if you do have to know, it is something you could use heavy doses of!"

So saying, she walked away to the dark insides of the *haveli*. Dhanush sat down near the three men who were still talking, wondering what her name meant. "Hey A.J." he whispered to his brother.

"Ask *Chachaji* what 'Leenata' means" "Me ask him? Are you crazy? I don't want to know. Do you?" "*Bhai*, I have to know! Please ask *Chachaji* or I won't be able to sleep tonight!"

"Alright!" "What are you two whispering about?" Arjun enquired, making place for Suhani and Bindiya, who joined the group just then. "Um, nothing important, *Baasa*" "Leenata-what a beautiful name! What does it mean?"

Suhani asked her childhood friend, Bindiya. Dhanush could have kissed his mother, as could A.J., for completely different reasons. Dan would now be able to rest after knowing what the name meant and A.J. wouldn't have to say something artificially awkward to extract the meaning of the name!

"We were childless for many years as you know. The Lord answered our prayers and blessed us with Vansh. And then, the goddess herself chose to come to our house as our daughter!"

Now Dhanush was confused. "So, 'Leenata' means 'goddess'?" Laughing at his remark, Bindiya continued, "*Nahi re buddhu*, (No silly) 'Leenata' means 'Humility'!" "Humility? Why would I need heavy doses of humility?" he said aloud, accidentally.

Everyone began to stare at him. As usual, A.J. came to the rescue. "We're tired and considering tomorrow is an early morning, may we call it a day?" Getting the permission of the elders, both brothers marched off to their room.

"What was that?" A.J. asked while taking off his boots. "Slip of the tongue. Tell me *bhai*, do you not think I'm humble?" "*Arre*, her name means 'humility'. What does that have to do with you?"

"She said I need heavy doses of what her name means!" "Oh, I see!" A.J. said, trying to hide his smile as he got ready to get into his cozy-looking bed. "*Sona nahi kya*? (Don't you want to sleep?)" he asked Dan, watching him walk to the huge window, frowning.

"In a moment" replied Dhanush, sounding distant. The room on the first floor had a light on, that looked like a lantern. Leenata was combing her hair and singing softly at her reflection, in the mirror.

She got up with a book, moving away from the seat by the window. "I sure need heavy doses of her" Dan sighed, his last words before he fell on his bed, dozing off within minutes. His mind was still whirling with the effect Leenata had on him, making him an ineffective charmer, a trait alien to him since he could remember.

The next morning was not quite what was expected. Everything that could possibly go wrong, did. Sangharsh and Nandish had to leave early for Delhi because the factory workers at Anand Creations had gone on a strike.

Bindiya's house-help was unwell, because of which Suhani and she had to cook and clean. Leenata was off to Gurukul. That left Dhanush, A.J., Arjun and Akash. All four set out wearing *dhoti-kurta*s, except Dan who wore his jeans with a black and grey, striped *kurta*.

"You have one son whose feet are firmly planted on the ground; the other's head is up in the clouds! What could you want more?" Akash jested. "Sure! Where is Vansh?" "He has gone to Viren's place. They will meet us near the sheds"

Turning to A.J., Akash said, "I think he feels like competing with you, Ajju! Be careful. My son has a killer streak!" "Your son is my brother, *Chachaji*. I have no fight with him" A.J. said, winning over Akash instantaneously.

"*Khammaosa* Tara *Chachiji*! Is your lazy son up yet?" Vansh asked, entering the hut "He has been ready since the last hour, *Chote Sardar*!" came Tara's reply. She loved pumping Vansh's ego for one, sole reason.

She had a secret ambition for her daughter Malika to become the *Chaudhrain* of the *Raikas*, by being Vansh's *Beendni*. Once, she had made the mistake of confiding in her husband of her ambition.

Simple that he was, he had reprimanded her into wanting too much. "*Khammaosa, Chote Thakur*!" Viren wished Vansh, bringing him down to reality. "You should address him as *Chote Sardar* when you two are alone at least. We all know he will be our *Chaudhary* one day!" Tara said, looking at her son sternly.

Viren was a soldier, following his general blindly. He didn't understand his mother one tiny bit. He went by what was factual, real. "Right. *Chalein*? (Shall we go?)" he ushered Vansh out of the hut.

"Where are we going?" "To the stables or sheds, I guess. I really cannot remember where the meeting point was! *Baasa* is showing the city folk around. I want you to be with me at all times"

Viren was flattered on feeling indispensable, but the truth was something else. Vansh was nursing a severe complex when it came to the Prataps, especially Ajju. He knew he would have to hand over the reins to him, for he was the real heir to the throne.

Nonetheless, he had made up his mind, he would retain his post honourably for as long as he could. They reached the stables but found no one there. "They must have stopped at Gurukul" thought Vansh out loud.

"Come on. Let's ride! A quick, short one. I'm taking Badal, *Baasa's* horse for a quick run. Hurry up!" Viren quickly saddled his horse Jigar, making a futile effort to catch up with Vansh, who was, by now, long gone.

Meanwhile, Dhanush was getting to see Leenata in the role of a teacher, as they were shown around the school. Malika was explaining a complicated construction to him, when Leenata gently interrupted.

"I think you all should leave now. My staff and students are getting disturbed" "Alright, *Maatsa*!" Dhanush folded his hands into a *Namaste*. "Do not call me that, please. You may call me Leenata if you wish to, that is" she added, awkwardly.

"I wish to call you Leena. I like it. Suits you" Dhanush said, walking past her, blowing a curl off her forehead that came stubbornly back where it lay before. "He likes you" Malika observed.

"He is full of himself!" Leenata cribbed. "So you like him too?!" "*Behan*, I like children who are spoilt brats also. He falls in the same category!" Laughing, they went off to their respective classes, letting the visiting group see themselves out.

"Now we go to the sheds. Or rather, let's go to the stables first. We will start with the horses first-our prized possession! We all commute with our own horses. They are kept over here in a cluster of stables"

"Turns are taken to groom, feed them by specially-trained village folk. My daughter rides too as does her friend, Malika. The women here shy away from horse-riding though. They say it is a man's sport. In fact, we will be participating in a fair, especially to show our horses off"

"We'll deck them up just like our camels and other livestock. They get a good price in the market nowadays. And…hey, where is my Badal?" Akash stopped his elaborate narration abruptly.

"*Chote Thakur* has taken him for a run. He should be back soon. Viren*ji* is with him" said the stable boy. "Now why doesn't that surprise me! He is always testing my patience. Has to have everything I own!" grumbled Akash.

"Relax! He will be back soon. There is the dust trail. Could that be them?" Indeed it was. Two handsome young men rode towards them in full fervor, conscious of the attention they were attracting.

Two young men of the city were watching in awe. A.J. could still ride a horse quite well. Dhanush could not ride a mule to save his life! "Forgive me, *Baasa*. We were waiting for you here and so thought we should take the horses for their daily exercise" said Vansh.

"You should have taken your own horse, Vansh. You do know it is forbidden to ride the *Chaudhary's* horse, don't you?" Snatching the reins from Vansh's hands, Akash walked away to the interiors of the stable, along with the city folk.

He was too far out of earshot to hear Vansh whisper, "Just practicing, *Baasa*!" Both Vansh and Viren walked triumphantly to join the silly group who, unlike them, preferred playing by the rules.

# CHAPTER FOUR

The India International Conference for Textiles and Apparel Designing or the ICTAD, was a ginormous deal for anyone who was in the apparel business. It was held annually in the Habitat Center at New Delhi.

Passes were exclusive, guest invites rare. The Anands always had access to this event, not only because the Chairman Mr. D'Souza was a family friend; but also due to the fact that Anand Creations was a name to reckon with, both in the national as well as the international markets.

Usually, Sangharsh and Nalini went for the final show, when the ramp walk displayed the latest handiwork of Indian designers. This time though, Sangharsh and Nandish went to the Habitat Center, while Nalini and Sarvani were ironing out the creases of the workers strike.

While at brunch with Suhani, Nalini voiced her concern. "These strikes are not healthy for the reputation of our firm. How do you manage, when there is a revolt of this sort?" "I'd like to say never, but you know me better than that!"

"We almost had a situation in our hands about a year ago. Abhimanyu, my assistant, handled it amazingly well. I'm telling you, that boy is worth every rupee he was hired for" she said, lighting up a cigarette.

Snatching it from her lips, Nalini said, "What's this? Since when did you start to smoke?" "Give it back, Nal" "Not a chance. Not in front of me, at least. What's the matter?" Nalini asked, momentarily forgetting about the worker situation at her firm.

"I can't put my finger on it, you know. I've been having these dreams lately. As if…as if something precious is about to be taken away from me. When I wake up, I feel hollow and more scared"

"You need a break, Suhani" "I just came from one! I need to design a new line. I'll call it **Strength of a Woman**, pump my ego a bit!" Back at

Anand Creations, Abhi walked in to Annie arguing as gently as possible with a handful of agitated workers.

"We are not interested in speaking with you. We want to speak to the owners, your parents" "They are busy at the moment. Tell me and I will help" she said, meekly. Unconvinced, they kept on shouting slogans.

Abhi loved Annie immensely refusing to let her be quashed this way for no fault of hers. "Make way! Excuse me! Here, here. What is the matter?" Abhi walked right into the heart of the crowd, stopping once he reached Annie, and stood next to her.

Annie tried to look stern, the veiled relief apparent to her saviour alone. "Who are you, Sir?" asked one of the workers. "Abhimanyu Shekhawat at your service. I am the spokesperson for Anand Creations. Let's sit down like mature adults to discuss the issues one by one"

"Once the list has been made, I will need signatures from everyone, after which one of you will represent your cause by coming along with me to the owners. So, shall we begin?"

The workers were mighty pleased at the responsible young man who seemed to have it all sorted out. "Thanks, but what on Earth are you doing?" Sarvani asked. "You are my damsel in distress, Annie. I am helping you get out of a situation. Call it territorial protection!"

Smiling, Annie said, "Flattering as it is, oh Prince of mine, do tell, how you propose to break this bit of news to my folks. You have just announced yourself as the spokesperson of Anand Creations!"

The weight of the gesture was finally dawning on Abhi. "Figure something out then. Be my lady, save your dude in distress!" That was the thing about Abhi. He could diffuse any situation, just like Sarvani's father, Sangharsh Anand.

Everyone liked him, mostly due to his affable temperament; everyone except Nalini. She did not encourage the proximity between her daughter and Abhimanyu one bit. Try as she might, Abhi would find an excuse to see Annie, if Annie didn't think of one already.

"There is something else I have been meaning to talk to you about. It's kind of personal" Nalini told Suhani, taking a spoonful of her *rasamalai*. "Go ahead. Oops!" Both began to giggle when Suhani missed a piece of her *gulab jamun* as it fell right back into the dessert bowl!

"It's about Abhimanyu, your assistant" "What about him? Not happy with yours?" "Nothing of the sort, Suhani. His friendship with Annie is increasing day by day. I think she too is overly friendly with him"

"Annie is simple, soft. She does not understand about our societal status, you know" Cleaning her mouth with a quick sip of sparkling water, Suhani said, "You have a problem with Abhi because he is an assistant, don't you?"

"You forgot you were once an assistant, as well. He is handsome, responsible, funny, affectionate, committed. If I had a daughter.." "But you don't. So you won't understand. All the qualities you mentioned fizzle out in front of two words- financial status!"

Resting her hand on Nalini, Suhani said, "What did I have when you both took me in? I made something out of myself, didn't I? Give him a chance, Nal. They both are in love. Don't be the one to keep them apart. Annie is like a daughter to me too, you know"

Nalini knew Suhani made sense, but the practical side of her refused to accept it. Suhani's phone rang just then, as they both got up, waving at the waiter who was just short of tap-dancing on seeing his generous tip.

"Yes, Abhi? Okay. Right. That's great! Stay there then. She's with me. I'm coming too" Biting her lip, Suhani tried to sound as forthright as she possibly could under the circumstances.

"That was Abhi" "Talk of the devil!" "Lady, if you knew how he saved your company from ruination, you would eat back your words!" On the way to Anand Creations, Suhani explained Abhimanyu's phone call.

"Spokesperson? Why did he do that? I am not hiring him." "You are missing the whole point here, Nal. He saved Annie, not to mention your firm in a way, as well. You owe him. I don't think he has time to work for you. Even if you offer him a post, he would decline it for sure"

"Then why did he do it?" Suhani's smile sufficed in answering Nalini's question, minus the words. They reached Anand Creations, walking straight into Nalini's office. The guard was ordered to call Annie and Abhi into the office immediately.

"Remind me to hire an assistant, who will double up as a spokesperson, as and when required" Nal addressed Sarvani, the moment she and Abhi were seated in front of her. Turning to Abhimanyu, she said, "Thank you for helping my daughter, young man"

Tearing a check worth a couple of thousand rupees, she slid it to him across the sleek, polished glass desk. "For your services" Suhani closed her eyes out of shame. Annie and Abhi's faces turned red.

Standing up to straighten his tie, Abhi said, "My name is Abhimanyu Shekhawat. I work hard for a living and do not accept *chanda*. Besides, it was my bounden duty to protect my would-be bride!"

"What?!" said all three ladies present there, in unison. "Annie, what in God's name is going on? How dare you even think of something like this? An alliance is between those who are of the same standard, if not above. Do you understand?"

"Be ambitious for yourself, but not through my daughter!" The verbal bashing was no sooner than over, that her targeted audience chose to put an end to it. Suhani got up, walking out with Abhi.

"That was real smart, Abhi" Suhani jokingly reprimanded him. "She is mean!" "Not one bit. She is a tigress protecting her cub" Liking her take on what happened, Abhi began to brief her about earlier happenings in detail.

Suhani now began to notice what Annie saw in him. He had traces of the one and only Sangharsh Anand in him. It was a trait that showed itself more than anything else in Abhimanyu, leaving her wondering, how come she hadn't noticed the similarity before.

Somewhere else in the city of Delhi, among beautiful models who walked their famous catwalk, dressed in yards of rich silk, satins and other flowing fabric, intoxicating everyone; the cameras flashed away to the sporadic applause showered time and again by the crowd.

"Your camera flash is going to trip one of the models for sure." came a husky female voice, from behind Andy. He had left his seat next to Sangharsh's, for want of better-angled shots of Anand Creations' pieces being catwalked.

"No way! They must be used to it already. Besides, I am not the only one. Look at that girl there. She has a brighter flash than mine. Crazy kid!" The lady came closer, standing besides Nandish.

"Myna" she said, introducing herself by putting her hand forward for a shake. "Andy" Nandish replied, shaking her hand. Pointing at the 'crazy' girl photographer with a single, well-manicured nail, Myna spoke.

"The 'crazy' girl there is my kid sister, Diana" Embarrassed, Andy apologized, which was immediately waived off by Myna. "How were you supposed to know?" "You have a British accent, but look Indian. Do you live in Delhi?" Andy asked, surprised at his own inquisitiveness.

"Just came to town a month ago. My sister is interested in Indian culture. Being NRIs, we have had no hands-on experience about the way India feels when you breathe her, you know" "Yeah, I know how you feel. I've travelled to foreign lands, many-a-times. Everything said and done, one's own country is always home." Sangharsh got a call from Nalini around that time, telling him all that happened at the office between Annie, Abhi and herself.

"Gosh, Nal, I asked you to hold the fort, not charge with a blood-curdling battle cry!" "Very funny as usual. Be serious, San! Where's Andy?" "Chatting with an exquisitely-beautiful woman" "Do not joke" "I am not. I can see him!" "Great! Both my children, out of my hands on the same day!" "Was that the intention to have the twins, my darling? So that we could control them?"

Nalini knew he was right, but her stubborn streak refused to accept it. "What's he doing now?" she asked San, who began to smile. "Tell you what. I'll take a video and then send it to you. Would that put your mind to rest, my love?!"

"My daughter is in love with Suhani's assistant, my son is flirting with a model. And, you find all this hilarious?" she asked, now slightly irritated. "I find how you are behaving hilarious. What the twins are doing is perfectly normal at their age"

"Now I have to hang up. I'll see you soon, Nal!" he said, blowing kisses on the phone before he hung up. "Dad, this is Myna. She is interested in opening her own apparel line. When I told her who I was, she wanted to meet you" said Andy, smiling at his father.

"Mr. Anand, you are an icon in the garment industry. I can't believe I'm actually meeting you in person! I have read everything there is to know about Anand Creations. The perfect 'rags to riches' story"

"You inspire people like us who wish to strive for perfection such as yourself." Sangharsh was flattered, as well as tickled with the enthusiasm shown by the young lady. "Well, thank you very much for showering so many compliments. Have you come alone?"

"No. My sister is here with me" "Well, in that case, may I invite you to my apparel house tomorrow, if you are free that is" "It would be my pleasure, Sir!" "Please don't call me Sir. And before you start, not even Uncle!"

"The thing is, abroad we call everyone usually by their first names. The concept of uncles and aunts is different, in relation to India. I'll call you Mr. Anand. Is that okay?" "Brilliant! Come on Andy. We got to go"

Wishing Myna, the pretty young girl goodbye, both left for Anand villa. "She is pretty" Sangharsh mentioned, waiting for Andy to respond. "Yes she is, isn't she? Quite attractive" "But not your type" "Dad!" "No, seriously! You like the quiet type, with streaks of conventionality. This one could turn out to be a handful." "I'm a big boy now, in case you haven't noticed."

"Try telling your mother that. Besides, I'm still your father, baby boy!" Sangharsh said, grinning along with his son, who suddenly looked all grown up to him. The moment they reached Anand villa, they were compelled to race up the stairs. Nalini was yelling at Annie, who was holding herself tight, sitting in a corner on one of the ornate oakwood chairs. "What are you doing?" Sangharsh asked Nalini, rushing to his daughter to hold her in his arms.

"I caught her talking to that opportunistic assistant of Suhani's" "*Maasa* he is not opportunistic." "*Chup kar, badtameez!* (Be quiet, you ill-mannered child)! Do you know what you're doing to your life, our reputation?"

"Enough is enough, Nalini. Annie, come with me" Sangharsh took her to the room they used to have family discussions in. It was an hour later that Annie's father understood, where the problem really lay.

"Let's make a deal. I will convince your mother. Promise to encourage him to better himself. Apologize to him, on our behalf. Your mother had no business offering him money, to hurt his pride so"

"Also, I have been hearing you mention about your interest in making dolls, for quite some time now. Don't you think your room has enough dolls already, Annie?" "Don't you think it's silly I make dolls in my spare time, when I am the Head Designer at Anand Creations, *Baasa*?"

"On the contrary, Annie. It just shows your heart lies in making dolls" her father answered. They chatted some more over a cup of tea, attempting to strategize as much as they could. Assured his daughter had calmed down, Sangharsh left to speak to the love of his life, the stubborn Nalini Anand.

"You know, you drive me crazy at times." he said, walking her to their bedroom.

"Likewise!" "Nal, she is crazy in love with Abhi. We've seen him for the last five years. I couldn't have found a better match, if I looked for one myself! What do you want? For her to run away? I want to attend my daughter's wedding, thank you very much! How about you?"

Nalini began to cry softly. Holding her close, Sangharsh asked her gently what the matter was. "Ramona used to make fun of me as Arjun's assistant. Since then I guess, all I've ever wanted is that our children, should be better and bigger than us"

"As a parent Sangharsh, I have the right to want that, don't I?" "Yes my darling, you do. But pushing our children into doing what you want, so that they live up to your expectations, is just going to push them further away. You know, they both love you"

"Annie loves you more" Nal, clarified, still sniffing. "Andy loves you more!" Sangharsh retaliated gently. "But you know what? We both love them equally, don't we?" he asked her softly. The look in his eyes was enough for her to know, it was time to show how much they meant to each other, in a way only two lovers understood. Unspoken words were conveyed by a mere touch, their minds in sync with their hearts.

Lying in each other's arms, they spoke for a while. "Why did you take Ramona's name after so many years, Nal?" Sangharsh asked, playing with her thick silver bracelet. "Because of the 'assistant' connection, Sangharsh. Why, what's wrong?"

"Nothing. Not thought about the 'Anaconda' for a while, that's all" Slapping his palm playfully, Nalini chided him. "You're incorrigible. Speaking ill of the dead is bad in every which way"

"Yes, Madam! Now let's go to sleep. We have an early morning tomorrow. Promise me you'll talk to Annie with a little more consideration and affection" Sangharsh asked her, turning off the bedside lamp.

"Can't promise. I will try though." Nalini said, giggling as he began to tickle her. Later on that night, Andy and Annie were having a cup of hot chocolate before calling it a day. Andy told his twin sister about the next day's visit, of his new friend and her sister.

"Does *Maasa* know about it?" "*Baasa* will probably tell her about the meeting, I'm sure. Annie, you might think she was unfair to you. But, do you know why she was harsh?" "Yes. She is a tigress protecting her cub. *Baasa* told me"

Andy chuckled at his simple twin sister, secretly hoping their father hadn't forgotten to mention the visit to their mother. Unfortunately, Sangharsh forgot to speak with Nalini about Myna and Diana's visit to Anand Creations.

He also skipped telling her at the breakfast table, not to mention losing his chance on the way to work, in the same car, as well! The moment Andy reminded him that he was off to the hotel to pick their guests up, Sangharsh got sweaty palms.

He knew it was too late to tell Nalini, but not telling her would surely make matters worse. Annie saw her father pacing up and down his office. She entered to ask him what the matter was. When Sangharsh told her his forgetfulness was going to be a catastrophe of historical proportions, Annie chose to bail him out.

"Let's tell *Maasa* that they are prospective buyers, who we are touring around. I'll text Andy, you text *Maasa*. Better yet, tell her. Let Andy explain the rest to his new-found friends" Sangharsh hugged his daughter, kissing her on the forehead.

"How did I get so lucky?" he asked, affection oozing out from father to daughter. "You got lucky the moment you married *Maasa*, I guess!" They went off to do as was required. There was something nagging Sangharsh though.

Something that he couldn't get out of his mind since last night. Something he had kept close to himself. The girl Andy was talking to, looked familiar. The question was - where had he seen that face before? No sooner had he begun to delve into his memory bank, Andy called, "I am on my way with our guests, Dad."

# CHAPTER FIVE

Evenings at Bassi splashed rays of the sun on all that was simple, like a stack of hay that glimmered and glistened, making it look like Rumpelstiltskin's golden thread. That was the magic that lay hidden in this land. Its beauty could be done justice to, by taking in the intoxicating effects in person, or by the well-trained eye of a photographer.

The last rays made the men and women look ethereal. Phantoms, whose silhouettes sang of dreams that are yet to be realized, their aching looks entwined with their daily miseries that shone through the eyes, freshly washed with brimming tears.

After being reprimanded by his father, returning the same with a hidden scoff, Vansh disappeared along with Viren under the pretext of some urgent business, that needed to be taken care of.

The city folk were left to be entertained by those left. Dhanush was enamoured with the horses, choosing to stay back at the stable, while the remaining left for the *Chaudhary haveli* to rest. "Greetings from the Hunter! That is what I'm called by fellow humans, oh majestic equidae beings!" he bowed at the centre of the stable, thrilled to be finally alone.

He loved his own company most of the time, considering others to be more of an intrusion. "A Hunter bows to horses in their stable. Beyond strange, wouldn't you say?" came a woman's voice, making him go stiff, with immediate effect.

Leenata walked towards him silently, in her *mojri*s made of camel leather. Her smaragdine-green *ghaghra choli* contrasting with her glaucous-like *odhni*; similar to the blue-gray or blue-green coating on grapes and plums. Dhanush noticed, how the sun was outlining her silhouette.

It caught the *gota* work to sparkle at the edges of her outfit, making her look special enough to give undivided attention to. "Will you keep standing still all through the night? That is how horses sleep by the way."

Leenata joked as she said this, but the fact that Dhanush, at that very moment looked devastatingly handsome, did not miss its mark; especially considering he was caught off - guard and was a tad less-guarded, vulnerable, thus losing his cloaked vanity.

"A lady doesn't sneak up the way you just did, Leenata. Why aren't you at the *haveli*?" he asked her, still trying to gain ground. "I went home straight from school. I wanted to ride Bijli" she replied, walking to her fawn horse with a dull gold mane.

"Bijli ought to be white, not brown in colour. Lightning is closest to white, is it not?" Dhanush threw another dart at a meaningless, yet oddly exciting conversation. "She was the fastest among the batch of foals"

"*Baasa* named her Bijli because of her speed, not looks or colour. You're so presumptuous." "I am presumptuous? Who gave me advice about needing heavy doses of humility?"

"I give advice only when it is desperately required" "Advice is to be given when asked, not when required." Frowning, Leenata turned around, planning to stage a walkout. "*Ruko*! (Wait!) Why don't we both ride together?"

"You can ride Bijli and I can ride any horse from the stable" Motioning to one of the stable boys, Leenata pointed towards a horse. "Sapheda *ko yahaan le aawo*(Bring Sapheda here)" The stable boy got a beautiful horse with white-markings of a blaze, right to where Leenata stood.

"You wanted a horse with lightning? Here you go." she said, mounting her Bijli, trotting off out of the stable. Dhanush leapt on Sapheda, who neighed at an unfamiliar rider, but accepted the decent horseman as a fleeting visitor.

The row of *kikar* trees hid a well-ridden horse trail, that looked as if it were used on a regular basis. It was there that Leenata looked back, slowing down to gape at Dhanush, hopping like a yo-yo on Sapheda's saddle.

"You are going to be in a lot of pain when you get on the ground." she said, stifling a smile as he came by her side, still hopping rather than riding. "Even more than I am in already?" Leenata burst out laughing, as Dhanush had intended her to, when he passed the remark.

"What do you know about our horses?" she asked him, pulling her *odhni* closer to the forehead momentarily, before the wind pushed it back down, again. "I read it somewhere that *Marwari* horses were on the verge of extinction in the first half of the 20th century"

"Maharaja Umaid Singh*ji*, followed by his grandson Maharaja Gaj Singh*ji* saved the breed" "Quite impressive. What else?" she asked, waving at a handful of children who were skipping on their way home.

"Their common colours are brown, piebald, skewbald. Black is unlucky, unless with markings like four socks, that your father's horse has. A virgin-white horse has religious significance and is used for processions only"

Dhanush parroted his knowledge about horses, courtesy either Andy, or the magazines he subscribed to. "That covers history as well as the colour-scheme of the *Marwari* horse. Other than their physical characteristics, is there anything else?" she enquired, sounding every bit the Gurukul teacher, that she was.

"Enlighten me." came Dhanush's jovial reply. "Some of our horses are trained to dance in marriages and religious festivals" said Leenata, pulling Bijli's rein sideways, to avoid rubble.

"I like the way your eyes dance when you talk. It's more like they are talking, before you even speak" Dhanush blurted out, as her horse came closer to his. Ignoring his personal remark, she continued, "The special breed between the *Marwari* horses called the *Natchni*, or the ones 'born to dance'"

"They are decorated in silver, jewels, bells.." Dhanush tugged at Leenata's horse's rein gently. "Leena, are you listening to me?" Her reins gathered in hand sufficed as a small whip, for the moment.

Rapping him on his forearm, she said, "I chose to ignore your statement, assuming your heritage would not allow you this impertinence." Dhanush quietened down thereafter. They reached the *haveli*, from where two young boys took the horses back.

"Where have you been, *behan*? It's past sunset!" Vansh said, looking at Dhanush walking in behind her. "Relax. She was with me" answered Dhanush honestly. "Do you mean to say, all this while you said you were going to ride Bijli, you were with him?"

Vansh glared at his sister now, shooting poison darts with his eyes at Dhanush. "*Bhaiya..*" "*Chup kijiye aap*! (Be quiet!) Go to your room" Vansh dismissed his sister, who scurried past him.

Eyes still ablaze, he walked towards Dhanush. "Viren told me he saw you both on the horse-trail. Is that true?" Vansh asked him. "Yes. Viren is correct. This was all my idea. Leenata is not at fault here"

"I asked to join her for the ride. Maybe she was too polite to decline" Dhanush spoke, uncomfortable with Vansh's menacing glare. "What's going on here?" A.J. walked in, watching Vansh and Dhanush, glare at each other.

"Ask your baby brother that. *Gaon mein sheher ka rang millane ki koshish kar rahein hai yeh.*" (He is trying to mix his city culture with our village's). "Dan.." A.J. looked at his brother for a clarification.

"I wasn't mixing anything, A.J. It was a harmless horse ride, with his sister as company, that's all. What is the big deal?" A.J. turned to Vansh. "He means no harm, Vansh. I apologize on my brother's behalf, for breaking *maryaada*"

"He may not mean any harm. But, I do not accept this friendship your brother is trying to build, with my sister" Vansh spat out rudely. "He is a child." A.J. said imploringly. "Then he ought to be escorted by his mother, don't you think?" Vansh spat out viciousness again.

"Alright, enough! Leenata *Bitiya, aawo humaare paas* (Leenata, my daughter, come here)" *Chaudhary* Akash walked into the courtyard, shouting at the three men, asking his daughter to join them. He heard both sides carefully.

"There is one more rendition we haven't heard. So far, both of you are justified in your own ways. Vansh is justified as a brother, to be concerned about his sister's whereabouts. Dhanush is fair in assuming a horse ride is just for enjoyment for the moment, with no strings attached. Let's see what Leenata has to say, to this argument"

Gulping hard, Leenata spoke, "*Baasa*, Dhanush was alone at the stable. I happened to have gone there to get Bijli. We rode and spoke together, that is all" she said, head bent down due to partial embarrassment, to the way Vansh was making insinuations against her.

Seeing his daughter being shamed by his son, Akash began to shout at Vansh. "Show your sister some respect! She has earned it in my eyes. While you fritter away your time, she teaches and trains at Gurukul"

"Does she not have the right to enjoy her free time?" "I have no problem with that, *Baasa hukam*" Vansh said with folded hands. "But as her brother, your son, my only question to you is this-are our customs, laws equal for all who come under them, or relaxed for a handful alone?"

Picking the connotation of his argument, Akash took a U-turn. "Dhanush is like a brother to you. Thus he is like a brother to Leenata too" *Chaudhary* Akash said softly, sitting to let the head-rush settle down.

Arjun, Suhani, Bindiya had joined the group by then. The elders chose to smoothen feathers with doses of heavy cajoling. Vansh was seething with rage by now. He left in a huff, but was careful not to be verbose about it.

"Before he leaves for the city, we must teach Dhanush a lesson, *Chote Sardar!*" Viren egged him on. Viren, loyal that he was, chose to give information about the two at the horse-trail, thus proving his loyalty to Vansh once again.

Bindiya gave Leenata a piece of her mind, advising her not to cross *maryaada* in the future, for it may bring shame on to the family. "You came here to work on a concept, Dhanush. Where is the progress?" Arjun asked him quietly.

"I accept on having other distractions, *Baasa*. Tomorrow I will get to work for sure" Dhanush responded convincingly. "You only have all of tomorrow. It is better we leave by nightfall, rest in a nearby hotel, and leave for Delhi straight from there. Enough of tension is in the air, as your mother and I can sense."

That night, Leenata was combing her hair with the window open, to let in the cool night breeze, as usual. She noticed Dhanush sitting on the window sill of his room, staring blankly at her. She pulled the *chatai* down after giving him a smile that spread a thousand moonbeams across the clear, night sky.

"Are you planning to count all the stars in one go, or do you intend to save some for tomorrow?" A.J. enquired offhandedly. "She smiled at me. It is morning already for me. Her smile is so bright!"

Choosing not to respond to Dhanush, A.J. drifted off to sleep, lonely again. Bizarrely though, he dreamt of a girl, perhaps born of his loneliness. He could barely make sense of the dream, except for the lonely feeling inside, which consistently gnawed his gut all the time, was no longer there. He woke up refreshed, buoyant, in high spirits.

The exact opposite of what Dhanush chose to open his eyes to. He slung his Sony Alpha A 7S Compact DSLR camera around his neck, packed an extra pair of lens, vowing to make every moment at Bassi worth the while, here on.

Some of the houses, albeit in cement, had interesting extensions of mud, in the shape of long benches, where one could just sit to watch passers-by, a significant way to spend time in villages like Bassi, all over India.

Across the road, under the huge *peepal* tree, there was a tiny *mandir*. The tree itself was surrounded by a raised, cement area where the *Panchayat* would convene whenever the need arose.

'*Jeevan yagya vishwa hith dharm, aahutiyan dainik shubh karm*' was written on one of the sides of the white platform. Dhanush was trying very hard to read it out, assuming he could rattle out his mother tongue, *Hindi*.

A lady with her *ghoonghat* pulled down to cover her face, read it out loud. "Leena, is that you?" he asked, dazed, delighted, expectant. "Hush! So it is. I am here to make sure you don't get yourself into any more trouble. I have had Ajju *Bhaiya* informed"

"You are not to be left alone. Viren and Vansh *Bhaisa* have their eye on you" "Thanks for looking out for me. I thought you came to see me" Dhanush flirted. "Yes, that too" she replied, equally casually, making his heart skip a beat.

"So technically, I am not alone anymore, am I? You are here with me." he said, attempting to sound innocent. She blinked, suddenly conscious of their proximity, moving away unhurriedly.

It was another blessing that the village was still waking up to the drudgeries of the day, as a result of which the streets were empty. "What do these words mean?" Dhanush asked, pointing at the inscription he had read out in *Hindi*.

Aware of the query as an attempt to prevent her from escaping, Leenata chose to stay and answer. "To want universal peace in the benefit of mankind, one must give in to little sacrifices on a daily basis. Beautiful, isn't it?" she whispered.

"Just like you are. Beautifully elusive!" "Pardon?" "I could not understand what it means but I love it anyways. Just like I cannot understand you but…" he said, feeling not as smart as he usually did, once again.

"What is there to understand about me? You are of the city. I am of this village. You are a guest here, in my home. Our parents are friends, our siblings practically enemies. Have I spoken enough?"

Feeling sufficiently rebuked, but yet eccentrically hopeful, Dhanush replied, "Yes. I can take a hint. You can go if you want. But first, let me a take a few pictures of you with your Bassi in the background"

Assuming Dhanush had a death-wish, Leenata gave in, asking him to come to Gurukul in the afternoon. In the meantime, he could enjoy Bassi waking up to a new day. A few buffaloes that were tied for the night were let loose by their drowsy owner.

They bellowed stridently, competing with a rooster who seemed to have synchronized his announcement with them. *Myena*s had gathered by the hundreds at the centre of the village, where grain would be strewn by the villagers for them, as an offering to their ancestors.

Routine, muscle memory brought both bird and man together for just that one hour; parallel to the superstitious belief of the simple folk, that their ancestors were somehow being appeased by this plain act of thoughtfulness.

Dhanush heard a roar behind him, that was rather startling. A tractor, with a mammoth amount of grain packed in a huge sack, was fixed on the carriage attached to it. For some quaint reason, a cane ladder was dangling at the back of the obese sack, as if someone was cuckoo enough to climb the grain mountain.

Just before he reached Gurukul, Dhanush was accosted by A.J. who had been forewarned about Vansh's ill intentions. "Stop gallivanting! Do you have anything to show yet?" he asked, trying to normalize the situation, on finding his kid brother roaming around by himself, with a potential threat from Vansh and Viren, as per Leenata.

"Somewhat. A.J. do you remember your stay here? As in, when.." Dhanush was at a loss for words, partly because his mind refused to register the hard fact that A.J. was his step brother. "Yes I do, actually. Don't tell *Maasa* and *Baasa* though"

"They think I've forgotten, which makes them feel they have replaced all my memories with good ones I owe to them both. Here, let me show you" A.J. walked Dhanush around explaining the changes.

"This used to be barren land. Now, there are houses made of cement. The tiny chicken coup, cattle shelters, also look ginormous compared to their original sizes since the last time I saw them. Everything has…changed"

The last word A.J. let out sounded vacant, unidentifiable. "Snap out of it, bro! We have to do work before those two clowns land up. The Hunter's reputation is at stake, after all." "I do hope you are not referring to us, city boy! Or, are you?" came a sinister voice, followed by a crack of *lathi*.

A.J. caught the *lathi* before another blow could fall on Dhanush. His scuffle with Viren got Dhanush's adrenalin charged enough to attack Vansh, just about the time that A.J. had overpowered Viren.

"Well now! What a wonderful sight! Are you all wrestling by any chance?" The heap of sweaty, dusty, men stopped in a jiffy after hearing the familiar voice. This was the first time that Arjun's sons had heard him yell at them, for as long as they could recall!

"Get up all of you, right this second! Now, apologize to each other. You should be ashamed of yourselves, fighting like common street urchins! Look at what stupidity has made you do! What are you fighting about this time? What is the problem here? Vansh, look at me"

Reluctantly, Vansh looked at the city man he loathed. The man who got Ajju to the village, that was rightfully his. "You are upset with Dhanush because he accompanied your sister on a horse ride. You have a problem with Ajju coming here because you feel threatened that your throne will be snatched away from you. Am I right about all of this?"

His eyes bore through Vansh, who merely scoffed, spitting simultaneously on the ground, showing his clear disgruntlement. "Well, then. Let me clarify once and for all. Your father is the *Chaudhary* of the *Raika*s as of now. He will decide who his successor shall be"

"As far as the city folk visiting Bassi goes, we plan to come here often. It would be best for you to get used to it!" Akash kept his hand on Arjun's shoulder, motioning him to calm down. "You shame us. All four of you" Akash stepped in to announce their sentence.

"Your punishment is to stay together till it is time for Arjun to leave with his family for the city" The evening that came was silent. Graveyard silent, to be precise. None of the four men spoke to each other.

Their raging hormones, cocktailed with an adrenalin rush, was enough to numb their speech. All the farewells happened as cordially as was possible, given the circumstances. All except one. Dhanush, claiming to have forgotten something relevant, ran up the stairs to the lobby where Leena was waiting for him.

"Here. Keep this for me until I return" It was his most precious possession. The trinket was spectacular to the naked eye. It was a brooch in the shape of a teardrop, with filigree work done on it. The diamond in the middle surrounded by tiny crushed diamonds, emblazoned a silent promise, freshly washed by Leenata's tears.

"Come back soon" she whispered to the wind, for the man who stole her heart raced down the stairs, joining the group to go back to where they came from. A man who had no clue as to why he gave in to his impulses so, doing the stupidest of things that he always ended up doing.

That's the thing about love. No one knows where the story began or where it would end; or whether it would ever end. But the fact that love was touching lives, hearts, souls, is something that no strength on the planet can control.

Comprehending the unfathomable is pure speculation. Living in the moment, is the priority that is beyond a shred of doubt. Whether one can participate in the making of their story hands on, or be a silent spectator and let nature take its course, depends on one thing alone-courage.

It takes courage to fall in love, to stay in love. It takes an immense amount of mental energy to attempt walking on air, assuming there is a wooden bridge, albeit rickety, that won't let you fall. Or better yet, a hand that will pull you up and let you soar high.

# CHAPTER SIX

The entrance to Anand Creations was studded with framed pictures, an odd bust here or there, breaking the monotony of design. The long, narrow lobby was especially designed to let each visitor take in the visual treats, laid out for them.

Chatting all the way from the car parking area, Andy escorted Myna and Diana, who looked like divas, straight out of a fashion magazine themselves. The chaperoning continued till the end of the lobby, where the ladies were eventually seated.

"So, you've told your parents we are prospective buyers?" asked Myna, seriously humored as to why a full-grown man had to fib to his parents. "I had to. Or else, the tour would not be possible" justified Andy, beaming on seeing his father walk in.

"Welcome to our world, ladies! My name is Sangharsh Anand. I will be your tour guide for today." he announced, kissing both their hands, with panache, flair. "No need for that, Dad"

"I have to finish this tour, then make a quick dash to DTD. The Prataps are back from Bassi. Dhanush has some ideas he wants me to take a look at" "Alright then. If I'm needed, you know where to find me" added Sangharsh, leaving for his wife's office.

"Where were you? Your *chai* has gone cold. I'll order for a fresh cup" Nalini began to fuss over him while he began to shower her with flattering compliments. "You look ethereal today. Have you done something new?"

"Not really. Everything is the same" "There must be someone out there who is supremely jealous of me being married to the most beautiful woman in the world!" The compliments, true as they were, sadly fell on deaf ears.

"Annie came ten minutes ago and told me everything. Do not make her lie. She is very bad at it" Nalini said, gathering her papers strewn into one pile at the teak desk. "I didn't have to ask her to lie because she volunteered." he reasoned.

"Well that's even better. You let her cover for your mistake." Nalini replied, enjoying every bit of the cornering of her husband. "Bottom line. You know" Sangharsh summarized. "Honey, the bottom line is that I always get to know. It is a given eventuality."

Amused, she hugged him, knowing he meant no harm. "You spoil them rotten!" she whispered, planting a gentle kiss on his cheek. "Hey Andy!" Annie took her twin's call, happily nested in her office, adjacent to their parents'. "Hi Annie, listen. Want to join us for lunch?" "Sure, Pick me up an hour after noon" "Done!"

Annie walked into her parents' office. "I have an appointment during lunchtime. I'll grab something from the fast-food joint" "Alright. See you later" Nalini waved without looking up.

She was neck deep in a set of designs that looked a bit flawed. Sangharsh was stumped at his wife's dismissal. "You let her go just like that? I have to tell you where I'm going, who I'll meet, when I'll return.."

"She is going to meet Abhimanyu. If she is not going to tell me, I won't belittle her by asking" Sangharsh took the marker chalk from her hand, pulling her close. "There is my Nalini. Show us yourself more often"

"The kids need to see this side of you too" he said tenderly, warming her with his words. Andy, in the meanwhile, was busy showing the ladies one of the leading fashion houses' intricate interior running.

"You've already seen the conference area. These are the offices" "Where is yours?" Myna asked casually. "I don't work here" "As in?" "As in I don't. I have a twin sister called Sarvani. We call her Annie. She is the Head Designer"

"My parents are the Joint Directors of Anand Creations. I am a photographer at a gallery called DTD. Ever heard of it?" "You work at DTD?" asked Diana, enamoured. "Yes! It stands for…" "Dare To Dream!"

Myna stretched the acronym for him. "The best photo gallery in all of Delhi. Can we go there too?" "Sure. After this tour, that is where I plan to take you both. We will be meeting my sister Annie and her close friend Abhimanyu for lunch, thereafter." Andy declared, mighty pleased with his itinerary.

The large door he opened next, left both ladies in awe. Rows of workers were busy whirring noisy sewing machines, to the specifications given by a handful of tailors, who also doubled up as their supervisors.

They crossed the hall silently into another back door, where all the finished products hung smugly, on labeled wooden hangers. "Where are the master designs kept, Andy?" asked Myna, abruptly.

"Nowhere actually. My mother insists on keeping it within the circle of Joint Directors, which are both my parents. No one knows if they exist for real, or are replaced with another idea Annie generates"

An earsplitting, consistent horn broke out soon after, declaring it was time for the workers to take a break for their noon meal. Taking the cue, Andy ushered the ladies back into the office area, to meet the senior Anands.

"Mom, this is Myna and her sister Diana" "Hello, Mrs. Anand. We've heard so much about you!" said Myna, smiling at the fine-looking lady who looked not a day older than her mid-twenties, smiling back casually at them.

"Well, hello! How was the tour?" "Quite interesting and insightful!" "Mom, we're off to meet Annie for lunch. I'm going to DTD afterwards. I'll see you at home" "Sure" "It was nice meeting you!" said Myna courteously.

The door to the office had closed as the young party left, leaving Nalini with a frown. One of the sisters looked familiar. Where had she seen that face before? "Working lunch, my pet?" came Sangharsh's voice as he popped in from the back door.

"Where were you? Andy just took the 'buyers' to lunch with Annie" Locking the doors and pulling the heavy drapes, Sangharsh walked to Nalini stealthily. "In that case, we have time to build our appetites now, don't we?!"

While fun and frolic prevailed between the Anands yet again, the lunch with Sarvani was beginning to get interesting. "What do you do with a design print after it is out in the market, if you don't mind my asking?" enquired Myna, twirling her pasta around the fork.

"Annie is a creative genius!" said Abhimanyu, interrupting in between. "Do you know she plans to open her own line of handcrafted dolls soon?" Andy looked at his twin, a bit taken aback.

"Seriously?" "Yes. Why not? I plan to one day. Might as well be sooner than later. Besides, my room at home can't handle any more designs or dolls anyways!" Now the entire conversation shifted to the new lines Delhi was about to witness.

One, was **Annie's doll collection** that she had suitably chosen it to be called so. The other, was Myna's indo-western men's apparel line called **Nara Apparels.**. Andy was bestowing almost all of his attention to Myna, an action that didn't go unnoticed.

Annie noticed it too, mighty tickled with how her twin was fussing over the gorgeous glam-doll. Besides, Myna came across as an affable, forthright person. Andy's phone began to ring halfway through dessert.

"Dan buddy! Welcome back! Yes, I'll be there in a half hour tops. See you soon!" "Let's make a move, ladies. Abhi, we'll meet up for drinks sometime soon, if that's okay with you"

"And baby sister, get back to work before Mom sends a search party headed by Dad, or worse…herself! Later lovebirds!" Everyone departed for their respective venues. Diana was the first to speak on the way to DTD.

"Who is Dan?" "Dhanush" clarified Andy." He and A.J., his elder brother, run DTD along with their father" "A family business just like yours." commented Myna. "It was due to snide remarks such as these that I chose to break away." said Andy, mildly irritated.

"No offence meant, Andy!" Myna smiled her sunshine at him. "None taken!" Andy semi-truthfully admitted. It was sort of a fleeting statement made by a third party that Andy was used to, since he could recollect.

The moment Annie chose to stay at Anand Creations, he chose to pursue his passion, which was photography. When teenagers his age pestered parents for bikes, he chose cameras. He got his Canon EOS 60D after winning a series of photography contests, which he prized to this day.

Anything worked towards a result, albeit tangible or materialistic, doubles in value after money and toil join forces. He had learnt that as his first lesson in life. The DTD layout was surrounded by sprawling lawns on all sides of the main gallery.

A valet took Andy's champagne-coloured Nissan Sunny, and they entered a world of lavish transformation; where simple was made to look everything but. The manager, Mr. Guha, came to greet them, offering to give the ladies a tour of DTD, while Andy went to meet Dan.

Myna and Diana didn't mind that at all. Pictures after pictures hung everywhere sporadically with speakers on the side that, when switched on, would explain everything there is to know about the photograph on display.

"Hey Hunter! Hope the trip to Bassi was lucrative?" Andy asked, sinking into the black leather couch, lighting up a smoke. "More than. Have a look at these" he said, showing the pictures he had clicked at Bassi.

After Andy took his own sweet time analyzing the photographs Dhanush had clicked, he shook his head. "I hope these are not the end products?" "No, you dope! I am the Hunter. My job is to churn an idea. You are the photographer"

"Assistant Photographer to Arjun *Chachu*" Andy corrected him, not waiting for an explanation. "So here is the plan. Dad has thousands of pictures to sieve through, that are at least two decades old. We can have a collection on display called **Regressive Progression**. Do you like it?" he asked eagerly.

"Yes I do! Have you run it by A.J.?" Andy asked. "We've been talking about this all morning. We three, that is A.J., you and I have to go to Bassi this coming week. You have to take shots of the exact same pictures from Dad's collection. How about that?"

"Sounds like a doable plan, Dhanush" "Excuse me, Sirs. The tour of the ladies is done. Is there anything else you would like me to do?" asked Bantu, who was entrusted to look after Andy's guests, by Mr. Guha.

"Which ladies?" A.J. asked as he entered Dhanush's office, smiling at Andy. "Hey A.J.! They are sisters from out of town. NRIs (Non Resident Indians). I just showed them around Anand Creations"

"Come on, let me introduce you to them" Andy offered, walking out of the office room already. "A.J., meet Myna and Diana. Myna wants to open an apparel line for men in Delhi" he added.

A.J.'s thick eyebrows and black eyes, were more than sufficient to intimidate anyone. Myna on the other hand, looked right into them, causing his cool stare to be cut short by an unexpected blink.

"Good evening ladies!" he wished them. "Your gallery is so much more charming than I had imagined" Diana said, waiting for her sister to join in. Myna was suddenly, perceptibly uncomfortable. "Dan is your brother?" was all she could ask.

"Yes. He is my younger brother" came the prompt reply. "Good. Diana is my younger sister" "Good" A.J. said stupidly, still holding Myna's hypnotic gaze.

Andy and Diana were wondering how much longer the ridiculous conversation would go on. "He is inside doing some work, otherwise he would have joined us" A.J. said again, still addressing only Myna.

"Right. It was nice meeting you. Could you drop us back to the hotel now, Andy?" said Myna, sounding downright dismissive. "Sure. A.J., I'll be late coming to work tomorrow. I've to ride Teja in the morning. It's been a while"

"Teja is his horse" A.J. found himself explaining quirkily to Myna again. "I gathered. I love horses too. Mine was called Pearl" "Well, I would love to pick you ladies tomorrow for a horse ride" A.J. found himself saying.

"Count me out. Horses and I are like chalk and cheese!" Diana intervened, leaving Myna to reply to A.J.'s offer. "I'll be ready. See you then" Andy left to drop the ladies to their hotel, slightly miffed at the way A.J. was behaving with Myna, who he himself was developing a soft corner for.

When A.J. returned to his office, he found Dhanush neck-deep in conversation with their father. "Where have you been?" he asked A.J., picking a handful of photographs. "Just seeing off Andy's guests. They came to see DTD. I'm meeting them for horse riding tomorrow" A.J. rattled out, praying his dumb streak would fade away soon.

"Alright, Listen up you two. We need to bring back DTD with a bang. I need pictures of these locations" said Arjun, showing them a handful of photographs. "You will be getting the soft version too. I will retain the Masterfile. Take as many angles as you can. We will select the best from those, later"

"How many are we talking about, *Baasa?*" "About a hundred" "A hundred!" A.J. exclaimed, looking blankly at the pictures in his hand. "The ones you hold are the main ones, a.k.a the showstoppers"

"The rest are fillers to complete the look. Dhanush has offered to go with you to Bassi. Do not, I repeat do not get into any sort of trouble with Akash's boy!" Nodding their heads in agreement, they watched Arjun go back to his office.

"The old man's gone crazy, A.J.!" "Watch your mouth, baby brother!" "The up side is the elation I feel. Back to Bassi!" Dan declared. "Back to

Leenata, you mean?!" A.J. replied, sifting through the pictures, his broad smile evident to Dhanush.

That night, Arjun briefed Suhani on what the plan for DTD was. "I will accompany the boys to Bassi. That way they won't be vulnerable, *Saheb*" "Let them be, *Beendni*. You cannot protect them forever. Besides, who will take care of me? I need you the most…in more ways than one!"

Arjun caught Suhani's *kurta*, pulling her close enough to let his breath fall on her glowing face. The night was young in the Pratap residence, where love seemed to have entered through each nook and corner of the house.

Annie sang to Abhi over the phone in between discussing her new doll-making ideas. Dhanush couldn't sleep out of sheer excitement. The prospect of meeting Leenata again, was enough to get his heart pounding, faster than any horse he had seen Andy ride.

A.J. was the most restless though. He had to get a hold over himself. He was beginning to act like a pup in front of Myna. The line between reality and dreams began to blur, with the onset of sleep in the household.

The next day, A.J. was up and about, ready to pick up Myna from the hotel. "Good morning, *Baasa*!" he wished his father, touching his feet as was the daily ritual for him, which was not as fanatically followed by Dhanush.

Arjun was making the morning tea for their mother, a sweet gesture of love ever since he could remember. "Good morning, *Betaji*! Andy called. He has asked you to come straight to the stables. He picked up your friend already" Arjun said, casually.

Ajju's immediate frown was a dead giveaway. "So, this 'friend' is a girl?" "Yes. She came to DTD yesterday" Feeling sorry for his son, Arjun gave him the same sage advice Sangharsh gave him, years ago.

"Word to the wise. Do not run after her. Stay aloof. Women like that kind of stuff" Surprised, Ajju picked a *jeera* cookie from his father's plate. Very few knew Arjun loved to bake, that too only various varieties of cookies.

He had no patience for anything more elaborate than throwing in some flour, sugar and essence together. "They do? Why?" "Beats me, Ajju. All I know is, if they think you aren't acknowledging them, they will begin to give you all of their attention"

"If you want to show attention son, first let the girl take the lead" Feeling confident, hopeful with this father's astute advice, Ajju left for the stables, dressed in his faded jeans, denim shirt and Hushpuppies.

Unlike Andy, A.J. preferred changing into his horse-riding rig at the locker room, for riders. Andy was overly proud of being an equestrian, flaunting whenever he got the slightest of chances.

On meeting Andy and Myna, A.J. acted as remote as his fine nature could possibly permit. He chose a chestnut horse to ride, loving the feel that cool morning breeze emitted as an instant natural energizer, all the while he rode.

Andy had shown off enough with Teja, his chocolate-brown *Kathiawari* horse. His show jumps won him several claps, not to mention vibrant grins from Myna. It was all an act though.

Myna was secretly disappointed. Every time she went anywhere near A.J., he stiffened up. It was as if she gave him the virus of displeasure, that he preferred to stay afar from. This was not how men reacted to her sensual charisma, usually.

All three sat at the club house to grab a bite, before calling it a day. Myna ordered for a fresh fruit juice and some bread omelet. Andy ordered for cold cuts, a milk shake and cinnamon bagels. A.J. had a cup of Darjeeling tea, with a pair of blueberry scones.

"Sorry about the morning, *dost*. If you want, you can drop Myna to the hotel. I'm off to freshen up and go to work" Andy announced, biting into his bagel. Feeling patronized, A.J.'s reply was precise, curt.

"No can do. I have to be off to the gallery, too. I need to be there before my father's Assistant Photographer" "Yes, I know that. I just don't want you thinking I got to pick and drop both, that is all" Andy retorted, hurt at A.J. pulling rank for the first time.

A.J. regretted the words, seconds after they audaciously poured out; not just because he knew he had insulted Andy, but by the way Myna reacted to being thrown around like a ball. She picked her hat, walked silently to the reception and hailed a cab for herself.

Andy didn't speak to A.J., leaving to say goodbye to Myna, who dismissed him casually, careful not to show any hurt felt by her. A.J. sat for a couple of minutes more, till he saw Myna come out of the Reception, down the cobbled path, cellphone in hand.

She talked all the way, right into the cab, but did turn to give him a glance. A girl knows when she has caught the fancy of a boy, as did she. He froze at the distinct look of disappointment Myna flashed at him through her blue eyes, before she donned her Coco Chanel sunglasses on.

That day, Arjun witnessed the not-so-subtle power play between A.J. and Andy, at work. Everything one said was counter-attacked by the other. This was a team that was being split right in the middle.

It was time to call in reinforcements. "Sangharsh, I need to talk to you" Arjun called Anand Creations. "So do I. Drop everything right this second and listen. Just don't react. These two new ladies are listed as not two, but three ladies!"

"Myna is listed as Mia Cotton. Diana is Diana Cotton. Both are travelling with their mother, Ramona Cotton!" Arjun sat down slowly on his chair, as his legs refused to take the weight of the information overload. No! No! NO!

This was either the beginning of the end, or the end of the beginning. Depends on how one looks at it. Being prepared to tackle a situation that is completely out of the blue, is possible only if there is enough mental strength, to chalk out a plan of action.

This isn't possible for everyone, for one simple reason. We are all built differently, wired differently. Therefore, we react to the same situation in more than one way. How we act or react is always typical though, to how we intrinsically are.

# CHAPTER SEVEN

The smooth waters of the river Bhairach, far from the tumultuous gushing near the dam, had a single row of brick houses; some partially painted, some just red brick. At the end point of this water body, was where the buffaloes were bathed.

Viren's family had the largest livestock of cattle, especially buffaloes. He was minding them as they swam around the shallow water, the occasional grunt revealing their pleasure, as their thick hides cooled down.

"Tara *Chachiji* told me I may find you here" Vansh announced, squatting on the grass next to Viren. *"Akal bina oonth ubhana phirein*! (Despite having the means, the job cannot be done!)" *"Kain?"* asked Viren, wondering what the context was in reference to.

*"Baasa* and I went to exercise our horses today. En route, he elaborately explained how I should be ready anytime now, to hand over my well-earned *pagdi* to Ajju *Bhaiya"* Astonished, Viren kept frowning, chewing on the long stem of dry grass.

"The city folk called last night. They are returning. This time for longer. Only Ajju *Bhaiya*, Dhanush, Nandish and two *bhaylian"* *"Chote Sardar, ab kya* (Now what, *Chote Sardar*?)" *"Na*. Call me *Chote Thakur*. Viren, if *Baasa* has asked me to be real, I do not have his support"

*"Maasa* is on my side, but she is just a *Panch* member. The final decision still rests with my father. I am not going after something that was never mine to begin with" Worried about Vansh's tone, not to mention his take on the conversation he had with *Chaudhary* Akash, Viren motioned the cattle helper to get the animals outbound, towards the sheds.

"My *Behan* was asking when you will come home to have *gajrela*. I told her you will come today" With a faraway look, deep in thought, Vansh followed Viren all the way to his home.

"I'll never get over how colourful your place looks, what with each wall painted a different colour!" Vansh observed, briefly humoured. Viren's house stood out among the other villagers, from afar.

All four corners were different colours, in stark contrasts, clashing with each other. Tara thought it would make her house stand out. Despite her husband Giriraj's repeated requests, she had it painted, only to regret her folly later.

"*Khammaosa, Chachiji*" Vansh wished Tara, who was busy preparing the noon meal. "*Aawo padharo Chote Sardar* (Welcome *Chote Sardar*)!" Irritated though, Vansh opted to ignore the intentional slip-up. "Malika made *gajrela* exactly the way you like it. Would you like some?"

Tara asked, pouring some of the pudding out in a steel *katori*, before he could respond. "Here. Try some" On seeing no visible change in Vansh's facial expression, Tara became anxious.

"What is wrong, *Chote Sardar*?" "Exactly what you just said. That is what's wrong!" he spat out, keeping the half-eaten *gajrela* aside. "*Matlab*?" Vansh shook his head, refusing to go into details, when Tara got up too.

"I'm going to Malika at Gurukul. She has left her lunch *potli* behind. Come with me. We will talk on the way" Already distressed, Vansh chose to avoid any confrontation with her. The effortless beauty surrounding them went unnoticed, courtesy the mood they both were in.

They met a villager carrying her *Bharauti*. Heavy as it were, she still managed a smile followed by a chirpy greeting. "*Khammaosa, behan! Khammaosa, Chote Sardar!*" Vansh flinched at being called the name he was asked to turn down, again.

Catching on, Tara began their talk. "Akash *Bhaisa* is the *Chaudhary* for now. Who knows what will happen tomorrow?" "He has asked me to be ready. As in, if Ajju *Bhaiya* wishes to succeed *Baasa*" Vansh said helplessly.

"*Arre, chodo*! (Leave it)! Ajju will never return to Bassi. He is of the city now. As per the *Raika* custom, Dhanush made Akash the *Chaudhary* on the condition that if Ajju were to return, he was to be given his rightful place"

"But, for all these years, your father, *Chaudhary* Akash has been our tribal leader" "What are you getting at, *Chachiji*? Speak out clearly" "Simply put, you have to focus on two things. Ensure Ajju does not return to Bassi as a permanent resident is point one. The other is a bit tougher to pull off."

Piqued curiousity emanated from Vansh, as he coaxed her into revealing the second requirement. "Take positive, known, noticed steps to show you are interested in the development of our village. Once your father sees you are working hard towards Bassi's progress, who knows!"

"He might rethink his stand" Newfound hope permeated into Vansh, like a ray of bright sun across a gloomy sky. "*Theek hai* (Alright). I will start planning right away. Ask Viren to meet me near the river. We will figure out something together"

Pleased she was being obeyed, Tara said, "And do not stop anyone from calling you what you are meant to become-*Chote Sardar*!" The path that curved naturally towards Gurukul, had Malika rushing up to meet her mother.

"Oh, thank God! I was beginning to think I'm going to starve for lunch today!" she said, hurriedly taking the *potli* from Tara, utterly famished. "*Pranam, Maatsa!*" Vansh teased his friend.

"*Jeete raho, Betaji*! Why haven't you worn your uniform?" Humoured by the touché moment, Vansh began to chuckle for the first time, since morning. "You always know how to make me laugh! And you make *gajrela* really well!"

Loving the playful banter between the two, Tara spoke. "Right then, children. I am off to meet my friend. *Chote Sardar*, please ensure she eats all of her *dal baati*. She eats like a bird!" Tara was, in fact, on her way to meet Bindiya; as Vansh's mother, not as the *Chaudhrain* of the *Raika*s.

"*Khammaosa, Chaudhrain!*" she greeted her, the moment their eyes met, on entering the *Chaudhary haveli*. "*Aawo baitho*, Tara. (Come sit, Tara) What brings you here?" asked Bindiya, filling her husband's *hookah* with pieces of coal for the evening.

Bindiya disliked Tara since she got to know about her clandestine affair with Dhanush, Suhani's late husband. She was not permitted to show it though. As per Akash, the *Chaudhary* and *Chaudhrain* are the father and mother of the entire village, barring no one.

Therefore, there could be no partiality, at any given point of time, favouring one person over the other. "*Khaana khaliyo kya*? (Have you eaten?)" "Yes, thank you" "Then let us have some freshly-brewed tea" Bindiya offered gracefully, which Tara accepted.

"So what is new in Bassi?" "Oh, nothing that deserves your attention. Normalcy prevails, as does peace all around. Our children though, are now all grown up." replied Tara, steering the conversation with gentle masterstrokes.

"Yes, Tara. I have noticed that too. Vansh and Viren are together practically every waking moment! Leenata and Malika are *Maatsa*s at Gurukul" Pulling her stool closer, Tara took the final step, sort of a leap of faith, to get a feel of *Chaudhrain* Bindiya's reaction.

"*Chaudhrain*, what do you think about '*Antaha kutumb vinimay vivaah*'? (exchange marriage between a pair of siblings)?" Bindiya's eyes popped out at the mere mention, but she let the information sink in. It was not a bad idea at all. Viren was a good boy. So was Malika, a docile girl.

She could control her own children through their spouses, if need be. "*Sochne do thoda humein.* (Let me think about it a bit). I will have to obviously speak to *Chaudhary hukam* about this" Exhaling in relief, Tara clasped Bindiya's hands.

"I knew you were a reasonable woman! My Malika cooks really well. She made *gajrela* for *Chote Sardar* today, which he liked immensely" Interrupting Tara's excited chattering Bindiya said, "I merely suggest to my husband, Tara *behan*. It is he who is the ultimate authority, as is our custom"

"Yes. That is true. It is also true, that a smart woman knows how to put things forth to her husband in such a way, that he has no choice but to do as she wishes!" Both laughed at this remark, after which Tara asked to take leave.

The afternoon brought with itself a gentle desert storm, the sand layering everyone, everything, with a granular layer of reality. Bindiya watched Tara rush back to her multi-coloured house.

Three village women dressed in *ghaghra choli*s, ranging from deep indigo-blue to tangerine, had their faces covered, to save themselves from inhaling the dust. They were in no tearing hurry, as they balanced their clay and copper pots.

She remembered how Suhani, her childhood friend, accompanied her when they were at Nagri, her *maike*, while they did practically everything together; be it depositing filled pots of water to their houses, to walking the fields all the way to the abandoned well.

Where did those days go? Deep in thought, she never noticed Akash walking up the path to the main door, where she now stood. "If you did not have this faraway look, I would assume you were waiting for me!"

Shaken into her senses, she replied, "Actually, I need to talk to you. Rest awhile. We will speak when you are awake" "What is it, Bindi?" Akash asked, studying his still well-adorned wife, turning the end of her brilliant fuchsia *odhni* around her fingers, over and over. "Later"

"Tell me now. The city folk arrive tomorrow. There is much to be done later" Giving in to his insistence, she narrated the entire discussion that transpired earlier with Tara. "It sounds like a good enough idea"

"We should speak to the children about it though" replied Akash, not very comfortable with the thought of Tara being their relative, if this idea was to be accepted. "Akash, what have you thought about our son?"

"Vansh is not to be *Chaudhary* if Ajju chooses to return. I had to talk with him about this today morning. Do not put ideas in his head that cannot be realized!" "But he is your son! You are the *Chaudhary* of the *Raikas*! Should he not be the successor to the throne?"

"There isn't much of a throne left, Bindi. Haven't you been noticing how many have left for the city, leaving our hard life behind? We are dwindling in number...and spirit, I fear!" "Hush! Do not speak this way. What will our village folk think, when they hear their *Chaudhary* speak in this morose way?"

"Dhanush *Bhaisa* made me the caretaker to his legacy, till Ajju would return. You may have forgotten, but I have not" Akash said, disliking the ambitious side of Bindiya rearing its ugly head again.

"Tara got the proposal assuming Vansh would succeed his father." she persisted the nag thread. "We cannot sentence our children to a lifetime of false assumptions. I know first-hand how frustrating it can get!" Akash yelled.

Years of pent up frustration began to finally find their way, out through his words. "You are frustrated with me because I speak my mind. Mine and our son's!" Bindiya hissed. "Well then, to hell with you and your son!"

"This entire discussion is based on two conspiring women-you and Dhanush *Bhaisa*'s mistress! Inform your co-conspirator, that I hereby reject her proposal!" Akash declared, stomping straight to the cool bedroom to lie down.

Not intending to aggravate the matter any further, Bindiya chose to stay silent for now. Akash may loathe Tara, but he had a soft corner for her straightforward husband, Giriraj. Bindiya sent word for Giriraj to join them for dinner, giving a note to the messenger boy for Tara.

The message was meant to urge Tara, to coax Giriraj into convincing Akash, about the familial alliance. The moment Tara received the message, she began to brim with enthusiasm, as she sweet-talked Giriraj into the well-thought out alliance.

She picked out a crisp cotton *dhoti kurta* for her husband with a *leheriya* turban in fulvous-yellow and fruity-orange. "What if *Chaudhary Saheb* refuses? It will be an insult I could not bear!" he panicked.

"Nothing of the sort is going to happen. You know he is fond of you from the very beginning. Besides, the *Chaudhrain* and I have had a talk only today. We both approve of the alliances"

"It will be good for both our families. As parents, isn't that what we want? Viren will mend his ways with the mature Leenata. Malika, as we both know, worships the ground Vansh walks on, ever since her childhood"

Convinced with all the convoluted logic his wife fed him, Giriraj left for the *Chaudhary haveli*, full of hope, confidence. "*Khammaosa, Chaudhary hukam!*" "*Aawo padharo*, Giriraj *bhai*! How have you been keeping?"

Akash welcomed him with open affection. "Very well. The fields have done well with the abundance of *bajra*. My buffaloes are healthy and get me good income. *Ma Bhavani* has been kind to my family"

Akash admired this trait of Giriraj's. His ambition was restricted, unlike his wife, who could go to any lengths to attain what her greed desired. Bindiya came with a tray of *thandai*, leaving as soon as formal pleasantries were done with.

"*Chaudhary hukam*, I assume you are aware of what I have come to speak to you about" Giriraj cut to the chase with utmost humility. "I do, *dost*. Like I told my *lugai*, I will not give my decision until I have consulted with my children"

"Those days when the parents would find a match for their children, are long gone. I do not want to give you my word today, letting it go in vain if not abided by, tomorrow" Shaking his head in agreement, Giriraj sipped his *thandai*.

"*Khammaosa, Chachaji*!" Leenata walked in, her fawn and copper zig-zagged *ghaghra choli* not hindering her quick gait, books in hand. "*Jeete raho Bitiya*!" Giriraj blessed her, as did he Vansh, who entered a few minutes after his sister.

"Leenata, Vansh..I need to speak with you both. Meet me in my room after you've freshened up, before dinner" "*Ji, Baasa hukam*" they both said. "There you go, Giriraj *bhai*. By tomorrow morning, you shall get your answer." Akash said, hopeful for the right decision that was yet to be made by him.

Giriraj returned full of ambiguity, much to the disappointment of his wife, Tara. "What gall! He is not even the real *Chaudhary*, but sure has airs like one! We suffer a sleepless night, while he chooses whether he accepts or rejects both our children?" she yelled, enraged at her passive husband and their pseudo leader.

"*Chup kar, bawli*! (Be quiet, silly)! The children will hear and that will be the end of it." "Then let them. They ought to know we care to secure their future. So what if our hopes depend on the wishes of *Chaudhary* Akash and his snobbish *Chaudhrain*!"

Viren and Malika heard each word spoken between their parents, lying in their respective rooms. They got the gist of the story, but were equally tensed. Viren was worried, because he knew Vansh would never agree to marry his sister.

That meant one thing alone-the end of his friendship with the future *Chaudhary* of the *Raika*s. The entire family was brewing with streaks of layered tension, sprinkled with plausible restlessness.

Meanwhile, in the *Chaudhary haveli*, Akash was sitting in the balcony with his children, speaking to them about the *rishta*. "Malika? She is like Leenata to me. How could I possibly marry her, *Baasa*?" Vansh replied.

"Besides, I have spent all day today making plans for our Bassi. I want to make subtle changes to retain our village folk; improve our living conditions, generate more revenue through our livestock"

"How can I achieve all this if you get me married? I am not ready now. Let me prove myself to you first. After that, you can choose anyone you deem fit. But, not Malika. I do not see her as my *lugai*."

Having heard his son, Akash turned to Leenata. Sitting quietly, she was turning her silver *kadha* over and over again. "*Bitiya*, what do you have to say?" Leenata was quiet. What could she say?

She had given her heart to Dhanush, but had no idea how he felt. Could she reject a marriage proposal on a whimsical possibility? Her place was in Bassi. If she married Viren, she could still manage Gurukul, be near her aging parents.

She loved Malika dearly and would never feel alone, either. "Well, Leenata?" Akash repeated himself. "*Jaise aap theek samjhe, Baasa* (Whatever you think is right, Father)" she said, her concurrence partially pleasing the *Chaudhary*.

"Well then, it has been decided. Vansh, you have one month to show me the changes you plan to make, in Bassi. After that, start preparing for your sister's wedding. She will be engaged to Viren shortly"

"Now let's go for dinner. Your mother probably has a stomach ache out of anxiety! Hope these pieces of news suffice" Bindiya was happy on seeing Akash elated, but not completely satisfied due to Vansh's rejection of the proposal.

When the news reached Giriraj's household, each one of them was equally unhappy. For appearances sake though, every member of both households faked anticipation.

Late, at that very same night, Arjun called to inform Akash that his boys were being accompanied to Bassi, by Nandish and two lady friends. "We are all set to welcome them, Arjun *Saheb*. You might have to join them soon though!" Akash said, sounding cryptic.

Arjun assumed he meant due to the prior, carnivorous encounter, but he was corrected shortly. "My Leenata's hand has been spoken for! She is to be engaged soon to Viren, Giriraj's son!" Arjun congratulated him, as did Suhani.

They promised to come to Bassi, both for the *sagai* as well as the *byaav*. "All packed?" Arjun asked Ajju, watching him frantically trying a number on his mobile with utmost sincerity. "Yes, *Baasa*. I am off to bed"

"Dhanush has slept off already" Ajju answered, watching his father look at the darkened side of the room where Dhanush lay on his bed, in his usual style, buried deep in blankets. "I don't know how that boy does it"

"The moment his head touches the pillow, he is oblivious to the world! Quite like his mother, I must say!" said Arjun, walking away towards his room, leaving the fresh information on Bassi for the breakfast table, the next day.

Ajju silently prayed for forgiveness from his Maker. He had fibbed to his father to cover up for his brother. Dhanush had heard the telephonic conversation between *Chaudhary* Akash and his father. He left home in his Hummer, to cool off.

His mobile was out of coverage area, which worried Ajju a bit. It was only in the wee hours of the morning, that Dan entered. He looked disheveled and stank of alcohol. "I will wake you in two hours. Make yourself presentable then" Ajju told him, understanding his plight.

When A.J woke him up, Dan freshened up without a fuss, chirpier than usual; as if nothing had happened less than 24 hours ago. In truth, he was about to face the biggest test of his life, far away from his own turf.

We all have defense mechanisms within us, that we colloquially refer to as masks. Depending on the level of comfort, proximity, we choose to change or shed our self-adorned masks.

True feelings are like savoured garnishings that can be shared, only with those we feel the closest to. Most men though prefer to keep their feelings to themselves. They don't adhere to this rule as they feel it is less complicated to open up to how they really feel, quite like the Pandora's box.

They weigh confidence, control, as being part of their manliness. But, like they always say, a split second suffices to reveal how one truly feels. In the blink of any eye, anything can change..everything can change.

# CHAPTER EIGHT

Ramona Rai was supposed to be a buried nightmare of the past. The phone call from Gerard Cotton which Arjun's previous assistant Tanisha had taken, while the Anands and Prataps were at Pushkar, was never followed up.

Neither did Tanisha's mysterious disappearance bother anyone much. Too many good things, at times, make us forget to take our rose-coloured glasses off, skewing the real into an altercation of the truth.

Arjun was waiting eagerly, for when the young lot would leave for Bassi. He had to get to the bottom of this sudden reappearance of the supposedly-dead Ramona. Why was she Ramona Cotton?

Why did the girls, Myna, correction..Mia and Diana, hide their true identity? Arjun trusted his sons not to give away any information about the gallery, in a fit of boastfulness.

Even so, he decided to call Ajju every evening, just to ensure everything was going as per their plan, of getting the desired pictures for DTD. "Your food is getting cold, *Saheb*!" Suhani's soft voice came from behind him, the moment he donned his jacket.

Taking her in his arms, he held her a bit longer than usual. "I love you my *Beendni*! You are the best thing that has ever happened to me" he said in an emotionally charged, shaking voice.

Smiling serenely, Suhani stroked his cheek, newly shaven and smelling enticingly of her favourite after shave that Arjun used, Old Spice. She kissed him ever so softly, whispering, "I love your loving me, *Saheb*. You are my dream come true."

"Now, let's eat before Shanti reheats the food again!" Arjun had gotten his old maid Shanti to their home after marrying Suhani. It was required too, for both spouses had lifestyles where the stereotypical home maker role of a wife, especially in the kitchen department, was an impossibility.

Usually, both husband and wife left for their separate professional venues in their respective cars; not just because their timings were different, or that their locations were poles apart; but also due to the fact that they would morph into thorough professionals, leaving home and hearth behind.

Today, Arjun offered to drive his beloved to Maya's Reality, her silver handcrafted jewellery store, after which he would proceed to his work zone, the Dare to Dream gallery.

Chatting all the way, Suhani told him about her latest collection of handcrafted pieces, painstakingly researched, intricately worked upon. She yearned to make pieces that would appeal to the younger generation, of both the Indian, as well as the international market.

All the information she was giving him, unfortunately, was bouncing right off of him. Arjun loved listening to Suhani's voice, his Braids' soft melody that washed over him like a fresh, cool, morning breeze; invigorating, intoxicating.

A few years ago, when they were holidaying in a quaint resort in the outskirts of Bangalore, she chattered about this and that for a while, indifferent to his consistent, sporadic nods.

Finally, she asked him why he was so annoyingly mono-syllabic. "Your voice calms me. It fills me up with hope, happiness, love. If I speak, it spoils the rhythm of the way you talk"

Charmingly convincing that he was, Suhani treasured this clarification of his. Arjun wasn't exaggerating though. He genuinely loved the way her eyes shone, when she spoke passionately about Maya's Reality.

"Thank you for the ride, my handsome husband! I'll see you in the evening then?" Suhani said, as they entered the gates of her office. "Hmm. Give me a kiss to get by the day, my queen, my love" She willingly obliged… sweet, soft, still lingering, long after it was over.

Now, Arjun had to take a detour. Unbeknownst to his better half, Sangharsh was meeting him at the hotel, the Cottons were staying in. Elite International was a seven-star hotel, embellished with all the frills needed, to maintain its reputation as one.

Sangharsh was already waiting in the lobby, dashing to meet him as he spotted his friend enter through the glass-copper door. Both had neither the inclination nor the intention to admire the plush interiors, with guests streaming in and out of innumerable doors.

"She is having breakfast. I saw" was all Sangharsh said, answering Arjun's unasked question. "I need to speak with her" Arjun said, shaken up by abnormally large doses, of curious discomfort.

"No, you don't! She is about to finish her meal, after which she plans to visit the gallery. Your gallery. Meet her on your turf, Arjun. Not hers!" Agreeing to his friend's justification, they both left to satiate their demanding professions.

The gallery seemed large, empty without his three musketeers-Ajju, Dhanush, Nandish. Sensing the same, Mr. Guha got him chatting on a thick file, with unanswered mail from journalists.

"We will have a gala soon, Mr. Guha. Dhanush is working on a brilliant concept along with Ajju and Nandish. This should be the masterstroke we needed to propel ourselves out of the abyss, just about keeping our heads above water, to ultimately bask in the glory of a well-earned success."

"Sir, the economy is also to blame" "Mr. Guha, when a business fails, it is wiser if the owner realizes his mistake instead of stay in denial, palming off the cause on external factors. If luck favours, one might even obtain the opportunity to rectify the error."

A few more semi-argumentative discussions later, Arjun's private line began to buzz. Mr. Guha took his leave, assuming his boss would want to converse with his wife, alone. "What a pleasant surprise, my love!" Arjun said as soon as he picked the mouthpiece, assuming it was none other than his *Beendni*.

"Of all the things I imagined you would say to me after all these years…I would never have guessed, this would be one of them." came a husky voice at the other end. "I'm sorry. I thought it was my wife calling. May I know who this is?" asked Arjun, apologetically.

"You are not entirely wrong, my pet. I am your wife still, aren't I?" Cold ice began to hit him from nowhere, shattering his rose-coloured glasses. That voice could have been no one else's but. He let her continue with her ramming introduction though.

"I am parked outside the gallery, Arjun. Won't you receive me, show off what you made, like your nephew did for my daughters?!" Repulsed as if a dollop of bitter gourd was put into his mouth, Arjun walked out of his office like a zombie, straight into his real life nightmare, to the main porch of the gallery.

A tourist taxi was parked, with a woman sitting behind. Ramona got out with her usual flair, tipping the driver. "Assuming you are my ride back, of course!" she said, intending for Arjun to understand the underlying meaning of her statement.

They stood in front of each other, like two people who were strangers. Familiar strangers. "I'm dying to see what you have done to the place, Arjun! The driveway is all spruced up. Come on, let's begin the grand tour!" she said, pushy as her old, usual self.

Walking through the long gallery, watching the still pictures, stopping to hear the description of a picture at random, she looked quite in awe at the giant leaps taken, to make visible changes at DTD.

"Quite impressed! So, where is my old office?" "The world thought you were dead. Before that, I acquired DTD from your father, if you recall. Here, I am the owner. And this.." said Arjun, opening the glass door to his cabin, "is my office"

Ramona tried to enter, but Arjun stopped her. "Only guests, business associates, are allowed to enter my office. If you would like to sit, we will go to the conference room" Snubbed, but in no position to retaliate, Ramona followed him to the well-equipped conference room.

"Won't you offer me a beverage?" "Sure. What would you like to have?" Testing him, she said, "A flute of red wine, maybe?" Arjun dialed the reception. "Bantu, a flute of red wine and a Hoegaarden at the conference room, please. Send Mr. Guha half an hour thereafter. Thank you"

"I admire your resistance, Arjun. You want answers to questions that only I have, right?" Ramona said, taking off her gloves and scarf. "Yes. It's obvious" "So it is. Alright, I am ready to be drilled. Ask away!"

"I thought you died in the car crash, at Greenwich village. How are you alive? No, that did not come out right" Arjun flustered, exasperated at being at a loss for words. "That's okay. Let me explain. I survived the crash"

"In the hospital, Gerard saw me broken, both mentally as well as physically. He was a powerful family's sole heir, back then. I was shifted to a private clinic in Scotland, accompanied by a well-paid nurse"

"For the world I was dead. Gerard ensured that by arranging my fake funeral, adopting Mia legally, shipping you off to India as well" A gentle knock announced that the drinks had arrived.

Arjun thanked the waiter, sipped his beer, opened a pack of Marlboros he pulled out of his pocket. "Still smoking the same brand, drinking the same beer. Some things never change!"

Ignoring her snide remark, he kept the box of smokes on the rectangular glass table, lighting one up. Ramona reached for the pack. "May I?" Arjun passed the Zippo to her, as an affirmative answer.

"So, where was I?" she said, inhaling the smoke and resting back on the swivel chair of the conference room. "Oh yes. We had Diana after that. Gerard and I, I mean. And, as they say, we lived happily ever after!"

Frowning, Arjun said, "What are you doing here, Ramona? Your 'happily ever after' is with Gerard, is it not?" "Was. He is dead. Besides, we were living in. Never really wanted to marry"

"It was bad enough, you and I were forced to marry, to legitimize Mia who wasn't even yours to begin with." she shamelessly owned up, not noticing the change in Arjun's complexion, that went from normal to pasty.

Smiling knowingly at Arjun, she said, "Which means we are still legally married. I heard you tied the knot with that nomadic girl and have two sons now. I am sorry, Arjun. I need to have my rightful place in your life, your home"

"What? What rubbish is this?" Arjun roared, springing up from his chair. Ramona, startled at his loud voice, sprung up as well, her hand accidentally hitting the glass flute, dropping it to the floor.

"Tch, tch, tch. See what you made me do, my husband. Sometimes things happen. Reacting in a hurry is inadvisable!" "Shut up! I am dropping you to your hotel right away. Then, get out of my life!"

Arjun stomped out, enraged. Ramona tailed him, straight to the front door. By the time Mr. Guha entered the conference room to meet his boss and the guest, all he was welcomed with, was a wine stain on the floor.

The two were silent in the car for a while, till Ramona chose to speak first. "I thought I had the patent for the silent treatment, Arjun!" she joked, trying to revive memories of yesteryears.

Arjun responded harshly, "Look here. I do not know what's going on in that brain of yours, as of now. But, if you come after my wife, my family…I will kill you myself!" Shocked, deeply insulted, Ramona went silent all over again.

She began to hum. A habit Arjun loathed in her, when they were married, earlier. It was strange how both knew what their pet peeves were, not making the effort in knowing more of what they liked, in general.

A silent battle based on ego, who ups the other threatened to begin. It had happened all those years ago and a repeat performance ensued, all over again. Picking up speed, Arjun's raven black Mercedes Benz got them to Ramona's hotel, Elite International, in no time.

Before she got out though, she parted with three sentences; or rather, three sharpened darts that landed right on the bull's eye. "I hope you realize bigamy is a legal offence. I am moving in with you in two days' time, whether you like it or not, as I am within my lawful rights as your wife"

"If that nomadic girl is still in the premise, make no mistake my pet, I will have her put in jail, along with you!" Slamming the car door, not turning back, the locust in Arjun's life returned. His head was reeling with all that had transpired.

He chose to go to Anand Creations to talk this out with Sangharsh and Nalini, his only family, his confidantes. "What in God's name am I supposed to do now?" "Ignore her!" blurted out Nalini, realizing how stupidly unrealistic it actually sounded.

Sangharsh was watching Arjun quietly, drumming his desk with a consistent finger rapping, like heavy rain beating on a window pane. What do you think should be your move now, Arjun?" he asked his old friend, not expecting the violent reply he got in return.

"Remove Ramona's existence from the face of the earth! But I cannot do that, can I?" Arjun shrieked, slamming his fist on the wooden table. "Neither can you wish her away, *dost*!" Sangharsh argued.

The slump in the conversation made all three think the issue out individually. "Leave Suhani at our place till the matter is resolved" Nalini said, concluding all three thoughts by uttering her well-thought out words.

"It's the only option-Hobson's choice!" Arjun replied, suddenly terrified of sentencing himself to pining for Braids, all over again. "Is there no other way, Sangharsh?" Nalini asked, tears welling up as she watched Arjun, slowly pull his car on to the road.

"I am sure there is. We just have to find it. In the meantime, if Suhani stays under the same roof as Ramona and Arjun, we both know the python is well within her rights by law to get them both arrested." he said, putting his arm around Nalini protectively.

Arjun chose to pick Suhani up in the evening, earlier than usual. Abhimanyu, Suhani's assistant was capable enough to take care of business. Annie too depended on Abhi, for he encouraged her to create the exclusive doll line.

Scattered thoughts pricked him off and on, during the entire drive back home. Suhani noticed it, but gave him the benefit of doubt. "Hard day at work, *Saheb*?" He waited till they reached their home. "Harder day at life, my love!" he blurted out, alone with his wife in their room.

Arjun knew it was time to break the ill-begotten news. He sat her down, held both of her hands, and said, "*Beendni*, what I am about to tell you is something you must support me in"

"Know that you and I are one. Nothing, no one can ever change that" "You're scaring me, *Saheb*!" "I'm a bit scared myself, to be honest, Suhani. But I must protect you, at any cost"

Arjun then went ahead, telling Suhani about the unwanted locust Ramona Rai, coming back to haunt them from the dead, in the literal sense. Suhani tried several times to move her hands away.

She couldn't for Arjun's grip was tight, albeit in a gentle manner. "Why didn't you tell me Ramona is in town the moment Sangharsh *Bhaisa* called, *Saheb*?" "I do not know" "Why didn't you tell me the girls that have gone to Bassi with our sons and nephew are Ramona's daughters, *Saheb*?"

"I do not know" "Why did you drop me at Maya's and then say you are going to DTD, forgetting to mention you were off to see Ramona, *Saheb*?" "I don't know, I don't know, I don't know!"

"What do you want me to say? I panicked! I wanted to see if it was her or someone else, I guess" "You panicked? Alright. Assuming you're fine now, the legal ramifications are crystal clear now, aren't they?"

"I cannot stay under the same roof as you. Legally, I am not even your wife!" Suhani sprung up, as reality slapped her on the face. "I don't love her. I never did. I love you" "Yes, I know. Love will not solve this though. Let's speak to the Anands about this" she said, calmly.

"I already did. They say you ought to go stay with them until this blows over" Enraged, Suhani spat out, "You had a family discussion without me. In your head, you have already moved away"

"Thank you very much. I will go and pack my things now." "I'll drop you at the Anand villa" Arjun offered. "And why would you do that? I have enough money to stay anywhere I choose!" "Don't be silly, Suhani. They are expecting you" Arjun reasoned.

"Well, to hell with them and to hell with you! To hell with all of you!" she shrieked, glaring at him, banging their bedroom door on her way out. Arjun went to freshen up for the night a bit later on.

He ate food alone, assuming Suhani must be sulking somewhere in their huge mansion. He finally got a call from Ajju that broke the deafening silence. "You sound tired, *Baasa*" "I miss you both, that is all"

"Everything okay there?" Arjun asked, putting his last bit of effort to sound casual. "Yes. As normal as possible. Dhanush is behaving eerily professional. Vansh is essentially being more than helpful"

"How are Andy's guests liking Bassi?" "Oh, Mia loves riding as you know. She looked so cute trying on a *ghaghra choli*. I took pictures too, *Baasa*. She is quite photogenic. The bluest eyes I've ever seen. And, she has a fantastic sense of humour too!"

"She has been trying to speak in Hindi, that charming foreign accent of hers just bowls me over!" Arjun closed his eyes, wishing he could shut his ears as well. Ajju was falling in love with Mia.

He wasn't even aware her name wasn't Myna, but Mia, his step sister! He had to warn his son, but feared it was too late already. He made a mental note to have a talk with his son, when he returned from Bassi.

Upon hearing the main door bang shut, Arjun peeped from the bedroom balcony. The chauffeur was putting a few bags in Suhani's car. She walked straight into it, although he knew she was aware he was at their balcony, watching.

He watched her mouth move as she gave instructions to the driver where to take her. Staring at her go, he blinked; not sure if what he saw for an instant was real, or a fragment of reality.

Suhani had turned back to look at him, her face contorted with grief, of a person who left something of great value behind- her heart. That night, Arjun realized how much pain and anguish Suhani had gone through, when he left her alone at Bassi.

The circumstances were such that he was a victim to Hobson's choice, again. Was this the beginning of the end, or the end of their beginning?

How was he to reason with reality? Who was he, but a puppet in the hands of the writer of his destiny?

He broke down several times that night. Dhanush Chand came in his dreams, for some strange reason. He was watching him from a distance, holding his *Chaudhary* stick for a long time.

He said something that Arjun could not make sense of. When he woke up and revisited his dream though, it made all the sense in the world. "These *Banjaran*s are hard to catch! They keep running"

"If you want to catch her, do not run after her. Let her come to you" And Dhanush in the dream transmogrified into a lookalike of Sangharsh, his words to Arjun years ago, reminding him of the battle to win the woman he loved with all his heart, had begun. Again! So be it!

Sometimes, a lesson from the past gives us bricks to pave with, for the road that would lead to our future. Not all choose to learn though, faltering, wondering why the same thing keeps happening to them, over and over again.

It is then that one needs to utilize what they have learnt, apply it in the current challenge, hope for a better outcome. Until that is not achieved, it is not considered a step forward. It stagnates the human.

Movement, forward or backward, is still better than being static. It is part of the growth process we all have to undergo, so as to fulfill the objective of being on this earth. Knowing is not good enough after a point. Doing what is known, is key.

# CHAPTER NINE

The early morning rays were reflected on droplets of water, felling from glossy leaves on the already dampened soil. There were puddles around the *peepal* tree in the centre of Bassi, which adults would try to avoid; children would splash on.

A.J. was sitting on a solid mud bunch, the extension of a random villager's hut, watching a beautiful lady dressed in candy-yellow and tangerine, touching one of the leaves and smiling.

"The *peepal* tree is considered to be one of the most sacred in our community. Even the tiniest of temples in India will always have one. Do you know why?" Mia turned to him, shaking her head in the negative.

"It is the only tree that gives oxygen both during the day as well as the night! Our ancestors figured it out quite early on, so in order to preserve them, a religious significance was bestowed thus"

"How do you know this? Do they teach you all of this at school?" she asked, impressed with the knowledgeable tidbit. "My biological father used to be the *Chaudhary* of the *Raikas*, here at Bassi"

"He would tell me all this and much more. For some weird reason, I retained most of what he said, as compared to anyone else who ever spoke to me, when I was a child" "Maybe it's because he spoke 'with' you, instead of 'to' you"

"That is the measure of our affection, often. I was expected to take care of my sister, the moment she was born. Responsibility was thrust upon me, as is done on a surrogate mother. Diana has seen more of me, than both of our parents put together."

The chat went on longer than they both expected, till Myna got conscious of the same. "Do I look ridiculous in this *ghaghra choli*? I thought I should try the tribal attire, since I came down here to get a taste of the life they lead"

68

"No one deserves a place in your life if they stop you from doing a harmless act such as this. You look…" "There you are! I've been looking all over for you! Hi, A.J.!" Diana looked flushed, bothered, as she interrupted the intimate tete-a-tete between the two.

"Come with me, Myna" "Sorry A.J., I have to steal her for a bit." she apologized, pulling Myna along with her, as she said so. "…beautiful" he exhaled the one word that could not be said, while looking into Myna's eyes.

Upon reaching their room, Myna saw sets of ethnic jewellery strewn on her sister's bed. "Planning to open a jewellery kiosk in the village, are we?!" "Haha! I am in a turquoise *ghaghra* with an apple-green *choli*, as you can see"

"But the *odhni* has *bandhni* work with both the colours, outlined with *gota*! What do I wear?" Diana looked beyond hassled, melting Myna into giving in to her silly whim. "Here, these pair of *jhumka*s teamed with the silver *hasli* will look great on you"

"Now tell me, why this nervousness on one plain outing?" "Plain? Anything but! Vansh, I mean *Chote Thakur* Vansh, is taking me around Bassi. He wants me to help him with suggestions to improve on his village. Can you believe it?"

Now, Myna knew her sister had no dearth of men swooning over her. But, if her memory served her right, this was the first time she had had the opportunity to witness Diana in the love-struck zone.

"Hmm, so you have a crush on Vansh." "What? No, don't say that!" "Honey, it's written all over your face. Not to mention the way you're behaving." "I could say the same about you and A.J., you know! You looked like a dashing pair from afar, if I may say so."

Myna pinched her sister's arm lightly, falling on the bed with her, giggling away. "What is happening to us logic-loving city girls?" "Don't you know?" Diana got up, wearing the suggested accessories.

"We are learning to defy it, Myna!" The duo stepped out looking like proud *Rajasthani* folk, with a pronounced pride on painstakingly attempting to emulate the original. Vansh was standing near the well, when he saw Diana walking towards him.

"You both could blend as beautiful village belles of Bassi, anyday! Myna, Ajju Bhaiya is looking for you. So is Nandish" "Who are Ajju Bhaiya and Nandish?" Myna asked, earnestly. "Who you call A.J. and Andy respectively"

Vansh answered, still ogling at Diana, who was blushing like an untouched rose.

Myna recalled she was to meet Andy, who would be clicking pictures for the gallery. Today was when he would take frozen shots of villagers, in their tribal finery. She was keen to take a look, hoping to be inspired by some of the ethnicity, letting it inject itself into her indo-western clothesline.

She left hoping she wasn't too late, just to find all three men together. A.J., Dan, Andy were looking at a picture, arranging the village folk in real life the exact same way. "We are calling it local simulation." Andy joked, looking at Myna.

"Why are you dressed up like that?" "You don't like it?" "It's not you" "That outfit is meant for the women who stay in these parts. You look like you've dressed up for a fancy dress costume party!" Dan put in his two bit, making Myna flush a deep tone of embarrassment.

"Well Ajju, what do you think?" she said, turning to her last ray of hope to save face. "You look very nice and comfortable in this, Myna. And boys, you owe the lady an apology. She may be an NRI, but your upbringing forbids you from being so blatantly forthright." he complimented Myna, reprimanding his brothers in the same breath.

It was time to experience the beauty of Bassi through filtered lens, another attempt to capture it's elusive charm. The bright morning sun was the natural prop of the carefully placed village folk, posing for pictures that depicted their daily lives clearly.

The natural light caught the spirit of the villagers, the landscape, making the moment magical. The arrows of colours darted in and out of all the outfits the *Rajasthani* wore, with silver or brass jewellery adorning their limbs, neck, even the forehead.

One such lady, a lookalike of Suhani, Vansh's sister Leenata, was sitting at the centre. She was the body double for Suhani, to perfect the set of the 'then-now' theme DTD was working on. "Could you hurry up, please? I have to get back to Gurukul after this game we all are playing, is over!" she said, irritated at sitting pretty in one place, doing nothing.

"Did you just say all this is a 'game'?" asked Dhanush, looking up from his fistful of notes. "What else is this? I had to be some place important. What could be more essential than educating children?" she replied.

"Being considerate is one thought that comes to mind, *Maatsaji*!" Dan blurted out in retaliation to Leenata's obnoxious behaviour. "You mock me? You, who works for his own father? Ironic!" "What is ironic is the fact that the namesake of 'Humility', is not practicing what she usually loves to preach."

Leenata glared at him, got up to leave, but Dan blocked her way. "Stay" "Say you are sorry" "If I say it will you stay? I'll walk you to Gurukul after the shot is over" he said, trying hard to sound gentle, caving into arrogance all the same.

Standing erect, she side-stepped him, walking away without uttering a word. "What was that?" Andy asked Dan. "Don't know. Don't care!" Dan spat out, walking away in the opposite direction of Gurukul. Andy tried going after him, but was stopped by A.J.

"Let him go. He has been acting strange lately. He might say something to you in his foul mood, that will worsen things" They quickly chose another setting, where Suhani's 'body double' would not be needed.

The shots came out perfect, but they stuck to Arjun's orders of taking multiples, for the purpose of clarity in selection. The noon break was welcomed by the ethnic models, photographers and the on-looking foreign lady, alike.

The scorching sun spared no one, as profuse perspiration served a grave reminder for all, to hurry indoors before the heat dehydrates their will power, along with the body. Sunburn was a matter of concern, only for the outsiders.

For those who toiled under it, the sun was a part of the landscape by default. "Where are Vansh and Diana?" Myna asked, sitting for the noon meal flanked by A.J. on one side, Andy on the other.

"Vansh has taken her to Gurukul, to have lunch with Leenata and Malika. At least that is what he told me" A.J. replied, dipping a morsel of *roti* into a thick *dal*. "You mean you don't trust him to tell the truth?"

A.J. watched her speak, his eyes progressing naturally towards her rolling the *roti* and dipping it into her *dal*, without tearing it. Humoured, he said, "Here, let me help you" He tore up the *roti* into pieces, placing them gently on Myna's plate.

Showing her how to dip a morsel, he encouraged her into aping him like a child, beaming when she managed in the first go. "Vansh is like Dan to me. I watch out for him like an elder brother should"

"Whether I trust them or not, is a completely separate issue" "Now this does worry me, Ajju. May I call you Ajju, as against A.J.?" Surprised at the question, he nodded. "Sure; although my family calls me Ajju, my friends know me as A.J."

The statement remained open-ended for a few silent moments, while each munched their hot meals with warm words, reveling a moment that could, with one false move, be lost forever. "Westernizing a name is quite a common trend. I do not understand it" Myna filled the conversational void.

"That's easy. Indian names are mostly tough to pronounce for them" "I am not 'them'. And a lot of my friends abroad are quite versatile in their pronunciation." Myna justified vigorously, though in a charming way.

Nandish was gorging on his meal, frustrated on being neglected, not a single loophole available in the dialogue between the two, so that he could barge in. By the time the dessert arrived, he was certain his loss would be A.J.'s gain.

He chose to give it his best shot though. After all, everything was fair in love and war. Bantu, was the grapevine of DTD. He was a regular source of information for Andy, a fact only Arjun knew about.

A.J. and Dan had a 'don't know-don't care' attitude, to any information other than photography. Bantu had called Andy, narrating the entire 'Ramona Rai incident'. This meant the world to Nandish, especially now.

He had a weapon to strike his opponent A.J. with! The opportunity came to him, as soon as the delicious sweetmeats of *boondi laddoos* were consumed as dessert. Walking to their room, A.J. and Andy were smoking, discussing Dan's mood swing resulting in the altercation of their plans, for the perfect shot.

"We still managed to pull it off, despite it all" said A.J. stubbing his cigarette. "More than! Arjun *Chachu* is going to love the original, not to mention the extra angular shots I took, for added effect " Andy said, pride sponging his words, as they poured out.

"I wish Dhanush comes around tomorrow" Concerned, A.J. continued, "We have to cover a lot of ground, if all the pictures need to be covered within the timeframe of a week. *Baasa* and I have our work cut out for us"

"Love makes us blind, like they say" Ensuring he had A.J.'s attention, Andy went on. "He should have realized, the shot was more important than taking shots at Leenata." Andy laughed at his own pun, turning completely serious a few moments thereon.

"I need to tell you something, A.J. Promise me, you will keep it to yourself, at least for the time being" Intrigued, A.J. committed, oblivious to the catastrophic truth that was about to be revealed.

The entire 'Ramona' incident flowed like the poison that she was, right through Ajju's veins, his newly lit cigarette hardly steady in his hands, as was his heart. "You mean the two…Myna and Diana, are related to us? They are my…"

Nausea did not permit Ajju to state the obvious. "I need to sit down" "I am sorry, *bhai*. I saw how close you were getting to her. If I withheld this information, it would be wrong on my part"

"Besides" he continued with his explanation. "Think of it this way. Better today than tomorrow. There is one more thing though, A.J." "Go ahead. Nothing can shock me more than this has anyway!"

Ajju's voice sounded resigned to his fate. "Her name is Mia. Not Myna. Mia Cotton" The despair rolled over, giving way to a hurricane of anger, deceit. He had no clue how to deal with the barrage of information, thrown at him by Nandish.

"Right then. I'm off to get some rest. I suggest you do the same. See you tomorrow" Nandish bade him a good night, walking away towards his room. When he reached, a flash caught his eye.

The mobile by his bedside had a message flashing from Mia. "Let's ride tomorrow. I'll see you at the stables. Six a.m. sharp!" Smiling, Andy responded and was about to put the phone down, when he received another message.

It was not from Mia though. Arjun had written to him, requesting that he not tell Ajju and Dan what Bantu had told him. At least Dhanush did not know yet, Andy thought. It was false respite, for Ajju had more to lose.

A fact both he and Ajju's father were well aware of, by now. He knew what was done would have a huge impact on so many, starting the very next day. There was no guilt or remorse in Andy, whatsoever.

He believed his information may just have saved Ajju from further heartache. Andy was genuinely interested in Myna, or Mia. He hadn't had the chance to explore his chances with her fully.

He was also aware that Mia was beginning to notice Ajju, a little more off late than his comfort levels would allow. Ajju's gaining ground was smashed by the knowledge, that Mia was his step-sister.

Nandish shuddered to think how Ajju must have felt, at that moment of realization. A bit of guilt, crept through his ego, pointing a stern finger on his false justification. His dreams were haphazard that night.

His conscience did not permit him to rest sound. Try as he might, tossing and turning wouldn't solve the problem either. The act done was like a crime committed, morally binding him in heavy chains.

The next morning saw two men, supposedly brothers, who had had a sleepless night. "You look like you forgot to shut your eyes while sleeping!" Dhanush exclaimed, looking at his brother walk to the *angan* for the morning *chai*.

"Work stress maybe. You have put us in quite a spot, Dhanush. Please refrain from communicating with Leenata. You know we need her for a few of our shots. Once we are done, we can return back home safe and sound!"

Dhanush was hurt with the uncalled for tone in his brother's usually affectionate voice. Andy joined in just then, looking equally groggy, making Dhanush feel guilty, assuming he did indeed cause a backlog in their professional plans.

He swore to make things right, gearing up for the new day. The women trickled out now, one after the other. The *myena*s on the roof had come for their daily feed, reminding Ajju of the namesake of the bird who stole his heart, just to fly away.

He felt stupid, at being so taken in by a fake. He wanted to question her, unendingly. That would give him some sort of closure, mayhap. But he knew he couldn't. Either ways, it didn't matter.

As far as he was concerned, she was out of bounds. He would readily hand her over to Nandish. Backing would be easy, when the head was still was intact while falling in love. Little did he know, the head has nothing to do with feelings as deep as love.

Ajju asked Nandish to lead the shoot for the day, while he coordinated with Dhanush. "There is a pile of rocks called the *tila* we will shoot at today. Let's get some children playing around it"

"Ask Leenata to get a bunch of candy to give to the children. In return, they must do exactly as they are told" Dhanush had half a mind to tell A.J. he had pretty much the same conversation with Leenata herself the previous day; except, she did not do as she was told.

Andy let A.J. leave to freshen up, choosing not to tell him about Mia's text message, inviting him to join her for a horse ride. He repeated the message about Leenata bringing a bag of candy to Dan, who grudgingly agreed to tell her.

Andy escaped for his rendezvous with Mia at the stable. She had chosen a fiery *Marwari* horse, which had recently been broken. Andy offered to exchange, as his horse was more docile, but Mia was confident about her horse-riding skills.

The first bend was the warm-up trot that every equestrian is familiar with. The pace of the horse is ascertained by the rider, the rhythm by the horse itself. That is where Mia faltered.

She pushed hers to a point where it sped away, galloping further and further away from Andy. A few piled up logs came as a respite, but Mia's horse crossed that too, leaving Andy's docile one to bow out of the sudden race.

Ajju had chosen *Chaudhary* Akash's horse, Badal, to de-stress himself alone before the photo shoot, or the subsequent confrontation with Mia that would occur. From a distance, he saw a rider galloping at break- neck speed.

It crossed him in a flash. All he heard was one word that came out more like a shriek. "Ajju!" His heart in his mouth, Ajju raced Badal with all his might, till it caught up with the now frothing horse of Mia's, who herself was sniffing now.

Ajju got off Badal and made Mia sit on it, taking the reins of her fiery horse in his hands. "We can ride back together if you want" Mia offered. A day ago, Ajju would probably not even need the invite.

The mind was not receptive to such offers anymore; especially from a person who was a trickster, albeit a beautiful, charming, disarming one. Ajju's heart ached all the way back to the piled logs where Nandish was still waiting, worried about Mia by now.

"Here, she is all yours" Ajju said, leaving the horse and Mia with Nandish, galloping away on Badal to complete his ride. "Are you okay? Did you get hurt?" fussed Andy, checking to see if she had any visible cuts or bruises.

Smiling, she said she was fine. Satisfied, Andy walked her back to the stables where they left the horses to be groomed. The silence all the way to the *Chaudhary haveli* was nagging Nandish.

Mia was not her usual self. She was different now, maybe even distant. Mia's thoughts were swirling around her head. She was eager to thank her savior, Ajju. More than that, she was eager to speak to him.

There were no cuts or bruises on her, but she had looked into Ajju's deep, dark eyes when he rescued her. He had deep lacerations that screamed her name. She wanted to ask him why.

She knew she could not. After all, blood is thicker than water. Her mother had trained her well to charm men. Mia was sent by her mother, Ramona, to get to Ajju. The problem that now arose was something Mia herself had not comprehended. Ajju had gotten under her skin!

How could she possibly explain that to her mother? How could she possibly explain this huge blunder to herself? She knew she had walked right into the spider's web without even knowing it existed.

Often, we are not prepared for a situation that we are bound to be a part of, or even cause. The effect of the situation does touch the lives of more than just us, the participants. When there is a hole dug for someone to fall into, it should come as no surprise if the digger falls into it himself; or, as in this case..herself!

# CHAPTER TEN

Life in a village is often hard to fathom, for those who are used to the perks of living in a city. Simplistically basic, the village folk always end up teaching a thing or two to visiting tourists, the most profound being not to take their luxuries for granted.

Dhanush began the day by walking up to Leenata amidst the humdrum, over a scrumptious breakfast of *mooli paratha*s and white curd. "I plan to practice being a gentleman, hereon"

"May I begin by apologizing to you?" he said, looking straight at Leenata, in his loose powder-blue short *kurta* teamed with a pair of dark mahogany khaki trousers. "I too would like to apologize, in that case"

"The blame is not entirely yours to take" the mystifying village belle said, breath-taking in a lavender-blush *odhni*, with a contrasted salmon-pink *ghaghra choli*. The brooch Dhanush had given her, was pinned with pride.

She wore it well, knowing he would notice it too. He had to be cautious with his compliments now, for she was about to be betrothed. Dhanush had to snap out of his dreamy state, infused by being in Leenata's presence.

"I have been sent to request your presence for the completion of yesterday's shoot" he said, turning his gaze to her eyes. "I will be there for sure. You have my word" she replied, silently leaving to the interiors of her *haveli*.

The solitary *gulmohar* tree with the fiery brick-red blossoms had shed their prized pride at Leenata's feet. Watching her walk away, Dhanush noticed her dainty attempt to avoid crushing any of the flowers strewn by nature, her embroidered *mojri*s peeping in and out of her *ghaghra* borders occasionally.

Akash had planted the tree when Leenata was born, to express his joy on being blessed with the goddess adorning his haven. It had blossomed along with his daughter, as if tied by an invisible thread, over time.

The *tila* Ajju had spoken of with Nandish, was to be pre-scouted by Dhanush. Determined devotion took over, as he observed the dry desert landscape, sprinkled with *ber* and *drak* trees, just off a curve at one end of the village road.

The stony hillock was more of a collection of boulders, carefully placed atop each other, giving it the appearance of a flat buttress. "We call it *badha pithoo*" came Leenata's soothing voice from behind.

"Yes, it does look quite a bit like that. I wonder if there were giants who lived here at one time, whose children forgot their piled-up stones, half-way through a game" said Dhanush, assessing the breadth of the wondrous landscape with his camera.

"What are you doing, if I may ask?" "Trying to figure out the best angles for a shot at this location. It's in our list of pictures to be taken. My mother and A.J.'s father used to sit here at times, away from the villagers to discuss important matters pertaining to Bassi"

Confused, Leenata pursued the original string of the conversation. "You mean your mother and father, right?" "I am Ajju's step brother, Leena. Didn't you know that?" "The topic never came up, I guess"

"You mispronounced my name. It's Leenata, in case you forgot" she said, watching him walk up to her. "Here, hold this" he gave his Sony Alpha A7S compact camera to her, garlanding the strap around her neck, lest it should fall.

Adjusting the lens, he asked her to look through the camera, focusing on the hillock. "What do you see?" he asked. "I see exactly what is there, except a bit closer, like binoculars"

Appreciating her honesty, he said, "When I look through the lens, I have to superimpose the picture that has to be taken, thus imagining the final shot. Only if it appeals to the 'Hunter', which would be yours truly as you know, is it then allowed to be clicked and displayed at DTD"

Impressed, she began to take the camera off, the strap of which had gotten tangled with a few beads sewn into her *odhni*. Attempting to help her, Dan pulled on the strap, his impatience clear in his action.

He managed to break a few of the delicate beads that now lay at Leenata's feet, just like the fiery brick-red flowers of the *gulmohar* tree at the courtyard of the *Chaudhary haveli*.

"I am so sorry" he apologized, bending to pick the broken pieces up, holding it in front of her upon his palm. "What will I do with broken beads? Leave them on the ground, please" she said, sounding normal.

"I owe you an *odhni* in that case, Leena" he said, putting the pieces in his pocket. "It was a mistake. We do not owe each other anything" she replied, this time noticing, he intentionally called her by a different name.

"I have not congratulated you yet. You must be excited about your *sagai*" Dhanush blurted out his usual silliness out of nowhere. "There is nothing to be excited about. The match was to be an exchange marriage"

"Vansh *Bhaiya* refused. I had no reason to offend" "Offend whom, Leena?" "Not whom. What. Logic, practicality, both demand that I obey my parents, for they shall always do what is best for me"

"Marrying Viren would mean I could continue teaching at Gurukul and live near my parents" "A very convenient practicality, *Maatsa*! But, pray tell, since when did marriage get into the groove of logic?"

"I would marry if I ever fell in love. Otherwise, nothing could compel me to pawn my freedom!" A sad veil fell over Leena's eyes, as she lowered them. "Yes, that is a luxury that you men, especially the city folk enjoy"

"I am not pawning my freedom, as much as securing my future" "Do you love, Viren?" he asked, all of a sudden, surprised at himself for asking such a question. "I like him" "That is not what I asked, Leena. Look up"

She regretted even as she obeyed him, her eyes locking into his in a deep gaze. "Now answer my question. Do you love him?" he asked, resting his hand on the slate rock beside him, hurt by her bottomless pools about to drop a precious drop of pearl.

"I cannot answer that" her quivering voice mouthed. "Why do you wear the brooch I gave you, when you will belong to someone else soon?" he inquired. "You ask too many questions!" she retaliated.

"*Mujhe jaane dijiye* (Let me go)" "Where to? The crew will be coming here soon. You will be comfortably lost in the crowd" Calming herself, she turned away from him, unpinning the heavy bejeweled brooch.

"It weighs heavily on me. Please take it back" she said sternly, softening as she saw a hint of hurt in the stone-cold man's eye. He smiled, put his hands in his pockets and turned away walking.

"Keep it to warm your heart when you think of me on cold, loveless days, Leena" were his last words. She watched his broad shoulders droop, his merry gait without his usual swagger.

The moment made her realize that which uptil now, her heart could not comprehend. Dhanush was in love with her too! He just didn't know it yet, simply because he had never fallen in love before.

"Hey! I have a few candy pieces. Would you like to share them?" she yelled out, watching Dhanush pause, turn around, smile and walk back, this time rapid, different. They sat on a boulder, a bit away from each other, chatting to pass their time.

They didn't realize how time flew, while they awaited the crew and the children to complete the vision of the 'Hunter'. When Ajju and Andy arrived, they were pleasantly surprised to see the pair chuckling and gossiping, like long-lost old friends.

The children wore every colour from mahogany-brown to rose-blush pink, breathing coloured life into the drab landscape; placed in pockets, rehearsed for their shots by their *Maatsa*, Leenata.

A.J. and Andy began to manipulate the visuals, a trait they excelled at. Dhanush walked around, watching his Leena crack jokes with the children, straighten a *choli* here, a stray strand of hair there.

A thought like an arrow pierced him from nowhere in particular. "She makes me feel something I would like to feel. And then some more. I cannot let her go" he ended up saying out loud enough for Ajju to hear.

Patting his hair, Ajju said, "Instead of declaring it to me and the winds of the Thar, I suggest you tell her first, little brother!" Embarrassed, Dhanush frowned, "It isn't easy. My brain, my stomach, my tongue are all in knots when I look into her eyes!"

"Would you rather she looks that way into another's then?" That did it. Dhanush walked up to Leenata. "We need to talk" "Later" "Now!" he said, making her freeze. "*Kya hua*? (What is the matter?)" "Call me Dhanush"

"No" "Say you love me" "No" "Is that the only word you know?" "No!" Exasperated, he shut his eyes, a silent prayer escaping his lips. "I feel for you. I do not understand it, but I cannot bear the thought of you belonging to anyone else but me"

He waited moments longer, waiting for the words to resound in his own ears, finally aware of how it felt to give in to one's true feelings without mashing them with logical thoughts. Upon opening his eyes, expecting to look into his gazelle's liquid pools of love, Dhanush was forced to blink when he saw Ajju standing in front of him.

"She left. Look" he said, pointing at Leenata running away, back to the village. Instinctively, Dan tried to run behind her, but Ajju's strong hand over his shoulder, refrained him from doing so.

"Wrong timing. You spoke. She heard you. Now, wait" "Wait for what? She is about to be engaged to Viren!" "Do you want to marry her?" "What? I like her. I want to know her better" "That is not what I asked, Dhanush."

"There is no dating or courtship period in villages. Either you like a girl well enough to marry, or you do not lead her on." Finding the theory a bit too hard to digest, Dhanush said, "Even if I do want to, she wouldn't"

"She gave me the exact logical reasoning as to why she is marrying Viren" "And you believed her?" Ajju was surprised at how gullible love had made his little brother. "I had no reason not to. I've never been dumped by a girl I'm interested in before. I do not plan to start now."

So saying, he lit a smoke, smoothly changing the topic. It was easy to sway Ajju with a topic that needed discussion with regard to the next set of shots with interesting twists. It was so much easier describing what one thought, as against what one felt, Dhanush thought to himself.

Lighting up a smoke for Ajju, Dan put the lighter back into his pocket, that landed with a distinct klink. "What's that noise?" "What noise, A.J.?" "Your trouser pocket just tinkled like the *payal*s of a village belle!"

Dhanush took out the broken beads, that had torn out Leena's *odhni*. "You got this in return? Didn't you give her that expensive-looking brooch?" A.J. asked, A.J. asked his lost-in-love brother. "It's the only thing I have of hers to keep for now"

"The brooch I gave her was something I wanted her to keep to remember me by" "Why would a woman keep a memory of one man and marry another?" wondered Ajju, logic supporting his statement.

He chose not to say it out loud due to the obvious turbulent expression on his brother's face. Their mother, Suhani, was a live example of the same. He thought it strangely ironic that not only did Leenata look like their mother, but was also being presented with similar situations.

"Morton's fork-marrying the wrong man for the right reasons, or the right man for the wrong reasons" Ajju said, leaving the sibling talk for later.

He wanted Dhanush to focus on work for now. Time was of the essence, for DTD depended on the team heavily.

Tara had a colourful youth, flaunting her beauty to the point of shamelessness. Despite enjoying an independent lifestyle even after her marriage with Giriraj, she wanted her son's *lugai* to be demure, docile, domesticated.

Off late, she had been noticing Malika excessively tired than usual. Assuming it was because Vansh had refused to marry her as of now, she never questioned her daughter. Up until Tara heard a rumour, that could trash her plans permanently.

It was from the other *Raika* women who spoke about how their *Chaudhary's chori*, soon-to-be *lugai* of Viren, was gallivanting about with the city folk. Time and again, there was another rumour that aided in adding fuel to the brewing fire.

It was believed that an expensive gift had been given as well to Leenata from *Chote Sardar* Ajju's younger brother, Dhanush. Tara went cold at the thought of another one of her offsprings being rejected, if there was any shred of truth in what she had heard, through the grapevine.

She knew Giriraj would never attempt to straighten things out, since he loathed gossip mongers himself. Tara knew she had to do it herself. She knew Akash loved the *lal mirch ka achar* (red chillies pickle) that Malika had made.

Quickly transferring some of it in a *katori*, she hurried to the *Chaudhary haveli*. "How have you been, *samdhan*?" she teased Bindiya, seeing her fill the *Chaudhary's hookah*. The immediate undercurrent of unpleasantness began to blow like a stale, gentle breeze between the two.

If there was one thing about Tara that Bindiya liked, it was the way she dressed. Her *ghaghra* was still tied seductively below the navel, the sienna *odhni's* translucence draping her prominent curves, smoothly.

Her printed *ghaghra choli* had camel motifs made on them in yellows of canary and antique white. "What brings you here? I was just getting ready to serve my husband his *hookah*. He should be back soon"

Bindiya spoke thus, after quickly greeting her 'forced' relative with plastic emotions. "I hope your daughter tends to her husband the way you do yours, *Chaudhrain hukam*. After all, the daughter usually does take after the mother."

Unclear as to what Tara was getting at, Bindiya asked her to elaborate clearly, latching on to the malicious sarcastic tone that spun a compliment more like a resounding slap. Tara was atrociously famous more for her sarcasm than anything else, especially for those she disliked.

"If I would have heard a rumour like this about Malika, I would have locked her in the house instead of letting her actions hang my head in shame." Tara rattled, still not coming to the point, faking a shiver to add weight to her words.

"I assume you have heard a rumour about Leenata. Tell me what it is" Bindiya asked, her maternal instinct ready to strike back any threat to her child. "Neeraj's wife saw Leenata with the city folk, one in particular, on more than one occasion" she finally said in hushed tones.

"That is not so. Leenata is always in the group where there are women as well. She knows her *maryaada*, now that her time for betrothal is near" "*Dekhiye samdhan* (Look), our families are about to unite" Tara said, interrupting Bindiya.

"The respect of my familial name is as important to me, as it is to you. Your daughter has been noticed, walking back and forth from Gurukul, with Ajju's younger brother Dhanush. They were also seen spending more than a few moments alone, at the *tila*"

"So? Do you know they think of each other as cousins? Why shouldn't cousins interact? Besides, they leave a day after the *sagai* anyway" Bindiya justified, irritated at Neeraj's wife now for spreading vicious fabrications.

Standing up, Tara said, "Malika made this pickle, so I thought *Chaudhary hukam* would like to have it with his dinner today" Folding her hands into a *Namaste*, she said, "*Behenji*, I too have cousins"

Before Bindiya could protest, Tara continued, "I have never been gifted an expensive jewel brooch by any of them on our first meet. The *odhni* of our daughters carry the pride of our tribe. That is all I have to say"

Bindiya was pacing up and down the courtyard, when she saw both father and daughter walk into the *haveli* together. "*Kahaan thi aap?* (Where were you)?" she asked Leenata. "With the city folk. Didn't I tell you before I left?" Leenata answered.

She had just began to sit on one of the large coir chairs, resting her head on the welcoming backrest, when the whole drama began. Akash didn't like

Bindiya's unnecessary questioning, so he opted to question his wife right back.

"What's all this about, Bindi?" "Ask your daughter! She has just spent the full morning with Dhanush." Before anyone else could respond, Leenata opened her half-closed eyes, springing up to face her mother.

"How do you know?" "Tara, your soon-to-be *saasuma* came. She was armed with chillies in her *katori* as well as in her mouth! She told me one of her *saheli*s saw you, sitting alone with Dhanush at the *tila*. Is it true?" Bindiya asked, now with her voice raised.

"Answer your mother, Leenata" Akash intervened, looking at his daughter sincerely. "So what if it was, *Maasa*? You both trust me enough to teach the children of our village at Gurukul, on one hand"

"On the other, you throw suspicious glances on a supposedly clandestine meeting rumoured by gossip mongers?" Bindiya took a step forward, pointing at Leenata's brooch. "Fine. Where did you get this from?"

"A gift from a friend" was all Leenata gave as a blunt reply, sitting back down again. "Is this gifting friend of yours Dhanush by any chance?" Bindiya carried the argument on. "Yes, *Maasa*. Here, take it. If that is what it will take for you to leave me alone."

Leenata, having spoken, attempted to unhook the brooch, freshly washed by large droplets of tears. Unlike the previous tears of sadness on the tiny diamonds, these bits of water were those of a hurt pride of an already raw, emotional wound.

"Leave it be. I have no such intention. Till you live under our roof, our reputations are dependent on our own, as well as each other's behaviour. Remember you are to start a family of your own soon, my daughter"

"I trust you, but I do not trust anyone else more" Hurt, Bindiya left to supervise the cleaning up of the fresh produce that was to be served as dinner. She knew Akash would wash off any hurt she had caused her precious daughter anyway.

Alone with his daughter, Akash pulled a chair sitting right in front of Leenata. "When did you realize you had fallen in love with Dhanush?" "How did you know?" "I am your father. I know more than you think! Now spill the beans, so that we can figure this out together"

Leenata spent an hour doing just that. Through the stained glass window, Bindiya saw the father-daughter talk, hoping Akash drives sense into Leenata. When she saw their daughter leave, it was understood her presence was required by Akash, her husband.

"Well?" she asked, sitting on her favourite ornate *jhula*, chewing on dry *amla*. "We have discussed everything in detail. She has told me all there is. Tomorrow, call both Giriraj and Tara. We will call the marriage off"

"What? Have you lost your mind? First, Vansh refuses. And now, Leenata. Do you think they will take it well? Giriraj owns almost all the cattle. If he wants, he could rebel" screamed Bindiya, frustrated at the soft-heartedness of her husband, especially when it came to their children.

"Well then, what do you propose I ought to do? Let my daughter go to another, without a heart, which she claims to have given away already? We were in the same situation once if you recall, Bindi. Have you forgotten?"

"Those were different times altogether. She is the *Chaudhary* of the *Raikas*' daughter. The clan will strengthen with this alliance. The dowry in terms of livestock has been discussed already. All the preparations have also been done. Leave Leenata to me. I will speak to her"

Bindiya spent the remainder of the evening explaining to her daughter how it was essential for her to accept the alliance. She was the link that would make the clan stronger.

She would be made the Principal of Gurukul, choosing to live as she pleases in the same place she was born in..Bassi. What she said next, rang in Leenata's years over and over again for several hours, after it was said.

"The brooch needs to be returned, *Bitiya*. Hand it over and I will give it to Dhanush. Steel yourself for what you are to endure, for only if you are strong in the mind, will you succeed in shining through"

Leaving the room, after having gotten the dazzling brooch from Leenata, Bindiya marched right out of the *haveli*, maintaining momentum. She saw Dhanush sitting with the rest of the city folk, plucking *ber* from the trees they sat under.

"Here. Take this back. Leave Leenata alone for now. Leave Bassi soon as well. She belongs to Viren. Try and remember that!" She marched off as silently as she had come to the group.

The tiny group of chirpy city folk went silent, waiting for Dhanush to say something to defend himself. He didn't. He couldn't. He had nothing to defend himself, or his love with. Not even the impenetrable armour of surety.

# CHAPTER ELEVEN

The Bassi Dam, along with the Orai Dam, were made to enhance the agriculture in the region. These man-made marvels were a God-sent to the farmers at Bassi, for it provided the necessary water, to quench the thirsty roots of the crops they grew.

Ajju was fascinated with the layout of the Bassi Dam, ever since the very first time he laid eyes on it. Arjun had gotten him to Bassi, just after Dhanush was born.

They had spent several hours staring at the white water, smashing against the turpentine-coloured rocks that surrounded it.

"Before you click pictures with a camera, learn to take in what your eyes can see, your mind can decipher into thoughts. That is how you make magic." Ajju could still hear his father's words, resounding within.

Sitting on a rock, staring at the water, he could sense her around. Turning sideways, he saw her walking slowly, lost in thought, entranced by the beautiful sight of the water contrasting with the rocky scenery.

She couldn't have seen him. There was a boulder, the shape of a blunt obelisk that was in her line of vision. She walked closer to the water.

He wanted to call her to be careful. What would he call her as? Myna? Mia? Her chartreuse-green *ghaghra choli* were getting playful sprays of fresh water, which she attempted to counter with her sienna-red *odhni*.

It was a memory worthy of retention, for no one could suspect an innocent beauty, such as what A.J.'s eyes beheld at that moment, of being a spectacular fraud!

She finally turned, backing away from the barrage of sprays, back pedaling and giggling at the same time. Before A.J. could get up from the boulder he sat on, she had somehow managed to cover all that distance while he was in deep thought.

Down they both fell, mercifully on mud slush, rather than a stony surface. The droplets from Mia's wet *odhni* fell on A.J., washing his face, maybe even the sourness he harboured at the point, in his mind.

She had her hands on his chest, her breath warming him in spurts. Their eyes were locked on to each other's, fearing a blink would steal some of the magical moment away.

Lowering her blue eyes, she got up, trying to dust out the mud stains. "What are you staring at?" she asked him, upset on getting her outfit dirty.

"Rubbing them is going to worsen the stains. I'm wondering why that never struck a smart person such as yourself" he answered, truthfully.

"Well, of course I know that! It's just awful to look at, that's all" she whimpered, moving a few strands of soaked hair from her face, caking her cheek with mud slush in the process.

"You still look as beautiful as the day you stood near the *peepal* tree" he said gently, forcing himself to forget at the moment that he was conversing with someone, who may possibly be a dubious character.

"Please don't patronize me. I honestly don't need that right now" "I'm not!" "What else is this? Your apparent kindness at this moment betrays your belief in your own superiority."

"You're being rude to cover for your vanity. I get it" "No, you don't!" This was apparently going nowhere. Sometimes the things that are left unsaid, can create havoc in a conversation, making it sound hollow.

Mia sat down quietly next to him by the water. He watched her take in the scenery bit by bit. It was then that he noticed what he was about to say out loud. "That's it! Your eyes are cornflower -blue!"

Alarmed at the sudden outburst, she turned to him for an answer. "I have a problem with describing a colour, as well as I possibly can. If I do so, then the matter ends there. If not, tossing and turning, I lose my well-required sleep"

Mia's heart melted on seeing the child in A.J., attempt to express himself intelligently. "I like it here" she said, trying to have a civilized conversation.

"I used to come here with *Baasa* often. We used to relax and talk for hours." he smiled, remembering the wondrous days.

"Hours?" Mia sounded surprised. "An hour is good enough for me. After that, this place loses its charm"

Countering her declaration, A.J. replied, "There is a saying in these parts. Water does not understand time. It feels and magnifies its emotions to those who are around it"

"We've been here for more than two hours, just to prove my point." he said, triumphantly.

Shocked, she checked her elegant antiquated watch, which confirmed A.J.'s claim. Before Mia could say anything more, Dhanush's call came on A.J. cell.

"He wants us to reach the *haveli* as quickly as possible. Your Nandish is just about to organize a search party!" Ajju said, trying to tease her.

"He is not 'my' Nandish, Ajju!" she laughed, almost getting him to use her real name by accident. Why wasn't he using it?

Was he afraid the warmth that emanated from her towards him would turn into an ice-cold breeze? These questions kept on playing in loop on his mind, until the moment was long gone.

They began to walk slowly towards Bassi, where the proximity they shared even now would be a mere, distant memory. "How lovely! I never noticed this before, Ajju!" Mia exclaimed, walking up to a row of red and yellow threads.

The threads were fluttering merrily in the breeze, flags claiming the sacred space of the wish of a memory. "*Kankad Dorda* are the sacred threads put on the hands of a newly married couple as part of the custom at Bassi"

"When they return to the village though, these threads are put on the boundary as a symbol of a new beginning" "*Kaise ho*, Ajju (How are you, Ajju)?" Neeraj, now older, greeted his nephew warmly.

"*Khammaosa, Chachaji*! I was coming to meet you. How have you been?" "I've been busy. The crops need my constant supervision, although I've hired workers to do the manual work. I will be off to Jaipur shortly"

"I am going to get tractors with attachments that can irrigate, sow, harvest, faster than humans or cattle. We plan to hire them instead of buying them in instalments. *Waise, Bhayli sundar hai*! (By the way, your lady friend is pretty!)"

Ajju burst out laughing at Neeraj suddenly changing the topic, from hiring tractors to admiring Mia. Bidding him farewell, the pair walked briskly to their destination. "I didn't understand what he said in *Marwari* at the end, Ajju"

"He spoke in Marwari, rather than Hindi so that only I could understand what he meant. You see, he did not want to offend you. *Rajasthani*s are gentle, polite and yet fiercely proud. The contrast is what makes us honourable, in a seaful of men"

"You still haven't answered my question, Ajju" "Because I too do not wish to offend you" he said, not slowing his pace to match hers. "I won't be. Either tell me what he said or teach me *Marwari*!" she argued.

At the wooden doors of the *haveli*, with the huge brass knockers on either side, chain in the centre, Ajju pulled Mia by the wrist to one side.

"Andy's told me who you are, Mia. I'm a village man raised in the city. I do not play games like you, so pick someone else to entertain yourself!"

He walked in thereafter, cool as a cucumber, straight to his room. Mia was still standing, her back pressed to the white boundary wall of the *Chaudhary haveli*, her refuge from the desert heat for now.

She wasn't angry. She wasn't hurt. She wasn't anything. When one is desperate to feel an emotion that eludes, the heart retreats, thus making way for the head.

She walked in, her elegant gait not giving away her screaming insides. "Hey, Myna! Where have you been? I've been worried about you!"

Instead of answering Andy's genuine concern, she kept on walking slowly, crossing the courtyard towards the guest chambers.

"At least answer my question, Myna. I was concerned about you, you know" Andy found himself getting irritated on this reiteration, not to mention the nagging feeling of being cast aside by the favoured.

"Concern is not the right word to use here, Andy. Try 'intrigued' instead. Also, if you know my name is Mia, why do you still call me Myna?" "So, Ajju *Bhaiya* has spoken to you, I see" Marching towards him with venom in her shiny blue eyes, she spat out.

"You see nothing. You know nothing. You have no idea what you have done and what I'm going to have to go through because you couldn't keep your mouth shut!" She stood for a moment longer and then turned.

"You used me, Mia. Shouldn't I be mad at you too? I have feelings for you. Haven't you figured that out yet?" Nandish groveled.

"Where I come from kiddo, we practice less of 'feelings' and more of 'business dealings'. I am sorry if you feel used. It was nothing personal. Means to an end, I guess"

"Thanks a bunch! That makes me feel a whole lot better. First you apologize on seeing me hurt. Then you acknowledge using me to get to where you wanted!"

"Oh stop with 'getting to the bottom of it' already. If it makes you feel any better, I failed in my mission, which by the way, was to get to know the Prataps!"

Tears betrayed her as they spilt over. Wiping them with her mud-crusted *odhni*, she stomped away, incapable of facing anymore showdowns.

Looking out of her room from the first floor after her refreshing bath, Mia was trying to see a common village scene through the uncommon way Ajju had explained.

Overlooking the back of the *haveli* was the area where saddled horses were stationed alongside their counterparts, the camels.

A *Rajasthani* woman in her attire, an unnamed shade between honey and tangerine, was feeding them *bharoont*, the balance of which was stacked up against a mud wall where all there fodder was being dried.

"You shouldn't envy them or their lives. We each have our crosses to bear" Turning to see who read her mind so, Mia saw Leenata standing at the small ornate entrance to her room.

"May I come in?" she asked, coyly. "Please do! I am a guest at your home. You shouldn't be asking me for permission to enter a part of your own house, Leenata!"

"We of Bassi believe a guest must be given the ultimate honour of space, respecting the same would automatically imply forfeiting some of our own!"

# CHAPTER TWELVE

Mia liked Leenata. She was an exotic creature of the land, with no idea how naturally stunning she really looked. Her wit, eloquence could easily be mistaken as weapons of vanity; but for those who knew her it was a different story altogether.

Her natural charms were but an add-on to the real Leenata. Close friends and family liked her calm reserve, peaceful demeanour and the ocean of knowledge she seemed to have never enough of.

"How did you know I was thinking on similar lines, of what you just said?" Mia asked casually, though deeply intrigued. "You were looking out of the window. Normally, it means one needs to necessitate deep thought, in order to come to some sort of conclusion."

"If you don't mind, may I help?" Leenata ended up enquiring, seating herself on the *baithak* against the wall, relaxed. "I doubt if you can. My problem is so complex, that sometimes I myself fail to understand where to untangle it from!"

Helplessness brimmed out of her eyes, as Mia walked to sit next to the epitome of calm, a trait she required most at the present moment. "Leenata, what does *bhayli* mean?" "It means a 'lady friend'. Where did you hear that?"

"An old man who seemed to be familiar to Ajju said '*Bhayli sundar hai*' to him" Leenata began to smile gently. "He told Ajju *Bhaiya* you are beautiful, assuming he would carry the conversation forward, thereby giving ultimate, or rather interesting information on you!"

"Then why didn't Ajju tell me what it meant, if this was all there was to it?" "Because, the men from these parts are cautious not to hurt the pride of a woman by crossing the line of decency"

Charmed, Mia nodded her head in approval of a much-desired masculine trait. "So, is Ajju *Bhaiya* the cause of that pretty forehead wrinkling?" "A part of it, yes." Mia accepted, surprising even herself.

"Myna, nothing is important enough to lose sleep over. If God gives a problem, he also packs its solution, sending them both together. The challenge is in finding it" "That's a tall order, Leenata"

"I'm too tired to play any more games. If I appease one, I lose someone who I never meant to wound" "What about yourself? Why are you walking through such a torturous route, when you know you are a vehicle and nothing else? Stop making yourself into one, Myna!"

That made all the sense in the world. Using the sage advice though, was not Mia's cup of tea at the moment. Slowly, Mia confided in Leenata, feeling the release in her nerves, being able to breathe freely without knotty tensions holding her back.

Leenata's expression was serene all through Mia's confession, proving she would not be judgmental about her. "I like the name Mia better!" Leenata said, smiling. "So, how do you propose I should resolve this?" Mia asked her.

"Never ask anyone else to solve your problems for you. The answer to your question lies with you alone. Someone else's answer may be the wrong solution" Seeing her visibly upset, Leenata continued.

"Having said that, here is what I would do. Mend the broken fence that matters to me the most. The importance of a relationship is ascertained, by how much effort one is ready to put, to remove the tiniest shred of misunderstanding"

"Agreed, but why would Ajju forgive me? I'm not Myna, but Mia "That's your beginning argument, right there. Myna was what your mother was trying to make you into. Mia prevailed " Leenata concluded.

"I feel so much better talking to you. Viren is a lucky man" The serene smile flashed a streak of sadness, albeit for a few split seconds. It was as clear as the brightness caused by her joyous smile as well.

"Compulsory choices are what they are. The good thing about them is that there are no give or take of expectations, others than what is the obvious" The vague statement was left dangling in midair.

Mia asked, "If you don't want to marry him, will your parents force you to?" "It's not just a marriage. Our tribe, the *Raika*s had an alliance a long ago with the *Banjara*s of Nagri"

"It was done to increase wealth by livestock. There is also a legend that the father of our late *Chaudhary* Dhanush Chand and Ajju *bhaiya*'s mother, Suhani *Chachi* did not even meet before the pre-arranged wedding!"

"At least I know who my husband-to-be-is, what he looks like…" "Are you convincing me or yourself?" "Both" she said, now walking to stand by the window herself. "I have confided in you, *behan*" said Mia, earnestly.

"It is time for you to reciprocate and lighten the load" Another hour of confessions passed, bringing them closer to the noon meal. "We both are in love with men who do not understand our chained compulsions" Mia concluded.

"Hasty judgement if you think from their point of view. They have never felt this way either!" "Valid point indeed. I do not believe in coincidences, Leenata. Believe there is a grand purpose in our meeting"

"I know my purpose as of now. I'm going to have a talk with Ajju *Bhaiya* post lunch" "About me?" "The topic will eventually come to you, of that I'm sure. So what's your role in my life going to be?"

"I could offer speaking to Dhanush, but it would be a futile attempt. I know Andy better than Dan, to be honest" confessed Mia, disappointed at her incapacity to return the humungous favour, Leenata was about to do for her.

"Then maybe the purpose hasn't revealed itself to you yet. Shall we leave it at that for now?" asked Leenata, walking out towards where the meal was now being served. The matter was considered discussed and temporarily buried, albeit unsaid.

The rich flavours of Rajasthan engulfed the worries of the ladies, who sat down to enjoy another lavish spread of *aloo pyaaz ki sabzi, boondi raita,* rice and *mirch ki tipore.* The women always ate separately from the men, but the arrival of the city folk had disturbed this dainty custom.

Everyone in the *haveli* who was present, sat down on the *chatai*s spread for them to eat. Diana had just gotten back from another village excursion, her tan showing the amount of involved enthusiasm Vansh was bringing out of her.

Mia hoped her statement of 'being a means to an end',did not apply to her sister Diana, as far as Vansh went. She was protective of her younger sibling, at the same time wishing her not to be caged.

Vansh seemed to be caring enough not to hurt her in any way. Besides, his sister was turning out to be a long lost friend, much wanted in her solitary life. Two siblings could be different, but their values would still remain the same.

With this hope in her heart, she moved her thoughts forcibly in the direction which worried her the most. Ajju was talking to almost everyone but her, as if everything was normal.

Maybe she didn't matter to him as much as he had begun to matter to her. She began to eat, occasionally conversing with Leenata over the texture of the food, exotic as it was. "Could you pass the *Lehsun ki Chutney*, please?"

Mia's mouth froze, the hot ball thudded against her heart straight from the pit of her stomach. "Here" she said, passing the pickle jar to Ajju, without looking at him, feigning disinterest.

His fingers touched her delicate ones that were wrapped around the jar. She thought he squeezed them gently before taking it from her, but couldn't be sure. What she knew was beginning to scare her enough.

He had begun to control her. He found herself thinking about him while awake. Her dreams were easier to experience than what she had done to her reality. It was a crime committed in complete innocence, unknowingly.

She was so utterly consumed with her own thoughts that she hardly paid any attention, to the vivid description Leenata gave, of each item that had been prepared for the meal. Leenata painstakingly continued describing all the same in spurts anyway.

"Ajju loves *Phirni* like his father does!" Akash said, smiling as he reminisced the days when they were younger. "It's been made just the way you like it, Ajju *beta*. For the rest of those who don't, there is *moong dal ka halwa*"

The desserts were enjoyed by everyone, since it was understood a nice siesta was to follow. Leenata had her work cut out for her though. She had to talk to Ajju about Mia in the afternoon.

"I'll have some more *Phirni*, please" Mia said, extending her *katori* towards Bindiya, who was closest to the dessert bowl. It was then that Leenata noticed Ajju's expression. There was affection written all over his face, the way he was looking at her blatantly.

He began smiling as he looked down into his bowl to resume his favourite *Phirni*, laughing at *Chaudhary* Akash's anecdotes of the younger days occasionally. But Leenata had caught on the few stolen glances already, Mia was oblivious to.

He didn't look like he hated Mia. It looked more like he was looking for a way back into her life, probably as desperate as she was. Now, all Leenata had to do was clear the air.

In order to do that, she needed the one-to-one with Ajju first. There was always a way, if it is well-thought out. Making it work though, took a lot more than just thoughts, as she would experience, in the due course of time.

# CHAPTER THIRTEEN

Before the satin sunset could touch the dusty hills that surrounded Bassi, Vansh was touring Diana around the land he grew up on. He had chosen to take her to the Craft Bazaar, where *Rajasthani* handicrafts were on display for sale.

The comfort level between the two was such, that they could talk to each other about anything. Crossing the space from where a part of the arid desert landscape could be seen, Diana stopped.

Four camels in a row, shaded from burly brown to bisque, were gliding across shrubs and *kikar* trees, a lone man escorting them in a white *dhoti kurta* and turban. The moment could have been captured by an oil painting called 'Serenity'.

Man and animal were lost in their own world; unaware they were providing a strange sense of peace to the one who was watching quietly. "They look like they don't have a care in the world!"

Diana exclaimed, her dark orchid *odhni* contrasted with a slate-grey *ghaghra choli*, the delicate tassels at the ends, fluttering in the breeze. "They don't have time to think, because they are just too busy throughout the day"

"By the time evening descends on them, they rest to gain the spent energy, much required to toil the coming day" explained Vansh with the utmost patience. Usually, he was curt when it came to explanations… but this was highly unusual.

"I've wanted to take you to a place where womenfolk love to spend the day shopping, since the day you arrived at Bassi. Luckily for you, craftsmen from neighbouring villages have also come with their specialties."

Diane was thankful for the last moment addition to her wardrobe-her wallet. The rows of shops with canopies supported by wooden poles, were lined as far as the eye could see. The very first kiosk was tiny, but power-packed with a lasting first impression.

It housed a *Rajasthani* woman in a yellow sari with rose-pink flowers, the mud shelves surrounding her were full of colourful toys made of papier-mâché. The famous epic, *Mahabharat*, was portrayed in a piece that looked like an ordinary box, at first sight.

On closer scrutiny, it opened up its folds like a peacock spreads his feathers to prance. The women looked sad on entertaining mere onlookers, who shirked buying any of their displayed items.

Diana went ahead and bought the most expensive toy, the epic-depiction box from her, making her pull out a forced, weak smile, courtesy their shy nature, in return of exchanging an ancient legacy, passed on from generations.

The next shop was bigger in length and breadth, the walls covered completely by mirror-worked cloth pieces, to be used as table cloths or as vibrant decoratives. She picked a square cloth piece, with several concentric circles on it.

The yellow and red elephants were complemented by the psychedelic pattern of a circle of flowers, supporting each alternate circle. She picked several cloth pieces of oval and rectangular designs as well.

These masterpieces were handcrafted with bright colours enhanced by carefully stitched mirrors. It was understood by the sellers, that whatever was being bought would be sent to the *Chaudhary haveli*, as the buyer was a guest there.

Diana could have paid in lump sum at the *haveli*, once all the items bought would have reached, but she chose to pay a little extra in each shop, not just as an advance, but also as appreciation, of a fast-dwindling industry.

Vansh decided on that very spot, in between two colourfully spiraled canopies, to call her Jiya-all heart! A couple of repetitive shops later, Diana screech halted. "Vansh, this might take some time" she said in a meaningful tone.

The shop they were standing in front of, was the shopper's paradise of any fashion-conscious woman- the jewellery section! Bangles with *lac* and *meenakari* work were stacked by the dozen, screaming to be tried on.

Some of them were glittering with faux pearls and rhinestones, to give it that extra special effect. The centre had an enormous carpet-like spread, with beads outlining them. Strewn on the spread were dozens of chunky neck pieces in brass, stone, silver and coloured glass.

The shapes and colours were such, that they could be worn with anything and everything, leaving hardly any room for Diana, to pick one over the other. She had to buy an extra bag, for the amount of jewellery she picked, for herself and Mia.

The last few rows of shops that beckoned the already overloaded Diana, were all terracotta. Hanging pots, figurines of man and livestock, gods and goddesses, were displayed. Nay, they were being flaunted by the craftsmen, few of who were still giving choice finishing touches to the brand new figurines, baked in small brick kilns.

"Can I record all of this, including the workers, if you don't mind?" she asked Vansh. "On the condition that you tell me why" "This will always remind me to stay focused on any goal I choose to pursue, however big or small it might be. If I follow the path of Diligence, it will eventually bring me to my destination!"

Impressed at the depth of understanding displayed by a person who was not even a resident of the country, leave alone his village, he decided to show her around Bassi a bit more, once the shopping bug had been satiated.

"Turn in the alley to your left. We are going to Gopal *Chacha*'s place next." The most jovial man in all of Bassi, Gopal *Chacha* was also one of the wealthiest *Rajasthani*s in almost five villages nearby.

Sangharsh had tied up with him a long time ago, maintaining his end of the bargain by sending him due payments on time. Gopal *Chacha* was the owner of the sole block printing house in the area of Bassi, as well as surrounding it.

There were three lanes in the courtyard of the place Vansh took Diana to, next. The first lane had workers with *palang ka paer*, beating into blocks of wood via a nail, that was moving with years of laborious precision.

The workers' art ended up carrying a plethora of patterns, making the one block, the magical beginning of a whole textile design. The second lane had workers equally spread-out in semi-circles; carefully chiseling the same blocks, smoothening out the rough edges, to allow colour to flow in and out of the pattern.

The third and final lane was where the pieces of plain cloth, some white, some coloured, were spread out, with Gopal *Chacha*'s son, Vijay, supervising workers printing designs on cloth, sporadically dipping the final masterpieces of wood blocks into vegetable dyes of all colours.

An approval nod later, Diana spent some time in recording the ancient art, rarely noticed by the customer who would finally buy it. "There ought to be a tour organized by the *Chaudhary* so that tourists like us can see, appreciate the effort put in to the beauty that results"

"Sounds like a great idea. We usually escort tourists into shops where *Rajasthani* crafts, ethnic items are displayed. It is nice to know the making also matters, not just the finished product"

"The journey is as important as the destination, they say" Diana said. "Yes. I am impressed by your astute sense, by the way you express how you feel with your heart. If I may, I would like to call you Jiya. It means 'all heart'. May I?"

The word suited her, as Diana shed her foreign skin, emerging into the epitome of the Indian woman. Jiya was born in broad daylight, on the same land that would worship her like a goddess, for years to come.

Malika had come to the *lac* bangle shop too, to buy a few new ones. The desert sun would sometimes fade hers, or even crack her bangles at the ends. It was there that she noticed, Vansh and Diana walking towards the narrow alleyway that lead to Gopal *Chacha's*.

She heard Vansh calling her Jiya, explaining why he wanted to do so. The evil streak of envy hidden deep in each human, reared its ugly head. Malika walked back briskly to her parent's home, threw her shopping bag on the bed and commenced wailing on the top of her lungs.

Her melodrama paid off when her parents came running to her room. "*Kya hua? Ro kyun rahi ho* (What's the matter? Why are you crying?)" they asked her, worried sick on seeing their offspring act out of her generally reserved character.

"*Baasa*, I wish to speak to *Maasa* alone" Sniffing in between air gulps, Malika made her choice apparent. Promptly Giriraj left the room, to sit with his *hookah*, ponder a while till Tara came to him with the information acquired.

"*Maasa*.." Out poured all there was to tell, of the observations that Malika had undergone, in the past few hours. Every once in a while, she would shudder and shake, her mother's touch keeping her together just a bit longer, the loop travelling all the way to the end.

Hell hath no fury as a woman scorned, was wrathful enough. To top it, both mother and daughter slid into the vengeful mode with the ease of vipers, ready to take back what they had presumable lost - Pride.

Tara convinced Malika to rest, leaving one of the house-helps to keep her company, until she slept off. Before she could reach her husband though, Viren was already seated beside his father. Their anxiety was over in an instant, because Tara's face said it all.

Whatever doubt they had, was removed the moment she began to speak. She narrated what Malika had told her, between bouts of pain, moments of anguish. Viren was not oblivious to Vansh and Diana's growing proximity.

He had his apprehensions as to whether or not Diana was the reason, Vansh refused to marry. At that time, Diana wasn't even in the picture. Vansh had confided in him, telling him the plans he had for their village, for the people who lived there.

"If he did have feelings for Diana, he could have told me. We never hide anything from each other" he defended his friend earnestly. "*Bawle*, do you really believe he will confide in you about his feelings for another woman, knowing he rejected your sister as his *Beendni*?" Tara said, disgusted at the stupidity of her son, probably inherited through his father's genes.

"Calm down, Tara. *Sambhalo apne aap ko* (Control your emotions). I am not happy about any of this. We must speak with the *Chaudhary* and get rid of these city folk, as soon as possible" Agreeing with the head of the household, the three went about their chores, hurt still throbbing in the back of their minds.

An hour or so later, word came within the *Chaudhary*'s residence, that Dhanush wished an audience with him. "*Chachaji*, I must speak to you about something that will probably get me into more trouble than I already am" he said, sounding like a schoolboy whose knuckles were about to be rapped.

"I am like your father, Dhanush *beta*. Speak your mind. What is it that troubles you?" "I wish to ask for the hand of your daughter Leena, I mean Leenata. I would like your blessings for the same, *Chachaji*"

From all the possible choices Akash was guessing was the 'problem', he had not expected one, as explosive as this. "You are as bad as your father! He did the same with Suhani. Dhanush, this is my daughter you are talking about"

"She is engaged to Viren already. Their *sagai* is due in two days, do you understand? Two days!" "Yes, I do..but.." "*Chup karo*! (Be quiet!) Do you expect me to call for Giriraj, informing him that we are formally rejecting both his children?"

Wiping his sweat, *Chaudhary* Akash continued, "They own a majority of the cattle at Bassi, Dhanush. Do you understand the ramifications of what you are asking of me?" Dhanush became silent, as he saw Bindiya walk slowly towards them.

From the way she looked at him, he was far from convinced that she was nearing to bless him. "Bindiya.." "Yes, I have heard everything. Akash is right, Dhanush. It will be better if you leave Bassi right away"

"This match is important for Bassi. Leenata will be engaged to Viren as has been decided, in two days' time. Leave tonight or early in the morning. End of discussion!" The moment she turned to walk away, Dhanush stood up to speak.

"I cannot leave without telling you this. I will be back in a day's time to bring my father to formally ask for Leena, I mean Leenata's hand. Better yet, I will ask Ajju to call Dad over, if that is what you want"

"Leena will marry me, not Viren. Ask her yourself. Let her choose" Bindiya turned to the gardener who was tending to the vibrant *gulmohar* tree, intent on his work, but ears following every word being exchanged at the *angan* of the *Chaudhary haveli*.

He looked up, nodded, running to get Leenata for the much-awaited response. Clad in a cyan-coloured *odhni* with patchwork on it, Leenata walked up to her family, the dark golden-rod coloured *ghaghra choli*'s mirror work catching the first rays of the sun.

Her *bindi* had the rising sun, which symbolized a ray of hope, how she felt after reading the tiny bit of confession from Dhanush. "Leenata, what is all this?" Akash asked, trying to sound harsh.

"*Baasa*, I cannot marry Viren. There has been a development" she said, shaking like a leaf. "The 'development' is standing right next to me. Am I correct?" asked Bindiya, in a louder voice.

Leenata's hung head, not out of shame, but out of humility cleared their doubts. "*Bawli ho gayee kya*? (Have you lost your mind?) Do you not know what will happen to your father and I, if Giriraj pulls away the livestock that belongs to him?"

"We will practically starve to death. Your father's *pagdi* is in your hands, child. Will you keep it aside when you are needed to honour it the most?" "But, *Maasa*.." "Hush, Leenata! *Dekho Bitiya* (Look my daughter), I know what you will say"

"Vansh's refusal was accepted. That was because he wants to do good, staying here. He wants to work, to improve Bassi. He was not being selfish, like you. Sure, your father and I wish for you to be happy"

"Don't you want to do the right thing?" The way Bindiya's artful flow of words came out, even Dhanush began to feel as if he was tearing Leenata apart, from the inside. Luckily, before anyone else could add any more fuel to the fire, Vansh walked in.

"My family luckily has the largest *haveli* in Bassi. If this shouting came from a normal hut, we would be attending the *Panchayat* tomorrow, to be chastened!" Grinning at his own joke, Vansh quietened, the moment he sensed the timing was wrong to crack one.

"*Padharo*! (Welcome!)" Bindiya said sarcastically. "You started this 'I don't want to get married business', Vansh. Now, your *behan* plans to follow in your footsteps" Vansh turned to Leenata, who still stood with her head down, turning one bangle after another, on her wrists.

"I don't understand" he said simply. "Dhanush Pratap wants to marry your sister" Bindiya said, adding, "How do you propose we react to his proposal?" Vansh looked at each person standing there.

He realized how awful it was going to be, for his parents to break the same news of another sibling rejection, to Giriraj's family. "If you wish *Baasa*, I can speak to Giriraj *Chachaji*, instead of putting you through it again"

"I am *Chote Thakur*, member of the *Panchayat*, after all. Maybe I can use that angle, since it hasn't been exploited yet?" It was the most convincing argument they had heard, so far.

"Alright, if you think you can do it, then go ahead. Now, what do we do about the main problem?" "This is not a problem, *Maasa*. This is a proposal. What is wrong with Dhanush? He's financially stable"

"He cared about my sister enough to ask for her hand. He lives in the city under better conditions. I give my blessings and suggest you do the same. If I know Dhanush correctly, he has done you a favour, by asking you once nicely"

"Should you refuse, he is capable of driving off with your daughter into the sunset! Where would the respect be in that then?" The way Viren turned his parents' thinking was admirable, even for Dhanush.

Mumbling, they agreed on Arjun being called for the 'formal talk' between the parents. "Thanks, *dost*! I owe you one" Dhanush said, when the elders and Leenata left. "I did what was right. My sister will be happy with you" Vansh said, smiling as he left the *haveli*.

No one knew that Vansh had won himself a strong ally, now that he was planning to make Diana, Mia's sister, his *Beendni*. Some things were better left unsaid though. Malika's envy-dripping overdose, Tara's hatred, were all on the boil when Vansh walked into their home.

He was not diplomatic like his father. Instead of beating around the bush, he exchanged pleasantries after which he asked to speak with Viren alone. Once Viren got to know that Leenata had rejected his proposal, he was keen to know why.

Vansh chose to keep the information to himself, till Dhanush and the rest of the city folk left Bassi. He then quickly went back, confiding in his father, who agreed with his point of reasoning.

Akash spoke to Arjun over the phone, telling him to come to Bassi soon. But first, he must speak with his son who would be joining him at Delhi by noon, the next day. All preparations were done as quietly as possible, so that the movement was known to a handful.

Vansh bid his goodbyes, albeit temporarily to Jiya, wiping her tears, promising they would meet very soon. He gave her a *jhola* that had seeds and shells outlining rows of different colours, held together at the mouth with a satin string.

In it, he put his favourite ring- a thick silver one with a tanzanite stone, carved in the shape of a 'V'. Diana took it out in front of him from the pouch, threaded a satin ribbon into it, made him put it around her neck.

Vansh was touched as never before, by a woman he was beginning to love more and more, with each passing moment. Dhanush walked to where Leenata stood to say goodbye.

"*Jaldi aana wapas* (Come back soon)" she said to him. "*Apna khyal rakhna* (Take care of yourself)" he said to her. The raw, gentle moment made them gulp together as he turned, "*Suno* (Listen)", she said softly.

He turned to her, tears shamelessly streaming. "I will wait by the *tila* every evening till you come for me" "Then stay safe. I will come soon, Leena" Andy, A.J. and Mia were the only ones who were unaffected by the current situation.

Bindiya had packed delicious *alu parathas* for all of them, along with bottles of *bel ka sherbet* concentrate, for Suhani to store. The dawn on the day the city folk left, was the beginning of a chapter in the life of Bassi, that cost sleepless nights to many.

More importantly, it created such havoc, that a human lost life out of sheer neglect. The *Panchayat* that sat in the morning included Tara, Viren and a few other prominent members of the village society.

*Chaudhary* Akash was accused of partiality, thus he voluntarily chose to step down. It was up to the *Panch* members now to choose the next *Sardar* of the *Raika*s. They asked him to continue reigning, until a suitable replacement was found.

The perplexity of the *Panch* was who to choose from. On the one hand, there was their previous *Chaudhary* Dhanush's son Arjun or Ajju, who lived in the city of Delhi. On the other hand stood *Chaudhary* Akash's son, Vansh.

Who would lead the *Raika*s next? That was a question that couldn't be answered easily for an obvious reason- both were equally deserving and undeserving at the same time. What happened next, was a classic example of a third party benefit from a chaotic situation, that remained unresolved.

# CHAPTER FOURTEEN

"Sangharsh…" Arjun pleaded, expecting his oldest friend to understand his pathetic condition. "Other than wanting to speak with Suhani *Bhabhisa*, ask me for anything else" came the hasty reply.

Sangharsh Anand was not being rude. He was in a tearing hurry to end the call, lest Nalini with her sharp ears should walk in on their discussion of the topic, that was forbidden once again-Suhani.

"Is she okay?" "She is now. She has been up all night talking to Nalini. Nalini won't tell me anything though. We have a trust issue when it comes to spilling the beans!" "Don't tell her I called"

"But if there is anything I should know, then I leave it you to do what's best" "*Dost*, my loyalties have and always will remain with you. Take care of yourself, Arjun. We will watch your *Beendni* for you"

The phone call was followed by another one, at Arjun's end.. The nature of the call though was the exact opposite. "I'm on my way, hubby dearest… bags and all. Make sure there is space in our house for your legal wife."

Ramona was a hot breeze in an already heated day for Arjun. He began to contemplate whether he should refer to her as El Nino in place of Anaconda, as coined by Sangharsh, all those years ago.

The situation did not permit him to do anything he really wanted to. Luckily, the boys were not at home. Ajju and Dhanush were on their way from Bassi, so he had until evening to figure out a way to break the news to them.

He wasn't even aware how Ramona, Mia, Diana, would all stay under one roof with the Prataps. Fitting them into Swarn Niwas, was easier than making all the unnecessary adjustments, of fitting them into his life.

By the time he managed to drag himself into freshening up for the day, the gate was opened for Ramona to enter the residence of the Prataps. "Be careful of the bags labeled in red, you dodo!" he heard her shouting at the guard.

"If any of my Danish glassware cracks, it will be taken out of your monthly salary!" Offended, the guard sternly asked, "Who may I say is calling?" "Your new mistress. That should suffice for you and the members of the household. What is your name?"

"Guru" "Well, quit looking at my face, Guru, and get my bags. I will show myself in" Her pushy nature was the first impression she imprinted quite well in any person's memory, irrespective of who he was.

Arjun saw her walk into the living room, sitting on the favourite chair that his Braids loved. The pang he felt of her absence, was quickly replaced with the hatred he felt for Ramona's forceful usurp.

"Get off of that!" Ramona flew off, standing straight, her purse falling on the carpet. "Mind your manners, hubby dearest. I will sit where I want, when I want. Aren't you going to welcome me home?" she asked, sarcasm dripping in her tone, as always.

Arjun could have manually lifted the elegant locust in her steel-gray jumpsuit, sending her flying off his property. Instead, he quietly walked down the spiral staircase, facing his foe as calmly as he could.

"I am not happy you are here. If my being happy is what you expect, then you're sadly mistaken. Given a choice, I would much rather Suhani was here" "You would prefer that pathetic nomad to me?" Ramona snapped, insulted at being compared to a commoner.

Arjun held her wrist tight enough to cause her Chambor wrist watch to snap open. "Never ever insult her in my presence. If you try it again, I won't really care whether I break a watch strap or your wrist"

"I will also not concern myself with the consequences you so eagerly remind me of. One more thing. Do not get too comfortable here. The moment you entered will not be far away, from the moment you will leave forever"

Releasing her stinging, reddened wrist, Ramona fluttered her eyelids, "Such passion is admirable as well as harmful, Arjun. I'm throwing a house-warming party tomorrow evening. I know the kids return today, so let's get our heads together to make all of this work"

A loud laugh which Arjun himself didn't recognize as his own, broke out in the middle of the dining room. "Do you really think Ajju and Dhanush will let you breathe, knowing you caused their mother to leave?"

"Have you completely lost your mind, woman? The stupid blackmail you used on me, will never work on them" "Yes, I know that sweetheart. That is why I won't be speaking to your sons. You will do it for me"

Arjun froze when he looked at her, sentencing him for a second time. He walked right up the stairs to his study, banging the door shut. It was noon already, and Shanti was made aware of Ramona's stay.

She had made a decent English spread for her and Indian food for Arjun. She had also had them sent to separate rooms they were in, at the moment. The meals were eaten quietly, the house seemed ghostly silent.

"Shanti!" A loud voice shattered the silence, just when Arjun was planning to take a snooze, to get over his headache. The house-help came rushing into the bedroom, where Ramona had currently stationed herself.

"I need black coffee after every meal. Someone has to arrange my cupboard. Send someone to take Arjun's clothes out, so that I can put mine" "Out, Madame? And keep them where?"

"Stupid old woman! He is staying in the study. That is where the clothes should be too. Now get me my coffee and bring the maid along" Shanti left quietly, straight to the study. "Who is it?"

"Shanti" "Come in" She told Arjun the gist of the orders rattled out by Ramona. "Do it, then" "But, Sir.." "I do not want any more complications. It's better this way. Ask Guru to have the car brought up front. I've to go out"

The maid was transferring Arjun's clothes bit by bit into the study, when Ramona heard the car whirr off. "Where did he go?" "I don't know, Madame" came the maid's scared reply.

"I'm not talking to you, you dolt! I was thinking aloud" she said, frowning into her coffee, repeating the same question to herself. Her mobile began to ring, as she almost began to nod off for her afternoon siesta.

"Mother!" "Mia! What a pleasant surprise!" "We are on our way to the hotel and…" "Stop, stop. There has been a change of plans. Can you come straight to the Pratap residence?"

"What?" Mia was hesitant to enquire, but did all the same. "Why?" "I'll tell you everything when you get here. Give the phone to A.J." Ramona asked, drumming her freshly manicured nails on her toned leg.

"He is talking to his father" "What?" "I said.." "Yes, I know what you said! What are they talking about?" Mia was done spying for her mother, especially since she had news for her mother too.

"I have to go now. I will see you soon" Mia hung up without giving her mother a chance to reply. Ramona was shocked at how her well-trained daughter had changed. She didn't even get a chance to speak with Diana.

Not that it mattered, of course. Her weapon was Mia. She would help her take revenge from the Prataps, for ousting her from their lives. Arjun had driven straight to Anand Creations. He broke down inside Sangharsh's office.

Nalini had handled the situation by instilling hope in what otherwise seemed hopeless. The plan had to be to keep the family together, somehow. The Anands made Arjun call Ajju, who was briefed as to how Ramona had annexed Suhani's status in their lives.

"The only way to protect your mother is to play along, Ajju. Do you understand?" "Yes, *Baasa*" "I am sorry I never told you who Mia really was" "Don't be. It's all in the past. We have important things to do, both at home and work"

"Is the lady coming to DTD as well?" Ajju asked his father, referring to Ramona. "Not if I have my way. Can't be sure though. You have got to convince Dhanush to be on our side. Bantu listens to Dhanush and will be more than happy to protect our trade secrets"

"Ask him to get all the important documentation to Anand Creations. Meet me here at DTD. Off load those two girls at Swarn Niwas first, though" "Can't do that. Let me get there. I'll explain everything when we reach. The traffic is maddening!"

Arjun knew, when Ajju was attempting at changing a touchy topic. Respecting his son for his graceful forgiveness, as well as standing by at a trying time like this, Arjun chose to wait for all five at the office of the Anands.

The cars were honking more in urgency than merriment, upon their arrival. The passengers in both vehicles totaled not five but six, the last to get off quietly walking straight into Nalini's office.

Arjun's heart skipped a beat when he saw his *Beendni*, who didn't even look at him. "I had to get *Maasa*, if we were to have a family discussion" was all Ajju said, as Arjun hugged him tight.

Everyone reached the conference room, to discuss what could be done about the current situation. "I don't understand what these girls are doing here. They are not family, Ajju" Suhani said, mildly upset to see Ramona's children.

"You will. Give me a moment and I will explain" came Ajju's reply. After his explanation was over, both his parents were staring at him in amazement. "Good Lord! Another complication." blurted out Sangharsh, laughing out loud.

"What's so funny? Ajju just played into Ramona's hands. She sent Mia to spy on us and get closer. So, mission accomplished, I would say" Suhani curtly said. "*Maasa*, Mia and I are married"

"Our registration in court is scheduled for tomorrow. We both want just the two of you to be there. Mia is not like her mother. Don't pass any judgement, without knowing how she really is" Ajju's earnest request was cut sharply by Arjun.

"Ajju, she is your step-sister. Did you think about that?" "Not from any angle, *Baasa*. She is not related by blood" "Ramona is still his wife legally" Suhani stood up, shaking as she said it. "She has moved in with your father and your father asked me to leave, which I did"

"Suhani, I never said that" Arjun was walking gently towards her. "Don't you dare come near me. I'm no one to you. Just a ghost! All these years we spent under a married home, that wasn't even there!"

The last bit of the sentence was muffled, as Arjun gathered his Braids in his arms, her tears wetting the front of his shirt. "Come on, everyone. Let's go to our place" Nalini suggested. Dhanush, Andy and Diana chose to go to DTD instead, but the rest were too drained to fight Nalini's suggestion.

"You never said anything, Dan?" Andy, the only one of the three not affected brutally by the situation, asked. "Too many have spoken in one situation. Another one would have complicated it a bit more, don't you think?"

Dan's reply, was unlike his usual headstrong ones. Both knew Leenata had made quite an impression on him. Andy was being a good friend to the hilt. He helped in getting the lovebirds elope, en route to Delhi.

The detour was straight to a temple, where a priest was rewarded sufficiently to conduct a quick ceremony, tying the knot of marriage and everlasting togetherness between A.J. and Mia. Diana was overjoyed for her sister, who finally did something her heart desired, wished.

Vansh would want her as his bride, someday. The thought was so sudden, that her blush was quick to show. Minutes after the ceremony was over, Ajju hugged Andy. "You will always have a special place in my heart for standing by me today, Nandish"

Andy knew Ajju meant it, as a promise to the end. For him, what mattered was that Mia had made her choice amply clear. She was in love with Ajju, not him. He didn't really have much of a choice on the matter, the way that he saw it.

He decided to dive deep into the world of photography along with Dan, who was equally keen to divert his mind. Amidst all the chaos, he could not bring himself to tell his father to ask for Leenata's hand from *Chaudhary* Akash.

His parents were temporarily separated. His elder brother just eloped and married the arch enemy's daughter. That was an enormous plate to digest, as it is. Where was their room for any festivities?

He knew his Leena must be waiting to hear from him. He chose to call her father instead, requesting for a few more days, as some urgent requirement had come up and he didn't want to burden his father.

"You are a good son, Dhanush. Take as much time as you want. Your *amaanat* is safe with us" He called Leena next, speaking to her as gently as he could, promising to tell her all in the call at night, just before he would call it a day.

"Take care of yourself" she whispered softly. "I can't. That's why I've got to marry you fast!" he replied, making her laugh instantaneously. Another long distance phone call was being made, in a separate room.

Andy was aware about the mutual affection between Vansh and Diana. He let them chat for a while, while he went out to the back room to have a look at all the hard work the group had done, at Bassi.

It didn't take much time for the young lad to divert his passion from a lost romantic interest in a person, into a reaffirmed romantic passion for his first love-photography. It was not a very well thought out plan though, as the diversion proved to be more of a reminder.

Glimpses of Mia showed in shots, either Ajju or Andy had taken. Besides the fact that she was photogenic, her blue eyes stood out in almost every picture of hers, dominating the entire photograph.

He chose to keep her pictures aside, to present them to Ajju *Bhaiya* as a wedding gift. He didn't want to put himself through any more pining. The beauty of the mind lay, in the flexibility of its usage.

One could use it either as a weapon for vindictiveness, destruction of lives; or, it could be used to enhance that which was good, worthy of retention, creative. One could be either constructive or destructive.

Both at the same time, were never possible. Both stemmed from thoughts, that swam the labyrinth of the mind. The Prataps and Anands were brainstorming at the Anand villa, when Ramona's call came on Arjun's cell.

"Let me take it. Haven't chit-chatted with Anaconda for a while!" Sangharsh said, tugging jovially at Arjun's cell. "And disclose where I am? I don't think she is aware. Mia is our daughter-in-law, Sangharsh. Let's be smart"

Arjun took the call out of the room, knowing Suhani would not like his tone when he spoke to Ramona. He needed her to be unsuspecting, unaware that there were plots being hatched to trap her.

"What happened?" "I'm all alone at home, Arjun. Where are my girls? Have your boys abducted my girls to teach me a lesson?" Arjun found her insinuation churlish. "Don't be absurd!"

"They are a young lot and must have stopped midway, for a bite to eat. Why don't you rest a bit, finish your settling down" "Will you have dinner with me? The kids will be here by then"

Arjun couldn't say no. "We'll all eat together" He hung up, turned around, closed his eyes. Suhani was standing, her arms like rubber attachments by her side, looking right into his eyes.

"*Saheb* has chosen *Memsahib* again" It was said in a flat tone. Aggression would have proven there was fight left. This was in a resigned tone. Suhani walked inside, picked her car keys and left.

"Where are you going?" Nalini asked. "Away" Ajju gently took the keys from his mother, offering to drive her any place she desired. Moments later, Arjun walked in and picked up his keys.

"Now where are you off to?" Nalini asked, exasperated at having to forever don the garb of the moderator in any situation that demanded maturity. "Away" came his reply, astounding everyone at how alike, he and Suhani truly were.

"If you allow me, I'll take you wherever you wish to go" came a tiny, but sturdy voice. Mia was standing near him, trying to smile. Shrugging his shoulders as if he didn't care, he walked off murmuring, "Whatever. But I am driving"

"Hi, you guys! What's going on?" Annie had popped in her head, wondering what was going on. Her new doll line, the galloping love life with Abhi, designing consistently for Anand Creations, didn't leave her with much time for anything else.

Her parents sat her down, telling her everything. There was one thing though that even they didn't know. But Annie did. How Andy felt about Mia. Regular calls between the twins, was enough to let the cat out of the bag.

# CHAPTER FIFTEEN

"Whatever happens, quit hurting her. I think she has been through enough already" Mia blurted out, expecting the man driving like a maniac, to lash out at her. Arjun chose not to though.

He could have given her a mouthful, but he knew he must conduct himself like the father-in-law he always wanted to be. Maybe Mia never got the love she deserved as a child from a vicious viper like Ramona.

"We used to call your mother Anaconda. Sangharsh and I" he said softly, smiling. A smile escaped Mia as well. "She does have that effect on most" "I missed you in the beginning so badly, that at times I thought I would either let my work drown my sorrows or drive me insane"

"Really? Mother said you replaced me with A.J. and Dan" Mia seemed to be quite comfortable talking to Arjun, about something she was usually guarded about. "Of course! I loved you from the moment you were born"

"Big, blue eyes, tiny fingers and toes. I thought you were all mine. And now, things have changed again. You've re-entered my life as a *bahu* and not a *beti*" Mia now understood the complexity of the situation, that the relationship caused.

This was the very reason, Ramona wanted her to get close to A.J. She confided some more in Arjun, telling him how she planned all these years to get back at him. How her mind was consistently poisoned, with the pictures of a happy family supplied by none other than Tanisha, Arjun's old assistant.

"Why did she want to get back at me, Mia? I never harmed her. On the contrary, she ruined my life but I still played along because…" "Because you thought I was your child. Yes, I know that part. What you don't know, is that Gerard Cotton is my father as well as Diana's"

"But, Ramona Rai is my mother alone. Diana is my step sister" Arjun screeched his car to a halt. "What?" Nodding her head, Mia told Arjun,

Diana was the product of an affair between her father and the nurse who was kept to look after Ramona, after the accident.

The affair was brief, as both Nurse Isabella and Gerard disappeared, a few months after the baby was born. "I have raised Diana as if she were my child. Mother never cared much about her"

"Well, actually she never really cared much about both of us." she said, laughing at fate. They were at a dimly-lit restaurant, with small round tables. City driving was taxing for Arjun now.

He didn't want to be too forward, so he ordered for a mocktail for himself. Graciously, Mia cleared the air. "I know all there is to know about you, Mr. Pratap! You love your Hoegaarden alone"

"Please go ahead and order it. I'll have a glass of white wine, if you don't mind" Arjun liked Mia, a lot more now. He also managed to convince her to call him *Baasa*, just like Ajju did.

"Won't Mrs. Pratap mind? I wouldn't want to upset her. We're already ahead on an awful start, her and I" Patting her wrist Arjun said, "Let me worry about her. We have much to do"

"Ramona has to be told, I have to convince Suhani you're to call her *Maasa* and there is a pending court marriage, followed by a honeymoon for you two." They were both upbeat, cheerful for those few moments, until the call from the gallery came.

Dhanush was on his way home. Arjun Senior and Mia had finished their drinks in haste, offering to meet him outside. They also decided to get Ajju to meet them up too. Dan would be returning with Diana as well.

"Say something, *Maasa*. You have been quiet all this while" Ajju protested, worried how quiet his mother had been throughout the drive. "There is nothing to tell, Ajju. I feel like I have been stabbed- twice"

"Once by your father and the second time by my own flesh and blood" she said, flatly. "Try and understand, *Maasa*. We didn't have a choice. We're in love like you and *Baasa* are, don't you see?"

"Just spend some time with Mia. Get to know her a bit more. She is…" "A snake like her mother. A daughter takes after her mother. It is a thumb rule, Ajju" "No, *Maasa*. She is nothing like Ramona Rai. You've got to trust me on that"

All his pleadings were of no avail, because Suhani was geared up to live a life full of hatred, for Ramona and her daughters. "Your father is waiting for you. *Jaao*" she left, walking up the stairs of the Anand villa, not even turning to wave goodbye to her son.

Hurt, Ajju sped off towards Swarn Niwas, to the party waiting for him outside the gate. The moment they saw him approach, they started their engines as well. All three vehicles entered Swarn Niwas, like a rally, a procession, an army.

Ramona was watching from the terrace, her keen eye completely sure something was not right. She saw them park their cars, walking straight in, stone cold quiet. It was confirmed then. They were indeed up to something.

"Welcome home, all! I've been waiting to say it all day" she said out loud, feigning to be cheerful. Sensing her discomfort, Arjun began. "Come down and join us, Ramona. Let's talk a bit before dinner" "Oh, nonsense! Let's talk after dinner and dessert"

"I have had everyone's favourites made, including yours, hubby dearest" she added, elegantly walking down the stairs in her flowing maxi gown, the shimmer on the sides catching the eye of all present, on her electric-blue outfit.

As everyone looked at Arjun, his nod of approval was enough for the party to proceed to the dining table. The Danish cutglass, Ramona's prized possession was laid in full splendor.

Arjun cringed at the faded memory of Ramona's cutglass obsession, sitting on his chair quietly. "That's quite a spread" Dhanush said, impressed with all the varieties displayed. There was *peas pulao*, two varieties of veggies, two baked dishes with chicken and two varieties of *dal*.

"'What's the occasion', you might ask. Well, I am back at my rightful place as your mother, Arjun's wife after so many years, that I just wanted to celebrate with my family"

Ramona seemed so earnest in her approach, that if it weren't for Arjun's true familiarity with her real self, as well as Mia's description of her mother's innate conniving nature, they would have all fallen for it.

The dessert was equally lavish, brought in by uniformed waiters. Both the house-helps looked uncomfortable in their freshly starched outfits. "I had them wear it, so that they know they're on duty when I call for them" she said, answering Arjun's unasked question, as she saw him looking at them.

"So now that the fanfare is over, shall we go to the living room to have our talk?" he said, his voice harsh, but firm. Ramona didn't really have a choice. Throughout the meal, she noticed how her daughters were averting her gaze, how the boys were eating quietly, just like their father.

"Alright then. What is it?" she finally set the ball rolling. "Mother, A.J. and I are married" Mia's first thunderbolt of a sentence, spiraled Ramona completely out of control. "What rubbish!"

"It's true, Ramona. They got married en route. I've accepted it, as should you" Arjun insisted. "They're step-siblings, Arjun. Step-siblings! This is an impossibility. Show me the marriage certificate" Ramona demanded haughtily.

"The court marriage is tomorrow. You can see the certificate after then" Ajju spoke, locking horns with the enemy. "You think you can get away with this? You are nothing but a common nomad's son!"

"Bred like a camel, like the one your father's tribe raised. How dare you even think you could marry my daughter? Mia, come upstairs this instant!" She got up, marching towards the stairs, stopping short of the first step.

Mia was holding Ajju's hand tightly. "You no longer control me, Mother. Ajju is my husband. I answer to him and him alone" Sufficiently snubbed, Ramona glared at Arjun. "You think you've won this round, right?"

"I took what was most precious to you. So, you took what was most precious to me. Well, here's a thought. It's not over yet. The games have just started. Tomorrow, I assume I'm not invited to the court marriage, since I strongly disapprove"

"I'll be going to DTD to have a look at the gallery, that originally belonged to me. Good night!" The collective sigh of relief by everyone at the living room, showed how pleased all present were, in a quick end to an unpleasant evening.

"Well, that's enough excitement for one day. Go on to your rooms. Ajju and Mia, take the guest bedroom at the end of the corridor, upstairs. Dan, come to the study with me. Let Diana have your room"

"We'll figure out the sleeping arrangements some other day" "No, *Baasa*. Dhanush and I will both join you, in the guest bedroom. Mia and Diana, can have our old bedroom. After the honeymoon, we'll shift in together" Ajju said, blushing slightly.

Proud of the way his son was handling each ridiculous development in the current phase of their life, Arjun agreed with his reasoning. Shanti served them light Darjeeling tea, missing her real mistress Suhani, who loved having her night cap, of lemongrass green tea.

"When will she return?" Shanti asked Arjun softly, keeping the dainty porcelain cups on the bedside table, in the guest bedroom. "Sooner than you think, my dear. Have faith" Arjun said, proud of the loyalty his old housekeeper displayed, towards his beloved Braids.

This kind of old-fashioned loyalty, could not be bought or demanded. It had to be earned, especially when it came to an old-fashioned, conservative person like Shanti. Suhani had steadily earned it, over a period of time.

Her actions were respectfully courteous towards each and every worker, who helped in the smooth functioning of their household. Once again, after decades, Arjun thought how different Suhani and Ramona were.

"Complete polar opposites" he said out loud, accidentally. "What was that, *Baasa?*" asked Ajju. "You mother and the crazy snake!" All three men chortled at the statement. "I want to call your mother. But, I know she won't pick up"

Arjun frowned having heard this from himself, not happy about the thought of having to spend another night without his *Beendni.* "I'll call *Maasa*" Dhanush offered, dialing her number, before anyone could protest.

Suhani was just about to switch her cell phone off, when it began to ring loudly. Close to midnight, she didn't have to wonder much who it was. Looking at the number though, she was secretly disappointed.

It wasn't who she hoped it might be. Could she have been replaced so soon, by Ramona? Were they together in the bedroom? Shaking her head away from those horrid thoughts, she went to take the call, but the phone went silent.

"What happened?" Arjun asked Dhanush, who was looking at his cell, puzzled. "She didn't take my call. Must have gone to sleep" Dhanush assumed. "Would you sleep soundly if Leenata were to be on a date, with Vansh?" Ajju reinforced.

"Point taken. Trying again" This time, Suhani did take the call. "You should've slept by now, *Betaji*" "We were missing you. How've you been, *Maasa?* Have you had your dinner?"

Tears welled up, as Suhani tried hard to control her voice. Calming herself, she finally asked, "How is your *Baasa*? Is he alright?" Bingo! "Why don't you ask him yourself?" Dhanush said, quickly handing his cell to Arjun.

"Him? What do you mean?" "He means *Beendni*, that our sons and I, are sulking collectively in the guest bedroom. We're all missing you" She couldn't help sniffing, when he came online.

"*Saheb*…" "I know. I'll fix this. Trust me, Braids" "How can you? No one can" "That is why I asked you to trust me. I know I will find a way. It's just a matter of time. We must stay strong, until then"

He took the call to the balcony, to talk to the love of his life at leisure. They spoke all the way, till both their mobile batteries needed charging. Suhani felt reassured, her faith in her *Saheb* restored, after Arjun's gentle cajoling.

"I love you my wife" "I love you my husband" These were the last words they uttered to each other, both warmed by the mutual love that engulfed them. Ajju was kicking himself for having offered to sleep with his brother and father, in the guest bedroom.

He knew it was the right thing to do, but found it difficult to follow. "Let's wake up early tomorrow and leave for the gallery. Ajju, drop the girls to Sangharsh's place. Nalini will get them ready for the court marriage"

"We'll have a small Vedic ceremony. Andy will take the pictures" Arjun hadn't realized he had drifted off to sleep soon, as did his sons. The girls were fast asleep, much before them as well.

The house was silent in slumber, except for one person who found it tough to close her eyes. Ramona couldn't let the party reach court. She couldn't even harm them by hiring goons or tweaking the car like she had with Gerard and Isabella, because Mia was with them.

Mia was blood, which mattered to Ramona, as she was the only family that was left. Diana was kept purely as a toy for Mia, because it helped to keep up appearances in public. She had to find a way to stop, or at least delay the court date.

And then, she sat up on the bed, glowing with an idea that had never occurred to her earlier! "Now why didn't I think of that?" Smiling, she went off to bed, putting the alarm for a time, when she would be up early.

The night was peaceful, like a lull before the storm. Come early morning, Ramona dressed up quickly. She pulled out an ethnic fusion outfit, made by an upcoming Indo-American designer, in seafoam- green and azure-blue chiffon with gold embellishments.

Accessories were all fit into an extra bag, along with her dainty heels. "Good morning, my beautiful girls! Rise and shine. Today is the big day, Mia" Mia and Diana got up with a start, on seeing their mother up and ready already.

"Mother? What are you doing here?" "What do you mean? I live here now, remember?" "No, I mean in our room" "How rude! How could I not be happy for my daughter, on her wedding day?"

"I have to show my face to your father someday, you know" Mia walked up and hugged her mother tight, happy to have seen her come around. "No crying on a day like today, my dear girl. Hurry up and get ready"

"Diana, that goes for you too. I'm going to the kitchen to give instructions for the day. See you downstairs!" The guest bedroom had three men who got up late and were struggling to look presentable.

Arjun went to the study room to tie up with Sangharsh over the phone, who was already waiting for the entourage. He called Suhani next, asking her to be with him the whole day. "Of course I will! Ajju is our son"

"The Anands are coming too. Annie will look after the store and Abhi will look after my Maya's. I have tied up all that I could" "That's my Braids!" Arjun was beaming, at the thought of seeing Suhani.

He really needed to spend an entire day with her, among all the chaos that had been happening, off late. When he returned to the guest room, he saw the boys talking in hushed tones.

"What's cooking?" "*Baasa*, Mia just called on the intercom. Her mother plans to chaperone the girls, all day today" Arjun didn't let irritation cloak a day, that was to be important for the Prataps.

"Son, when we have a choice between worrying about what might happen and enjoying each moment that is actually happening..I say, let's shelf the former and work on the latter, yes?"

"You're right, *Baasa*. I'm not going to let anything affect my happiness, for today. I'm a bit nervous, but that's my problem." Arjun was fixing his tie, something he was used to seeing Suhani do.

"Nervous? Why's that? Are you in double minds or something?" Dhanush asked his elder brother. "Not at all. I am nervous but I don't know why. Isn't that stupid, *Baasa*?" Arjun made his son stand square, in front of him.

Fixing his silk, marsala-red tie, he said, "Anxiety and nervousness are signs of insecurity, not immaturity. These feelings show you're now responsible not just for yourself, but also for Mia"

"Let these feelings come. Accept them as they are. They will help you as they helped me" Ajju touched his father's feet, to take his blessings. "Thank you for supporting me. I don't know what I would've done, if either of you would've put your foot down"

"We love you too much to hurt you. Now let's get a move on. We have one more unwanted passenger with us" The entire party got in chirpily in their cars. Ramona was thoroughly ignored, as she was chauffeur-driven along with her daughters.

Arjun and the boys went in Ajju's Eco Sport, driven by Dhanush. While Ajju and Arjun were talking about married life, Dan suddenly interrupted them. "Dad, I'm taking you out for a drink in the evening"

"Keep yourself free. If Mom wants to come along, that's fine by me too. I need to talk to you both" Dhanush had to get his parents to speak to *Chaudhary* Akash, now. He wanted Leenata, now more than ever. Love had struck the Pratap household manifold, out of the blue.

# CHAPTER SIXTEEN

Ramona was standing out in her outfit, that was a tad elaborate for a court marriage. Mia wore a soft watermelon-red sari with a medium thickness *zari* border, complemented by elegant gold jewellery.

Diana wore a dull-orange *Patiala salwar* suit, with a *chunni* full of *phulkari* work. The moment they got down at Anand villa, the fuss started. Nalini pulled Mia and Diana to her back room workshop.

They came out without any change in their current outfits, but glowing a bit more than before. "What prank have you pulled now?" Arjun asked his *rakhi* sister, who looked lovely in an off-white and vintage-gold sari herself.

"Mia's soon to be mother-in-law, selected outfits to choose from. The jewellery she'll be wearing for the ceremony, will be from Maya's!" Instead of smiling with pride at his Braids' compassionate heart, Arjun panicked.

"Where is she?" "Upstairs. Why?" Arjun didn't answer, but sprinted down the hallway, up the stairs. "*Beendni*" he knocked on the closed door of her room. "Why is she here?" came a soft voice, a tired voice.

"I don't know myself. Please don't change your mind. I need you to come" "As what? She will be there as your wife and Mia's mother." "Then come as Ajju's mother. I swear to you, during the ceremony, you will sit as my wife"

"I swear on our sons, or you will never see my face again." She opened the door. Arjun pushed it further. An ethereal beauty stood before him. Her sari had mild brush strokes, as if from the palette of a painter.

Her *kundan* jewellery, made her look like a divine goddess. "Wow!" was all he could say. Slapping his arm lightly, Suhani said, "Flirt!" "I'm flirting with my wife. That's no crime" he said, walking down the stairs, holding her hand.

"*Maasa*, you look beautiful!" the boys exclaimed, proud of their mother, who carried herself like a queen, despite the circumstances. "Where is 'she'?" Suhani asked, referring to Ramona.

Nalini replied to her query, "Sangharsh has driven her and the girls to court. We are following behind them. He didn't want you and Arjun to have a fallout today. It would have been unfair to Ajju"

Blessed are those, who have friends who care so much about feelings that matter. Suhani and Arjun thanked God to have the Anands as their anchor, at a time like this. They were family more than friends, with each passing day.

In a world where there were opinionated critics as relatives, friends like these were desperately required, to keep the faith in the goodness of humanity alive. "It's a huge sacrifice to make for Sangharsh"

"Considering he still thinks of Ramona as an Anaconda, he must feel like a zookeeper." Arjun declared, making everyone slip right into the realm of being jovial. The truth was that which Sangharsh chose not to disclose to anyone, because of the purity of its nature.

Sangharsh had committed into getting Ramona out of Suhani's sight, as an act of chivalry from a brother for his sister. It cost him far more in reality, because keeping calm within the vicinity of Ramona, was a trait not very many possessed!

"No pot shots at me today, Sangharsh?" Ramona asked him, curious as to why he was quiet in the car. "Not really. Maybe some other day. Today is Ajju's and Mia's day. No one has the right to spoil it"

"Well now! It looks like family life has matured someone" she said, waiting for a jibe, which never came. "You were far more interesting earlier though. Age has made you boring"

Sangharsh knew she was goading him to start an argument, so he simply said, "Thank you for the compliment. Mia, how are you feeling?" "Fine, Uncle. A bit nervous. A bit excited" Mia replied, wiping her sweaty palms, yet again.

"It is a lifelong commitment, dear child. Are you sure you want to go through with it? If you change your mind at any point, I will stand by you" Ramona said, sounding like a supportive mother.

"Ramona, quit playing with the kid's mind. She knows what she is doing. Am I right, Mia?" Sangharsh said, glaring at her mother. "Yes, Uncle. I have never been surer of anything more in my life"

"It's just that I hope I don't disappoint Ajju. He is very conventional, set in a few ways. I hardly even know him" "Then get to know him better first, Mia. That is what I am trying to tell you"

"Doubting is a bad sign. A delay is still making up your mind completely" Ramona had finally managed to push Sangharsh off the edge. "One more word out of your mouth, and you can hire a cab to the venue."

Ramona wanted to pound Arjun's annoying friend, but chose to keep her façade of a caring mother intact, smiling at Mia, keeping quiet then on, all the way. When they reached the office of the Registrar, it was almost mid-morning.

Sangharsh asked Diana to walk her mother, to where everyone was waiting, at the steps of the courthouse. He wanted to walk Mia alone, so that if any more brainwashing were to be done, it would be one that would enhance the positive.

"Mia, I got married here too. I don't have any parents. Arjun and I are orphans. I want you to know, that if you ever need to talk, talk to Arjun. He loves you a lot too, as I'm sure you know"

Mia felt reassured, her footsteps confirming a confident gait. "I am not attempting to please her anymore, Uncle. I think she has realized that" "If I know your mother, she will come up with something or the other, to keep us all on the edge"

"Now off you go to your Prince Charming! Smile and be happy, *beti*" Sangharsh pinched her cheeks, watching her big, blue eyes light up, as they locked into Ajju's. Suhani was nowhere to be seen.

Arjun whispered, "I've dropped Suhani and Dhanush at the *mandap* in the temple, where the *byaav* is to take place" Sangharsh patted his friend. "Bravo! Another confrontation avoided."

"How was the drive?" Arjun asked casually, as they all walked in. "I just drove a snake around. Leave it at that!" Ramona was watching the two childhood friends cracking jokes, as if everything was alright.

Nalini and Ajju, were walking along with Mia and Diana. She felt left out of the festivities, but was also glad there was no requirement to make small talk. That time would come too, as she saw it.

The signatures of the witnesses and the couple, solemnized the wedding by law. Mia was the new Mrs. Pratap, glowing with joy, Ajju smiling sheepishly by her side. Andy would be meeting them at the temple, so Nalini took as many shots as she could take of everyone.

Everyone, excluding Ramona, of course. Noticing the same, Ramona began to stand closer to Ajju. "Aren't you the lucky one! Take care of my daughter or you'll have me to answer to" she said, intending to sound like she was joking.

Ajju flashed a boyish smile at her, saying, "I am the son of Arjun Pratap. We know how to take care of our *lugais*" Feeling chastened, she turned to Mia. "I always wanted a Christian wedding for you"

"I would have gotten a gown in Venetian lace from the House of Dior.." "Mother, Ajju and I are very happy this way. You should be happy for us too" "Well, of course I am! I'm just saying a church wedding would have been better. You are half-Christian"

"Not anymore, Mrs. Cotton. She is a *Rajputni*, from now onwards" Ajju said, holding his bride by the hand. "Alright. Off to the next venue then!" he said, regretting his words, the moment they slipped out of his mouth.

."Next venue?" Ramona caught on immediately. Sangharsh unknowingly barged into the conversation, saving the day again "Sure! We are all going back to my place, for drinks and lunch"

"Come along, Ramona. Don't you want to chit-chat with me, all the way to Anand villa?" Disgusted at his offer, she said, "I am tired. I thought there was to be a another wedding, the Hindu way"

Curious, she asked, "Is it happening today, or at a later date?" "Maybe a few days later. We will have to contact a *pundit*, for an auspicious date" Arjun joined the fabricated explanation.

Convinced surprisingly, Ramona said, "You guys carry on with your celebrations. I have no time to play, as you all know. I'm going to the gallery to have a look at it, now that it is partially mine"

"After all, I am the owner's legally-wedded wife!" She walked off in the chauffeur-driven Merc of Arjun's, straight to the Dare To Dream gallery. "I don't know whether to be relieved she bought our story and isn't going to be present for the *byaav*"

"Or should I panic knowing there is no one to guard DTD, while Ramona is there." "Relax, Arjun. Just be glad she is out of our hair, for now. I'll call and ask Andy to stay put there"

"If there is anything at all, he will handle it. Just go with the flow" Sangharsh was right. Andy knew how to hold the fort. But, Ajju wasn't so sure. His absence during the court marriage and now the *Vedic* ceremony, was beginning to disturb him.

He hadn't even had a proper talk with him, about any of this. By the time they could all enjoy the air-conditioning of the cars they were in, it was time to get off for the second ceremony.

The temple of the Goddess *Durga* was in the heart of Delhi, very popular for its architecture, as well as religious ceremonies. It had a garden at the back, with an outhouse that had a few rooms on rent.

Arjun had hired the rooms, so that everyone could change into their ethnic attire. It was a clever move, as these attires were far more elaborate than the ones they wore, during the court marriage.

If Ramona had gotten a whiff of their plan, she would want to participate in it, for sure. Just like everyone was trying to keep Suhani away from her, Ramona was aching for a face-to-face, with the *Banjaran* herself.

Dhanush was assigned the role, of the one who was to captivate all memorable moments of the ceremony. He was dressed in a mellow, turmeric-yellow *churidar kurta*, his Sony Alpha A7S Compact, slung around his neck.

He was now ready for the shoot, that would capture real life moments, of one of Ajju's life-altering days. Ajju had changed into a chocolate-brown coloured *sherwani* suit, the tones matching beautifully with Mia's caramel-brown and strawberry-red *ghaghra choli*.

"You look like a pair of strawberries and chocolates!" Diana commented, astounded at how glorious love made her sister look. Suhani and Arjun looked like a match made in heaven, as they stood beside each other, throughout the ceremony.

The *pundit* announced for all to be seated, as the chanting began. The *phera*s were next, which went off smoothly, as the couple did exactly what they were told. It was finally time for the newly wedded couple, to take the blessings of the parents.

"Where are the girl's parents?" the priest asked. "They need to bless the couple too" "We are her Uncle and Aunt; sort of her Godparents. Is it alright if we bless them?" Nalini intervened.

The priest accepted the explanation, asking the couple to touch the feet of the elders. Suhani froze, when Mia touched her feet. Graceful as she was, she took out four heavy *kadha*s in gold, inlayed in diamonds, with green and red *meenakari* done in places.

Slipping them into Mia's elegant wrists, she looked into her eyes, for the first time. "*Bahu*, you are my son's *ardhangini* now. Learn the customs of our family. Abide by them. My blessings to you, for your new life"

"May *Ma Bhavani* protect you both, keep you happy with each other, for each other" Mia hugged Suhani, who had to response to the spontaneous warmth the girl exuded. Arjun in his turn, blessed the couple on similar lines.

"I am not as eloquent as your mother-in-law, but Mia…you are to call us *Baasa* and *Maasa*, just like Ajju does. I would like a change of residence too, so you can start a new family, where we could come, visit often"

"But, for now, as per tradition, your name has to be changed. Your *patri* has been read by Suhani's astrologer, who suggested a few names for you. Do you mind, if we address you with a name other than Mia?"

"*Baasa*, as long as I am a part of a family that loves me, I have no issue with anything else" Ajju chose the name Aradhana for her, which everyone approved of instantly. "It means 'prayer' in *Hindi*" he explained to her, smiling.

"Are you alright?" "Yes, this is all fairly new, but so far I'm enjoying every bit of this whirlwind adventure! How about you?" Aradhana asked Ajju. "I'm waiting to taste those lips alone, drown into those cornflower blue eyes.. Other than that, I am good!"

Mia, or as she was now to be known as, Aradhana, blushed a deep, crimson-red at Ajju's remark. "Alright people. Group photograph time." Dhanush announced. There were several pictures clicked of couples, as well as several permutations of those present.

Dhanush was included on pics with set timers as well, for he was Aradhana's brother-in-law now. "Where will they stay, *Saheb*?" "We're booking them in the Taj hotel, as of now. From there, they leave for their honeymoon"

"By that time, something should turn up" Arjun senior replied, still ogling at Suhani. "Why haven't you worn this *sari* before?" he asked her out of the blue. "It was something simple, so I thought you may not like it"

"Your simplicity has an incomparable beauty hidden inside it, *Beendni*. Anything you wear turns to gold, because of how you are within. How you blessed Aradhana today shows your nature, reflects on your character"

"I am proud to be your husband, my love" Arjun's honest words brought tears to Suhani's eyes, a reminder once again that they were not legally spouses yet. Moving closer, he whispered, "Trust. Faith. Hope"

He walked away without turning, rage tearing at him from the inside. He detested watching his Braids cry, knowing he was momentarily helpless to do anything about it; knowing he was honestly not to blame, for the pain and humiliation she was being put through.

Dhanush had witnessed all of this and taken shots. He wanted to have that talk with his parents, as soon as possible. Seeing them hold on to each other made him realize, how any relationship is frail, tender like a new born.

If not tended with the utmost care, sincerity, the thread of silk that holds two hearts together frays, breaks. His brother had taken a huge leap of faith, marrying a woman who he hardly knew.

She entered their lives with the intention to con, ending up giving her heart to the one she was supposed to deceive. Life can never be planned, to a complete extent. Even if it is planned to a certain degree, it is still crucial to make room for adjustments.

In reality, flexibility is key, to maintain the status quo of happiness and contentment. It was time for lunch and drinks, to celebrate the new addition to the family. A few cursory calls later, everyone hopped into their respective cars, to drive towards Anand villa.

Dhanush had sneakily tied empty cans, balloons, coloured crepe paper that said 'Just Married' on A.J.'s Eco Sport. Laughing, the couple got into their SUV and drove towards the Taj, where they would stay until they left for their honeymoon.

No one was to utter where Mia, Mrs. Aradhana Pratap was staying, so that Ramona could be kept away from her. The rest of the party reached the Anand villa, one beer after another being opened by the men, the women laughing at old stories and anecdotes.

Dhanush let loose with the camera there too. It was surprising to see how the two families had taken a day that could have gone horribly wrong, changing it to celebratory, but short. Everyone was tired and moved in for a short nap.

Arjun walked in with Suhani, spending time alone behind closed doors after a long time. He made promises to her in words no more as they brought the forces of their love together again, their passion igniting what they treasured, nurtured, into the forefront. Early evening, everyone met up for tea at the balcony. A special glow had rekindled between Arjun and Suhani, happily noticed by all.

Against all odds, keeping the flame of a love within the realms of passion, is the onus of both partners, when they are in a situation where all they really need, is to hold on to each other and walk through time.

Sometimes, that is all that is really needed. To walk through time knowing, that the length and breadth of a situation has been put at that point of time, to merely test the strength of the bond two people share, and how much they are willing to work towards each other, rather than shirk.

# CHAPTER SEVENTEEN

Ramona wasn't exactly dressed in her work clothes, but she managed to move around DTD all the same. She walked into her old office, disappointed at how masculine it now looked.

There was no feminine touch in the interiors of the gallery from any angle. The outside that was open to visitors had quite a bit of art, apparel flowing from here to there, typical of something Sangharsh would do.

She could also have bet her bottom dollar, that Suhani had chipped in with the interior designing as well. Arjun's office had Suhani's picture on his desk on one side, his sons' on another side of his desktop.

Behind his chair was a huge mural of the Lord Shiva, who seemed to be smiling straight at her. "I know you think I'm crazy. I'm not. I just want to feel like I'm needed. Like I belong somewhere"

"As if someone wants me badly enough that I feel…" She began to laugh hysterically. "Maybe I am going mad, speaking to a mural of a God, that Arjun of all people worships!"

"Not crazy. Just desperately lonely. I know how it feels" She swung around to face Nandish standing behind her. "I was informed you are to be expected, Mrs. Cotton. Welcome to DTD"

Ramona didn't know, whether to be angry at being welcomed to a place that originally belonged to her, or embarrassed at having been caught off guard, by a boy half her age. "You are Sangharsh and Nalini Anand's son, Andy"

"Yes" Andy was visibly uncomfortable being in her presence, making it clear to her that Sangharsh had brainwashed his son well. "Did he tell you I can cast a spell on you too, or swallow you alive like the Anaconda that I am?"

Andy released a smile in return. "Two halves make a whole" "So, both then. Well, I am not surprised, considering I haven't done much to win his trust or respect" Andy put his hands in his pocket and shrugged.

He found it hard to believe, that the venomous Ramona Rai was showing her normal, human side to him. "Mia looks a lot like you" he said. "Except her eyes. They are like her father"

"I am not Mrs. Cotton, by the way. We were not legally married. So, technically I am still Mrs. Arjun Pratap. That has upset a whole lot of you, I bet!" "You think?" he replied, turning away to go to his office.

She followed him to the lobby. "I like you, Andy. Show me around, won't you? So much has changed, that I fear I might lose my way" Andy didn't buy her story at all. At least, the part where she wanted him to show her around.

He knew that she wanted to carry on the conversation with her to avoid boredom, loneliness, both. They walked through the displayed pictures, Ramona occasionally waiting to take a look at a picture, up close.

She had already had a look at quite a bit of the gallery displays, when she came to meet Arjun for the first time. There were two places she was interested to explore-the Accounts Department and the back room.

The back room was where, the negatives of the original photographs used to be kept. She knew Andy would guard them both, not letting her see what she actually came to have a look at.

The only way she could gain leverage, was by getting at his soft side. He was immune to her charms, but by now she had gathered, that he too felt left out. The question was from what?

"You work here as the manager? Mr. Guha used to be here in that post" "He is still here, as is his nephew Bantu. I am here as one of the photographers; assistant to Mr. Pratap actually"

"But they let me take pictures off late" Nandish had to subconsciously ask himself to keep quiet. He had no business rattling out information to someone, who wasn't even welcome in the first place.

"So, how do you find my girls? Diana is still alright, but keeping boys off Mia was a tough task to pull, since she was a teenager." Ramona said, bending over to look at one of the displays.

The unique display caught her eye, as it showed a 3D view of a beautiful hill full of a variety of trees, swaying in bloom. "This is pretty" "That is a shot I took, while everyone was resting. Mr. Pratap liked it so much, that he insisted it be displayed"

"If I had my way, I would have all your pictures displayed, not in bits and pieces" Andy liked the thought, which was his secret ambition as well. But he knew, she was playing mind games with him.

"We don't have any rights or silly personal attachments to the pictures we click, for the gallery. Is there any place else you wish to see?" "Yes, I do. But I'm afraid, it's something that a soldier like you, would have to take permission from his general for"

"Unless, you think my harmless look around is of no consequence, to the strength of your masses!" Now Nandish was stuck between the devil and the deep sea. If he were to call to take instructions, two things could happen.

Either Ramona would get to know about the Vedic ceremony and try to get there; or, it would weaken his claim of being an intrinsic part of DTD. "I can call Arjun if you want. After all, he is my husband"

"No need. I am sure they won't have any issue with you, wanting to look around. I am to escort you at all times though" "Oh, I quite like your company. I'm sure you must have been great company, for my daughters too"

She walked into the back room, to have a look at the working of roll development of films. "So much has changed. There used to be just one room. One dark room. It's more like a hallway with cubicles now"

The computer screen began blinking, showing there was an incoming message from Dhanush. Panicking, Andy switched the screen off. "What was that?" Ramona asked, suspiciously.

"It must be Dhanush, sending picture of the court marriage. I'll have a look at them later" Andy said, casually. "Let's see them together" "I'll have a look at them with the rest of the photo editors"

"Now, what is it you wanted to see here?" he asked, sounding guarded. Not wanting to upset him or raise any kind of alarm, she simply said, "I wanted to have a look at some of your latest work"

"Do you have any finished pieces for me to have a look at?" "As a matter of fact I do" Andy replied, flattery finally getting in through the cracks. He pulled out a tray of tagged memory cards and started moving his finger through them.

"Okay. Let me show you this one. We took this off late at Bassi. Some pictures are of the drive to Bassi too. They are not edited though" "Doesn't matter. I wouldn't know the difference" Ramona said, reassuring Andy's sluggish opening up.

"These were en route to Bassi. Those are the road pics" Mia was laughing at Andy, while she threw water at him, soaking his t-shirt. A thin smile came on his lips, that did not go unnoticed.

"That's the only bridge we crossed, where Mia had to stick her head out to take a picture. Her hair looked funny after that" Another smile got him, right there and then.

"This one is Mia and Diana conspiring to get me off guard, when in reality, I was standing right behind them" This time both Ramona and Andy laughed together. Laughing brought back pangs, that Andy failed to hide.

"Does she know you're in love with her?" Ramona asked, still staring at the screen. "I don't know what you mean" came an ineffective reply. "I'm her mother, Andy. If I had my way, I'd have chosen you any day over A.J"

"It wasn't up to you. It was Mia's choice to make. As we both know, she has made it already" Andy played right into Ramona's hands. He heard her sniffing next. "What's wrong? Are you crying?" he asked, surprised.

"They'll change her completely. She has started listening to them already. Before you know it, she will forget all about me. A.J controls hers now. I am to be left behind in the past"

"There, there. Don't be silly. No one can take Mia away from you. She is your daughter after all. Don't be cynical about all of us. We're not all that bad" he found himself saying, wondering what his father would say, if he saw the 'anti-social' interaction with his own eyes.

"Wait and watch, Andy. Arjun will try every trick in the book, to make Mia forget me completely. I have never been needed by anyone, as much as by Mia. Arjun, Gerard, everyone used me and then abused how I felt, about them"

"The only person to have loved me exactly the way I am, is Mia. And now…" Another bout of wailing, made Andy rest his palm on Ramona's. "I need to make a few calls. Why don't you go to your old office?"

"There is a rest room, where you could freshen up. Perhaps, rest for a while?" "Sure, thank you. Where would you be?" "I have to go to a couple of places. I should be back in an hour, maximum two"

"I'll probably be asleep by then. Wake me up if I am, Andy. I feel so drained out" "Sure I will. Let me escort you to the office" "Aren't you disobeying your general's orders, soldier?" she asked in a tiny voice.

"Only a fool would think you were a threat. I do not make mountains out of molehills. If you need anything, call Mr. Guha. His number is on the glass desk" He left in a hurry, so that his work could finish earlier than his estimate.

Andy left a lady, who could not believe how gullible the offspring of a cunning person like Sangharsh, truly was! She now had access to Arjun's office. The only person who stood in her way, was Mr. Guha.

That man saw her and almost had a nervous breakdown. She managed to convince him to take her to the Accounts Department, as Andy had to cut the tour short, due to some urgent business to attend to.

Poor Mr. Guha tried to put two and two together, falling on his face. He was told not to let Ramona out of the premise at any cost, by both Mr. Pratap as well as Nandish Anand. The Accounts Section was just a room, with cabinets full of files.

"You have all become supremely organized." she complimented. "Bantu, my nephew helps out a lot, Madame" "Mr. Guha, how are things in DTD? Arjun is busy, so he could not brief me completely"

"He did tell me you were the right person to ask" Falling for her lie, Mr. Guha said, "Well Madame, it's not going very well. There is a lot of competition, courtesy the galleries that have opened up close by"

"The market is not as DTD- friendly, as it used to be. All the clients your father had, are now big multinationals, who refuse to associate with us. We have become more like a boutique gallery"

Ramona looked supremely pleased with the news. "Hear me carefully, Mr. Guha. I plan to sit on this chair one day soon. Arjun was never a good businessman. He was a good photographer, no doubt"

"Now, I can get DTD back to its status it enjoyed, in the golden days. I'll give you a raise, make you Senior Manager. Your nephew will take your place. You will handle the photographers, the business"

"Bantu can help with anything else" "I do not understand, Madame. Mr. Pratap will not be coming to DTD anymore?" "Of course he will! I will buy him out. Once this place is mine, he will work under me"

"If he chooses to continue, he will be working under you too." "I am sorry, Madame. I do not think DTD is for sale" "Oh no? You told me yourself the gallery is suffering losses. How long before you think Mr. Pratap will throw in the towel?"

"What do you plan to do then, Mr. Guha? I know all about your family. Your needy relatives, your greedy son-in-laws…" "Please don't drag me into this. Mr. Pratap has been good to me" Mr. Guha pleaded.

"From what I see, he may have been good to you, but he has been better to himself. Your salary has hardly been increased, your leaves hardly sanctioned on one hand"

"On the other hand, Mr. Pratap has been taking world trips to exotic destinations, under the pretext of working for the gallery, squandering all of its profits"

"He has nothing to show. Where is the business, if DTD is what I left it as?" Mr. Guha had no reply to her accusations, purely as there were elements of truth inside her argument.

Everyone knew the market slump, the competition had nothing to do with the business being generated for the gallery. Arjun Pratap was a photographer, not an entrepreneur. He detested accounts, meeting people to advertise DTD.

He loved the gallery per se, but that is not what it needed to stay afloat. "I am taking some of these files and leaving. Have a cab called for me. Andy will be back any moment. Do not let him know I have taken these documents"

It was then that Mr. Guha realized, the depth of his folly. He was to ensure Ramona was to stay in Arjun's cabin, not to venture to any place else; least of all the Accounts Section. He wanted her to go away quickly.

The cab came within a few minutes, as Mr. Guha escorted her out. "Here is my number. Call me anytime, if you need anything. I stand by my word, Mr. Guha. When I take over, you will be my Senior Manager"

"Until then, I want to know about every little detail. You will call me every evening and give me a report, as to what transpired during the course of the day, in the gallery. Am I understood?"

A tiny 'Yes, Madame' escaped Mr. Guha's chapped, thin lips, hardly audible out of guilt and shame. Ramona left for Swarn Niwas thereafter, leaving Mr. Guha to clean up the scattered files after her.

Andy arrived in half an hour, ordering for two black coffees for Ramona and himself. "Mrs. Cotton has left, Andy Sir" Mr. Guha spoke into the intercom. "What? Why did you let her go?"

"I gave you specific instructions to detain her within DTD, at any cost!" Andy yelled at Mr. Guha for the first time. Unable to control himself any longer, Mr. Guha yelled back. "What was I supposed to do?"

"She said she was feeling sick and wanted to go home. I called her a cab like she asked" Andy was taken aback with Mr. Guha's shouting. He couldn't remember the man every raising his voice.

Maybe Ramona did have the lethal effect on most, after all. He went into the back room, still wondering what got Mr. Guha so wound up, when he saw the light in his cubicle blinking.

Remembering Dan had sent him pics of the Vedic ceremony, he began looking at all of them. Mia looked so happy with Ajju, that Andy forgot for a moment that he was in fact, head over heels in love with her.

Everyone looked so happy and content. They didn't seem to have missed him, in either of the ceremonies. Annie was taking care of their parents' business for the day. He was stuck in the gallery.

Abhimanyu at Maya's was holding the fort for Suhani. Andy felt used, unwanted at that moment, empathizing completely with the one they called Anaconda. He liked her from their interaction, albeit short-lived.

Why was everyone mean to her? She just wanted to be counted in. He knew how she felt. Maybe her methods were a bit extreme, but it was quite possible she was pushed, to become who she was now.

Nandish was slowly becoming Ramona's ally, as his thoughts convinced him she was being branded, as something she was not. He decided to call her on her cell, over his coffee.

"Hi! Where did you disappear to? I ordered coffee for the both of us" "I'm sorry, Andy. I started going through all the pictures you had taken, of your trip and the girls all over again"

"My heart broke and I felt so guilty. If I knew you were so much in love with Mia, I would have done everything in my power to stop the wedding. Ajju can never love her the way you could have, dear fellow"

Nandish spoke to her some more, confiding in her as to how he felt. He felt less burdened with the thoughts that were beginning to weigh him down. It was good to have someone on his side, who understood his feelings.

Ramona and Andy developed a strange friendship that no one else could have understood. They both felt the same sense of not belonging anywhere, unheard. The question remained, as to what they were going to do about it.

# CHAPTER EIGHTEEN

Dhanush saw his parents sipping tea while talking in the balcony. He had forgotten how reassuring it felt, to watch his two pillars of strength together. He decided to be spontaneous, as he walked up to them.

"It's good to see you both together! *Maasa*, I'm taking *Baasa* out for a drink in the evening. Please join us. I'd like both of you to be there" "What is it about? Is there something wrong?" Suhani asked, concerned.

"I'll tell you everything once we three are alone. Let's move around 7 in the evening" he said, leaving in a hurry before his parents prodded him again. "What's this about? Do you have any idea?" Suhani turned to Arjun, after their son left.

"I think I know what he's up to. He wants to talk to us, about Leenata" "Akash *Bhaisa* and Bindiya's daughter? But she was supposed to marry Viren" "That's the puzzle that can be solved, if we sit with Dhanush"

They talked some more, like the old times. There was no threat of any harm to their relationship, whenever they spoke openly to each other. Over the years, they had begun to realize how crucial communicating was, in their lifelong companionship.

"*Namaste, Chachaji, Chachiji*!" Annie walked in beaming, with a huge cup of hot tea, smartly clothed in an Adidas t-shirt and Levis jeans. "*Namaste, Bitiya*! Have you lost weight?"

"I'm on a new diet. Abhi says I've to lose my puppy fat. It seems to be working, isn't it?" "Sure does! You look lovely!" Pleased with the compliment, Annie began to talk about how busy she had been, with her new doll collection.

"Abhi encourages me a lot, although he is bordering pushy at times" "Sometimes we need that extra push from our men, to shine. Your *Chachaji* does it at times too" Suhani looked at her *Saheb*, with unmasked affection.

"She can be a bit lazy at times! So, have you set a date? Get engaged to him, at least!" Arjun teased Annie. "He wants to marry directly, without any fanfare. He has a few relatives, who might come from his hometown"

"We want to keep it simple" Annie confided. "Looks like you have it all figured out!" Suhani exclaimed. "Seems to be a trend, off late. Keeping it simple, I mean" Arjun said, watching Annie float over to Sangharsh's arms.

"Yes it does. It's practical and quick. I for one, am for it" Suhani said. "Then it's settled. Once Ramona is out of our lives for good, we'll marry following the latest trend." He kissed her gently, making them both happy at the mere thought, of being inseparable once again.

The phone beside Arjun rang, announcing the intrusion of none other than the Anaconda. "Hello? Arjun, where are you guys? Mia's phone is switched off, as is Diana's. What's happening?" he heard an over-anxious mother blurt out.

"They're all here. I'll be home late at night. No need to wait up for any of us. You wanted to move in yourself. There was no clause that required all of us to attend your stupid circus!"

"That was a bit rude, *Saheb*" Suhani chided him. "It's the only language she understands" he replied, harshly. It was almost time to keep their word, of going out with Dhanush for the mysterious talk.

They got ready and met up again in the living room. Suhani was dressed in a cocktail dress, long, flowing in cascades of vermillion and fawn. She burst out laughing when her *Saheb* walked in wearing Sangharsh's palm tree beach shirt and dockers.

"I wasn't carrying any change. This is all the idiot gave me! He doesn't share his clothes. Can you imagine? He'll share his food, his home, even his wallet. But never his clothes!" Arjun said, loud enough for Sangharsh to hear.

"You complement her, *dost*!" he yelled from the vicinity. Dhanush walked in, wearing a pair of tailored trousers, with a starched white shirt from Marks and Spencer. "Dad, drinks in a classy restaurant, not the beach"

"I thought it was understood." he remarked, joining in pulling Arjun's leg. Sangharsh chuckled again, coming out to meet the trio this time. "Alright, that's enough leg pulling for now"

"Come on, buddy. Let's try something else on you" Grumbling, Arjun left with him, only to return after a quarter of an hour, completely transformed. It was these moments that reminded Suhani, how magnetic Arjun really was.

Bottle green trousers, cream half-shirt, Hushpuppies footwear. "Perfect!" Dhanush spoke for both himself and his mother. He drove them in his Humvee, to a perfect place for dinner called 'Sublime'.

The seating was both indoors, as well as outdoors. It was fast becoming a popular culture in Delhi. They chose to sit inside, in a pre-booked corner, with a red and gray leather seating area.

Suhani ordered for a mocktail while both father and son ordered for a beer. "Alright, out with it. We've been patient enough" Arjun started the conversation. "A few minutes more of patience, please"

"We have a couple joining us any moment now" The moment he uttered the words, the doors of the restaurant opened for a tall, slender, sparkling couple holding hands, while they walked towards them.

"Ajju! Mia!" Suhani exclaimed, standing up to greet them. "She is Aradhana, *Maasa*" Ajju gently corrected her. "Right. What're you two doing here? Has your brother summoned you two, too?"

"Guilty!" Dhanush said, pulling a chair for his new *bhabhi*, kissing her on the cheek. "Alright. You are my family and know me in and out better than anyone else. I have not been the best son or the best brother either"

"You have seen me with many girls too. But this time, I have fallen in love with someone I would like to spend the rest of my life with. I would like all of your blessings, to marry Leenata"

There was hushed silence for a few seconds, but it was not out of shock. Everyone present had an inkling, Leenata would be the topic of discussion. The way Dhanush spoke, caught them completely off guard.

"All this elaborate planning was unnecessary, *beta*. We would have supported you anyway" Suhani said, resting her hand on his wrist. "I'm aware of that, *Maasa*. But I wanted to show you the change in me"

"I'm willing to walk the extra mile, do whatever it may take, to make her part of our family, your *choti bahu*" Impressed, Arjun said, "Alright. Consider it done" The waiter interrupted, with drinks for everyone.

Mia had a cocktail too, but Ajju chose a soft drink. "I have to drive" he said, making both Arjun and Dhanush feel guilty, about their mug of beer. "What happened to Viren?" Suhani asked, munching on the sesame-coated finger chips snack, that came with the drinks.

"*Chaudhary* Akash will speak with Viren's family, to call the wedding off. He wants you both to come to Bassi, to ask for Leenata's hand formally" "We'll go as soon as it is possible. I'll call him to tie up and.."

"*Baasa*, I've been in touch with him on a regular basis. I think you should go tomorrow" Dhanush spoke. "Tomorrow? Ajju gets married today. Tomorrow we go to talk to your would- be in-laws"

"Where do you mother and I get any breathing space?" Arjun protested, irritated at being mentally taxed, at this age. "*Saheb*, we can do this. I'll get a few *thaalis* ready, by tomorrow afternoon"

"We'll leave around noon siesta. Dhanush will come along with us" "*Maasa*, Aradhana and I wish to come along with you" Ajju said, not wanting to miss out on a chance, to go to his dear Bassi.

"Of course. Be ready by noon then" Arjun intervened. "Anyone else wants to hop in for a ride?" "We have a few shots to figure out in Bassi, so Andy needs to come too. He's been away from all of us, for quite some time now"

"And, Vansh gave me clear instructions to bring Diana along, as well. He seems to have a thing for her." Dhanush said, expecting the next statement from his father, who was predictable enough to give it.

"It looks like your generation has gone into a pairing-up mode, all of a sudden!" Suhani noticed Aradhana was wearing the bangles she gave her, as *ashirwad*. They were a complete mismatch, with the black velvet and grey *anarkali* salwar suit, she was clothed in.

"Why didn't you match your hand accessories, Aradhana? Everything else is coordinated expertly" "*Maasa*, these are not just bangles for me. It's the very first time, that someone has shown me love and acceptance"

"I must earn their trust and respect, in return" Aradhana's wisdom reflected in her words, as well as her actions. Nodding at Ajju, complimenting him on his choice silently, they ordered for dinner.

"Ramona called to say she wanted to speak with you. Yours and Diana's cells were switched off" Arjun mentioned casually to Aradhana, while Suhani left to powder her nose.

"I've no wish to speak with her. Feel free to say anything you want. There is nothing urgent, of that I am sure, *Baasa*" "*Bitiya*, she is your mother. Call her once a day, to assure her you're alright"

"If she says something you disapprove of, then gently brush it aside. That's not too much to ask, is it?" Arjun reinforced the age-old custom, of respecting the elders. "I'll call her when we get back to the hotel, *Baasa*"

"Great. No mention about where you are or where we are all off to, tomorrow. If she tries to pester, cut it short" The dinner was served like Suhani used to have it laid out, while she was the queen of Swarn Niwas.

"Why is it called 'Swarn Niwas'? It means a mansion of gold, right?" Aradhana enquired. "Actually we never thought of it like that. There's a brilliant perspective for you!" Arjun said.

"Braids' father was *Chaudhary* Swarn Singh, a great tribal leader of the *toli* of the *Banjaras* of Nagri. The villa is named after him. It…holy moly!" Arjun dropped his lobster on the plate, with a thud.

"What? What is it?" Suhani asked, scared. "*Beendni*, I think I might have found a way out of this mess!" he said, beaming. "The house is in your name. If you want, you can reside there"

"You can choose who can stay, who must leave" Suhani was astonished. She had totally forgotten this minor detail, that was a major cause for elation, at present. "But, under the same roof, Arjun? I mean.."

"Everything is fair in love and war, *Beendni*. She is in the master bedroom. You and I can stay in the study. Or flip it. I don't care. If there is any way for you to move in legally, I want it done"

Arjun's stubborn streak flashed through, to his beloved. "I'll tell you what. Let's finish the Bassi visit. Once Dhanush's *sagai* is done, we'll have to give a reception for Ajju and Aradhana"

"By that time, we'll formulate a plan, with zero loopholes. I'll check with our lawyer, get the deed in order, till then" Everyone agreed to Suhani's offer, beginning to pray, hope that their plan takes shape soon.

Arjun hated to break the party up, but he knew he had to go back for now, without Suhani. "No alarms need be raised" he justified to Suhani, who nodded quietly in agreement. "Doesn't mean I have to like it though" she answered.

"For what it's worth, I don't either" he said, kissing her tenderly, ever-lovingly. Walking her up the stairs to Anand villa, Arjun left with Dhanush back for Swarn Niwas, talking to him about the Bassi visit.

It proved to be a good distraction, up until the moment they reached their home. Loud voices came through the hallway, as both walked up the stairs to the bedroom. "What is going on?" he asked Ramona, who looked furious, glaring at Diana.

"It's none of your business! Stay out of it!" Ramona snapped at Arjun. "You're in my house. It damn well is my business!" Turning towards Diana, he asked, "What happened?"

Diana had tears in her eyes, which she closed shut, refusing to let them fall. Arjun understood she was being interrogated mercilessly. "Dhanush, take Diana to her room. I'll speak to her mother alone"

They had already discussed that the Bassi trip would be disclosed to Diana, later on at night. She was the only one, who hadn't gone to Anand villa with them. Aradhana wanted her to spend time with Ajju and herself.

Back in her room, Diana was told not to mention, that the couple were staying at the Taj. While Dhanush was briefing Diana about the trip to Bassi, Arjun led Ramona by her forearm, dragging her inside the master bedroom.

"Leave me! That hurts!" she squealed. "Why were you shouting at the poor girl?" he asked. "Who are you to ask me anything? Are you my husband? Are you Diana's father? What right do you have to ask me, to conduct myself properly?"

Before Arjun could interrupt, she walked up to him and inhaled deeply. "A woman knows, when her man has been with someone else. Even if you didn't smell of her, she is written all over your face."

Arjun was agitated, though he managed to speak in a calm tone. "Firstly, you are the other woman. Secondly, I'm not answerable to you, of all people. Thirdly, there are rules abided by, by all who live here, that you are not above"

"Now, I have had a long day. I'm leaving tomorrow for an outstation trip for a day or two. When I come back, I'd like some peace and quiet. There is Ajju's and Mia's reception to think of"

Arjun almost said Aradhana instead of Mia, but was quick to check himself. One word, would have given away the entire Vedic marriage ceremony, that was conducted in Ramona's absence, but Suhani's presence.

"Where are you going?" "On business" "I'll come too" "Please! There is no need" What am I supposed to do here?" "Hatch eggs, plot and scheme some more, jump off a cliff etc. Don't know. Don't care"

Arjun walked off into the study, relieved one job was done. He waited for Dhanush to join him, who told him Diana had kept quiet about the wedding. She was eager to go to Bassi, with them.

"Leave the packed bags in the car at night. I've told Ramona that I'm going on a business trip" Strange as it was, Ramona enquired only about the wedding, not about Mia's whereabouts."

"Maybe she knows, we are trying to keep them apart" Dhanush shot in the dark. "No, there is something more to it. Do me a favour.. Call Bantu tomorrow morning. Ask him to report anything strange, at the gallery"

"If I know Ramona correctly, she will be eager to spread her fangs, all over my life. Once she puts me in a spot, the power is what will satiate her" Arjun and Ramona were a perfect example, when it came to studying vices in the other partner.

In a healthy relationship, each person ought to encourage the qualities that bring out the best in them. In the reverse, each person attempts to injure the other, with ammunition that badgers the worst out of them.

Arjun and Suhani were the polar opposites, as were Sangharsh and Nalini. The reason why Ramona was unable to find a partner who could accept her for what she was, was because of her innate nature.

Her nature, was to poison everything she touched. The fear of being unwanted, had blown a crater into her core, causing her to cause pain to everyone around, irrespective of whether she cared for them, or not.

She had been getting calls from Mr. Guha, who had informed her no one had come to DTD, except Andy. She had already spoken with Andy, who by now had become not just a strong ally, but also a dear confidante.

Mia was out of her league now. Ramona chose to shift her focus to the weakest link of the Prataps and Anands-Nandish. She would teach him how to make himself feel important, be noticed, counted.

Then she would use him as a weapon, to destroy her daughter's marriage and subsequently Ajju's life. In the meantime, the next morning was as important for Ramona, as it was for the Prataps. Ramona was going to meet her lawyer.

She wanted to discuss buying DTD, thereby gaining ownership over all of Arjun's assets. It was late at night when all slept sound in body, but their minds were restless "What is going to happen now, Ajju?"

Mia asked while she lay in her husband's arms, finger-doodling his chest. "We are going to forget about the world, its problems. Let's just focus on each other. I want a child with you, Aradhana. Will you bear me one?"

She hid her face in his chest. He engulfed her in his arms, his passionate embrace leading from hot intensity, to tender love. They were above the drama that surrounded them, for now. Their minds, souls were uniting through their bodies, till sleep and exhaustion took them to the realm, of fantasy-like dreams.

# CHAPTER NINETEEN

Early next morning, Suhani quickly briefed the Anands, about the Bassi plan. They opted to help in any way possible. Suhani needed the *rasam ki thaali* to be prepared, which Nalini took responsibility for.

She knew exactly where to go to, for all that was required to fill the two brass plates of the ceremony. One would have apparel, namely a *sari* and a *ghaghra choli* with jewellery to match.

Another would have sweetmeats called *mithai*, with dry fruit and silver foil on them. Suhani had to rush to Maya's, to check on how Abhi was handling her business. He had managed to get a few new accounts, including an ad campaign, which pleased her immensely.

Arjun, along with his boys, had gone to DTD early, to check on their gallery. Mr. Guha was told not to let Ramona in at any cost, during their absence. Bantu was taken aside and told the same.

"I trust you the most, Bantu. I want you to think, you are the protector of DTD in my absence" Dhanush told him, making the simpleton who followed him blindly, feel largely important.

"I'll make sure you are the first to know in case of anything, Dhanush Sir" he said, short of saluting him. They got together at the Anand villa and left after an early brunch of *alu paratha*s and curd with white butter.

They took the Humvee and the Eco Sport. All seven were enthusiastic to revisit Bassi, for different reasons. *Chaudhary* Akash was informed previously, that they were on their way for the formal talk, to ask for Leenata's hand in marriage, with Dhanush.

Ajju and his wife were enjoying the ride, as were Arjun and Suhani. Dhanush and Diana were excited to see their respectives, who were equally anxious to meet them. Andy was the only one who was faking being chirpy, enthusiastic.

He was still hurt about being treated as the fort holder during the marriages. Unfortunately, everyone assumed he would be understanding of the situation, not questioning whether or not he'd prefer to be participative, in any other role.

Another example, where the lack of communication was increasing the gap between those who genuinely cared for Andy, and himself. He had already messaged to Ramona, mentioning he's being taken to Bassi.

Ramona didn't show she was eager to come as well, for she knew Andy would be her eyes and ears. Preparations were on in full swing, at the *Chaudhary haveli* for the city folk, who were now soon to become relatives, by wedlock.

Leenata was dressed in a sunny-yellow *sari* with golden *gota* stars all over, a thin border keeping the chiffon in place. *Kundan jhoomka*s adorned her ears, matched with a plain *mang tikka* and a necklace, to add to the ensemble.

The bangles were a gift from her mother. They were of gold, their sparkle encasing the lovely inlay-work, typical of *Rajasthani* jewellery. Vansh had worn a pair of jeans and a long, cotton *kurta* in turmeric and green stripes, a smile that had his Jiya's name on it.

Akash and Bindiya had no idea of all that was transpiring in the city, so they assumed as always that the Prataps, were still husband and wife. News of Ajju and Mia was also not known to them, as everyone wanted Dhanush and Leenata to be in the spotlight.

When the city folk arrived, the *haveli* broke into a loud noise of jubilatory welcome. Dhanush knew his Leenata would not be permitted to come out blatantly, as it was against the *maryada* of the *Raikas*.

Vansh nodded at Diana, who looked refreshingly pretty in a fawn and opal salwar suit. Bashfully, she returned his nod, smiling right back. "Welcome, Arjun *Saheb*! Looks like Lord Shiva wanted our clans to unite, after all!" stated *Chaudhary* Akash, embracing his old friend.

"It is an honour to be associated with a family such as yours, *Chaudhary* Akash. Your daughter will never need anything, for as long as she shall live. She will get the respect and honour of a *Rajputni*, in the Pratap household"

Bindiya ushered the group in, complimenting Suhani on her complexion. "I've been resting for long hours, off late. Maybe it's that I stay away from the sun, or the city's polluted air"

"No, Suhani. This is the glow of love. I see it on my Leenata every time your son calls, to speak with her" They basked in the pure silliness of romance. "*Beta* Nandish, come sit with us" *Chaudhary* Akash said.

*Bel ka sherbet* was being served to everyone present by Leenata, who was the centre of attention for the day. "I'll have a look around and return soon. Bassi is like a second home for me too"

Believing his story, the families began their exchange of gifts, as acceptance of the *rishta*. "Dhanush *beta*, take care of my daughter. Protect her from the evils of the world. Let her purity remain untouched"

Bindiya spoke these words, a wave of maternal emotion overcoming her momentarily, making her voice shake a bit. "I give you my word" was all he said, mostly because the moment she walked in, he lost his power to think, within the vicinity of practicality or logic.

"When do you plan to set the wedding date, *Chaudhary Saheb*?" "As soon as the *sagai* is over, of course. We will get our *panditji* to suggest dates for the marriage" "Then why don't we get them engaged, right away!"

"We could have the *sagai* ceremony tomorrow, if you are okay with the idea" Arjun watched Akash frown for a few seconds, till the wrinkles on his forehead cleared again. "Yes, it can be done"

"The *byaav* must be as per the *muhurat* though" "Alright, that's settled then. Come, let's have your *hookah* and discuss some more about our children. Let the ladies figure out, how to pass their time"

Arjun was led away to the *palang*s with the *hookah*s in the private courtyard, situated at the back of the *haveli*. Ajju and Aradhana broke the news to Bindiya, who was happy for them.

They preferred the name Aradhana to Mia. "Sounds less of a *firangan!*" Bindiya said, watching her blush, every time Ajju glanced at his new bride. The youngsters chose to go for a walk around Bassi right to the *tila*, literally in pairs.

Leenata changed after the *muh dikhayee* was over, into a rust-red salwar suit, to join them. While sitting at one of the boulders, Dhanush opened his palm. "I think this belongs to you"

He handed her the beautiful brooch, studded with crushed diamonds, that had been returned to him, by Bindiya. She picked it out of his palm, smiling, "It will suit me well for the dress that has been picked out for me, for our *sagai*"

"You'll look good in western wear too, Leena. Once you join me in the city, you'll have to wear clothes like city folk do. Are you prepared to change your lifestyle as you know it completely, for a man such as myself?" Dhanush asked, looking into her dark-kohled eyes.

"Are you discouraging me, or testing to see what I say?" "Neither of the two, my love. It is a matter of great pride, that someone like yourself finds me worthy enough, for such a drastic change"

"If it is okay with you, maybe we could stay for one half of the year in the village, the other half in the city. That way, we could both adjust, as well as appreciate each other's backgrounds"

Leenata's suggestion almost got taken seriously by Dhanush, were it not for her burst of tinkling laughter, that showed she was merely jesting. "You will never leave my side, Leena. Once we are married, I will take you everywhere with me"

Flattered, she smiled at him once again, making his heart race and skip beats, like never before. "This village is like a magnetic memory bank, for me" Ajju was talking to Aradhana, holding her hand and walking slowly around the smaller boulders of the *tila*.

"Every time I return, Bassi gives me a gift, almost as if..." "As if what, my darling?" Aradhana coaxed him to continue. "As if my memories open up here alone, but lock themselves up tightly as soon as I reach the city"

"I don't even think I'm the same person, in both places" "You look and feel the same to me, Ajju" Aradhana's purse had a few items that a lady ought to carry. She also had a mobile that was perpetually switched off, lest Ramona should call.

Noticing the same, Ajju asked, "Do you feel I'm keeping you away from your family?" "How so?" He looked at her mobile, gaping out of her embroidered sling purse. Pushing it in with her translucent fingers, she said, "You are my family"

"Like I said earlier, I've only gotten conditional love from her. If I listened to her, only then would she let me near her, or be nice to me and Diana. I had to be the circus monkey for both of us, for years now"

"It's exhausting, both mentally and physically, to try and appease someone who replaces one ambition with another, with no breaks in between" She did have a valid point, not that Ajju could relate to it.

Most parents he knew, tried their level best to live their ambitions through their children, making it look as if they were doing their offsprings a favour, by bringing out the best in them.

Instead of letting them enjoy their childhood, learn the art of living a simple life, they taught their kids all about competition, how to stand out in a crowd, par excellence. It was a trend Ajju disapproved of thoroughly and had sworn never to follow himself, once he became a father.

Andy was desperately looking for a signal that his cell showed, close to the time. He had seen the young group walk in the same direction, so he chose to stay away. Proximity had hurt him already and he had no intention of putting himself through it, all over again.

"Hi, Andy! Where have you been?" He almost dropped his cell, instead of putting it back into his pocket, when he faced Malika, Viren's sister. "Hi there! Where did you come from? You village folk are spooky!"

She giggled at his remark. "You city folk are jumpy, in that case! I was returning from Gurukul. This is a nice place to sit, when one needs to be alone. I come here often, when I'm out of ideas and need to generate few new ones, for our school.

"You're welcome to the spot. It is your village, after all. I was just walking around to see if I could find some nice ideas, to click pictures" "Photography is your passion. Teaching is mine"

"They are fields that need more than just hard work" Malika said, sitting on one of the boulders, smoothening the crease of her *salwar*. "That is true. When I first started, I thought the camera was a magic box, that worked once clicked"

"The more I learnt about how it works, what it can do to an ordinary snap, it made me want to learn more and more. If I ever enter a shop with cameras and accessories, someone has to manually pull me out of it!"

They both laughed at Nandish's remark. "I have a similar problem with bookshops and libraries. There is a huge bookstore in Jaipur where I go to occasionally. Feels like I could turn invisible right there and stay forever"

The word 'invisible' reminded Andy about Ramona. He had to update her, but that could wait. It was nice to have company, he seemed to enjoy. "How come you're not with your friends?" Malika asked him, taking a *churan* out of her bag, offering some to him.

"They are in pairs, if you've noticed. What's this?" he said, popping a *ram laddoo* into his mouth. The sweet sugar exterior was a disguise, that cloaked the sour-spicy interior. "It's something we use as a toffee and is also good for digestion"

"Do you like it?" she asked, trying not to peek over his shoulder to look at Vansh, laughing with Diana. He noticed her eyes, gazing over his shoulder. Not wanting to offend her, he gently said, "For what is lost, is best to leave behind"

She looked at him directly, knowing he must feel what she did, as well. It was obvious during his previous visit, how much into Mia he was. "Mia cares for Ajju *Bhaiya* more" she said, innocently.

"Mia is Ajju *Bhaiya's* wife now, Malika. They got married in the city. Her name is now Aradhana" Andy said, slapping his pocket, as it began to vibrate. "Ah! Looks like my cell phone has obliged me with a signal, after all"

By the time he pulled it out of his trouser pocket, it began to vibrate crazily. "Sorry, I have to take this call" "Go ahead" she said, getting off her perch. "Don't go. Stay if you can. It will only take a minute" he semi-requested, making it sound casual.

But Malika knew they both had one thing in common. They lacked company they both enjoyed, more than loneliness. He walked away from her, to speak to Ramona. "Hi" "Where have you been?"

"I have been wondering, why there's been no contact. Everything alright out there?" "Yes, it is. There might be a delay in our return. Dhanush is getting engaged tomorrow. We might return after that"

"Well now! The Prataps sure are in a hurry, to get their children married off. Do the village folk know, Dhanush's parents are not legally wedded?" "No, they don't. I have to go. I will call you a bit later"

Not wanting to push her budding new informant, she agreed. "Sorry about that" Andy apologized to Malika, who had sat right back on the boulder. "Don't be. It was my choice to stay or leave. I chose to stay"

"You village folk are so simple" "Not really. We like to show you we are simple, so that you end up feeling silly!" "Silly? Why is that?" "It's just something we do to remind ourselves, that being forward, modern, does not necessarily imply being out of touch, with who you really are"

It was true. Villages had more of cultural richness, the bustle of a city would never permit. "Besides, we hold honesty in high esteem. Among other unpardonable acts, one would count deceit, as something which oughtn't ever to be practiced"

Taking the hint as if it were meant for him, he said, "All this for taking a phone call?" she laughed saying, "It was a general statement. My life got disrupted, once you city folk arrived"

"Earlier I found it impossible to fathom, but now I am thankful for it" "Thankful? Why is that? Hey, give me another *churan*" Offering him a few more, she continued, "If it weren't for Diana, I would have assumed Vansh would stay loyal to me, as I to him"

"I know now, that he could never belong to me completely. In a way, I'm grateful to her, as should you, to Ajju *Bhaiya*" A sense of shame came over Nandish, when he heard Malika speak.

She wasn't as street smart as he was. Neither was she as qualified, educated as he. But, she did make all the sense, in the world. "Malika, where have you been? *Maasa* is looking for you. Hurry up and come along!"

Her brother Viren had come hunting for her. Finding her chatting with Nandish, infuriated him further. Running, she turned around to shout, "Nice talking! Don't eat so much, that you fall sick"

Waving at her, he noticed she had left her bag of *ram laddoos* for him, seeing how he liked them so much. He knew, just like too much of a tasty sweet digestive wasn't good for him; similarly, doses of Ramona in his life had to be curbed, or better yet, exterminated before he reached the point of no return.

He chose to confide in his twin Annie completely, for want of lessening the burden of guilt he'd been carrying. He knew his sister understood how he felt, since he could remember. She was fair, just, dependable.

These were qualities, he was beginning to become the antonyms of. He had to reconnect, with who he was raised to be. He wished it wasn't too late. Ramona's call vibrated his cell once again, but he chose not to take it.

A few more calls later, the persistence ceased for the time being. A message came from Ramona saying she expected messages if not calls, by the hour. He sent a message back that was curt, but clear.

'Enough. No more games. Do not contact' Understanding his implication, the next message made it clear, that he was on quicksand. 'Too late, my boy. All is recorded. Do as you are told'

He closed his eyes shut, knowing he would have to live his nightmare, until shame or guilt would eventually catch up, with what he had been made to do, by sheer blackmail.

An impulsive action that is not well thought out, will bring one to the brink of disaster, each and every time. Once the step is taken, it is next to impossible to retract. The real challenge though, lies in maintaining sanity, at a time like this.

To be accountable for your actions, is a sign of maturity purely for those who believe, they have to face the consequences later on. Being accountable, is possible only when the action is made in full knowledge of the fact, that impact is imminent.

# CHAPTER TWENTY

Brilliance lies, when mere art is turned to magic. Every craft has artists, who aspire for that one moment, when the transformation from normal to surreal, takes place. Other than Arjun, strangely Nandish of all people had the ability to pick a shot, after the Hunter Dhanush had spotted the location.

A mother dressed in a powder-blue sari, was giving instructions to her daughter, who was dressed in a salwar suit for Gurukul; while the father-in-law was desperately attempting to wash his knees, that were muddy under the rusted hand pump.

He looked arthritic, as he was hardly able to bend his joints, but he continued to try, till his son walked up to help him. "Is this part of your shoot?" Andy looked behind to see Malika standing.

"I thought I was supposed to be out of bounds" he said, smiling at her, with a wicked glint in his eye. "My brother isn't a huge fan of the city folk, as I'm sure you'll understand"

"And you?" he asked, wondering if she was over Vansh, not that it bothered him. "I'm still standing, aren't I?" That was reassurance enough for Nandish, as he turned to click some pictures again.

"Why don't you take some pictures of our school, Andy? I don't think the crown achievement of Bassi, has been given its due attention by you city folk" "True. I'll go there next"

"Alright. I'll see you there" she answered, turning to leave. "Are you going to Gurukul now?" "Yes, I am. Leenata has her personal life brimming, so I must fill in for the both of us" she said, not sounding as much exasperated as helpless.

Softening to her, surprised how they were in similar situations that had to be struggled to come to terms with, he chose to walk her to Gurukul.

"Are you going to run away if your brother comes looking for you again?" he asked. He was adjusting his camera strap, which kept slipping down, like the ill-fitting strap of a dress.

Malika noticed it, unable to control her giggle. "What's funny? You ran away the last time" Andy said. "That's not why I'm laughing. Your camera strap reminded me of something. And no, I won't. He knows I will never cross our *maryada*"

They crossed several locations that were worthy of a camera capture, but Andy didn't want to stop her from talking.

It was strange how her voice silenced all his doubts, troubles, grievances. The gates of Gurukul were the first place he took her shot.

A simple village girl in an off-white and yellow salwar suit with books in her hand, smiling. Looking away from the lens, he looked at her standing through the naked eye, then back through the lens again.

"What are you doing?" she asked, impatiently. "Just focusing, wait a minute" He zoomed in on her and clicked a few pictures, from different angles.

Walking in, they went into the Principal's office, since Malika was forced to be the Acting Principal in Leenata's absence. The room was sparsely furnished, giving it a spacious, neat appearance.

The table had a pen stand, a few registers stacked on one side, the calendar behind the chair, the national flag. "I'll take a picture of you sitting on the chair" he declared, beginning to adjust his camera.

"Please don't. It's not my chair. Take it anywhere else you wish, but not in this room" Impressed by her honesty, he complied. The corridors had a few children, who were either entering their respective classrooms, or coming out of them.

A few teachers crossed Malika, wishing her a good morning. Andy found it disturbing, how he found it offensive to take pictures of such a naturally normal day.

Upon Malika's insistence, he began at the staff room. Malika began to read out instructions given by Leenata, to ensure the smooth functioning of Gurukul.

"Try and encourage hygiene. Make sure all students bring their handkerchiefs from home. We have tissue boxes that can be given, but only if the child is not a regular defaulter"

Malika highlighted each point, taking pains to explain the relevance of the same. Andy was introduced as a friend from the city, who would be taking random clicks of Gurukul.

His camera though had something planned already. Nandish Anand was clicking each and every picture, with Malika as the centre of attention.

He made it through the day, without anyone noticing it though. The pillars of the corridor were quite unique.

Whitewashed, they had artistically-inclined students who had painted small, simple pictures like the sunrise, a pair of swans, a nest on a palm tree, that showed how precious the temple of knowledge was, to each one of them.

The glow Malika had every time she spoke to a student, caught Nandish'a attention as he tried to take natural shots with no artificial poses, like his lens had to endure at times.

A shrill bell announced the recess period, where everyone could grab a bite from their tiffin. Malika opened her *potli*, offering Andy *roti, sabzi* with mango pickle, that her mother had packed for her.

The *peepal* tree in the centre courtyard gave them ample shade, from the harsh desert sun.

Having a conversation was completely out of the question, simply due to the fact that there was the shrill voice of children playing in the open to shout over.

"We have another Nandish in our school. Would you like to meet him?" Malika asked. Andy nodded, grinning at having to hear her scream on top of her lungs, to be heard over the noise.

A little boy was screaming at one of his friends, to pass a torn tennis ball to him, in one corner of the courtyard. Malika didn't have to tell Andy, that the boy was his namesake.

His hair, along with his uniform was ruffled, sweat soaking him from top to toe. "Nandish, come here for a minute please" Malika called him.

The little boy quickly ran up to them saying, "Sorry, *Maatsa*. Arun doesn't pass the ball unless I shout for it" Smiling, Malika asked, "Did you ask him why?"

"No. I forget every day. But when he doesn't, I get angry!" Little Nandish sounded excitedly annoyed at having to repeat himself to his friend daily.

"I feel ignored which is not a nice feeling, *Maatsa*" "If it was important, then you would remember it. Like when you study for your tests, isn't it?" Malika explained.

"Why don't you tell him today after you finish playing, that he needs to pass the ball to you so that you can give it back to him? He must learn to catch and not just throw after all, right?"

Andy came up with this idea, that impressed the little boy. "Who are you, Sir?" he asked inquisitively. "Please mind your manners. Are you supposed to ask grown-ups their name?" Malika reprimanded him.

"It's alright" Andy said. "Nandish" "Yes?" the boy said. "My name is Nandish" Andy corrected himself. Wide-eyed, the boy looked at him from top to toe, astounded. "I'm Nandish too!"

"I've never met another Nandish in all of my life!" Laughing at his innocent remark, Malika ruffled his hair.

"Well you have now. Go on and get back to playing, before the bell rings" Little Nandish ran off to play, stopping midway just to run right back, to where Andy and Malika stood.

"Is that a camera?" "Yes, it is" Andy replied to the little one's query. "Can I touch it?" "Sure" Seconds after touching Andy's camera, Nandish ran off to boast to his friends, about the achievement of his day.

"Simple pleasures of life" Malika said, smiling into the crowd of the next generation. "Adults adulterate it though" Andy said, enamoured by Malika's lost look. Conscious she was being stared at, she blushed.

"Stop staring at me, Nandish" Suddenly conscious that he was indeed staring at her, Andy got up to walk away. "I better go and have a look at what the others are up to. I'll see you later"

His hasty retreat sent a pang of disappointment through Malika, which she didn't care much for. Letting him go, she turned her attention to the school and all the responsibilities that came along with it.

Andy found the entire lot of city folk sitting over the noon meal. "Hey Andy, where have you been? Have you eaten?" Ajju asked, as he entered the courtyard of the *Chaudhary haveli.*

"I've been walking around Bassi, to see how simple folk live around here. I've had my lunch. What's the plan for today, Ajju *Bhaiya*?" Ajju was happy Andy was speaking to him, in what felt like a long time.

He chose to encash on the moment a bit longer. "Dhanush and I are going to the backyard for a smoke. Come along and let's plan for the evening. We have to be back an hour before dark for Dan's *sagai* though" Ajju said, getting up to wash his curry-stained hands.

Taking his cue, Dhanush too followed his elder brother, motioning to Andy to come along. "Where are the elders?" Andy asked, noticing that their meals were eaten, but they were not to be seen.

"Gone to rest already. Aradhana and Diana can't take the heat, so they're resting too. That leaves us three. Let's cover Bassi step-by-step. I wanted to take a few shots of Gurukul. Every time we come here, I keep forgetting it's considered to be the crown of Bassi, its biggest jewel!" Ajju said, passing his Zippo to Andy.

"In that case, I saved you a trip because that's where I've been all this time. I bumped into Malika, Viren's sister in the morning. Or, she sneaked up on me just like yesterday near the *tila*. Or...anyway..."

Ajju and Dhanush had lit cigarettes that were now dangling loosely from the sides of their mouths, while they stared at Nandish.

He lit his, took a long drag and looked up. "What? What are you staring at?" Andy asked, handing over the lighter to Ajju. "Dude, you've been bitten by the love bug too!" Dan exclaimed, slapping him on his back.

"Don't be crazy. It's nothing like that. I've been supremely productive. Take a look at the shots. I might have killed the complete roll" Andy justified, aware he was turning a shade of pink.

Ajju and Dhanush began to chuckle, when they saw the pictures Andy had taken. "This is proof, you dodo" Ajju said, grinning at Andy.

"There is more Malika here, than Gurukul!" "What rubbish! Giver it here for a second" Andy said, taking his camera back from Ajju.

He was thunderstruck when he saw the pictures he had supposedly clicked. Malika was in the middle of each and every frame. "Oh my Lord!" Andy said, slapping a palm on his head.

"Oh my Lord, yes! Welcome to the jungle, little brother!" "No, no. You don't understand. I'm heading for a heartbreak again. She made it clear she belongs to the rules laid down by her family, from the start. I mean..."

Ajju kept his hand on Andy's shoulder. "Where is she now?" "Still at Gurukul, I presume" "Then I will talk to her for you, if you want" "Let it be" Andy said, flattered at Ajju's offer. "Let it be" he repeated to himself, walking away.

He went and sat on the *tila* that evening, after the afternoon snooze tortured him, with snippets of Malika. The cool breeze of the early evening made him close his eyes, as he sat on one of the boulders, serene thoughts crossing his mind, until the bubble burst.

"*Ram laddoo khaoge aap?* (Will you have a ram laddoo?)" Waking up with a start, he saw her standing in front of her.

"You've changed your dress" he said, looking at her dressed in a *ghaghra choli*, that was in sapphire-blue and shocking pink.

"Yes. I walked home thinking I would see you on the way, but…*koi baat nahin* (Doesn't matter)" she said, sounding disappointed. Andy took the *churan* she offered, popping one in. "I like them" he confessed. "I'm addicted to them" she added.

Laughter engulfed the two, until Andy cleared his throat. "I'm sorry I left earlier in such a hurry, Malika" "Will you make up a story as to important work that needed to be taken care of, Nandish?" "No. I'm also sorry I didn't walk you back home"

"I'm glad you weren't there in a way. If Viren would have seen you…" "May I ask you a question?" he asked her gently, standing up to take a step towards her. Taking a step back she said, "Ask"

"Why do you keep popping up every time I'm alone?" he asked, taking another step forward, this time smiling at her gaze. Taking a step back again, Malika answered, "I don't know"

Her eyes were lowered and she didn't realize Nandish was closer to her than ever before. "I like your company" "I like yours too. But you're not to come any closer" she said, timid like a deer about to run to safety.

"Don't be afraid of me, Malika. I won't hurt you" he said, ever so sweetly. "I'm not scared of you. I'm afraid of how you make me feel" she said, moving away from him to sit on a boulder, with her back towards him.

"I am of the village, Nandish" "So was my aunt, Malika" "I'm nothing like her. The courage of *Chaudhrain* Suhani is still spoken of far and wide" "True. You show courage by letting your heart get stolen by one man, when another had attempted to break it"

"You're very good with words, Nandish" she said, turning to face him. "Say it again" he said, turning to face her as well.

"What?" "My name" "Nandish" "I like it when you say it. I've always preferred Andy; but, when you call me by my real name, it sounds different"

"I have to go. It's getting late" "Me too. I've a *sagai* to attend. Aren't you coming?" "I want to, Nandish. But my family won't allow it" "Come along, Malika. I'll ask the elders, so you can attend"

"No, I cannot. I am sorry. Goodbye" she said, stopping as he held her hand. "When do I see you again?"

She pulled her hand free, walking away with a hint of a smile. Nothing was said between them, although the silence was perfectly understood.

Two completely different people, were forming a new bond of friendship that would play a pivotal role in transforming almost all the negativity, that was suffocating the lives of those who mattered.

Whistling, Andy entered into the *haveli* and was ushered to the men's area where everyone was getting ready for the *sagai*. Small *diya*s were lit all around the courtyard, as Leenata walked in.

She was dressed in a gorgeous shade of virgin-peach with a shimmer of silver, bordering her veil. Dhanush was dressed in a *khadi* silk *angarkha* and looked anxious, until he saw his Leena walk out with her mother.

The *sagai* was over within an hour. Everyone sat down to see what the *pandit* had deciphered from both Dhanush and Leenata's *kundali*s. "Their *Gun Milap* is very good. But the girl is a *Manglik*"

"She must be wedded first with a banana tree, after which the boy will have a long life" "No way. Forget about it!" Dhanush said sternly. "Be quiet, Dhanush!" Suhani scolded him.

"No, *Maasa*. She's not marrying any tree. All this is utter nonsense, not to mention humiliating" Arjun looked at Leenata, who was struggling to keep her chin up. "Let Leenata do what she wishes to"

Leenata was contemplating the same thought. She knew exactly what she had to do. "I would like the ceremony to be conducted. My pride would be hurt, if I were not given the opportunity to prove, that I honour and follow the *maryada* of our society"

"I cannot play with the life of someone I have dedicated the rest of my life to. That is all I have to say" Suhani rushed to Leenata and hugged her tight. "Welcome to the family, Leenata!"

"I respect your thoughts and am proud you and Aradhana are my daughter-in-laws." Arjun seconded his *Beendni*, relaxing everyone else with their words. Andy's mobile began to ring.

Everyone assumed it was Sangharsh, calling to see if all was well. He saw the screen, excused himself to take the call. When he returned, Arjun asked, "Spoke to your father?"

"Yes, *Chachu*. I speak to him once in the morning, once in the evening. If I don't, I wouldn't be surprised if he lands up here himself!"

He left with the others for a stroll outside the *haveli* soon thereafter, leaving Arjun and Suhani alone in the corridor outside their room. "What's wrong, *Saheb*? You're too quiet on a happy day like this" Suhani asked him, as he played with her hair.

"Nandish is in some kind of trouble, Braids" "What? How do you know that?" "I've been in touch with Sangharsh on a regular basis. Nandish has not spoken to his father, since we've arrived at Bassi"

"He disappears for hours, runs when he gets a phone call, lies about whose call he received; add them up." "Yes, you're right. What do we do now? He's like our own son. Shouldn't we tell the Anands?" Suhani said, forming a similar conclusion.

"It could make matters worse. I think we should just be careful. Send Dhanush to me when he returns from his walk" Arjun said. Leaving him to his thoughts, Suhani walked outside to get some fresh air.

She found Andy hissing on the phone outside his room. "I don't care what you do anymore, do you hear me? I'm done with you as well as your stupid phone-calls. I'm planning to tell them myself anyway"

He hung up and stomped into his room, leaving the corridor empty again. But not without leaving Suhani's mind with a flurry, of a dozen thoughts.

Could *Saheb* be right in his assumption that something was indeed wrong with Nandish? Who was he talking to, in such a harsh tone? Why was he lying about these phone calls?

There was one thing she was aware of. Time was the best answer to questions that needed to be answered, mysteries that needed to be solved.

She believed it was just a matter of time, until Nandish would have to figure out, how to include those who care about him, one way or another.

# CHAPTER TWENTY ONE

Ramona was raving mad at the way she was being treated by her newly adopted prodigy. She had seen tall dreams for Andy, similar to the ones she had had for Mia, earlier. What had happened to the boy since he had gone to Bassi?

That village had the audacious capacity to turn all laid plans completely topsy-turvy. Thank God she still had Mr. Guha under her thumb. Even her lawyer was extremely positive about buying out the gallery, agreeing to keep the matter under wraps, until she contacted him to set the ball rolling.

All the planning was beginning to take a toll on Ramona, as she noticed in the mirror. Her wrinkles began to show again, her hair needed colouring, her face needed to look younger, more carefree.

Money took care of all of that. The only thing that money could not buy, was the peace of mind she secretly craved. Her father took his revenge on her, by giving away what mattered to Arjun Pratap- The **Dare to Dream** gallery.

Gerard was her saviour, up until the nurse Isabella proved to be far more satisfactory to him, than she was. Mia slapped her mother's affections on the face, by refusing to let her in to her new life, as the daughter-in-law of the Pratap household.

Andy had turned out to be a blunt knife, even before she had begun to sharpen him. She still needed to figure out what caused that boy's sudden change of heart. She felt let down for years and was beginning to tire. She had to bank on herself for everything, all the time.

Now, she wanted to be the owner of the gallery, that once belonged to her. It was the only thing that wouldn't let her down. She decided to focus all her attention on the acquisition of the **Dare to Dream** gallery.

Yes, she not only dared to dream to be sitting on the owner's chair again, but she promised herself that soon she would live her dream as well. She chose to make Mr. Guha her weapon, who would do her bidding, for fear of losing his job.

She called him immediately, asking to meet at the gallery. "Madame, Bantu has been assigned to report any untoward incident to the Prataps. It is not safe to meet you here. I'll meet you someplace else"

Agreeing with him for the time being, she asked him to meet her at a hotel's coffee shop, in the evening. It was the day when the city folk had arrived from Bassi, after Dhanush's engagement.

Everyone was busy trying to get back into the daily grind, until the *pundit* would inform *Chaudhary* Akash about the *shubh muhurat* for Dhanush and Leenata's wedding. The ring Dhanush had gotten was plain gold.

He didn't want anything fancy and neither did Leenata. "Why do you call me Leena?" she had asked him on their walk to the *tila*, after the engagement. Glad she finally noticed and asked, Dhanush replied.

"I always thought it suited you better. It's what I shall always address you as" Watching his ring, he remembered this conversation, smiling into nothingness. Love always leaves memories in the hearts of lovers when they're apart, to keep that special flame alive.

Ajju and Aradhana were practically inseparable, never getting enough of each other. They were just getting ready to have a drink by the pool after their laps in it, as a part of their strict workout routine, when Mia, or as she was now known as, Aradhana, gripped Ajju's hand.

"What happened, darling?" he asked, surprised at the change in her facial expression. "I think my eyes are playing tricks on me. At least I hope they are" "What do you mean? What did you see?" he asked, looking in the same direction.

"Behind the drapes, I think I saw my mother standing. Then I saw her walk in. How on earth did she get to know we were here?" "Cool down. So what if she knows? You're my wife now. There's no need to be afraid of her"

"If you knew her Ajju, you wouldn't be saying that to me. You've no idea what she's capable of!" "I don't need to have any idea, Aradhana. I want to get to know you better, not your mother!"

Realizing she was indeed over-reacting, she chose to sip her drink again, opting to let her guard down for the moment. Ajju had seen her as well, but didn't let Aradhana know. He wanted to contain the situation, instead of aggravating it.

He was prepared for any sort of confrontation. Watching Aradhana closely, he knew the same topic was troubling the woman he had sworn to protect, for as long as he would live. "Let's go to our suite upstairs, freshen up, and then come down later. What do you say?" he offered.

His smile made it clear to her, the want to shower his physical reassurance, possible only behind closed doors. They raced upstairs like little children, giggling all the way.

After an hour or more, they felt more of each other's souls, bonded, satiated. Meanwhile, downstairs at the coffee lounge, Ramona was in a meeting with Mr. Guha, the manager of DTD, currently the mole of Ramona.

"Madame, this has gone far enough. I doubt if Mr. Arjun Pratap is going to forgive me, if he ever found out" "How would he, dear chap? Unless a bout of conscience made you clobber yourself in the foot!" she snapped, wondering why she had to encounter stupidity, at a time like this.

"It's better to come clean, than having to watch my back like a common criminal, continuously, Madame. I am a God-fearing man" "Even God can't save you now. There is nothing to be afraid of, Mr. Guha"

"All I'm asking for, is the accounts of the last decade. It is in the blue drawer clubbed together. Just walk in, put them in a bag, bring them to me. That is all I am asking you to do"

"It is easy for you to say. My own nephew, who holds me in high esteem, is keeping a close guard on every single movement, within the gallery. How do you think I would feel, if he finds out his uncle is the one, who did the entire spy work?"

Pushing an envelope towards him, she said, "This is for all your sleepless nights, so far" Watching his eyes grow wide, after counting the thousand rupee notes stashed in a fat envelope, she relaxed a bit. Greed assured Ramona this would be a cakewalk, hereon.

"Mr. Guha, you used to be loyal to me once. Arjun was just a photographer, who I elevated to the position of a fiancé. He tricked my father into willing everything to him, leaving me with no choice but depend on Gerard Cotton, my childhood friend"

He looked up at her. "Really? I never knew that. What happened then?" "After our daughter Diana was born, poor Gerard and his mother died in an accident. When I tried to contact Arjun, I was informed he was already married to that nomad, Suhani"

"What was I to do, with not a penny to my name!" she said, her crocodile tears working beautifully, into melting Mr. Guha's loyal armour. "Please don't cry, Ms. Rai. I mean, Mrs. Cotton. I mean, Mrs. Pratap. I mean,..."

Watching him flustered as he tried to address her, she smiled innocently through her fake, yet believable tears. "Call me Ramona" "Oh no, Madame. I shall always call you 'Madame'!" "I need the old Mr. Guha, who worked for me in DTD"

"I need his loyalty, his courage. Only then can I bring the gallery, our gallery up to the standards, as I deem fit" He looked at the envelope again. Its weight would lighten the load in his life, as he saw it.

Looking up, he saw the fine lady wiping her tears, with a dainty lace handkerchief. "Alright. A week's time and I will get the files for you" "I knew I could count on you. Thank you!"

"My name must never be mentioned though. Please understand, Mr. Pratap has been good to me and my family in his own way, whatever you may think" "You have my word. No one will ever know" Ramona assured the man.

"Know what?" Mr. Guha and Ramona flew off their comfortable seats for an instant, as if they heard a collective explosion. When they looked up, they saw Arjun's eldest son, Ajju or A.J and his bride, Aradhana or Mia, looking at them both, smiling.

Both Mr. Guha and Ramona, had been caught with their hands in the cookie jar. At least that is what they looked like, at that moment. "Sir, good evening, sir!" Mr. Guha stood up in attention awkwardly, as his fat envelope that was resting on his lap, fell down on the floor.

"Good evening, Mr. Guha! What a pleasant surprise! Meet my wife, Mrs. Aradhana Pratap!" Wishing them both, Mr. Guha left after faking an untied shoelace, under the pretext of which he picked up the envelope, literally swooshing out of the hotel thereafter.

Turning their focus towards Ramona, Aradhana began. "Hello, Mother" "Mia, what is this 'Aradhana' business?" "We got married the Hindu way and Ajju changed my name" "I don't like it" Ramona grumbled.

"You don't have to. I love it" "Mia.." "I am sorry, Mother. I do not respond to that name anymore. My name is.." "Aradhana, yes. I got that! What have you done to my daughter?" she almost shrieked, looking at Ajju who was still standing as calmly as possible.

"I married her. Is it my turn to ask you a question? Shall we sit down first, just to catch up?" he said, sitting where Mr. Guha sat prior, patting the seat next to him as a signal for his better half to be seated.

"I'm in a bit of a rush. We'll catch up some other time" Ramona said, picking up her Gucci clutch. "Sit down, my dear mother-in-law" Ajju said sternly, glaring into her eyes with his dark, piercing black eyes. His knitted eyebrows were in a frown, making Ramona conscious of being closely scrutinized.

"Well?" "Well, let's begin with what I am to call you. Since you have wounded my family, displaced my mother, used my wife while she was still under your wing, shall we say Mrs. Cotton or Ms. Rai?"

"I am Mrs. Pratap!" Ramona insisted, glaring right back at Ajju. "The only two Mrs. Prataps I know, is my mother Suhani and my wife Aradhana. Suit yourself then. I will call you whatever I wish"

"Call me Ramona in that case" she said, praying some miracle would let her leave. "I have unfortunately been raised in an environment, where we do not address elders by their name"

"But you are allowed to disrespect them, is it?" Ramona added, sarcastically. "You haven't done much to win their respect, Mother" Aradhana intervened. "Be quiet, child!" she snapped at her daughter.

"I would be very careful if I were you, as to how to address the *badi bahu* of the Pratap *khandaan*, Mrs. Cotton" Ajju said, his voice calmly stern. "And now for my question. What are you doing here?"

"It's a free country. I am not answerable to anyone, about my whereabouts. "Fair enough. It implies you have something to hide, in that case" he said, watching her get more irritable.

"I have nothing to hide" Ramona's flat statement got Ajju speaking again. "Then state the purpose of your visit" "It was personal" "I am your son-in-law. You can tell me" "It was a surprise for you both"

"I wanted to host a reception at the Taj for the two of you. That was not possible, since alone I would not be able to afford it" Watching them both almost getting sucked into her fabrication, she continued.

"I called Mr. Guha here, so that he could give me the dates, when the gallery is free. I wanted to host the reception for you both, there. And now, you two have completely ruined my surprise!" she bawled, her mascara flowing down her cheeks.

"Oh Mother!" Aradhana went up to Ramona, embracing her. "Go away, both of you! I can't even throw my own daughter and son-in-law a reception, without being questioned? It was bad enough you all tricked me into depriving me of your Hindu wedding and God only knows what all…"

Ajju felt silly when he heard Ramona's explanation. "I am so sorry. I thought.." "I know what you thought. You are Arjun's son. You will always think I am up to something. Why would I meet Mr. Guha of all people? To reminisce about the past?" she scolded them both blatantly, enjoying their shamed faces.

Mellowing down, she continued, "I'm tired. If your interrogation is over, I'd like to go home" They both walked her out to her car, waving her goodbye. "Did you buy that?" Aradhana asked, still waving out to her mother.

"Not in the least!" Ajju said, smiling and waving too. When the car disappeared out of sight, Aradhana turned to Ajju, smooching him in full view. "Rule number one of tackling Ramona Rai Cotton. Never, ever underestimate her. You just proved you're smarter than I thought!"

Pulling her by the waist, Ajju's husky voice said, "I'm a lot more than that. I plan to show you tonight. Get back upstairs Mrs. Pratap, before I carry you all the way myself!" Ramona heaved a sigh of relief as the car turned towards the main road, away from the couple waving frantically behind her.

"Mohan, drive slowly. I need time to think" Ramona told the chauffeur hired by Arjun, but on her secret payroll especially kept to spy on the Prataps, since the beginning. "Yes, Madame" Mohan replied, slowing down his speed.

He hated Ramona Rai Cotton for all the unpleasantness she brought along with her. Any outsider would never believe how calculating, apocalyptic, her mere presence could be. He wished in his heart, he could drive Arjun and Suhani Pratap the way he used to, earlier.

"Didn't you hear me, you fool? I said take me to the gallery. Stop day dreaming, you moron!" Putting his foot on the gas, he drove her straight to

DTD, without any delay. Mr. Guha was just about to lock up, when he saw Ramona pull up in the car.

Running up to her, he said, "I told you not to come here! I am in enough trouble already" "Oh, shut up! I have already pulled you out of it" "Really? How?" "That doesn't matter. You are too slow to understand and I don't have much time. All you need to know is…"

Ramona quickly briefed him about the upcoming reception and how she would be speaking to Arjun about it. Mr. Guha was quite impressed by the way Ramona's brain worked. Impressed and scared at the same time.

"Thank you, Madame! I can't tell you how scared I was, since Ajju sir saw me with you. And since the envelope fell, when I stood up.." "Alright, alright. I'm off now. Just play along when I come to the gallery tomorrow, understood?"

That evening Arjun spoke to Suhani for a long time, over the phone. They couldn't meet after lunch, since their work backlog didn't permit them to do so. Sitting in the balcony of the Anands, Suhani asked him, "When will we have the evenings we used to, *Saheb*?"

"Soon, Braids. Trust me, I'm working on it" Arjun answered, struggling to maintain composure, as he walked in the garden of his mansion. "The roses are in bloom. I'll bring some for you tomorrow" he said, smelling them.

"No, don't pluck them. Let them be as they are. Take a picture and send it. I would love to see them" Arjun spoke some more and hung up, clicking a picture of the rose bed and a few of the garden, from his mobile phone's camera.

"Who are you clicking these pictures for?" Ramona came from behind him, dressed in a sleek chiffon dress, her curves dangerously accentuated. "Just for myself. They will wither eventually" he said, in a matter-of-fact manner.

Ramona picked up the rake that the gardener had left by mistake at the corner of the toolshed, charging the flower bed that held a dozen roses in different shades. Arjun had reached his room by the time the deed was begun, oblivious till it was done.

In the morning, the wails of the gardener woke him up as he rushed down. "Madam*ji's* roses! She loved them. Someone destroyed the entire bed!" Arjun turned up to see Ramona curve her thin lips into a smile, as she turned away from the window. Running up the stairs in a fury, he charged into the master bedroom, shaking her hard.

"Why did you do it? Tell me why? What do you want from me?" Shaking herself free, Ramona yelled back with all of her might. "I will not allow my husband to have a rose garden kept for his mistress!"

"You've no right to still give her the status in your life that is mine by law!" upon his Braids being called a mistress, Arjun Pratap's rage knew no bounds. He slapped Ramona hard across the face, walking away briskly before he could harm her beyond repair.

"Before you leave this room Arjun, hear this. I know you went to Bassi for Dhanush's engagement" Arjun turned around and opened his mouth to speak, but Ramona spoke first.

"*Chaudhary* Akash and his family are not aware that Dhanush, their future son-in-law is born out of wedlock. I am aware you are smart enough to figure out what I imply, as I say this. I would be very careful if I were you, especially knowing there is a carpet of landmines that could cause some extensive damage"

"Mr. Arjun Pratap, looks like the Rais and the Prataps have a business deal, repeating history" The sting of her words were far worse than the sting on her cheek. Arjun knew the downfall of the Prataps was imminent, by now.

# CHAPTER TWENTY TWO

A flower has always epitomized natural beauty. Its fragrance enhances its aesthetically pleasing colours, shapes that usually signify a powerful emotion. Some flowers are given to the Lord as offerings while one prays, some to the ones we love as a sign of affection.

Roses, over a period of time have been symbolic of the passion one feels, when in love. Suhani's first gift received was a rose bed, with especially imported shades. It was a gift she treasured not just because they were her favourite flower, but also because it was a thought germinated by her *Saheb*, the love of her life.

Arjun decided to tell the gardener to plant roses quickly in the same rose bed, after cleaning up the havoc created by Ramona. Considering it was the least he could do to cover up for Ramona's stupidity, he walked up to the dining table to have his breakfast. Ramona was already sitting, eating silently.

Dhanush was strangely reading the newspaper. The moment he saw his father, he jumped up. "I got an urgent call from DTD. Let's go, *Baasa*. We'll have something there" Not wishing to argue, Arjun left with Dhanush in his Humvee. Instead of going to DTD, they went off to a completely different road.

"Where are you taking me, young man? Just because I'm not driving this monster truck doesn't mean I don't know where I'm being taken!" Laughing, Dhanush said mysteriously, "A few minutes more and you'll know yourself"

They parked at the Taj, walking straight in to be greeted at the lobby by Ajju and Aradhana. "We thought it would be nice to have breakfast together, as a family" Ajju explained, watching his father smile back at him.

"Still one missing" Arjun said softly, not intending to ruin the children's surprise. "Are you sure about that?" Arjun looked up to see his *Beendni* standing behind Ajju, his bulky frame covering almost all of her frail silhouette.

"Suhani!" he rushed to her, holding her tight. "So, this was the surprise!" Arjun said, thanking his luck on being blessed with loving, caring children. The buffet was built to satiate the appetite of a very hungry king.

The family had an array of breads, cold cuts, eggs to order, that they enjoyed over tiny anecdotes, followed by lots of laughter. "A great way to start the day" Arjun said, looking at Suhani, still holding her hand under the table.

"We were hoping you would say that, *Baasa*" Ajju said. "As in? More surprises?" he said, smiling at his eldest. "Kind of. *Maasa* has found the deed, that clearly states Swarn Niwas belongs to her"

"Legally she can move in with all of us and Mrs. Cotton will have to leave!" Arjun was thrilled at the news, congratulating his courageous partner on her effort. His cell rang on the table, making everyone frown around them.

They all saw whose call it was. "Where are you, Arjun? I'm at DTD waiting in the office" "Why are you there?" "I'll tell you when you get here, my darling husband" He cringed at Ramona addressing him as something he was used to hearing Suhani call him.

"I'll be there in half an hour" he said. "Ajju, Dhanush, let's go. Aradhana, take care of my property" he said, smiling at both the lovely ladies. On the way, Arjun told the boys they had to get DTD into shape fast.

"If my hunch is right, Ramona will try to annex the gallery next" "*Baasa*, I've something to tell you as well. Bantu called me early this morning to say, that Mr. Guha has been behaving, and I quote him, 'unreasonably jumpy off late'"

"He says he texts to someone, but jumps if Bantu calls him or tries to come near him" Dhanush said, eyes on the road, but his mind wandering to the conversation. "Suhani told me the same thing about Nandish"

"He was talking to someone in the corridor of the *haveli* at Bassi. Could there be a link between these two sightings, or is it a mere coincidence?" Arjun wondered out loud. "There are no coincidences, *Baasa*"

"You've taught that to us yourself. I have to tell you something more. Aradhana and I spotted Mr. Guha and Mrs. Cotton in the coffee shop at the Taj. When confronted, Mrs. Cotton claimed she was planning a surprise reception at DTD for us"

"She said the Taj was too expensive for her to host the party alone" No sooner had Ajju finished, that Arjun clapped his hands together. "Ha! I knew it! The common factor among all of them is the gallery. So, that is the link as I see it"

"*Baasa*, Mr. Guha walked away with a thick envelope that day as well" "It could be documents, plans…" Dhanush parked the Humvee and turned to them. "I think it was money. I think the Anaconda is using Mr. Guha's financial obligations, to gain a backdoor entry into our gallery"

"All that is fine. But, how does Nandish fit into the picture?" Arjun asked, walking with his sons into the gallery. "There you are, husband!" Ramona stood at the entrance, looking bright and sunny in a lemon top teamed with an A-line off-white skirt, summer heels in dull silver, matching her belt and earring studs.

"I told you not to call me that!" Arjun snapped, literally pushing her aside as he walked in. "I'll call you what you are to me, Arjun. Now, let's talk shop, shall we?" Dhanush remembered how often his mother would scold them never to talk about work, when they were together at home.

The stark contrast between the two, left him blank momentarily. Ajju felt the pain of a distant memory too, stopping alongside his brother. Arjun sensed his children missing their mother, but continued to walk towards his office.

"I'll see you boys in the backroom at lunch. Order in. Get Andy on the loop about what we discussed" he said, marching right into his office. "You used to hold the door open for me once" Ramona complained, having to hold it open for herself, lest the swing would knock her senseless.

"You had trained me well. Now leave, or speak what you have to say and then leave" he snapped, checking to see his mail. "What's this?" he saw a mail from a corporate lawyer, claiming his client wishes to buy him out.

"Rubbish!" he said, about to delete the email. "Before you do that, I suggest you give it a long, hard thought. I'm sure you need to consider how the gallery has been struggling to keep its neck above water, off late" Ramona said, sitting in front of him.

"I don't need you to tell me how to run my business. Now leave my office, if there isn't anything substantial you have to discuss" "I plan to host the wedding reception of Mia and her husband at DTD. I've contacted Mr. Guha with regard to the dates and should be getting them today"

"Her name is Aradhana, not Mia anymore" Arjun checked her. "I named her Mia and that is how I'll always call her. It's shocking how you allowed your son to marry his step-sister" She hit him with this statement, right below the belt.

"They're not even remotely related, Ramona. Think before you speak, or you might just get labeled crazy!" "Moving on" she said, ignoring him completely. "I have a budget to work within. When the DTD dates come to me, I'll require all of you to be present and not disappear to your favourite getaway village resort!"

He looked at her, smirking at him. "That's right, Arjun darling. I know you had all gone to Bassi, like I mentioned. And when I say all, it also includes that nomad!" "It was foolish of you to destroy the rose bed, Ramona" he said, looking at her still.

"And I know you'll go that extra mile, just to make it alright, for her sake. This family matters to you, doesn't it?" she asked him, a contemptuous look on her face. "We never mattered to you, Mia and I" "That is not true and you know it!" he sparred.

"Is it? Which husband leaves a day after his wife's funeral, quietly handing over a newborn baby girl to a set of total strangers?" "So, that is the rubbish you've been feeding Aradhana. Poor thing. And Diana? Do you have someone who she is to take shots at, like her elder sister?"

"Don't compare them, Arjun. Diana could never be like my Mia. She isn't even mine, for that matter" "What does that mean?" he asked, intrigued if she would corroborate what Aradhana had told him, while they were driving together. Correcting herself quickly, she said, "I meant, I focused much more on Mia, who in turn took care of Diana"

"And you're proud of that?" "I raised them single-handedly, Arjun" "You raised them with an army of governesses and nurses, Ramona" "When I tried to get in touch with you after Gerard's death, I was informed you were happily married"

"I did get a call once, but not from you. My assistant then, Tanisha, said it was from Gerard" "It was me. Not him. How could he have the gallery's number? Anyway, I'm off to speak with Mr. Guha. Try staying in town, when I get the reception dates"

He let her walk out, not wanting to continue wasting any more time on her. Wondering who this corporate lawyer was, Arjun thought he would discuss this offer with the boys. Better yet, he chose to email him, asking him to meet at the gallery premise along with his client, the next day.

The screen popped the signal of a new mail, minutes after Arjun shot the email out. The lawyer's name was Mr. Patil. His client was out of town, but quite eager to seal the deal, as soon as possible.

Frowning, Arjun called for the boys, including Nandish and discussed the matter with them. "I think you should look into the client's profile, *Chachu*. What if he is a mafia don or someone who wants to tear down DTD and set up a residential building instead? Andy argued.

"That is a concern that is of no consequence, once the gallery is sold. You three have not been paid your salaries, for the last two months. Mr. Guha and Bantu's salaries have not seen an annual bonus, in the last two years"

"Some parts of this building need renovating desperately, as you all are aware of. How do we get the money to do all of this? There is no business. I tried, but.." "Try harder" Andy said softly. "What?" "I said, try harder"

"Where will all of us go, once you sell DTD? This is our home away from home. We don't know anything other than photography" he said, justifying his stand. "Alright. So, Nandish is against DTD's sale"

"Those who are with him, raise your hand. Those on my side, keep your hand down. Let's take a vote on this" Both Arjun's sons kept their hands down, leaving Andy in the lurch, yet again. "Kind of ironic, isn't it? DTD is not even mine, but I'm begging you to keep it"

"It is your legacy to pass on to Ajju *Bhaiya* and Dhanush. Anyway, if that's what you want to do, then go ahead. I have nothing more to say" Andy sat back on his chair. "Let me ask for the client's profile, to set the ball rolling. I won't carry the matter forward, if this lawyer withholds information on his client"

"*Chachu*, what is the lawyer's name, if I may ask?" Andy enquired, pushing his chair back as he got up to leave Arjun's office. "Mr. Patil" Arjun answered, absent-mindedly. They went to the backroom to have their take away lunch, in some peace and quiet.

That was not to be the case, unfortunately. Ramona landed up with her salad bowl. "Hello boys! You wouldn't mind a lady joining you fine gentlemen, would you?" Ajju pulled a chair for her, ensuring she sat between Andy and him, which was on the opposite side of Arjun Pratap.

"Mr. Guha says the only date available is day after tomorrow. The gallery is busy for a month after that" Not getting any response from anyone, she continued forking her cherry tomatoes for a bit.

"Fine. It is possible. How much would it cost?" Arjun finally broke the silence. "Don't worry about the cost. I'll take care of it. It is my gift after all" "It's my gallery, Ramona. Ajju is my son. We'll split the costs"

Laughing Ramona said, "Sorry to burst your bubble, but you can hardly make ends meet, pay the salaries of these poor boys..." "How do you know this? You've been snooping around, haven't you?"

"Why would I need to snoop around a gallery that belongs to my husband?" she raised her voice needlessly. "You really know how to throw a party, Ramona. But, you can also spoil my lunch!" Arjun dropped his half-eaten club sandwich, walking towards the door.

"Come home early today. I need to talk to you alone" Ramona said, not turning to look at him. Hand still on the brass door knob, Arjun replied, "Actually, we all will be there early tonight. And by all, Ramona.." he watched as she turned around to face him.

"I mean the *Banjaran* who you hate not as much as I love!" Seething in fury, Ramona left her salad bowl, storming out behind Arjun. "Why do you always insult me in front of others? I know you go to meet her every single day. No need to rub it in"

Arjun walked up to her glaring. "It is because of you that I have to meet her occasionally. If I had my way, you would be blasted off to space!" The whole time they argued, Ajju, Dhanush and Nandish were still in the backroom. "Don't let *Chachu* sell DTD off" Andy looked at the brothers.

"Andy, we can't be emotional about a business that is about to become a sinking ship" "I can't join Anand Creations. What would I do? Become a freelancer photographer? Who would hire me?"

Andy sounded anxious as he panicked, while he contemplated what the future held in store for him, the life he knew, the gallery he had grown to love. They dispersed after having a small dessert of frozen *rasgulla*s.

Ajju and Dhanush had to go to the camera accessories shop, to window shop and invariably, possibly buy a miraculous piece of equipment, to fit in their magic-making machines. Andy had found a few magazines with some breath-taking shots of a landscape, quite similar to what he saw of Bassi.

His cell rang just once and went silent. A few minutes later the same thing recurred. Intrigued, Nandish pulled his cell out to see an outstation number that flashed two missed calls. Opting to dial the number, he heard a female voice, "Hello?" "Malika!" "How did you know it was me?"

"I'd recognize your voice anywhere. How have you been?" They chatted for a few minutes, till Andy had to cut her short. He could see Ramona walking towards him, through the reflection on the glass panes. He didn't want anyone to know, or use how he felt about his lady love.

He promised to call her in the evening, hanging up just in time. "Mr. Guha's cover is blown. Bantu has caught up with him. It's just a matter of time before Arjun does too. I need you back on board" Ramona said, her blunt, straightforward manner, easy for Andy to see through.

"You'll do anything to make your plan work, isn't it? Count me out. I avoid complications and you're one with a capital 'C'!" "Like I told you earlier Andy, wishing nothing happened will not affect the recordings"

"I'm not asking for something which you can't do. There is a lot to gain if you're on my team though" "I doubt that. No one gained from stepping on a sinking ship!" "Whatever. Are you in or out?" "In or out of what?" Arjun asked, walking towards them, with a file in his hand.

"Oh, Arjun! You scared me. I was asking Andy whether he would like to help with the arrangements, since no one else is helping me" Ramona covered up cleverly, once again. "Well, Andy?" Arjun asked this time.

"*Chachu*, …" Andy almost spilt the beans, but back tracked out of pure shame. "Fine. I'll do it" "Great" Ramona said, leaving Arjun and Andy for the time being. "*Chachi* is far better" Andy declared as Arjun added, "I completely agree"

The blue file Arjun had in his hand, was to be returned to the Accounts Department. Andy wanted to run some pictures by him, so he went to Arjun's office to wait for him there. Ramona was sitting on the boss's chair, swiveling it round and round, like a school girl.

"What do you think you're doing?" Andy asked her. "Behave yourself. If you wish to continue here, better learn how to speak to a lady" Pleased with the progress, Ramona said, "Mr. Sahu has all drafts and plans in order"

"Arjun's already been contacted by him. Soon all this will belong to me" Andy was still standing with his hand on the office door, watching the lady waltz out of the office, humming to herself.

Walking into the washroom, looking into the mirror atop the basin while washing his hands, he said to himself, "If Mr. Sahu is Mrs. Cotton's lawyer, then who is Mr. Patil?"

"More importantly, who is his client who doesn't wish to disclose his identity?" His questions were to be answered, faster than he would have imagined. This was another mystery that was bound to unravel, sooner than anyone would have comprehended.

When there are situations created by one, that are not acceptable by some, the result could go either for, or against them. The creators of this situation though may have an end result in mind, but they do not have the surety of the same.

That is when a single act, could transform the end result that was wished by the creator of the situation, into something that could not be speculated in the beginning. It is then that the quick response of those caught in the cobweb, would steer the course of their destinies.

It is true that, plotting and planning has a path that needs to be followed. It is also true that scheming and conniving, is meant to take away more than just an object from the target, something which not many of us are aware of. It takes away the plotter's peace of mind.

# CHAPTER TWENTY THREE

"Arjun, the reception is the day after tomorrow. No other dates were available. I've already begun to send out the invites, that have been mostly accepted. We.." "Stop, stop!" Arjun raised his palm at Ramona, still struggling to wake up.

Looking at his watch, he saw it was an hour before his alarm was to ring. She was standing in her nightgown, that was almost as sheer as the lace night-slip under it. "Cover yourself, for God's sake!"

"There are people in my house, who aren't used to such obscene displays", he spat out, motioning further with his hand. "Close the door on your way out, softly. We'll talk when I'm awake, at the breakfast table"

Pulling the opaque chocolate ottoman close to her, Ramona sat down on it. "Dismiss me all you want. But I'm going to finish what I came to say. After that, I'll leave you to your beauty sleep" Fisting his pillow once, Arjun got up on his futon.

"Fine. Talk" "I'm going to divide the work between Mr. Guha and Andy. Bantu fumbles too much and I don't want to spoil Mia's special day. She will be dressed in a wedding gown, decorated with white lace and pearls"

"A.J. in a tuxedo will compliment her, of course. If I couldn't give her a Christian wedding, at least a reception looks doable" "Do you have dress codes for the rest of us, or we can actually wear what we want?" Arjun grumbled.

He was irritated at how Ramona had the uncanny knack to pick a happy occasion, twisting it to a possibly explosive one. Getting up with her notepad and pen, Ramona whispered, "You can 'Aradhana' my Mia all you want, Arjun"

"Do not forget the age-old saying though-Blood is always thicker than water!" Walking out of his study, she took his peace of mind with her. What was she up to now? Why couldn't she ever talk straight?

Shaking his head, he tossed the thought aside for later, planning to catch a snooze before his alarm behaved like Ramona! The corridors were dark and dimly lit in places in the mansion, giving it an eerie look, straight from a horror movie.

Dhanush, who had been feeling restless off late, had just returned from an early morning jog. He saw Ramona dressed in her skimpy nightgown, coming out of the study quietly, smiling to herself.

A shot of possessiveness took over him as he walked briskly towards her, dripping sweat all over the floor. "What were you doing in the study?" he asked, bluntly. "What do you think?" she said, her lewd wink making him want to throttle the demonic diva right there.

He walked into the study to pick up his change of clothes. The keys to his Humvee slipped from his last night's jeans to the floor, disturbing his father's snooze. "I'm tired, Ramona. Stop sneaking into the room and let me get some sleep"

"I'm not as young as I used to be" Turning his face, shielding his eyes to cover the lamplight, he recognized the silhouette of his son. "Finished your jog?" he asked casually, closing his eyes again.

Dhanush stood staring at his father a few seconds more, packed his bags, leaving quietly. By the time he revved up his Humvee to leave, Arjun was getting ready for the day and couldn't hear the roaring vehicle zoom away.

Diana, Ramona and Arjun were the only occupants of Swarn Niwas now. Dan had driven straight to his mother, at Anand villa. "Hello! What a lovely surprise!" Sangharsh welcomed him, quietening down the moment he saw tears in his eyes.

"What happened? Are you all right?" "*Baasa* spent the night with Ramona..I think. I was feeling restless and was speaking to Leena on the couch downstairs. I went straight for a run from the living room itself. When I returned…"

Dhanush went on to mention what transpired, including what Ramona was wearing and what Arjun mumbled, thinking Dhanush was Ramona re-entering the study. "I'm sure there's more to it than meets the eye, *beta*. Go to your mother, but do not speak with her about this"

Seeing his luggage, he frowned. "Stay here if you must. But running away from a problem is not the best solution. You and your mother are just the same!" he said, smiling. "Who were you chatting with downstairs?" Nalini asked.

She had slipped on her gypsy peep-toes in matte grey suede, her sleek trousers and strawberry -pink top making her look a decade younger. Sangharsh, since the very beginning, loathed the very thought of having to keep secrets.

He spilled the beans to Nalini within a few minutes, watching her casual smile change into a concerned frown. "I don't believe Arjun *Bhaisa* spent the night with Ramona. Do you?" "He did it at Bassi all those years ago"

"What makes you think he won't do it again? He is a man after all" "What kind of a friend are you, Sangharsh? Doubting someone who you've known since childhood is extremely unbecoming!"

"What Dhanush narrated sounded like Arjun and Ramona spent the night together. I'll get the truth out of Arjun. You…" Time seemed to have stood still, suddenly whirring them to several moons ago, when a young *Banjaran* was running away from seeing, what she never should have.

Bumping into a city couple, in the pouring rain at Bassi. "Suhani! How long have you been standing here?" Nalini asked, not knowing what else to say, to break the silence. "I came to ask why Dhanush has left Swarn Niwas. I got my answer"

Her calm tone matched her cold expression. "Don't jump to conclusions. I know Arjun well. He would never cheat on you" Sangharsh defended him. "That's not what you said five minutes ago, Sangharsh *Bhaisa*"

"Besides, technically he wouldn't be cheating on me. She is still his wife, is she not?" Leaving the Anands stumped, Suhani left for Maya's in her car, alone. Meanwhile at Swarn Niwas, Arjun was wondering where Dhanush was.

He asked Diana at the breakfast table. "Where is Dan? We're getting late" "He left quite a while back in his Humvee, Uncle. I thought you knew" "Left? Where to? Why didn't he tell me?" he said, calling Dan's number.

Frustrated at finding Dhanush's cell was switched off, he proceeded for DTD alone, finding his two sons arguing along with Andy, about pictures and other paraphernalia pertaining to the gallery.

"Dhanush, come to my office!" he boomed. "Where did you go early morning?" "To Anand villa" "Why didn't you call me?" "You were in no shape to be informed, *Baasa*" "What kind of a statement is that?"

"The kind where a son has to watch his father cheating on his mother" Dhanush blurted out, his voice shaking, along with his legs. "Have you gone crazy? What do you mean? I have not and do not ever plan to cheat on Suhani! How dare you even suggest that! Did..."

Arjun went cold all over, afraid to finish the sentence. "Did you tell your mother?" "Not yet. She is smart enough to figure it out eventually" "Dhanush, nothing happened. She walked in to talk to me. I was groggy, but she wouldn't leave. So, I let her..."

"Spend some time with you alone in her see-through nightgown? How dumb do you think I am, *Baasa*?" Dan screamed, storming out of the room, before he would burst into tears like a little girl.

At Maya's Reality, Suhani rattled off instructions to Abhimanyu, who had been handling the business quite well "Our new line is to be named 'Strength of a Woman'. I want the media to gobble up each picture of a few pieces that will be focused upon"

"The sketches are to be protected at all cost and given to our artists to make. Have you checked the stones and *Kundan* required for the pieces?" she asked, stubbing her smoke. "I've supervised them myself"

"Your sketches and stones are safe. They're in the locker behind you" Softening his business-like tone, Abhi asked, "Ma'am, you smoke when you're upset. What's the matter?" Suhani wanted to divert her mind, by nose-diving into work.

She had no intention of washing her dirty linen in public. "Nothing, except the competition seems to be so profound, that I've had to design a line that is quite unlike the handcrafted jewellery I had begun Maya's Reality with"

"It is a deviation Ma'am, but I have a feeling it will work well for us" Abhi smiled at her, knowing she was not comfortable pouring her heart out. "I'll have your breakfast sent for you" he said, getting up to answer the question Suhani was about to ask next.

"Annie called to say you left without it" Suhani moved her eyes to the laptop screen's slide show, of her happy life with Arjun. There were thousands of pics that she never tired of, that inspired her.

Today, every time she saw his picture, her imagination painted Ramona's slender arms around his neck. The rage of a *Banjara* took over her sanity, as she dialed her lawyer's number. "Send the eviction notice to Swarn Niwas"

"I want everyone out, except the staff by today evening. Yes, you heard me right. Keep me posted at all times. Thank you" The click of the phone felt like a thread, a fragile thread that shook a bit, resisting to be cut.

Suhani had her biscuits, dipping them into her fragrant Darjeeling Tea, leaving the rest of her breakfast to be taken away. She had cut a dozen calls Arjun made to her cell since morning, trying to make sense of it all herself.

The previous night, she had decided to have the eviction notice sent for Ramona, done. Today, she wanted to punish Arjun too. Was it jealousy, insecurity, a bit of both? Whatever it was, she didn't let it take over her senses at work and began to pay attention to her business in full gusto.

Arjun knew that the link between Suhani cutting his calls and the misunderstanding Dhanush had created, had to be quashed before it would affect his relationship with Braids. He had enough on his plate already, an unwanted extra that could fuel an unwanted fire, not in his preference list.

He called Sangharsh to inform him, he'd be having dinner with Ajju, Aradhana and everyone else at the Anand villa, around 8 p.m. Sangharsh and Nalini heard him on the loudspeaker at Anand Creations, convinced he was coming to clear the air.

They chose to keep the information to themselves, lest Suhani should run again. They also offered to invite Ajju and his wife to avoid any more scandal, to which Arjun agreed. It was important to have family around for the Anands, when it came to matters relating to the same.

Ramona was stalking Mr. Guha and Andy all through the day at the gallery, prodding them to check if all was moving the way it had been planned by her. Try as they might, she looked extremely displeased with their level of performance, almost all of the time.

"Andy, Mr. Guha is used to my style of working. I do not like sloppy slip-ups. Please ensure tomorrow you tie up all the loose ends, so that day after would conclude a splendid reception" Ramona said.

She walked around the conference room airily in her tube skirt and melted Swarovski top. "A bit more time would have been good. The caterers, decorators are all charging extra because of the time constraint" Andy cribbed.

"Then sweet talk them into believing they will get plenty of business from us hereon, if they deliver as requested. You are Sangharsh's son, so I assume you could sell ice to an Eskimo!" Ramona said.

She checked the balance amount she had left, after the payments. "Keep my father out of this" Andy hissed, glaring at Ramona. "Hush, little boy. Your father need not know how you've backstabbed his oldest friend"

"I'll keep your secret, providing you do as you are told" she smiled at his whitened face. Annie and Andy, unbeknownst to anyone else had been continuously updating each other. By default, Abhimanyu became a part of their discussion, as did Malika.

Annie wanted Andy to talk to their parents about how he felt about Malika. "How can I, Annie? Eventually Dad's going to find out, about my leaking out information to Ramona!" "Then tell him yourself" Annie intervened.

Suddenly, it made all the sense in the world, the weight of guilt he had been carrying around would be off his conscience, making him normal again. He chose to speak to his parents in the evening over dinner about this.

By the time it was evening, the setting sun seemed to have drained the energies out of all the hard-working people in the city of Delhi. Everyone looked far less bright and enthusiastic, as compared to how they came to work in the mornings.

A series of cars and SUVs parked in the Anand villa, much to Suhani's surprise at a quarter to eight. "Are you expecting guests?" she asked Nalini, walking with her towards the living room. "More like house guests, I suppose" came an honest, yet cryptic reply.

"*Pranaam, Maasa*" Ajju and Aradhana entered, touching her feet as she welcomed them, happily. Dhanush walked in with Andy, seconds before Annie walked in as well. Abhi chose to stay out of the dinner invite, politely declining due to the pending paperwork at Maya's Reality.

The bell rung once again, much to Suhani's surprise. "Who can that be?" she said out loud, as the housekeeper opened the door. Arjun walked right towards her, before she could utter a word, grabbed her by the hand, literally dragging her to the balcony.

"What do you think you're doing?" she snapped, jerking her hand out of his grasp. "Why did you not take any of my calls?" he snapped back at her.

"I'm not answerable to you for anything anymore, Mr. Pratap" she said, her ice-cold tone back again.

"Yes, you are" "Oh, really? As what?" "As my wife" "Your wife is waiting for you in her skimpy little outfit at Swarn Niwas. Go to her" Arjun's suspicions were confirmed, as Suhani began to shake when she uttered the words.

"*Beendni*, it was nothing like you heard. I swear on our children" "You did it to me once a long time ago and drove me into the arms of another man. Now, you did it again. Maybe I should have a man kept aside for me too" she said softly.

"Be quiet, woman! How dare you utter such nonsense!" Arjun shook her, unable to digest what she just said. His fingers seared through her thin *Lucknowi kurta*, as she jerked herself away from him again.

"Do not touch me. I…" The phone rang at the wrong moment. Arjun had half a mind of throwing it out of the balcony when he saw who it was. Seeing his expression, Suhani's temper flared again. "She wants you to go to her. Go! What're you doing here?"

He disconnected the call, but was compelled to read the message that came thereafter. It said, 'pick up before it's too late'. Intrigued, he took Ramona's call, "What do you want?" he screamed on the phone.

"Don't shout at me. Point your frustrations someplace else, Arjun. There is a lawyer at our doorstep with an eviction notice. Come home. Diana is with me, and I…" "I what? Leave with or without Diana. How do I care?"

"Arjun, I've read the notice carefully. It says all except the staff ought to evict the premise by midnight today to avoid being prosecuted. That means the nomad you stupidly willed our house to now, wants you out too!"

Arjun froze at the insinuation, refusing his mind to let it seep in. "It's not true. You're fibbing to make me come there. I know how your mind works, Ramona" "Oh, I see. You're with her right now"

"Well Suhani, if you can hear me, let me tell you what happens every night after he has finished talking to you. I…" Arjun hung up to avoid any more unpleasantness. But, the damage had been done already.

"Don't believe her" "Why did you disconnect?" "Because she'd have lied through her teeth" "You should trust me more" "Trust, Suhani? You speak of trust to me? Do you trust me?" "Yes, I did. I don't know anymore" she said, resignedly.

"Did you want me out of the house too?" he came closer to her. "Yes" was all she could say, turning to walk into the living room. Two people who were inseparable, began their separate paths once again that day.

Suhani ran upstairs to her room, Arjun walked out of the Anand villa quietly. Everyone present was quiet, until Andy spoke. "Dad, Mom, I have something I need to discuss with you. In fact, replace 'discuss' with 'confess'" he said, nervous as the moment of truth came nearer.

All eyes turned to him, "Fantastic timing, Nandish! Let's eat at the table. No, Aradhana. Leave your mother-in-law alone. Nalini will go to her with her dinner later. We've been through these fights before"

# CHAPTER TWENTY FOUR

When one's conscience begins to feel weighed down, no strength on earth can help unburden, without the nagging fear of being misinterpreted. Nandish knew he was taking a leap of faith, trusting his parents to pardon his folly.

He wasn't so sure how Ajju and Dhanush would react though. Although Mia was converted into Aradhana, having won over almost everyone in the bargain, Andy still had his doubts since he had seen her mean streak at Bassi, a trait he assumed was a genetic inheritance from her mother, Ramona.

Once everyone was seated, the food was served. He waited half-way through the dinner, until his mother reminded him about the talk he wished to have. "With you both, alone" he said, making Ajju look up immediately.

"I don't know what's been going on off late in both the families, since Aradhana and I got married. Care to brief me a bit?" he said, quietly sipping lemon water to clear his throat, of the *dal makhni* he had served himself with.

"*Baasa* spent the night with Aradhana's mom" Dhanush exploded, unable to contain himself. "I'm the mole you guys have been poking Bantu to catch red-handed at DTD!" Nandish exploded with equal fervor.

"Great!" Sangharsh banged his napkin on the table. "Dhanush, bad timing. Ajju, I'll talk to you later about this. Arjun came to clarify, but your mother's stubborn streak transforms her into a jungle cat, when she's mad!"

Looking at his son, he waited for an elaboration to his claim. Nandish told them from the very beginning, as to how Ramona had tricked him into becoming one of her pawns. "Why should we believe you now?" Dhanush snapped, shocked at how many back-stabbers he was amongst.

"You should. Mother is quite capable of everything Andy said" "Your mother is the root cause of all the darkness in our lives right now. Why don't you take her and disappear?" Dan yelled at Aradhana, who was soon reaching the end of her tether.

"Dhanush! Do not speak to your *Bhabhisa* this way!" Ajju screamed. "*Bhaiya*, while you are honeymooning with your wife at the Taj, I at home have to witness our father cheat on our mother…with this one's mother! I'm sorry but an apology is the last thing you will get from me"

His anger couldn't be contained as he stood up from the table. He went upstairs to his mother's room, away from all the chaos. Ajju had never witnessed Dhanush being so openly rude to him. "I'm sorry on his behalf" he apologized to everyone present.

"Why should you be sorry for Dan? He's a grown man and not a child anymore. Let him be accountable for his actions" Aradhana said flatly. "Stay out of this" Ajju said sternly. "Why Ajju? Am I not family? Don't I have the right to express my opinion?" she pleaded.

"Yes. But only to me in private. In public, I will speak on behalf of both of us" "That is not how I was raised" "It is apparent then that you were raised wrong, considering who raised you. I wouldn't be surprised if you end up being your mother, after a while!"

Ajju snapped at his wife, who looked mortally wounded. "Baby…" he was immediately apologetic. But her thin smile and curt 'excuse me' from the table meant only one thing- a war between the newly-married couple was to ensue, that was to last a while.

The couple left for Annie's room, where the extended balcony was enough to have a private chat, without being overheard. With the Pratap boys gone, Andy began to speak but was hushed by his twin sister, Sarvani.

"I am equally to blame. Andy and I have been in constant touch. I should have told you but chose not to, because you two are either too busy with your work or each other" Nalini glared at her daughter.

"Don't you dare palm this stupidity off on us, young lady! What you and your brother did was horrible. Do you know what the ramifications could be? We could lose the Prataps forever as friends"

"Arjun could lose the DTD gallery to Ramona. And a sorry may not fix all of this to begin with, so having this conversation is in itself, a waste of time! Why don't you both think about that for a while, until I go sort out the mess upstairs"

The trend of napkins banging on the dining table was once again followed by the first lady of the Anand household, as she marched up the stairs to address all the escapists. *"Baasa*, we're sorry" Annie looked at her father, imploringly.

"It is in the past now. Focus on damage control. How do we fix this? Nandish, how much information does Ramona have about the gallery already?" Sangharsh enquired. "Enough to take over the business. Buy it hands down" Andy replied honestly, still ashamed of himself.

Gulping hard, Sangharsh decided to shelf the thought of a possible takeover of DTD by Ramona, leaving Arjun helplessly jobless for now. "I never understood why you opted to stay at the gallery, on Ajju's wedding day" Sangharsh thought out loud, forking the remainder of his pasta.

"He was in love with Mia, *Baasa*" Sarvani offered the clarification, much to Nandish's chagrin. "What? You were in love with Mia? Why didn't you tell me this earlier? We could have done something, *beta*" he said, feeling sorry at the state of his son now.

"What could you have possibly done, Dad? Change her mind and make her fall for me? She told me herself that she fell for A.J. unknowingly. It was her mind to make and so she made it" "I'm proud of you for being mature about a heartbreak, Nandish" Sangharsh voiced himself.

"My 'mature' self, joined hands with the enemy, its ugly head rearing to fan the flame that'd destroy the link between the Prataps and DTD forever, Dad" Holding his head in his hands, Andy whispered, "All is lost"

"Not yet" came Annie's reply, who looked like an angel with a ray of hope. "As in?" "As in tell *Baasa* about the lawyer who isn't Ramona's" she said, holding Andy's arm tightly. Andy's face lit up like a dozen lanterns were set aglow.

"Yes! I forgot all about that. The email that came for the offer to buy DTD was from a lawyer called Mr. Patil. Mrs. Cotton's lawyer's name is Mr. Sahu!" Hitting the napkin playfully on his son's head, Sangharsh smiled for the first time that evening.

"You are one crazy boy! How could you forget something like that?" "Just got completely bogged down by how to confess my sin to you both" Nandish replied honestly. "Alright, I'll take it from here"

"Let me go and see what's happening upstairs. Ask the cook to serve dessert at the living room, a half hour from now. Hopefully, I should have everyone under my roof seated for it, by then" Sangharsh went up the stairs, partially relieved at one of the problems resolved.

Matters of the heart were a whole different ball game altogether; of that, he was certain as well. Knocking on Suhani's door, he entered to find Dhanush looking out into the skyline of Delhi through the tall French windows.

Suhani and Nalini were talking in hushed tones, obviously about Arjun. "May I join the conversation?" he said, smiling at both the ageless, lovely ladies. "Only if you promise not to ruin what I've accomplished. Our Suhani is ready to speak with Arjun" Nalini declared, triumph showing on her face.

"Well done! I see you've learnt well!" Sangharsh said, ducking a pin cushion his wife threw at him. "You taught me nothing, mister!" "When I met you, Mrs. Anand, you were a hurricane chaser. Now, you're a simultaneous hurricane coordinator! I would call that 'learning well'"

Suhani would have smiled at Sangharsh's charming wit, a weapon he used often to diffuse tense situations. She looked up at him this time with no smile and spoke. "*Bhaisa*, I had an eviction notice sent today at Swarn Niwas"

"Good for you! Let Ramona do her plotting and planning elsewhere" he said, proud of her for taking such a bold step. "Wait, there's more. The notice mentioned everyone ought to leave the premise immediately, except for the staff"

Suhani watched Sangharsh's face turn sober again. "You threw Arjun out of Swarn Niwas?" he exclaimed. "I was angry because of what I overheard when you were.." "Whoa! After you came upstairs Andy owned up to being part of an espionage plan, deftly orchestrated by Ramona"

"Yes, *Bhaisa*. I'm aware of that. Nalini just told me" "So, Arjun is to leave his home, give up his job, and then do what? Go where?" he asked her, bluntly. "I don't have all the answers alright!" Suhani started to cry softly, ashamed at what she was putting her *Saheb* through.

"Leena says there can be either room for worry or faith. One cannot harbor both. Muddy water is best resolved for the purpose of clarity, purely by giving time to the mud to settle down" All three elders looked at the spoilt young boy, who spoke with the utmost sagacity and sobriety.

"He is right. Nalini, take Suhani downstairs. I have to go and get Ajju and Aradhana to come down as well. We are going to have sundaes for dessert!" "Shall I come too?" Dhanush offered. "Promise to be quiet. Leave your anger here, in this room"

"Take your cloak of affection, compassion with you" Sangharsh replied. On not getting any response to the knock outside Annie's room, Sangharsh entered with Dhanush. Ajju was standing on one extreme of the tiny balcony, Aradhana on the other side.

"Are you staring into oblivion to compare whose view is better?" he said, seeing them both turn towards him. "Forgive me, *Bhaisa* and *Bhabhisa* for shooting my mouth off. I had no business disrespecting you both this way" Ajju patted Dhanush's back, breaking into a smile.

"Water under the bridge" Ajju merely said, making it evident that all was forgiven. Ajju sobered when he turned to Aradhana though when she spoke. "It's not so easy for me. I've done everything I can to win your trust, Ajju. Somewhere in the back of your mind, you have this fear that I will prove I am my mother's daughter someday"

"I spoke in a fit of rage. I'm sorry, but some things you said were uncalled for as well" justified Ajju. "Be that as it may, I've never taken potshots at your parents" "Yes, for that I ought to apologize, I know. But your mother deserves no apologies, considering what she has done"

"I'm not taking her side, Ajju. But that doesn't mean you bracket me as her. We are very different, her and I" Aradhana continued the pointless argument. "You were behaving like her at the dining table. She too speaks more than required, out of turn!"

"That is a trait most women are born with, I'm afraid!" Sangharsh interrupted. Not paying attention to his sense of humour, Ajju looked at Aradhana. "Why are you behaving like this?" "Like what, Ajju? Don't act like you are the victim here"

"Oh, you're doing a perfectly good job being the wounded deer" Ajju's voice was raised again. Aradhana turned swiftly to leave for the hotel but Sangharsh stopped her. "Have your sundaes first. Leave after that and I won't stop you"

Once everyone was gathered downstairs, Sangharsh had everyone's sundaes served. Quietly, everyone ate up their ice-creams, sinking deeper and deeper into their own thoughts; up until a sound other than the clinking of the dessert spoon to the glass was heard.

It was Sangharsh who spoke, slowly. "There is a barrage of information hurling itself on us. We have no control over that. The intention is to damage, break, crack our families. That, to some extent, we do have control over"

"By the time we are ready to react, it might be too late. Have you noticed a trend off late? How often we listen to the person who speaks to us, purely with the intention of replying back. There are two sides to each story"

"Similarly, there can be more than one truth as well. It is time for each of us to choose whether family comes first, or jostling to come to terms with the hurling cannonball of emotions. Which one is it going to be?"

Like a stack of cards placed atop each other, all present whispered "family". "Aradhana, I speak on behalf of all of us. We have accepted you as family. You have our trust, our love, our blessings. Treasure them, protect them tooth and nail like you did today"

"But, we do have certain customs and traditions that make us who we are. Never break them in a fit of rage, even if the one in front eggs you to" Moving on to Nandish, he said, "You wanted to work for the gallery and not me. I was hurt at first, but was glad you were following your dream"

"Carve your niche on the basis of trust. Loyalty has no value for one who belittles it. When it comes to love, stepping aside and wishing the one you care for, was admirable on your part" Nalini nodded at Andy, as did Suhani.

Sangharsh it seemed, had briefed them upstairs. A.J. and Aradhana were visibly uncomfortable with the old story of Andy cropping up. Before Sangharsh could continue his impressive sermon, his cell rang.

Arjun had called to say he was packed to leave for DTD, where he'd stay until he found a place for himself. He also asked him to inform Suhani, that *Chaudhary* Akash's pundit had fixed the *shubh muhurat* for Dhanush and Leenata's wedding.

They were to expect three guests from the village shortly-Vansh, Leenata and Malika. "Why don't you tell her yourself, *dost*?" Sangharsh gently suggested. "Don't even go there. Your stubborn sister can stay in her mansion, with her guests from the village"

"I don't need to be humiliated anymore!" Arjun hung up, sounding hurt more than agitated. Sangharsh parroted the entire information out, further mentioning that Ramona had left with Diana to Elite International, the first hotel they stayed in.

Everyone was now looking at Suhani, who was staring at her palms. She didn't have the courage to look up, leave alone speak. Her palms were filling up with droplets of tears, like her rose garden did during the monsoons.

A sorry sight for anyone to watch. Aradhana walked up to her mother-in-law, hugging her hard. "It'll all be okay, *Maasa*. We'll fix each and everything. Soon, life will be normal again, you'll see"

Looking into her big, blue eyes, Suhani found herself asking, "How will I stay in Swarn Niwas alone?" "We'll come with you, *Maasa*" Ajju offered. "Your father will be alone" "I'll stay with him then" Dhanush said quietly.

"You know, you are one melodramatic lot! Arjun is staying with us. Dhanush, you cannot stay under the same roof as Leenata before marriage, as you are already aware of. You stay here as well" Nalini said, sounding like a pretty General, commanding her emotionally distraught troops.

Everyone dispersed, exhaustion taking over their senses for another day. Suhani left with Ajju and his wife who planned to stop via the Taj to pick up their luggage. Dhanush left for the gallery with his sleeping bag, under the strict instruction not to get into any argument with his father, for the night.

Annie and Andy went off to their respective rooms to speak to their sweethearts, who eagerly waited to hear from them. The senior Anands retired to their room, holding each other's hands with their fingers inter-laced.

"Why does this keep happening to them?" Nalini asked her husband. Putting his arm around her, he pulled her close. "I don't know, Nal. I just know they will pull out of it, one way or another" "It's going to be tough this time, Sangharsh. It's far more complicated"

"True, my love. But, that is the real test then, isn't it? Is their love strong enough to help them bounce back to life? That is what remains to be seen" They talked some more with their words, their eyes, their bodies, till finally sleep got the best of them.

Suhani tossed and turned the whole night at Swarn Niwas. She was used to cuddling up to her *Saheb*. The bed was too big to sleep in alone. She walked like an apparition into the study, wore Arjun's night suit and slept off on his futon.

Ajju found her curled in the study, the legs and arms of the night suit covering her, much more than her height. She looked vulnerable and innocent at the moment. Click! Aradhana was standing beside him, as she took a snap.

Tiptoeing out of the study, he asked her why she took a picture. "Send it on Whatsapp to *Baasa*. He should see that the fierce tigress can sometimes be a gentle lamb too. Go on, Ajju" Ajju kissed her softly, promising a generous reward for her brilliant idea.

Arjun woke up to the beep of his mobile. He saw Suhani's picture of Ajju's message. 'She was missing you, so she slept in the study wearing your night suit, *Baasa*' Ajju replied, constantly removing the droplets of water, that kept falling from his eyes.

'Take care of your mother for me, my son. I will come for her. But first, I must finish what I started'. Arjun had decided to do, what he ought to have done a long time ago. This was one action of his, which would change a whole lot of equations.

There comes a time when we all believe there is a way out of a situation, but we can't seem to reach it. It is then that we must envision what courage and trust in ourselves, can make us do. A solution comes to the one, who has clarity of thought alone.

# CHAPTER TWENTY FIVE

Divorce is a word that implies the death of a relationship. It is a word that is unwelcome in conventional societies, where compromises, adjustments are admired, irrespective of the happiness quotient.

Besides, a divorce also means one more thing. One of the two in the marriage chose to give themselves a better chance, or put their foot down at being treated in an undesired way. Arjun had made up his mind to speak to his lawyer, to file for a divorce from Ramona.

The lawyer advised him to consider, how it would affect the current condition of his family, as well as its upcoming occasions. "I'll handle that, Mr. Yadav. Go ahead and file. Let me know when to reach court and I will"

He was still a bit groggy when he went into the washroom, to get ready for the day. The corner of his eye noticed something moving on the sofa, in his office. It was Dhanush. "What're you doing here?"

"I thought you were at Sangharsh's. How did you get in?" he asked, still not pleased with the way he behaved earlier. "Sangharsh *Chachu* sent me. All of us have spare keys, because we all have different timings at times"

When they both took turns to get ready, Dhanush ordered for breakfast, over which he mentioned the Anands wanting him to stay at their place, along with Arjun. "Something about Leenata and I not being under the same roof" he murmured, watching his father struggling with a soft paisley tie.

"Here, let me help you" "No need. You have helped enough. Go to your office if you're done" Arjun said, fully aware of the harshness in his tone. As per him, Dhanush had no business making a mountain out of a molehill. A molehill that didn't exist in the first place!

Feeling suitably chastened, Dan left for the backroom, where A.J and Andy would land up shortly. Until then, he had pictures to Photoshop, getting busy with them. A,J reached a bit later than Andy, who had his hands full of papers.

"I'm helping Mrs. Cotton with Ajju *Bhaiya's* reception" he said, imagining the pleasure he would feel in dancing around a bonfire lit, by all the papers he had collected! "How is *Baasa?*" Ajju asked Dhanush, who shrugged saying, "Still in a temper. How is *Maasa?*" he asked in return, to which Ajju replied, "Quiet. Very quiet"

"Dan, Andy, work on the pictures I gave you. If Mr. Guha or Mrs. Cotton walk in, switch over to the reception work she has detailed you to do, just to keep up with appearances. I need to go talk to *Baasa*. He needs to be updated on the latest"

He didn't want to belittle Andy, by saying he was going to tell on him. Ajju was an expert in handling Arjun, from the very beginning. The uncanny understanding, connection both had for each other, was par exemplary.

Behind closed doors, Arjun was appalled by Andy's espionage fiasco. "What is wrong with that boy? I took him under my wing and this is how he repays me?" "*Baasa*, Ramona conned him into it. Just like, I'm sure she conned Dhanush into believing that she spent the night with you" Arjun looked at his son carefully.

"Do you believe me, Ajju? No one else does" "It doesn't matter, *Baasa*. If your conscience is clear, the truth will eventually present itself" Ajju's fierce loyalty and mature thinking, made Arjun's chest swell with pride.

"Alright. I still want Bantu to watch over both Nandish as well as Mr. Guha" Nodding, Ajju was about to leave, when Arjun called him again. "How are things between you and Aradhana?" "We have teething problems like any other newly married couple"

"But we do love each other. That's what matters, at the end of the day. If given a choice between walking away and walking towards each other, we prefer the latter than the former" "True. Very true. After this godforsaken reception Ramona is hosting is over, I want you to go for a honeymoon with Aradhana. Choose where you want to go"

"We already have, *Baasa*" "Really? Where would you like to go?" "Nowhere. We want to stay here. Our honeymoon can happen later. There is so much of restlessness in the air right now, that we would be there leaving our minds here"

"Right, then. Let's get to work. I believe you have to go for a last minute tuxedo fitting. Go ahead. I'll meet you back here for lunch" Ajju left for the outfit to be finalized at the tailor shop, that customized all of the Prataps' formals.

Ramona was back at DTD with a long checklist that she was busy ticking, when she locked eyes with Arjun. Cold ice waves would have felt warmer, in comparison to the way they looked at each other.

"Madame, the caterers and decorators representative is waiting in the conference room" Mr. Guha announced. She left to discuss the details with Mr. Guha still standing in front of Arjun, sweating profusely.

"You look unwell, Mr. Guha. Are you?" "No, Sir. I'm fine" "You don't look fine to me. Andy and Dan will cover for you. Go home and get some rest. You'll be required at your best, tomorrow"

Fearing the consequences, Mr. Guha said, "Sir, if I leave, Madame will be furious!" "Madame was born furious. I'm your boss and I say you must take the rest of the day off. That is all" Arjun's lawyer called him some time during the day to say that they have a court date, but there will be a letter sent to Ramona, stating Arjun had filed for divorce.

"It's better if you inform her beforehand, Mr. Pratap. At times, these things can get quite messy" "Mr. Yadav, it couldn't possibly get any messier. I'm willing to take the risk. Go ahead and have it delivered at DTD after lunch, if the paperwork is ready. She should be here around that time"

Hanging up, he turned around to face Dhanush. "Who was that?" "No one you know" "Fine. These are the pictures we've shortlisted. The blue memory card has the ones we scanned from some of the old pictures you had taken of Bassi"

"Good. Now, listen. Your brother has gone for his tuxedo fitting and I've given Mr. Guha the rest of the day off. Do me a favour and keep Ramona away from me. You and Andy are henceforth detailed for the same"

Astonished at his father's selfishness at over-burdening the two, Dhanush remarked, "How on earth are we going to do that? Do you want the security guard at the main entrance to be stationed outside your office?"

"*Badtameez mat baniye*! (Don't be shameless!) Stay within your limits. Do as you are told. At home, I am your father. Here, I am your boss. Both places, you will respect me. Do you understand?" "Yes, Sir!" Dhanush gave a mock salute and marched out of the room.

Arjun sat down, wondering how long he would have to endure being away from the one who made sense of it all-his Braids. Putting the memory card, he began to look at the pictures one by one.

His obvious obsession with Suhani showed in each and every picture, making him miss her even more. The situation they were in at the moment didn't even permit him to call and ask how she was, whether she had eaten or not. Before he could sink into his thoughts further, in barged the demanding Ramona.

"How could you give Mr. Guha an off without consulting me? Are you bent on sabotaging the wedding reception, Arjun?" "Firstly, lower your volume. You're standing in my office. And secondly, Dhanush and Nandish have been detailed to assist you for the day. That ought to suffice"

"Suffice? Do you know how tiresome Dhanush is? He is not as dumb as he acts. Before I came to you, I asked him where you were. Do you know what he said?" Ramona said. "No. But I'm sure you'll tell me" "He said to look for anywhere in the premise but not in your office!"

Arjun unexpectedly burst out laughing, at Dhanush's response to Ramona's query. "What's funny?" she asked, puzzled at his reaction. "You won't understand" he said, getting up to leave. "Where are you going?" "Lunch with the boys!" "I'm off to help Mia with her gown fitting. I want her to look like a knockout tomorrow"

"You'll be back soon, I hope? There's still a lot to be done" Arjun said, walking away from her. "Most certainly will. Although, I've no idea what these two are going to do with the jobs I've given them"

Arjun was still smiling when he hugged Dhanush, who in turn apologized for his childish behaviour back at the office. "I'm just mad about everything" he declared, munching on his cheeseburger.

"I know. I am too. But let's stick together through this. I love your mother with all my heart and did not do anything you were made to believe" Nodding, Dan acknowledged the truth finally. The fitting of the tuxedo was much faster than Mia's dress fitting.

"I look like a doll on a cake, Mother. I am not wearing this. Ajju will be mad at me. It's too low at the top, too flared at the bottom." "Don't be silly, child! This is a designer-wear wedding gown"

"It's too low" "It is highlighting your assets" "My 'assets' are what Ajju will not want me to flaunt!" The argument continued, till the seamstress quickly came up with a solution. A bolero jacket, studded with pearls, was fitted to her size.

Her hat had lace falling partially on her face, with her hair pinned in a French knot. "Chic!" Mia declared, but Ramona was not pleased. "You look older than you actually are" Ramona gave in to her daughter finally.

She rushed back to the gallery venue to pick up the arrangements for the next day, where she left off. "Excuse me, are you Mrs. Ramona Rai Pratap?" enquired a bulky old gentleman. "Yes, I am. May I know who is asking?" Ramona asked politely, hoping it was a prospective buyer.

He quickly handed her an envelope, walking off without saying another word. Shocked at how rude he was, she carried the envelope addressed to her to the conference room, using the paper knife to slit it open.

Arjun was in a closed door meeting in his office with Ajju, Dan and Andy discussing their pet project of the renovation of the old pictures, when Ramona stormed in, all guns blazing. "Get out all of you! I want to talk to this conniving trickster alone."

Humoured, all three looked at Arjun, who nodded his concurrence. The moment they left, she threw the envelope on his table. "What is this?" she screamed. "No shouting in my room. Sit down and drink some water, or you'll bust a nerve and end up looking as ugly as you are…on the outside."

Ramona kept standing, glaring at him mocking her. "You're trying to show me down. You want to ruin Mia's day. First, you gave Mr. Guha the day off. Before that, changing my residence through that nomad's eviction notice. And now, this!" she said.

"You are quite shameless, you know. Nothing seems to be working" Arjun said intently. "Let's talk about this after tomorrow, Arjun" she tried reasoning with him. "No can do. I've filed already" Arjun said, walking out of the room, holding the door open.

"Get out of my room, Ramona" She walked up to him and hissed, "I'll make your life a living hell. You'll regret having ever met me, or crossed my path!" "Well, for what it's worth, I regret having met you already!" Coming closer to her, he hissed back.

"As far as crossing your path goes, I plan to do just that!" before she could answer back, Arjun walked to the back room, where the boys were busy with the adjustments he had given them. The reception day arrived with a buzz, from the morning itself.

By evening, everyone wanted to harm Ramona in an unimaginable way. Suhani chose to stay back at Swarn Niwas as Vansh, Leenata and Malika were to arrive that very evening. She was gracious enough to bow out of the wedding reception, so as not to cause any kind of unpleasantness, for Ajju and his bride.

She had no desire to face Ramona either. Arjun was a separate issue altogether. She wanted to meet him and didn't, both at the same time. When Aradhana walked into the gallery hallway, all eyes were expectantly on her.

She looked stunning, in her sharp white gown with a mermaid-trail, that followed obediently behind her. Her hands held a bouquet of spray-painted blue and pink roses, with pearl attachments on it.

Ajju loved how she looked, up until she turned around to kiss her mother's cheek. "How do I look?" Aradhana asked him coyly. "As beautiful as ever, my darling! Your bolero jacket is beautiful"

"Was it part of the outfit?" Ajju asked, trying to sound casual. "Not really. The dress is low, cinched at the waist. I thought you wouldn't approve. So, the bolero jacket was a last minute alteration" Aradhana explained, all the while thanking the assembled guests for coming.

"You look astoundingly gorgeous, my dear!" Arjun complimented her, as did the Anands who chose to attend the event to support Arjun. "What an unpleasant surprise!" Ramona, dressed in a dull red and rose pink fishtail gown, said.

"Your dress looks stained, Ramona. Bought it from a flea market is it?" Sangharsh threw the ball right back at her. "I stand by my previous statement" Ramona said, with her nose up in the air.

"The feeling is mutual, as I am sure you know!" responded Sangharsh, dapper in his black tie outfit holding Nalini's hand, who was dressed in a beautiful long, shirt kurta with a crop jacket from their own Anand Creations.

"Behave everyone" Arjun said. "Keep your claws to yourselves or the press in going to feast on your carcasses!" The couples moved away from each other for the time being, holding fire temporarily.

"Looks like the assistant and the nomad have both done quite well for themselves" Ramona's comment was venomous enough to gain a retort, but

Arjun chose not to react. He was watching Ajju and Aradhana arguing in one corner.

The quarrel didn't look like it was about to end, anytime soon. Choosing to intervene, he hurriedly walked up to them. "What is going on?" "Why don't you tell him, Aradhana?" "And steal away your sadistic pleasure? No, I couldn't do that!"

"Stop bickering like children. Start smiling, you two. Everyone has noticed that you two have disappeared" whispered Ramona looking at Mia's red cheeks. "What's the matter, my dear?" she asked her daughter.

"Ajju has a problem with how I'm dressed!" Mia said, annoyed. "But you're wearing the bolero jacket to cover your cleavage" Ramona reasoned. "Mother, he doesn't like what is written on it at the back"

Turning around, Arjun and Ramona both noticed the letter 'N' sown in pearls right in the centre of the jacket. "So? It doesn't mean anything" Arjun said, frowning at Ajju, who clarified curtly. "'N' stands for several things such as names. The one that comes to mind as of now-Nandish!"

Ramona glared at Ajju, "Don't you dare make it look like this is Mia's fault. She has been trying to please you, since day one. You are the one who is insecure and difficult"

"Alright, everyone. Just fake it, till the evening is over. We'll figure this out later" Arjun said, trying to end the argument. "The evening is over for me, as far as I'm concerned" Ajju said, walking away to the parking.

Turning around, he looked at Aradhana, "Come along" She stood still and replied, "I'll be staying with my mother and sister at the hotel, for the night" The entire evening was ruined, as was the reputation the gallery carried.

The first scandal the press caught, was that Ramona was the real Mrs. Pratap. The second scandal they noticed, was Suhani's absence. The third and most delicious scandal was the altercation on the alteration, that they witnessed first-hand between Ajju and Aradhana.

The Anands took Arjun home, where Dhanush was waiting already along with Andy and Annie. When they heard what happened, Andy spoke first. "This was completely uncalled for. Ajju Bhaiya has no reason to be jealous or insecure in any way. Mia loves him a lot. And I am in love with Malika, who I plan to marry, if she will have me"

His open declaration of love, seemed to have spread its wings and flown over the gates of Swarn Niwas, to welcome the much-awaited guests from Bassi. Suhani greeted them with open arms, along with Ajju. She missed Arjun by her side that night again, crying herself to sleep…just like every night.

She wondered if he missed her too, whether sleep had become a stranger to him, the way it did for her. She wanted to touch him, to speak with him, to smell him. She wondered, if he yearned for her as well. If only she saw how Arjun pined for her, in the exact same way.

# CHAPTER TWENTY SIX

Delhi, officially known as the National Capital Territory of Delhi, is the capital of India. A few neighbouring cities like Gurgaon, Noida and Ghaziabad, are among those included in the status of NCR (National Capital Region), as per the Constitution of India.

Delhi is largely demarcated into two parts- Old Delhi and New Delhi. Today, the group was to see the visual treats of the historical monuments, at Old Delhi or *Purani Dilli*. This group entailed the youngsters from Bassi, as well as their escorts.

Ajju and Suhani, wanted their guests from the village, to see the timeless beauty of the city they lived in. The obvious chaperones were chosen for them as well. Diana was to be with Vansh, Dhanush with Leenata and Nandish with Malika.

Ajju had to go to DTD, as Arjun needed one of them to be there for the day. Aradhana was busy recovering, from what transpired at the reception. Ramona was busy convincing Mia to break out of the new identity of Aradhana, that the Prataps had shackled her down with.

"You will never become one of them, Mia. They will always have that one percentile doubt, because you're my blood. Somewhere in your heart, you know it as well. I wish you'd have spoken to me sooner, so that I could save you the heartbreak that you now endure"

Aradhana's cell beeped, making her read a message from her husband. 'Distance isn't a big factor in a relationship. Communication is. But, most of all, commitment is the most important one'

'No matter where I am, know this. I'm me. You're you. The 'we' is what is, was, always will be'. Her smile warmed her heart, at what the man she loved wrote. From a distance she heard her mother, still attempting to poison her mind against the Prataps, especially Ajju.

"I'm going to design a new Indo-western men's apparel line called **Nara**. What do you think?" Aradhana's out of context statement, caught Ramona off guard. "Where did that come from? You don't know anything about business, or men's apparel!" she said, condescendingly.

"Well, Mother… I guess you don't know me as well as you think you do, then. I plan to launch it very soon. Ajju is supporting me in every which way, on this" Ramona wanted to smack her across the face for her insolence, but left the room of the suite for now, instead.

Bumping into Diana, she saw her getting ready to leave. "And where are you off to, may I ask?" Diana was dressed in ethnic attire which was non-festive, but appealing all the same. Ramona thought her dress sense was as distasteful as her mother, the nurse's, used to be.

"I'm going to meet some friends. Since Mia is here to babysit you, I have some time to myself" "What friends?" Ramona asked, inquisitively. "No one you know. Some girls I met at the hotel. I'll see you in the evening. Bye, Mother"

Kissing her on the cheek, a forced ritual Diana disapproved of as more artificial than necessary, she left the hotel in a cab, straight for Swarn Niwas. Vansh was impatiently pacing the lawn, stopping the moment he spotted her cab park, in the driveway.

"Jiya!" "*Namaste*! How are you?" He hugged her spontaneously, embarrassing himself in the bargain. Such public displays of affection were uncommon, where he came from. "I missed you" They giggled upon realizing they had both said it together.

Back at Anand villa, Andy had been trying to decide what to wear since morning, up until his father noticed a hillock of shirts on his bed. "Are you opening a second-hand shop for shirts?" "Haha! Not today, Dad. I have to get ready and meet Malika"

"I am taking her to view in some of Delhi's historical sites" "Alone?" "No, Vansh and Diana, Dhanush and Leenata will be with us as well" 'Three pairs of lovebirds, as I see it!" Sangharsh duly noted.

"Are you happy with her?" he asked his son. "More than" "Well then, bring her home for dinner. Your mother and I would like to meet her" Hugging his father, he shooed him away, seconds later.

"Thank you for being the coolest! Now go away and let me choose, before I'm late for my date" Keeping up the rhyme, Sangharsh replied, "Try the lime-green *khadi* shirt mate, with the fawn dockers..don't be late!"

Tickled by their rap potential, father and son split until the evening. When Malika, dressed in a peacock blue and green *anarkali* suit, saw Nandish drive in, in his champagne-coloured Nissan Sunny, she had the broadest grin on her face, that she could ever remember having.

He matched her happiness, waiting for her to walk to him. "*Ram laddoo*" she said, handing him the packet that was brought, as a gift for him. Laughing as he took the packet, he hugged her gently and watched her push him away out of shyness.

Dhanush raced his Humvee, zig-zagging through the traffic, finally reaching Swarn Niwas. He saw Leenata reading a magazine, that had a write-up of the gallery. The sun shone on her hair, making a halo that seemed to emanate more out of her.

Her eyes were accentuated heavily with kohl. She wore a short-printed kurta with a flared *patiala*, her *chunni* wound like a soft serpent around her neck. The engagement ring Dhanush had given her, reflected the sunlight well.

Five diamonds, all shaped differently, looked truly exquisite on her long, slender fingers. "Are you planning to stand there all day?" Leenata asked, still looking at the magazine. Smiling, Dhanush walked up to her.

"And how long have you known I've been staring at my fiancé?" "Since he came in" They held hands, touched each other's faces, smiling happily all the time. "You grow more beautiful with each passing day" Dhanush said, moving a stray strand of hair from her face.

Leenata blushed a charming shade of pink, his touch once again, reminding her she now belonged eternally to him. "May I ask you a question?" "Ask, my heart" "Why aren't you staying here? Is it because I'm here now?"

"I understand you're trying to follow a custom, but I feel bad for you having to move out for the few days I'm here" Touched by her innocence, simplifying everything right down to the grass root level, he decided not to tell her the truth for now.

He knew well, how catastrophic it would be, if Leenata found out that he was technically born out of wedlock, courtesy the reappearance of the vicious Ramona. "What are you thinking, Dhanush?"

"How lucky I am, to have someone like you, to share the rest of my life with" The entire Swarn Niwas was drowned in the ocean of love, with the three couples planning to leave for their much awaited 'Delhi Darshan'.

They left in three separate vehicles, to maintain their level of private chats. Vansh and Diana had hired a taxi for the day. Dhanush and Leenata were in his yellow Humvee. Nandish was in his Nissan Sunny with Malika.

They had their GPS coordinated along with their watches, to ensure they would stay in touch, although they chose to go every place together. The convoy left the mansion in high spirits, wishing the day would go as per their plan of sight-seeing and entertainment.

They visited the Qutab Minar, the world's tallest free-standing brick minaret, that stood at 72.5 metres. "It has been declared by the UNESCO as a World Heritage Site" Dhanush said, as all three couples walked towards the enclosure.

"Can we climb right to the top like the Eiffel Tower in Paris?" Diana asked. "It was possible earlier. Both A.J and I have raced up and down till we were breathless, when we were children. Now, most of it has been closed for safety reasons"

Dhanush said, turning out to be the guide for the group. "Muhammad Ghori, a Tajik invader from Afghanistan, defeated Prithviraj Chauhan and had his bloodline reign till 1206. On his death, the Turkic slave-general, Qutb-ud-din-Aibak, broke away from the Ghurid dynasty"

"He became the first Sultan of Delhi and constructed this monument, as a symbol of his power" Leenata finished speaking and watched how all looked at her in awe. "I am a teacher and ought to know history!"

Next, the group went to the Old Fort, also known as *Purana Quila*. "An excellent example of Mughal military architecture. Built by the Pandavas, renovated by King Humayun, with later modifications by King Sher Shah Suri, the Purana Quila is a monument of bold design which is strong, straightforward, every inch a fortress"

They circled around Leenata, while Dhanush and Nandish clicked pictures, just like they did back at the Qutab Minar. "Tell me more, Leenata.

Your information is amazingly accurate" Vansh genuinely encouraged his sister, walking around the red stone building.

"It is different from the well-planned, carefully decorated palatial forts, of the later Mughal rulers. *Purana Quila* is also different from the later forts of the Mughals, as it does not have a complex of palaces"

"Neither does it have administrative or recreational buildings, as is generally found in the forts built, later on. The main purpose of this now dilapidated fort was its utility, with less emphasis on decoration"

"The Qal'a-I-Kunha Masjid and the Sher are two important monuments inside the fort. It was made by Aqeel in 1853" On their way to the next destination, Nandish asked Malika, 'How come Viren didn't tag along? He is quite possessive about you"

"I have been wondering as to why you haven't asked me this, yet!" "I don't want to ever put you in a spot, make you feel uncomfortable around me, Malika" Conscious of his look, Malika answered his query.

"Viren *Bhaisa* has been tending to the cattle that have been newly acquired by my *Baasa*. His age does not permit him to handle the entire livestock we own, alone. Since Vansh is here as well, *Chaudhary* Akash asked him to stay back in order to help out my father"

"That must have really gotten his goat!" Andy said, chuckling at the last swerve before they were to park at the Red Fort. "Goats? No, we have cattle like cows, oxen, buffaloes…" "My dear, it's a figure of speech which means 'to annoy someone'" he clarified patiently, knowing Malika was a simple, true village belle.

Intending to impress Andy, Malika took over the guide status from Leenata to describe the Red Fort. "The decision for constructing the Red Fort was made in 1639, when Shah Jahan decided to shift his capital from Agra to Delhi"

"Within eight years, Shahjahanabad was completed with the Red Fort. It was called the Qila-i-Mubarak or the Fortunate Citadel and was Delhi's first fort, ready in all its magnificence to receive the Emperor"

Pointing at the Fort on which they stood, Malika continued, "This entire architecture is constructed of huge blocks of red sandstone. Though much has changed with the large-scale demolitions during the British occupation of the fort, its important structures have survived"

"On every Independence Day, the tri-coloured flag of India is hoisted by our Prime Minister right here" They walked to the Bahadur Shah Gate that linked both the Red Fort and Salimgarh Fort, through the arched bridge.

Malika began to narrate information, the same way that she taught at Gurukul. "Salimgarh Fort, which is now a part of the Red Fort complex, was constructed on an island of the Yamuna river, in 1546.

"But, the Bahadurshahi Gate was constructed in 1854-55 by the last Mughal Emperor, Bahadur Shah Zafar. As you can see, this gate is built in brick masonry, with a moderate use of red sandstone. This fort was used during the Uprising in 1857, by our freedom fighters against the British Rule."

"It was also used as a prison for Zebunissa, daughter of Aurangzeb. The British imprisoned the freedom fighters of the INA or the Indian National Army too. Now, this fort is renamed as the red plaque you saw at the entrance- *Swatantra Senani Smarak* (Monument dedicated to the freedom fighters of India)"

The group was now restless with grumbling stomachs and aching soles. They unanimously voted to go to Asia's largest wholesale market- Chandni Chowk, to grab a bite, as well as shelter themselves against the sun.

They went to Karim's, arguably Old Delhi's most famous culinary destination. The hotel waiter who escorted them to their seats, introduced himself as Abu. "I recommend you try our *Alu Gosht* with *dal*, served with *rumali roti*"

"In fact, this restaurant began with just these dishes in 1913!" They ordered a mutton dish as well, since Diana had read about Karim's non-veg cuisine in an international magazine. Luckily, a table was vacated the moment they entered the restaurant.

It was bustling with hungry guests and busy waiters screaming orders over the chatter of the crowd. Leenata was keen to try the *jalebi* and *chaat* that was displayed as street-side delectables, in the food lane of Chandni Chowk.

Dhanush refused to let anyone eat, not just for health reasons, but also because there was no place for them to sit, if they ate. "You look tired, Malika" Andy whispered, watching her drink ice-cold water, to satiate her parched throat.

"I am. Sight-seeing is exhausting as it is. The narration has taken the breath out of me as well!" she replied. "Listen everyone. Since I am a regular in these parts and have my lady love tired of narrating… here is a tidbit on Chandni Chowk to chew on, before our orders arrive"

Sipping on the chilled coke, he began. "It is the city's sole living legacy of Shahjahanabad. Created by Shah Jahan, the builder of the Taj Mahal, the old city the Red Fort as its focal point, the Jama Masjid as its praying centre, and this fascinating market we are in, at present"

"Legend has it, that Shah Jahan planned Chandni Chowk so that his daughter could shop, for all that she wanted. The market was divided by canals, which are now closed. Over time, intense cultural harmony began in Old Delhi, courtesy small temples, mosques co-existing alongside each other"

The aroma of the meal reached the table, before Abu came with them. They almost burnt their mouths, gulping mouthfuls of the delicious food, that was piping hot and out of the world. It was time to head back to Swarn Niwas, where they chose to laze around, until it was time to call it a day.

En route, Nandish told Malika about the invite for dinner, extended by his father. "How nice of him to say that! I'll surely come, but.." "But, what?" "I have nothing to give them. I believe the city culture requires that the guest must never arrive, empty-handed" "We'll pick up flowers on the way, then"

"Now smile so that I can focus on the crazy traffic and get us out of here in one piece!" They welcomed the cool mansion with its tall trees and quiet surroundings. Darjeeling Tea was served at the balcony, where Dhanush and Nandish showed the pictures they had clicked of everyone.

Not surprisingly, Vansh had told Diana during one of his conversations about how Malika and he were matched, paired with Viren and Leenata. He wanted her to get to know from him, rather than anyone else.

"It's called an exchange marriage that's quite convenient. Wrap it up, all in one go!" he had said. Diana chose to extend her hand of friendship to Malika, who was polite, but clearly distant. "I cannot take any guarantee for Viren *Bhaisa*"

"Personally, I wish Vansh well and am happy for you both. But, Viren I'm afraid is not as forgiving or understanding" Dhanush called the gallery to check on his father and Ajju. "*Baasa* has been busy almost all day, over the phone. I know he's speaking to two lawyers, simultaneously"

"Corporate lawyers, you mean?" Dan asked, shutting off his camera. "One corporate. One divorce. Dhanush, he is filing for a divorce from Ramona" The ray of hope in Dhanush's heart, glimmered a bit brighter.

He enquired about his sister-in-law next, but Ajju was tight-lipped about it. "I'm going to the Anand villa after dinner with Leenata. Give my love to *Maasa*, A.J"

"Will do. Give my love to *Chachu* and *Chachi*" Hanging up the call, both brothers began to ponder, how life moves on mercilessly. There are relationships that change, break and mend simultaneously that need an adaptable, flexible nature to soak in all of it.

Whoever doesn't possess such a nature, is left behind. Ajju decided to call Aradhana and drive sense into her, offering to drive Diana back to Elite International. Dhanush decided to speak with his father about his new nagging worry of the leakage of the truth, that could possibly damage his secure future with Leenata.

But, what Ramona had decided, turned out to be lethally crushing, endangering everyone else's interests, except of course, her own. It was a brutally blatant example, of how desperate one may get, so as to realize a dream they have envisioned for themselves.

# CHAPTER TWENTY SEVEN

The next day was dedicated to exploring the Lutyen's zone. Dhanush and Nandish had discussed the places to visit there, so that by lunchtime they could be seated at the Nirula's hotel, at Connaught Place.

When Ajju came to pick Diana after dinner, he noticed a drastic change in her. From the normal silent, she had now transformed into a chirpy sparrow. All he had to do was ask what she saw around Delhi.

She began to chatter about the monuments visited, the history behind the magnificent structures, providing enough entertainment till they arrived at the hotel. "Won't you come upstairs, A.J? Mia will be happy to see you"

"Do you think so?" "I know so!" she said, pulling him out of his Ford Eco Sport, letting the valet slip in behind the wheel. "Hello? Anybody home?" Ramona was nowhere to be seen, but the television was running in Mia's room.

Diana and Ajju stood at the doorway watching her fast asleep, holding on to the stuffed toy tiger cub he had gotten her. He smiled, turning to go back when Diana stopped him. "She has been through enough. Don't lose what you have over something that won't matter in the long run, A.J"

Touched, Ajju turned to pull a wicker chair lightly. He sat to watch his Aradhana, who was smiling in her sleep. Diana left them alone, closing the door behind her. She had to recuperate, before the onslaught of the next day.

Ramona had been dining with her lawyer, to discuss the progress of her takeover bid. "Mr. Sahu, I know the gallery has hit rock bottom. You can see yourself as the accounts show, I'm right. What I don't understand is, why it's not out at the market yet?"

"Madame, your husband is a very stubborn man. Anyone in his place would have declared bankruptcy by now. He's trying to keep the gallery's head above water, making it sink even further in the process"

"Make no mistake though. There are others who are interested to purchase the gallery, for themselves" "Others?" Ramona looked up from her plateful of Mediterranean salad, tossed in extra virgin olive oil.

"Who would be interested in an almost written-off gallery?" "You forget the land cost has appreciated in value. The gallery is standing on prime property. I'd be interested if I had the money"

"Alright. Do you know of any bidders so far?" "Yes. Once I get to know more about the client of my old friend Mr. Patil, I will let you know" Moving on to the divorce case, the lawyer assured her things would work out, to her benefit.

"If he loses the gallery and this case, I will be grateful to you, Mr. Sahu. In my books, as you know, that translates to you and yours being looked after for the rest of your days on this earth" Mr. Sahu convincingly reassured her once again, as their meeting came to an end.

When Ramona reached her suite, she noticed something was wrong right away. She remembered shutting Mia's room door with the T.V. on, when she left. Walking towards the open door, her face paled when she saw her daughter's bed made, her luggage gone.

Panicking, she was about to call for help, when the note on the bedside table, caught her eye. It said, 'Diana was fast asleep, so I didn't wake her. Ajju has come for me. I am leaving with him. Take care of yourself. Try staying out of trouble! Love, Aradhana Pratap'

Ramona tore up the paper into tiny shreds, anger blinding her for those moments. "She signed off as Aradhana Pratap, to show me Mia Cotton does not exist anymore" she said to herself. Now that she has chosen which side she's loyal to, Ramona decided not to allow her maternal emotions, get in the way of her skyscraping ambitions.

Swarn Niwas, on the other hand, was once again richer by another pair of lovebirds. Suhani welcomed Ajju and Aradhana with open arms, going back to her room to count her blessings before and after she began to miss her *Saheb* again.

Andy got Malika for dinner at Anand villa, where she was greeted with a great deal of affection. Annie kept teasing Andy, wondering how he managed to get such a good catch. "Just lucky I guess" he said, warming his eyes as they rested on her.

"You must be tired. I'll get dinner ready. Why don't you freshen up, Malika? Nandish, show her to the guestroom, please" Nalini began to flutter around the kitchen, while Sangharsh and Sarvani discussed Annie's doll collection, that was almost ready to be launched.

"There you go. I'll wait for you downstairs" Andy told Malika, opening the door of the guestroom for her to enter. Dhanush and Arjun were freshening up too, on Sangharsh's insistence.

"Our prospective *Bahu* is coming to have dinner with us for the first time. Let's not scare her, with how we end up looking at the end of the day!" he had said to them, earlier. "I don't like lying to Leena, *Baasa*. It feels wrong"

"You're not lying to her, Dhanush. Shielding her from the truth is your duty, which you are doing, as I see it" "If she finds out that Ramona is still your wife, she will put two and two together. It would mean I am born out of wedlock, which would mean…"

"*Chup karo*! (Be quiet!) You are my son. Nothing can change that. We will figure out a way to resolve the matter. Now, finish up quickly before Nalini decides to starve us as punishment!" The door of the guest room closed silently, as Malika washed up in a hurry.

She had heard everything across the door that interconnected both the guestrooms, one of which was occupied off late by Arjun and his son, Dhanush. Earlier, this information would have been a goldmine, but now she didn't see the value of it.

She was in love herself, which by definition implies focusing on what matters, as against what doesn't. Choosing wisely to push what she heard aside, she joined everyone downstairs for a scrumptious dinner of *chole bhature* and *raita*, followed by *moong dal ka halwa* as dessert.

The evening was successful, the sporadic pleasant head bobs making it evident to Nandish's parents. They knew Bassi had to be revisited, this time to get a bride for their son. The next morning, everyone was rested enough for another tour around the city of Delhi.

Unlike the previous day, when the group of three couples toured Old Delhi, they were to sight-see New Delhi now. Ajju and Aradhana had chosen to join the group for today, much to everyone's delight.

Ajju was the expert of the day as he and his father had coordinated, studied several photo shoots in the area. "Edward Lutyen was a British architect, who, along with the team he led, laid out the central administrative area of Delhi, with the plan of retaining one-third of the area as green space"

Parking the convoy of cars, the group stood on the pavement. "On your left is the Rashtrapati Bhavan where the President of India resides, as you all know. Straight down this road is India Gate. Formerly, the Rashtrapati Bhavan was known as the 'Viceroy's House'"

"This straight stretch of road that connects the Bhavan and India Gate, is called the Rajpath or the 'King's way'" The enormous buildings looked as impressive to the group, as any other tourist visiting to see them.

"The LBZ or the Lutyen's Bungalow Zone is something we'll drive through next. It covers approximately an area of 26 sq.kms. All land and buildings in the LBZ belong to the Central Government, except for about 250 acres which belongs to private firms or individuals"

While they drove across the LBZ, they noticed around its great green expanse, a thick swath of trees, manicured lawns within the area watched over by grand buildings. Dhanush remembered the iron pillar at Qutab Minar that made Leenata laugh, when he saw a long black pole near one of the roundels.

"If you can touch your wrists with your back pressed against the pillar, a wish will be fulfilled" Everyone had tried but couldn't pull off the feat. "My turn now" Dan announced, holding Leenata's wrist with his back towards the black iron pillar.

"That is cheating!" Diana shouted. "Not if you give it a thought. Leena is a part of me, so if I touch her wrist, technically it would mean I'm touching mine." She smiled again, sharing her thoughts with Ajju and Aradhana, who were sitting with them in Dan's monster truck.

"I hope you plan to change your mode of transportation after marriage, little brother" Ajju teased Dhanush. "Why would I do that? Leena loves my Humvee" "Dhanush, Ajju Bhaiya is right. Can't you get something a little less intimidating, that looks more like a car and less like a tank?" Leenata said.

"I'll get you one of your choice. My Humvee stays" "So many rules and annexes happened in the old days. Was Delhi always the Capital of India through it all?" Diana asked Vansh, who looked at Leenata as they stepped into the Nirula's Hotel, to eat their lunch at leisure.

"Calcutta was the capital of the Britishers who came to India under the garb of the East India Company. Delhi was made capital in 1911. Lutyen's Delhi or New Delhi came into existence around 1931"

They ordered continental for everyone except for Ajju, who was following his father's footsteps. He fasted every Monday to pay his respects to the Lord *Shiva*, opting to have fruit or milk. "What's the latest at Bassi?" Ajju asked Vansh, sipping his chilled cold coffee.

"Not much as of now. Some ideas Jiya, I mean Diana churned, seem to be what we need for our village to rise up, like the glory days. I plan to speak with *Baasa* about them, when I get back" "Get back? Aren't you staying for a few more days?" Dhanush asked.

"Not this time. Since your marriage date has been fixed we have a lot of work to do, including stopping on our way at Chittorgarh, where Leenata's bridal jewellery is being made" Vansh said. sounding proud, nostalgic at having to give his sister away.

"What about you? Any plans to tie the knot?" Aradhana asked, knowing he held the key to her baby sister's heart. "I haven't asked her yet. But I will after I've given away my sister and spoken to my parents" Frowning, Aradhana revealed yet another difference in custom.

"Where we come from, the man proposes to the woman and then approaches the parents" Vansh wiped his mouth with his napkin, saying, "I'm aware of that. Where I come from, I need to take my parents' blessings, before I approach her or her parents"

Worried the casual conversation might escalate into a full-blown argument, Ajju threw in an idea, that was adopted greedily by the women. "In case you are not aware, there is a place here called Janpath, which is the paradise of bauble shopping, not to mention an underground shopping area alongside it, called Palika Bazaar!"

They cleared the bill, sprinting across the traffic to the street shops at Janpath. Rows and rows of endless shops flanked the streets with artificial jewellery in white metal, colourful cloth and apparel, hung high enough to catch a passerby's eye.

There was a shop where you could pick a t-shirt and have anything painted on it, by the local artist. They noticed Ajju disappear into one of the shops, choosing to follow him in there. It was a kiosk, where black and white sketches of parts of Delhi were sold, by a pair of brothers.

Ajju seemed to know them well, and was bargaining on that base, for the sale of a few of the sketches. All four couples bought a pair each, happily leaving the shop to get back to their cars, when a sharp voice stopped them from their prolonged merriment.

"Diana!" Ramona was standing on the other side of the road, sunglasses in her hand, glaring at her. "Mother! What're you doing here?" she asked, using the time to come up with a possible explanation herself.

"Me? Forget about me! Come here right now! We are leaving!" Years of submissive obedience forced Diana's head down as she said, "Yes, Mother" "Wait a minute. This is your mother?" Vansh looked at the lady standing across the road.

She looked quite upset, but he couldn't understand why. "Shouldn't you be introducing me to her?" "No, she shouldn't. Let her go, Vansh" Aradhana interrupted him. "No, I won't. Not like this. It doesn't feel right"

"I don't have all day to wait around. Get here fast!" Ramona screamed over the traffic again. "Are you sure she is your mother? Such an over-bearing, aggressive jungle cat!" "Come along, Diana. I'll drop you to her side and join back" Aradhana put her arm around Diana.

The two weren't related by blood from their mother's side, but had a common father. The bond they shared over the years, made Mia treat her with affection one showers on one's offspring, rather than sibling.

There wasn't much of an age difference between the two, but the way they were treated, was a different story altogether. "Stay out of it, Mia" Ramona yelled. "Pipe down or you'll bust a nerve, Mother! This is getting us nowhere" Mia yelled back.

"Mia, I don't want to go with her. I want to stay here with Vansh" Diana's heartfelt plea melted her, as well as the man who had grown to love her so dearly. "Let's go over and talk to her. She is capable of creating a public spectacle, of all of us"

"So, just play along, will you? Come on, trust me" Mia pulled Diana while they crossed the road, avoiding the traffic. They found a clear space and were rushing across when two cars with equal speed came from opposite directions.

Mia pushed Diana out of the way, Vansh pulling her completely off the road. Ramona ran to the road to save her only daughter and got hit by one car, Mia with the other. Ajju was already by their side, Dhanush froze in those moments, but was the first to call for an ambulance.

Ramona was badly bruised, but Mia…Aradhana didn't have a scratch on her body. She was still, cold like leather. The wail that Ajju let out was no longer human, for he knew Aradhana had left him to live through their promised eternity, alone.

The ambulance arrived at the hospital where the staff tried their level best to revive them both. Ramona was put in the Critically Injured List. But Aradhana Pratap, the previously known Mia Cotton, died with a smile on her lips, not a scratch on her angelic face, her big, blue eyes never to open again.

Dhanush had called his parents as well as the Anands who rushed to the Lilawati Hospital. When they found out who was injured, who deceased, they turned to look at Ajju. Hollow eyes stared back at them, her purse and glasses still in his hand.

They tried to talk to him, but he was still in shock. They took him home to Swarn Niwas. Dan and Leenata followed them as did the Anands. Diana and Vansh chose to stay back. Someone had to be there for Ramona when she woke up.

"Don't tell her Mia's gone, Vansh. She always loved her more. I'm afraid she's too weak to take any bad news" Agreeing with her, Vansh let her cry on his shoulder. Diana had lost the only mother she ever knew.

The world knew Mia and Diana to be sisters. In reality, Diana learnt everything from Mia, who was her best friend, teacher, all roles in one. We live all our lives, refusing to believe everything as we know it, can be taken away from us at any given point of time.

Breath, life, time can never be replaced. Choices cannot be made once these are snatched and all that one can hold on to, is memories. Enduring the pain of the loss of a loved one is something we have all been through.

They say time is the best healer. They are not completely wrong. Ajju chose to go to Bassi with the village trio after the cremation was over, a week after the accident. He watched Ramona cry shamelessly, howling till she was hoarse, wrapped up in bandages, being held by Diana on one side, Vansh on the other.

He knew he had lost Mia, but chose to keep Aradhana alive in his mind and heart. He wouldn't let her memory die along with her body. Suhani and Arjun watched as he quietly packed, leaving with the others for Bassi.

Before leaving, he took his father's hand and placed it into his mother's. "I'll be back soon. Look after each other until then" The large-heartedness of Ajju brought tears to their eyes, as they awaited the return of their son, healed and ready to take on the life he was sentenced to live.

# CHAPTER TWENTY EIGHT

When *Chaudhary* Dhanush died, his *Chaudhrain* Suhani's life changed completely. After marrying Arjun Pratap, her life changed again. Now that Ramona's reappearance made her slip down a notch from the spousal status, Suhani was determined to prove herself through the new line she planned to launch-**Strength of a Woman**.

She decided to show the sketches to Nalini, who had similar taste as hers in jewellery, asking her to pick out a dozen of each accessory, to accentuate in the line. "Why don't you ask Arjun to do the shoot for you? He was the original photographer who launched Maya's Reality. A comeback would be déjà vu, don't you think?" Nalini proposed.

"Mia's death, Ajju's leaving for Bassi, has left him empty. I don't know what to say to him. If I could, I would hold him tight and never let him go" Suhani's anguish poured through every word she uttered.

"Well then, here's your chance, *behan!*" Sangharsh was standing beside Arjun, who looked pale, thin, aged. Suhani walked up to him quietly, putting her palm into his, resting her head on his chest.

"*Maafi, Saheb*" Arjun wrapped his arms around her, tears dripping on her long, braided hair. "*Ghar chalo apni Beendni ke saath* (Come home with your wife)" she whispered softly. The Anands let their beloved couple walk hand-in-hand to the car.

Arjun was quiet through the entire ride. Neither did Suhani say a word. At times, silence plays a soothing tune, that healing hearts need to hear. The balm that was required to ease the pain Arjun felt, was within the presence of Suhani.

They explored each other reaching their home for several moments, rekindling the togetherness that once seemed to slip into oblivion. "I love you, Suhani. Please don't ever leave me alone" Hugging him, she promised never would either let go.

After lunch, they were lazing around their home when Arjun asked, "What were you talking to Nalini about?" "I took some sketches to show her. Her taste and mine are pretty much the same. I wanted her to choose a few select pieces, which I plan to highlight in my line"

"And who is to take the pictures for your new collection, may I enquire?" An impish smile spread on her luscious lips, as she slowly kissed her *Saheb*. "Why on earth would such an option even cross my mind?!"

"I have an idea that might just work. Give this job to Nandish instead of me, *Beendni*. He's never gone solo on any shoot. This might just be the break he needs" Suhani liked the idea very much, choosing to make it formal, by having a letter shot out from her firm to the gallery.

Andy was neck deep in paperwork, the next day. He got the fax from Maya's Reality that evening. He needed to get busy because his mind was still reeling from Mia's loss, Ajju's absence and the gallery in limbo.

He immediately sent a fax back, accepting the offer. Suhani asked Nalini to take the sketches home and show them to Nandish. "He's the photographer for my new line" she ended up saying, making Nalini smile, at how happy she was for her son.

"Is Dhanush coming back, or do you two need some time alone?" Nalini enquired, referring to the current living arrangement, wherein Dhanush was living at the Anand villa and the senior Prataps cozily tucked at Swarn Niwas. She knew what the answer was going to be though.

"We need to be together, Nalini. Keep him there for some time. We'll have to go to Bassi soon, to speak about the marriage date. We'll get him back home by then" Nalini was happy for Arjun and Suhani, but worried about their sons.

"Ajju's heartbreak is irreplaceable. But Dhanush's life is on the line. If the Ramona fiasco leaks out.." she confided in Sangharsh while they were waiting for their children to return from work. "It'll all be okay. Things always have a way of working out"

"Maybe not in the way one would envision, but they do all the same" Annie walked in with Abhi and Andy, with a handful of ribbons and bows. "Abhi and Andy are to look at the sketches together" she said, trying to justify his presence at the house.

"Please join us for dinner, in that case" Nalini invited him graciously. Abhi replied, "If you don't mind, as what? As Annie's soon-to-be husband or Mrs. Pratap's assistant?" The bold move Abhimanyu made could be interpreted as brash by some, but Sangharsh was impressed all the same.

"Touché! Let's discuss your terms of surrender over dessert, in that case. Hope you like crème brulee?" "I do, since your daughter loves it" Sangharsh excused himself, walking over to the kitchen, where Nalini was busy with the dinner.

"Why the sudden change of heart?" "I don't want my child to suffer the way Mia did" she answered plainly. Andy didn't want to use any models for the jewellery pieces. Instead, his unique idea blew everyone away.

"I want to put them on flat pieces of furniture, as if they're lying around lazily to be picked up" "I like that concept. But, won't that be bland?" Abhi asked, not sure he understood the concept completely.

"Look, the line is called **Strength of a Woman** right? If we show an office table, an oven in the kitchen, crockery, a conference hall, it would mean that today's woman is versatile enough to pull off any look at any place she wishes, with confidence!"

An applause made them both turn to face Annie standing beside her parents. "That's a fantastic concept, Andy! Promise me you'll cover my doll line as well?" "Whoa! One job at a time, Annie. And yes, thanks I will"

The dinner was simple, but the company at the table made it quite interesting. Andy and Abhi got along quite well, chatting merrily through the main course. The dessert was when the senior Anands began to ask him pointed questions.

"Tell us a little about yourself. Who all are in your family, where are you from…" Sangharsh sat down next to Nalini, as he asked the boy who stole his princess's heart. "My name is Abhimanyu Shekhawat"

"I have no one in my family except my father who is a doctor, running his practice in Jaipur" "And when can we meet him? We plan to visit Bassi very soon, to ask for Malika's hand for Nandish"

"We could look your father up then, as well" Nalini said, offering him some more crème brulee. Declining politely, Abhi welcomed the offer of the visit, assuring that his father is fully aware of Annie and would be very happy to meet her parents.

Annie went to see him off to his Bullet mobike, making Andy yell from the balcony. "Dude, time to promote to a four-wheeler!" Abhi responded in the same vein. "There's a debate between your sister and I whether to buy a black Scorpio or a red one. The moment that's decided, I'll get it!"

Waving goodbye, Abhi left the happy venue for the day. Suhani decided to call Nalini, late that night. "How is Arjun?" was the first question Nalini asked. "Much better now. What's the progress with the sketches?"

"You are in for an amazing surprise, Suhani. Nandish is coming to you in the morning with a revolutionary concept. I love it!" "Then I'm sure I will too!" Suhani smiled into the phone, moving her free hand up and down Arjun's back, as his head rested on her lap.

"Has Dhanush returned from the gallery?" Suhani asked. "He called to say he was on his way. Since both Arjun and Ajju are pre-occupied, all the work pressure has come on him" Nalini voiced her concern.

"He is doing a good job of handling it. I'm glad he's learning the ropes now" Suhani added. Wishing each other a good night, they slept off in their respective beloved's arms. Dhanush was exhausted while driving back to the Anands' mansion.

His mind and body were completely out of sync, leaving him looking like a zombie. He tried telling Leenata several times before she left, about what was eating him up from the inside, but he just couldn't bring himself to do it.

Trying to divert his mind again, he called Diana to check on how she was doing. "I'm alright. A bit lonely since Vansh left. Trying not to think about never speaking to Mia again" "I know. How's your mother?"

"She's still in Intensive Care, though the doctor says she's out of danger" "That's good to hear" Dhanush said, honking at a scooterist who jumped the light, almost bumping into his Humvee. "I hate it when traffic rules aren't obeyed!"

"Did you know there's a rule that says the bigger of two vehicles will be charged when involved in an accident, irrespective of whose fault it was? Ridiculous if you ask me!" He noticed the silence over the phone, realizing what he had just said.

"I'm so sorry. It just came out of my mouth. I'm tired in every which way and..." "It's alright, Dhanush. Please arrive safe" She hung up on him, not intending to be rude. The lump in her throat did not allow her to speak.

All alone at the hospital, not wanting her mother to wake up and see nobody there, she went to the cafeteria to get something to eat. When her phone rang, she thought it was Dhanush to repeat his apology out of guilt, but found it was thankfully Vansh's.

"Jiya" Just hearing his voice, the way he called her by the name he had chosen, set her crying. She couldn't control herself, try as she might. "I'm coming back" "No, don't. You're needed there. I'm needed here"

"Nothing is more important than being next to you, my darling" Vansh said, wishing there was a way he could be with her, sooner than he had planned. "I'll come to Bassi, the moment Mother is up and about"

Pacifying each other was the purest form of unconditional love and support, both Vansh and Diana needed at the moment. She wished he were with her too, but wasn't selfish enough to say it. "How's A.J.?" she asked, concerned about her late sister's love.

"Quiet. Very quiet. *Baasa* says we must give him time to come around. He's completely expressionless at the moment" Feeling sad for him, Diana said a silent prayer at the chapel that night, for God to give courage to those who were left behind to deal with the void in their lives, that Mia had left behind.

She met Ramona's doctor checking the daily roster on her way back to Intensive Care. "Doctor, any change?" "Why don't you go home and rest Ms. Cotton? She won't wake up anyway before tomorrow, or maybe even the day after"

"I assure you if she does wake up, you'll be contacted immediately" Diana was hesitant at first, but the trauma had taken a toll on her as well. She took her mother's belongings, kissed Ramona on the forehead, left for the hotel.

It was late at night when she finally managed to drag herself to freshen up and wait for some tea and walnut brownies, before sleep would take over. Her mother's mobile was still intact in her clutch purse.

It was blinking with messages and calls. Most were from a gentleman called Mr. Sahu. The cell ran again with the same name. No sooner had Diana picked the call, that she heard a man begin to rattle off.

"Where have you been, Madame? I've been calling all day. Mr. Pratap's making his move pretty fast. His grounds for divorce look solid too. We need to know how to proceed further. When can we meet?"

"I'm sorry my mother can't come on the phone right now" "Who's that? Is that you, Mia?" "No, it's Diana" "Diana? Madame only has one blood relative listed as her daughter. That's Mia Rai Cotton"

"What nonsense! Who are you anyway?" Diana snapped, irritated at the stranger for not knowing who she was. "I'm her lawyer. Who are you?" "Her daughter. Mia was my sister!" Diana screamed into the phone.

"Was? What you mean by 'was my sister'?" "She's no more. There was an accident. My mother is in the Intensive Care at Lilavati" The click of the cell concluded the conversation, making Diana's head spin.

Choosing to sleep it off, she dreamt all night of her childhood with Mia, always watching over her. Building sandcastles on their beach holidays, helping her with homework, school projects, bullying school bullies in return, who tried being mean.

Her subconscious sent silent tears into reality, that trickled down her soft cheeks, quickly soaked by the pillow she rested her head on. The phone rang in the morning, jump starting Diana for the day. Assuming it was her wake-up call, she picked the receiver, managing a sleepy "hello" into it.

"Good morning, Ms. Cotton. There is a gentleman here to see you. Would you like to meet him downstairs, or shall I have him escorted up?" Not comfortable with entertaining strangers, that too a man, she asked for him to be informed to wait, till she came to the lobby to meet.

Diana wore a long A-line skirt with a vegetable-dyed turmeric *kurta*, her heels clicking on entering the lobby. "Someone's here to see me?" she asked the receptionist, who quickly escorted her to the heavily built man, on the couch.

"Sir, Ms. Cotton is here to meet you" The gentleman stood up, letting the magazine he was glancing through, fall to the side. "Ms. Cotton, my apologies and condolences" he said, holding her hand sandwiched between both of his podgy ones.

"And you are?" "I'm Mr. Sahu, Madame's lawyer. We spoke last night if you recall" "Oh, yes. Please have a seat. What can I do for you?" "I'm sorry to come at a time like this, but there are some pending issues that need Madame's immediate attention"

"Alright. I'm ready when you are" Shifting on his seat, Mr. Sahu cleared his throat, "My apologies Ms. Cotton. In the absence of our client, we discuss their issues with either the next of kin, or the one that holds Power of Attorney to act on their behalf. I'm sorry, but you're neither"

"Have you come here to annoy or insult me? If you have, let me tell you you're doing a very good job at it! Mia's gone. I'm handling everything hereon. If you like it, we can talk further. If you have a problem with it, then please show yourself out. Have a nice day!"

Diana got up to leave, when she was stopped by Mr. Sahu. "Do you have any proof Madame is your mother?" "I'm sure I do somewhere. I'll have to look for it" she said. "Ms. Cotton, you are Gerard Cotton's daughter"

"But you're not Ramona Rai's daughter. All your documents, you half-sister's and Madame's are with me. She had them transferred from the Cotton family's lawyer to my firm" Watching her fall down on the sofa, Mr. Sahu spoke with as much softness as his broad voice could hold.

"I'll wait for a few days, put all urgent matters on hold. I'm sorry I had to break the news to you this way. If there is anything I can do, let me know" "Yes, you can. You can show me the files that pertain to me alone. Leave them at the hotel reception. I have to be at the hospital"

She left for Lilavati, biting her fingernails all the way. If Mia were there, she would have slapped her palm. "It's not ladylike Diana. Besides, it's a sign of nervousness" Simple things reminded her of Mia.

She had family. Ramona was her mother. How could she not? Mia would have told her at some point. If it were true, who was her mother, then? The questions kept swimming in her mind till she reached the hospital.

The hotel called her before she could enter the room Ramona had been shifted to. "Ms. Cotton, there are some faxes that have come for you" "Send them to the hospital. I'll send you the number of the fax machine"

When Diana took the handful of sheets, she sat to stare at them for a long, long time. She held her Birth Certificate, her hands shaking so hard that it was a task to hold on to. Her father was Gerard Cotton.

Her mother was Isabella Jones. She remembered the nurse who took care of her and Mia. Her mother was just like that lady? Why didn't anyone tell her? She wanted to shake the woman who lay in front of her, attached to tubes and respirators, on the hospital bed.

Her world came crashing down in an instant, with no one to hold her up. She called the only person she knew Mia trusted, completely. "Arjun Uncle, this is Diana. Can I speak to you if you're not too busy?"

She told him everything that had happened, leaving him speechless as to how low Ramona could fall. Mia had told Arjun herself during their drive alone, but to hear it from Diana was heart-breaking. "Do you want to come stay with us, *beti*?" he offered kindly.

"No, thank you. I've to learn to live alone. I'm an orphan as I just found out. I need to deal with it by myself" She hung up, walked out to the window, looking at the world outside. She was to dive into a sea of people, who she could never get herself to trust again.

For the first time in her life, she wished she were never born. Feeling helpless, she sat back on the chair, dozing off while surfing the channels on television, wishing she could switch modes in real life as smoothly.

# CHAPTER TWENTY NINE

Nandish was up earlier than usual the next morning. He had a few pics picked up by Bantu from Maya's Reality. Abhi chose to accompany the masterpieces of the new collection on Suhani's insistence.

Andy borrowed Arjun's Nikon D3S for a better zoom and picture quality. Arjun never lent his camera to anyone as a rule, but he made an exception this time so that Andy's confidence remained intact.

There were sheer-snow silk curtains in tissue and lace, that the gallery picture display area had in several places, on a permanent basis. Andy had four fan blowers on stands, put in a cross with his favourite piece, first.

It was an enormous neckpiece in silver, of antique design, with a sunflower at the centre, made of Belgian glass. Tiny *ghunghroo*s added to the ethnic charm as well as the length, attached deftly to the lower half of the flower.

Once the blowers were switched on, it looked like a very windy day. Andy got to work, grabbing his chance to make magic. He clicked several angles of the neckpiece, that was placed on a wooden chair.

It was propped up with a black appointment diary. The faux leather sheen complimented the silver and glass perfectly. The curtains added that extra bit of feminine touch for class and finesse.

Three slim watches in rubies, emeralds and *kundan* with dainty dials of different shapes were to be shot next. He rolled up a calendar, winding up a lace curtain carelessly around ; placing all three watches in such a way, that the dates on the calendar peeked out through the lace, but the focus remained on the dazzling timepieces with their glittering jewels.

The four rings he was given were all floral. He got fountain pens from Arjun's office, removed their caps, slipping in the rings into the pen's bodies. They were made to stay standing, spread like an open palm with fingers wide apart.

Luckily, he had all pens in silver or white, so the rings were once again accentuated. "Something's not right, still" Andy murmured, looking around him for the missing piece of the puzzle.

"Put the cover boxes you got along, Abhi" Once the pretty boxes were placed in front, the shots were taken. The *Maharani* or the Queen's necklace in rubies with the square centre neckpiece, had *navratnas* or nine gems embedded in them.

Little pearls and emeralds hung freely at the lower half of the square centre, to add colour and charm to the entire look of the piece. Andy shot the necklace that was fitted on the edge of the dull golden-beige sofa, in the private enclosure of Arjun's office.

The window was open, rewarding them with rays that reflected on the piece well, making it dazzle almost as if it were alive. The rattlesnake design of multifaceted precious stones had seven lines of sapphires, rubies, emeralds and topaz.

Andy opened the window, hanging it on the knob outside. He sat on the sill and clicked the piece several times again. The last to be shot were a pair of ethnic earrings or *jhoomka*s. Silver pieces with blue *meenakari*, had agate stones circling the lower half of each earring.

He fit them on the tissue curtain in the conference room that was steel grey. Paperclips held them steadfast as the blowers, this time two only, were switched on. Once this shot was complete, Andy declared the shoot over.

"If you don't have any plans for lunch, we could grab a bite together" Abhi did have to get back, but he decided to spend more time with his future brother-in-law, for now. From what Annie had told him, he had come out from quite a pickle smoothly.

Abhi needed some pointers as well because he was getting pretty close to the pickle zone himself! He hoped Annie would be as understanding the day the truth revealed itself. "Burgers or pizza?" Andy asked.

"Anything will do. I've to be back within the hour though" Waiting for their lunch, both men began to talk about the shoot, then moved to Annie and finally to Andy's forgiven fiasco. "Must have been hard on the family. You must've had sleepless nights too" Abhi empathized.

"Until one isn't in the situation, one can never even remotely fathom. I hope you never reach the point I was in" Andy wished. "Too late, brother. Same shoes, same size!" "Do you want to talk about it?" Andy offered.

He knew he shouldn't speak to Andy before he had a chance to talk to Annie, but the burden was too much to hold on to any longer. "It's not that bad. You've withheld information, not participated in corporate espionage"

"And Annie? Will she be as understanding?" Abhi voiced his biggest concern. "She'll be hurt at first. Never tell her you've told me. I suggest you tell her as fast as possible, to clear the air. There's no right time to be truthful" Andy's words hit home.

Abhi quickly ate up his pan pizza, leaving with the jewellery collection for Maya's Reality. "*Baasa?*" "Abhi! After so long! How're you, *betaji?*" "*Baasa*, I called to tell you, that I'm telling Sarvani everything today"

"This hide and seek game is not meant for people like me" Silence on the other side, compelled Abhi to ask "*Baasa*, are you there?" "Yes, I am. Can't you wait a bit longer? Her parents are about to come before which I have a transaction, that is just about to conclude"

"No, *Baasa*. Forgive me, but my mind is made up" "I thought this is what you wanted" "Things have changed. I'll call you later" Hanging up, Dr. Shekhawat called his lawyer. "Mr. Patil, push for the takeover or withdraw completely"

"Sir, the gallery owner wants a merger, not a takeover. He's ready to meet you anytime, if you agree" "Alright. I'll come to Delhi tomorrow. Meet me at his office at the gallery, in the morning. Keep me informed, in case there's any change" Arjun had a lazy morning with Suhani, both lost in their own world where dreams were far rosier than reality.

They left for their respective offices, promising to return earlier than usual to slip into their dreamland once again. Mr. Guha walked into Arjun's office, before he even had a chance to sit. "Good morning, Sir. Someone called Mr. Patil has called a few times, wishing to speak with you"

"He says its urgent. I didn't give your mobile number, since I don't know who he is" "Good you didn't, Mr. Guha. My mobile was switched off anyway" Arjun said, asking him to have his *adrak ki chai* sent, with a few butter biscuits.

Arjun picked up the landline to dial the lawyer's number, but put it down a few seconds later. He chose to call from his mobile, in case the landline had been tapped. "Good morning, Mr. Pratap!"

"Good morning. You called?" "Yes, I did. I spoke to my client. He would like to meet you tomorrow morning at the gallery premise, along with me. As you know he lives out of Delhi, so.."

"Alright. No need to inform anyone else. Also, maintain this number to pick up and leave information. The gallery lines are under repair" "*Baasa*, I need to show you something" Dhanush walked in just then.

"Now is the right time, so go on ahead" Arjun said encouragingly. Dhanush showed the finished slides of the theme they had chosen eons ago- **Regressive Progression**. "I'll watch them with your mother in the evening again. She'd like to look at them too"

"Are they like you had envisioned?" "Yes *beta*, they are. Dhanush, I'm sorry for being hard on you at times. I won't be around forever, so I keep trying to perfect you" "It's alright, *Baasa*. You're my father, well within your rights to treat me any way you choose"

"You're not a little boy anymore. Your marriage is to be fixed soon. Are you ready to start your own family with Leenata?" "I truly am. I've grown a lot, knowing Leena will be with me through thick and thin. If I make a mistake, I know you'll watch over me"

Arjun called *Chaudhary* Akash to ask how Ajju was doing, after his talk with Dhanush was over. "He's better today. He's gone off with his camera alone. I've sent two men at a distance, to watch over him" "Alright. Tell him I called and that his *Maasa* and I miss him very much"

Dr. Shekhawat called Sangharsh Anand at his office, introducing himself as Abhimanyu's father. "I'm coming to Delhi on business tomorrow. Is it possible to meet you someplace?" he asked, sipping his hot coffee before ringing for the next set of patients, to be permitted into his doctor's chambers.

"We'll be happy to meet you at home. Please have lunch with us. Would you like to stay the night?" Sangharsh suggested. "I've to get back to Jaipur. The clinic invariably malfunctions without me!" the doctor replied, showing he too had a jovial side, just like Sangharsh did.

The busybodies of the city of Delhi were engrossed in their work the rest of the day, losing track of time until the sun had set on the concrete jungle. Abhimanyu had tied up to take Sarvani out for dinner.

He had his navy blue suit on, which Annie liked best on him. Annie was wearing a floral halter-neck dress, looking like Audrey Hepburn, with her hair up in a satin pushpin. They drove to the newly-opened 'Punjabi Tadka' restaurant *dhaba,* where the seating was outside under dull, lit Chinese paper lanterns.

Most of the conversation hovered around Annie's now ready doll collection. She had to wait for Andy to have the photo-shoot, now that he had completed that of Maya's Reality. "I was with him during the shoot, Annie"

"Your brother is a genius! The way he put the pieces, was like an artist painting on canvas" Abhi described what he saw at the gallery, making Annie feel proud of her twin's achievement. Their dinner was a simple butter chicken with *tandoori roti,* since Annie was a fussy eater, as Abhi had grown to love, as one of her many quirks.

"Speaking of the gallery, I've to tell you something. Just promise me there'll be no violent reaction to it" Abhi said, breaking his hot *jalebi* into the cold milk bowl. Annie assured him she was in a good mood.

"The biggest problem your mother has had is that I'm Suhani Ma'am's assistant. The second biggest problem she has had is that I'm not rich enough for you, considering your family is quite wealthy; am I right?"

"True. But it's all in the past now. My parents have accepted you, in case you haven't noticed" "I have noticed, Annie. But there was a time when what I just said was how they felt. Now, my father is a doctor in Jaipur who owns his clinic"

"What you don't know is that he is one of the richest men in Rajasthan because he runs the Shekhawati Group, a series of clinics built only within the state itself" Annie looked at him, leaving her dessert aside.

"Why didn't you tell me this earlier? When we began dating you…" "Annie, I left Jaipur because I was sick of being treated as the prince, the heir to the throne. I never wanted to be a doctor, which disappointed my father"

"He thought I would handle the business, so I told him I'd work for a business house in Delhi to gain some experience. I came here under the pretext of learning to be a Hospital Administrator, but didn't get a job anywhere. Maya's Reality had an opening, so I decided to give it a shot. I haven't looked back ever since"

"Does your father know you're an assistant in a jewellery house?" "Yes. Another disappointment for him, I'm sure" "Is that all? That you stem from a rich family?" Annie asked. "Not really. *Baasa* has been looking for investment in Delhi"

"His lawyer suggested a couple of places like restaurants, stores, galleries. Since I've been keen on photography as a hobby, he thought of a photo gallery" Annie's sixth sense had forewarned her where the conversation was leading to, but she wanted to let Abhi finish before jumping to any conclusions.

"The Dare to Dream gallery was well within budget and prime time property to invest in as well" "You mean to say your father has been the secret client who made his lawyer communicate with Arjun *Chachu*?"

Abhi was caught off guard this time. "You know?" "Of course! Andy is my twin. We tell each other almost everything" "Annie, *Baasa* is coming to Delhi to meet Mr. Pratap at his office, with his lawyer"

"But what will happen to Andy, Ajju *Bhaiya*, Arjun *Chachu*? Does he want to breakdown DTD?" she asked, hoping she was wrong. "Of course not! You know I won't let him do that" Annie was quiet, checking the length of her fingernails, until Abhi paid the bill.

"You're quiet, baby. Talk to me" "Abhi, you made me believe you were a struggling youngster who was working hard to make it big. I should be mad at you, but I'm not. Do you know why?" "The fact that you've taken all of this so well, is blessing enough!"

"You told me something just now that makes me proud. Not wanting to be treated like the heir to the throne. I know how it feels being treated as someone born with a silver spoon. When I became Head Designer at Anand Creations, Andy got to follow his dream of being a photographer"

"My dream had to be locked up because I was trying to be fair to my parents. And then…you came along. Your constant encouragement gave me the boost I required to follow my dream too" Sitting in the parking lot, Abhi watched Annie express her heart to him.

"You're the one for me, Sarvani Anand. I know I said we won't get engaged, but propose I will. Right here, right now!" Bending on one knee, Abhi began his journey into manhood. "Sarvani Anand, I've loved you more and more each day"

"You've been caring, loving, understanding throughout. You love me for all my flaws and I love all your crazy quirks. Calling me in the middle of work because you finished the dress of a doll, forgetting to take off your glasses like right now, puckering up your nose…I love all of that"

"Will you let me love you till eternity? Marry me, Annie!" She had the broadest smile on her lips, the sweetest of tears that rolled down her delicate cheeks. She squeaked a weak 'yes', her vigorous head nod untangling her hair, making the curls fly everywhere.

The cool evening breeze brought the two close enough for their lips to touch briefly, sealing the promise they made silently to each other. They sped off for a drive, before he could drop her at the Anand villa.

Annie skipped into the balcony, knowing her father would never sleep till she got home. She saw Andy standing with him as well. Racing up the stairs, Annie gave them the news of Abhi's proposal.

They looked happy for her, but it wasn't as enthusiastic as she wanted them to be. "What's wrong?" she asked bluntly. "Did Abhimanyu tell you why his father chose DTD of all photo galleries in Delhi to buy out?"

"Of course he did. It was the only one within budget, since it isn't doing as well as some of the other galleries. Plus, the property it stands on is worth a fortune" "Sounds plausible to me, *Baasa*" Andy chipped in.

"To me too. But the coincidence is a bit too much to digest" "How is the doctor supposed to know the connection?" "I don't have all the answers, Nandish!" Putting her purse down to pull a chair, Annie spoke to both.

"What's going on? Fill me in right this second. If it has to do with Abhi, I have the right to be a part of it" Sangharsh told her what someone he had entrusted to find out who Mr. Patil's client was, had informed him.

Abhi's father was a very rich doctor who resides in Jaipur. He also has a son who works in Delhi. Prior to all of this, many years ago, he was the doctor who said he couldn't do anything for *Chaudhary* Dhanush at Pushkar after the camel race accident.

He had returned to Bassi, since he opened a branch of his hospital nearby at Chittorgarh. Annie's hands began to grow cold. "What does all this have to do with my Abhi?"

"Nothing. But it may have something to do with the gallery" The conversation was abruptly ended, but Sangharsh knew it was time to talk to Arjun. Dr. Shekhawat had been spotted with a lady very often time and again.

This lady was not of any city, but a village. She was known to control his life and finances through her feminine charms to keep him enticed, obedient. Tara was smarter than she looked, Sangharsh thought.

He had photographic evidence and sent it to Arjun immediately, faxing it to his locked office. The message read 'Stall the merger. Introduce me as the lawyer. Let's get to the bottom of this'. The mystery had to be cleared and Sangharsh hoped his daughter was going to a sane, stable family.

The fax lay at the floor as Sangharsh messaged Arjun's cell. 'Reach earlier than anyone else at DTD in the morning. Call me en route'. Sangharsh hoped Arjun would play along the next day. He wanted to find out the truth for himself as a father, and for Arjun as a good friend.

# CHAPTER THIRTY

The mornings when lovers wake up to each other is termed in their own words as paradise. Arjun loved waking up to Suhani's gentle breath on his chest. She looked peaceful, when in his arms.

The previous night, they stayed awake till late, watching the finalized photographs Dhanush had given him of Bassi. Suhani greedily watched the entire slide show many times over, admiring the pictures taken, voicing her pride of the place they were taken in.

They'd also discussed the meeting at Arjun's office, with Mr. Patil and his mysterious outstation client. "I thought you had told him to reveal his client's identity?" she asked, gently running her fingers through his hair.

"I did. Tomorrow I will get to know anyway. Besides, I could always refuse" Arjun justified. It was then that they received Sangharsh's message, beginning to wonder how he fit into the picture.

Choosing to untangle all the knots in the coming day, they satiated their desire for each other, sleeping off blissfully, without a care in the world. Arjun remembered he had to reach the gallery earlier than everyone else.

He got ready without waking Suhani up and drove off in Ajju's Eco Sport. Following Sangharsh's instructions, he called from the car. "Hey, hi!" "Hi, hey! Where are you, dude?" "On the way to the gallery, like you said"

"Get here faster then, because I am parked outside!" "What? I thought you're coming later" "I thought I would too, but it's better this way" A few traffic lights, unruly vehicles and honking horns later, Arjun reached the gallery.

They walked in together straight to his office, where Sangharsh briefed him on the information he had on Dr. Shekhawat. "Small world! He is to be your *Samdhi*?" "We'll see after this meeting is concluded. I don't want to marry my daughter into a dubious household!"

Understanding the concern of a father, Arjun dialed a number from his cell. "I'm calling my lawyer to be present at the meeting too. Just hope Mr. Yadav isn't busy" "Hang up. I'm the lawyer for today" Sangharsh said, pulling a chair to sit on.

"You!" "Yes, me!" "You're joking, right? Since when did you start practicing law?" "A fake lawyer if you must know, Arjun. Listen, the doctor has never seen me. We've spoken only once. I'll introduce myself as Mr. Yadav, your lawyer"

"Let me see how he is and accordingly accost him with the information we have" "Tara is just a coincidental link, Sangharsh. What could she possibly want with DTD?" "I do have a theory in place, albeit long shot. Let's wait for the duo, until then"

Both friends had an hour more to kill, before their guests would arrive. Mr. Guha and Bantu were there already, but they weren't surprised to see Sangharsh with Arjun, as it had happened several times earlier as well.

Arjun showed Sangharsh the pictures of Bassi, that had been finalized for display. There were no snaps of Mia in a few of the group pictures though. Sensing this, Arjun clarified, "Ajju has the ones that have her in the shots"

"Dhanush couldn't bring himself to ask for them" Realizing he hadn't spoken about Mia at all, Sangharsh enquired. "How're you coping?" "I saw her when she was an infant. The next time as a young lady" Arjun said honestly.

"Feels like I've lost two people I'd grown to love" he replied, staring at his friend. "I'm here if you need me for anything, anytime" Sangharsh said, meaning every word of it. "I know. I do have other things on my mind, too"

"Such as?" "I've filed for divorce. The court date was delayed because of Ramona's accident" "Don't have compassion for the enemy, Arjun" Sangharsh said curtly. "I don't. But if she refuses like her lawyer said she might, it could go on for a long time. What'll happen to Suhani and I?"

"That's far-off thinking. Deal with the now first. When Ramona comes around, she will be a changed person. Mia's loss must have hit her as well" Agreeing, they sipped their coffee until Dr. Shekhawat walked in with his lawyer, Mr. Patil.

"Good morning, Mr. Pratap! I'm Dr. Shekhawat. This is my lawyer, Mr. Patil" Pleasantries were exchanged wherein the fake Mr. Yadav was introduced. The fax that Sangharsh had sent to Arjun the previous night, was kept face down on the table along with a pile of books on photography.

The doctor looked like a friendly, down-to-earth, fun-loving man. Adding to the list of mysteries was, how a person like Tara managed to get to him. "Let's get to business now, shall we?" Arjun said, after tea and snacks had been served.

"Sure. I'm on a deadline too. I've a lunch to go to" Smiling, Arjun asked him point blank. "Why did you choose my gallery to invest in, when there are other bigger, better galleries doing well in the city?"

"Yours was within my budget, from the approximate estimation of sale given to me by my financial consultant. Apparently your gallery value has depreciated, because you are a better photographer than a businessman"

Handing over the torch, Arjun said, "My lawyer would like to ask you a few questions, if you don't mind" "Absolutely. Clarity is crucial, if this business deal has to come through" the doctor insisted.

"This is being considered as a merger, not a takeover. I hope that's clear?" Arjun reiterated, looking at his potential partner. "Yes, understood" the doctor answered, turning towards Sangharsh. "What are your future plans with DTD?"

"To bring it back to what it used to be" "So you're interested in photography?" "Yes, courtesy my son. He work for a silver jewellery house as an assistant, although he left Jaipur saying he'll find work as a Hospital Administrator"

"Kids of this generation have smartened up. He mustn't have gotten a job at any of the hospitals, so he decided to choose a job that sustained him, growing to enjoy it in the bargain" "You're probably right, Mr. Yadav"

"I still don't get why my boy had to leave his home at Jaipur, come here, lead a common life" "It is the makings of a great man, to leave his home to preserve self-worth. You're lucky for not having an offspring, that squanders your hard-earned money" Arjun said.

"That is true as well. He is very secretive though. Hardly tells me anything about his life here at the city. He told me he likes a girl, wants to marry her…" Watching him speak freely, both Arjun and Sangharsh realized Dr. Shekhawat was an honest, upfront man.

"Sir…" Mr. Patil, his lawyer got him back to business. "Just one more" Sangharsh pushed the photograph of the doctor with Tara, that he had faxed earlier. The poor man turned white as a sheet, shifting on his seat uncomfortably.

"Where did you get this? Have you been tracking me?" he asked on regaining composure. "It is every father's business to conduct a thorough background check, when it comes to a family his daughter plans to marry into"

"Surveillance without legal permission is an offence!" Mr. Patil objected, attempting to protect his client. "Wait, Mr. Patil. Mr. Anand is your client too, Mr. Yadav?" he asked, looking at Sangharsh.

"No. I am Sangharsh Anand, father of Sarvani Anand. Abhimanyu works for Arjun's wife Suhani's jewellery store, as her assistant" The raining bullet-like information seemed to surprise the doctor at the odd point.

"Suhani? He said Maya" "Yes. Maya's Reality has Maya as the owner. She had her name changed when she came from her village Bassi" "Bassi! That is where Tara is from!" "That is right. Suhani Pratap used to be *Chaudhrain* of the *Raika*s of Bassi and the *Banjara*s of Nagri Suhani Chand, *Chaudhary* Dhanush Chand's *lugai*"

The doctor looked stunned to the core. "I was his doctor at Pushkar. Tara came to me a few months later to ask for a loan. I used to give out loans to poor villagers in Jaipur and found myself in love with her"

"She used to visit on a monthly basis. I was a lonely widower since Abhimanyu was born. As I'm not blessed with looks such as the two of you, it was flattering to get the attention of such a beautiful woman as Tara"

Gulping water to soothe his parched throat, he continued, "I asked her several times to leave her husband, but she refused, saying her children were to be her legacy. She began to show interest in my business expansions in terms of opening hospitals all over the state of Rajasthan"

"One day, she asked me to start investing in land in metropolitan cities outside the state. Delhi being the closest, we chose to begin here. Abhi's interest in photography meant, I needed to look for a photo gallery, that he could perhaps own someday"

"It's better than being an assistant in a jewellery house. No offence meant" "None taken" Arjun replied, nodding at Sangharsh. "We think Tara has an ulterior motive to push you into focusing on DTD, doctor" Sangharsh declared, matching his honesty.

"She doesn't come across as scheming to me, Mr. Anand" "That is a trait women have. Cloak their true identity with what they intend their victims to see. The only way as I see for the truth to reveal itself, is if the merger does come through"

All parties got their minds together collectively and agreed in plain terms on a partnership of fifty-fifty. The Shekhawati Group would finance all of DTD's ventures, Arjun would retain his status as the owner with a slight correction of Joint Owner now.

The doctor was asked not to breathe a word of Tara's link to anyone, to which he agreed. Scandal was bad for his business as his impeccable reputation was now at stake, not to mention Abhimanyu's future with the Anands' daughter.

Nalini was at home with Annie to welcome Abhimanyu and his father for lunch. Sangharsh landed up along with the doctor, declaring what a small world it was after all. He also spoke of the merger, careful to leave out the Tara angle.

Everyone was happy with how things worked out and the families blessed the young couple. Nalini and Dr. Shekhawat decided to check with their *kul pundit*s, when the marriage could take place.

"Mrs. Anand, we want a plain court marriage followed by a *phera* ceremony. Nothing elaborate, please" "You won't deprive a mother of realizing her dream of dressing her only daughter up in bridal finery and getting her married the traditional way, would you?"

"Besides, we could use a change of scene with all the court marriages, including ours!" Annie looked at the family who sat in front of her, nodding her consent to Abhi. "Nothing over the top though" he still insisted.

Sangharsh called Arjun and Suhani to give them the good news. They expressed joy on Annie's betrothal, beginning to think it was time for them to go to Bassi for the dates they needed to know. Dhanush and Leenata had to be married at Bassi, as per *Chaudhary* Akash's insistence.

The Prataps were okay with the suggestion. Back at the Lilavati hospital, a dragon was awakening from one, long slumber. "Water.." came a feeble voice from Ramona. Diana jumped out of her single sofa, by her mother's bedside.

"Water.." Ramona mumbled through cracked, parched lips. "Here" Diana gave her a sip from the disposable glass after propping her up on a pillow. "How do you feel?" "Like I've been hit by a truck" she answered slowly.

"How are you, Mia?" Choosing not to correct her, she said, "I'm fine. Let me get the doctor" she said. Diana ran down the hallway, to the nurse who knew where all doctors- on -call were. She then found the one detailed for her mother.

Dr. Krishnan was sipping his black tea, reading the newspaper, when Diana found him in the cafeteria. "Dr. Krishnan?" "Yes?" "I'm Ramona Cotton's daughter. She is awake!" "That's great. Why don't you chat her up?"

"I'll join you both shortly. She could use exercising her vocal chords after the long silence" "Doctor, I need to ask you if you're aware she was in an accident where I lost my sister, Mia Cotton"

"Yes, I am aware of everything. Sorry for your loss, dear child" Exasperated Diana came right to the point. "She's just called me Mia!" Frowning, Dr. Krishnan shut his newspaper, put his stethoscope around his neck and left at a quick pace for the patient's room.

"Mother.." "Mia, where did you go?" "I got the doctor. I told you before I left" "Doctor, my daughter was in the same accident. I want to see her. Try as I might, I want to open my eyes, but they don't seem to open!" Ramona said, frustrated at her fumbling.

Dr. Krishnan and Diana looked at each other. He walked up to her, pulled out a pencil torch from his pocket and shone it into her eyes. "Anything?" "Anything what?" "Madame, your eyes are wide open" "What? Mia is that true?"

"Yes, it is" "Nothing to panic about. Sometimes traumatic situations make part of our body mechanisms dysfunctional. We'll conduct a few tests and then take a call" he said, walking off to make preparations for the same.

"Mia.." "Yes, Mother" Diana sat beside her on the bed. Ramona caught her hand, feeling her face quickly. "Not a scratch on your beautiful face, my darling child! What a relief! Where's Diana?"

"She should be here too. If you're looking after me, she should be looking after you!" "Diana has gone out of town for a few days, Mother. She needed a break" "A break? We were in an accident that almost killed us and she needs the break?"

"This is what happens when you raise a thankless child. To think she is the daughter of a two-bit nurse and prances around saying I am her mother!"

Ramona's contorted expression showed the ugly side of her, "She loves you though, you know"

"She better! Everything she eats, wears, sleeps on, is mine. It's my money that she enjoys. I kept her for your company. Now look how she has repaid us" The doctor was back with a wheelchair and attendant, to take her for the tests that needed to be conducted.

The moment she was wheeled away, Diana called Arjun. She briefed him on the latest, wondering what to do next. "She'll ask you where Ajju is next. Tell her he is with me as of now. The only one I see who can be a potential threat is her lawyer, Mr. Sahu"

"Let her keep calling you Mia. Take care of yourself. Let me know when you get the results. I'm sending Bantu with some things for you. Take care, Diana" She spoke to Vansh next: her constant and credible companion, her sole source of strength.

"I think the Prataps are coming to Bassi along with the Anands, the day after tomorrow. Can you come?" he asked, hoping against hope that she would agree. "How can I? It's too early. She can't see and the tests will show how she fares"

"Fine then. Either you come here or I'm coming there. If you can't come here, you know what the other option is" Diana started sniffing, ready to cry. "Alright, I'll be there by the evening. Have me booked in the same hotel as yours" he said.

Diana was happy to have Vansh around at a time like this. Off late she'd been feeling lonely. Every time he called her, she felt like she mattered, was counted, was alive. An hour and a half later, Dr. Krishnan led the way.

"As of now, Ms. Cotton, your mother has lost her vision temporarily. There is no damage to the eyes whatsoever. But, the concussion to the head and neck seems to have jolted a nerve. By God's grace, her eyesight should return over time with good food and rest"

Thanking the doctor, Diana called Arjun again, transferring the information to him. "Shall I come there to give you company?" he asked. "No, Uncle. Vansh should be here by the evening. He said he doesn't want me to be alone, at a time like this. He also said you might be going to Bassi soon"

"Day after tomorrow to be precise. Take care of yourself, *beti*" That evening, Vansh reached the hospital directly to find his Jiya seeing the pictures of Bassi, which had Mia that were sent by Arjun through Bantu. She fell into Vansh's arms crying at a past that never was for her…a future that never will be for Mia, her sister.

She stood at a juncture in her life where all that mattered to her, that she identified as her own, was snatched away untimely in a cruel twist of fate. What she had left now was a barren land that couldn't even grow weeds.

She had nowhere to start from, knowing one day Ramona would know she was not Mia. That day she would lose her forever, severing the last tie that bound her to the concept of a family. Now, she felt like a complete, isolated, orphan.

# CHAPTER THIRTY ONE

Thick twigs, thin branches of the acacia, *kikar* trees, were dried to be used as four-poster holders for the tarpaulin roof for the village folk to sit under. They needed to keep a watch at all times, when the cattle were grazing.

There were sightings of hyenas, leopards which hunted the bovines as prey. A man with a camera was clicking pictures of a group of young children, muddy from playing on the sandy terrain, laughing at him with his camera.

He recalled how he used to play with his friends in the same place, how his mother would yell at him for being late for Gurukul, how his father would insist on him learning more and more each day.

"*Aap Ajju Bhaiya hai na*? (Are you Ajju?)" a shy girl in an almost brownish *ghaghra choli* that used to be orange once, asked. "*Haan*" he said. "What's your name?" "Dhara" the little girl replied.

Before he could compliment her, the group of children yelled for her. "Come *Ajju Bhaiya,* play with us!" She invited the six-foot hulk to join them.. Smiling at her generosity as she gave the torn rubber ball for *pithoo*, Ajju conceded.

He ran behind them, as they squealed and dispersed. Their giggles permeated into his skin, laughter washing away the tears his sorrows had brought him. He chased each and every one of the little players, gently hitting the ball on their legs so as not to hurt them.

"Wow that was great! Thank you for letting me join your game" he said, pulling out his handkerchief to wipe his sweat. "Dhara! Come along! *Chachi* is calling you for the noon meal" The shrill voice of a female caught his attention. Before he could turn to see who it was, Dhara rushed past him and toppled the big man over.

Sunlight hit his face as he tried to cover his eyes from the glare. "*Baasa* used to say, that a man who has his foothold strong on the ground, will never know how it feels like to have his back on the earth!"

The silhouette of a village belle was all Ajju could make out, who laughed as if nothing else mattered. In an instant, she ran off as an elderly woman, perhaps the same *Chachi* she referred to earlier, bellowed for her.

Dusting himself, he got up, but the girl was nowhere to be seen. Shrugging, he went to the *Chaudhary haveli* to have his noon meal too. "I'm hungry. What's cooking?" he asked Leenata, who was elated Ajju finally spoke, that too to her.

"I made some of your favourites-*gobi paratha*s with *alu ki sabzi..*" "Sounds great" Taking in all of Ajju covered from top to toe in dirt, Leenata asked, "Did you fall down?" "Not exactly. I was pushed down"

He walked in to wash up, had a quick smoke and came downstairs to the courtyard. He heard the same voice chatting with Leenata. His pace quickened, as did his heart. He wanted to see her face, ask her name.

"Here he is. Give it to him yourself" Leenata said. The girl turned to face him shyly, extending one hand. "You dropped your camera" A forest-green *odhni* covered her forehead, a flirty yellow *ghaghra choli* draped around her nymph-like figure.

He took the camera and thanked her. She stood for a few seconds more, just to run away abruptly. "How do you do it in the village? Talk to a woman, I mean" he asked Leenata, after their noon meal was over.

"Just like in the city, I guess. Introduce yourself and expect one in return" she smiled, saying, "Her name is Rati. She is the blind *Daisa*'s granddaughter; the one who raised *Chaudhary* Dhanush Chand.. And she has no one but Dhara, her younger sister"

"Her entire family was wiped out in one of the desert storms, including *Daisa*" Feeling sorry for her, Ajju chose to rest a bit and switched on his camera. Apparently it had been fiddled with, as there were several hazy shots.

He stopped at one, then two. He saw Rati's face, clicked probably by her sister Dhara. She had the kind of, smile that made you want to smile back. Drifting off to sleep, he dreamt of Aradhana. They were talking normally at first, but an argument ensued soon thereafter.

Waking up with a start, he realized his siesta was over. He left again, this time with the intention of sitting by the calm water of the River Bhairach. He watched how the waters became like liquid Mercury, as the sun played with its sparkle.

The other side of the lake had lush greenery, short bushes being devoured by a handful of cows and horses. "*Bas, bas! Ghar chalo* (Enough already! Let's go home!) He heard her again. She had no *odhni*, but wore the same *ghaghra choli*.

Her hair was freshly washed and open. He zoomed his camera, as she tried to get her animals to obey her. He smiled at how she laughed at the foal, who kept trying to nibble, despite her pulling it away from the shrub he was feasting on.

She turned to go, when her *ghaghra* got stuck in a few horns jutting out of the bush. Bending down, she noticed the camera flash and turned. He was clicking away at the glorious beauty of the nymph-like creature.

She picked a stone and threw it in the water, expressing her annoyance. Ajju ran all the way to the rickety wooden bridge, till he caught up with her. "*Ruko*! (Wait!)" he yelled, as she quickened her pace on seeing him.

"Rati!" she stopped immediately and turned to him. "What else did she tell you?" Rati asked, still pulling the foal. "Can I help with that?" he asked, pointing at the stubborn foal. "You can't even hold your ground. How can you pull a foal, when a little girl dropped you?"

He didn't mind her laughing, but gave her a stern look. "That was because I was caught off-guard. You are not that smart either, by the way. Throwing a stone from a distance, when it was bound to fall into the lake"

"If I were aiming, I would never miss" "Well then, I am glad you weren't" Gaining half a smile from her, he remembered Leenata's words. "Hi, I am A.J. or Ajju. My real name is Arjun" "You have three names?" she asked, surprise showing in her eyes.

He didn't notice how clear the white of her eyes were earlier. An *odhni* he saw Leenata wear, would have matched the colour of her eyes well-cornflower blue. Just like..Mia! Guilt raced up and down his spine.

What was he doing? It had hardly been a few weeks since his wife had passed away unnaturally, in a tragic road accident. "Why do you grow so quiet, Ajju?" she asked him. "You reminded me of someone"

"Really? Who?" "My wife" Horror, anger shot through her blue eyes. "A man who already has a wife oughtn't ever to look at any other woman" she said, reprimanding him with her words. "Let me guess…your *Baasa* used to say that?" he said, smiling at her again.

"Stop smiling at me all the time!" You don't like it, Rati?" "I don't think your wife would like it either!" she said, running away. Ajju didn't follow her because his legs turned to lead, rooting him still on the ground.

He went straight back to the *haveli*, this time remembering to take his camera back with him. Leenata had just finished speaking to Dhanush and looked fresh as a daisy. "Ajju *Bhaiya*, I just spoke to Dhanush"

"They're coming here the day after tomorrow!" she said, aching to see her beloved again. "That's good" Ajju's flat reply clearly indicated he was disturbed about something. Leenata left him alone with his thoughts.

He looked like he had some serious thinking to do. Climbing the staircase with the *gerua* boundary, Ajju met *Chaudhary* Akash. "Your father called me asking about you. I told him you're better today"

"Thank you, *Chachaji*" he said, walking with a slouch to his room. Vansh was waiting for him inside. His pacing showed his impatience, which stopped the moment he saw Ajju enter. "Where have you been? I've been meaning to speak with you" he said.

"Speak. I'm here" "*Bhaiya*, I have to go to Delhi. Jiya..I mean Diana is alone at the hospital. I cannot let her feel lonely, at a time like this. That crazy old lady is the only family she has" "Alright. Go then" Ajju said, wondering what the fuss was about.

Sitting down on the *baithak* by the window, Vansh's handsome features contorted into an intense frown. "It's not that simple. I can't just leave. What do I tell *Baasa*? I just came back!" Ajju lit up a smoke, began to look out of the window.

"Ajju *Bhaiya*, did you hear what I just said?" Vansh asked. "Loud and clear, Vansh. I'll speak with *Chachaji* and tell him *Baasa* wants you to come there, with regard to Leenata's wedding. I know they're finalizing where to have the wedding reception"

Exhilarated on having found a solution to his problem, Vansh hugged Ajju. "Thank you, *Bhaiya*!" He rushed out to tell his father, while Ajju quickly called his, in case *Chaudhary* Akash called him to check on the authenticity of the excuse.

"*Baasa*.." "Ajju *beta*, how are you?" "I'm fine. Better I think. How're you and *Maasa*?" "We are all fine. We've all been worried about you. Are you sure you're okay?" Assuring his father, Ajju managed to squeeze in the real reason for calling.

Arjun informed him that he was in regular touch with Diana and knew that Ramona was not her birth mother. They chatted for a while and hung up, both glad to have touched base. Ajju was going through the pictures he had clicked so far at Bassi, that evening.

There were more people than the landscape, in the shots that were taken earlier. He saw Dhara playing with her friends, laughing as the wind threw more sand on them. He saw the picture of two women, orange and red *odhni*s covering their faces partially, watching a spread cloth piece with *haldi* left out to dry.

The toddler squatting in front of them was pointing at the camera and smiling, as if only he knew the secret to that mysterious object. He was deleting the hazy shots Dhara had taken, when Rati began to show up in his pictures.

She was naturally photogenic, considering he had to have Andy spend hours on Photoshop, trying to make his models in a photo shoot look flawless. He zoomed in on one of the headshots and noticed an *Om*, at the dent on her throat.

He was aware a lot of the *Raika* tribals used tattoos to adorn their bodies, wondering why he never had one for himself. Rati's *Om* tattoo moved in the next few shots, as she breathed heavily. The desert wind had her cotton *ghaghra choli* stick on one side of her lissome figure, making her silhouette even more enticing.

Shutting his eyes, he chose to switch his camera off. Taking his headphones playing Santana's Maria, off from one ear, he heard voices near the *gulmohar* tree at the centre of the courtyard. "What do you mean it doesn't matter?"

"Of course it does! I don't want anyone assuming Rati Singh Rana is rude!" Before Leenata could stop her, Rati had raced up the stairs, bumping into Ajju standing with the headphones in one hand, camera in the other.

She head-banged his chest, making his arms cross over each other, as a defense mechanism. Seconds later, they flew away from each other. "I'm sorry!" they both apologized together. Ajju was stunned at how natural it felt, wrapping her in his arms.

Rati was shocked at how safe she felt for the first time, in a long time. "I came to say I'm sorry" "You've said it already" Ajju said, smiling at her. "No, no. This was an apology for banging into you, clumsy oaf that I am" she said, watching Ajju walk a step towards her.

"I'm not sorry, Rati. Now, tell me, are you?" Blinking hard at his insolence she said, "Leenata *di* just told me you're a widower. I'm sorry I didn't know" His expression changed again, as he turned.

"Apology accepted. Now leave me alone!" he snapped, walking away. "*Ajeeb insaan hai*! (What a strange person!) Rati said, coming down the stairs. That night, Ajju dreamt of Mia again. She was on a boat without any oars, looking into his eyes, as it floated away from him.

The strange part was, that he didn't even try to stop or talk to her. Just watched her fade away into the horizon. The early morning rooster was loud enough to get Ajju up and about. He walked right out to enjoy a run in the cool morning, when Bassi was still struggling to be awake.

He stopped near one of the wells for a sip of water before he would run all the way back to the *haveli*. He bent down as one of women poured water from her steel pot. Looking up on hearing the neigh of a horse, he saw the rider flying off from sight, like a flash of lightning.

He thanked the kind lady with a *Namaste*, jogging back through the wide alley on the peripheral boundary around Bassi, to make the trip back a bit longer. The horse-rider was trotting along the other side of the low brick wall.

"What're you running from?" Keeping his jog steady, Ajju turned to see Rati perched on her horse. "You, I think!" "Is it working?" "You caught up with me" "I sure did!" she said, stopping her horse to get down.

Ajju stopped, crossing the low wall with a sprint. He got up on Rati's horse, giving him his hand to sit behind him. She got up and they sped off to the *tila*, where the sun was just about to come up. They never spoke; just sitting there made both feel like they were a part of something big.

"I think I'm falling in love with you" Ajju said, still looking at the carnelian globe, ready to bestow its richness to the land. "I don't know what that means. I like you a lot. More than anybody else" Ajju liked her honesty.

"Haven't you ever been in love before?" he asked. "No. You have though. So, what was her name?" "Mia. She was named Aradhana after we were married" "Aradhana. I like that name" Conversing with the innocent beauty next to him, Ajju found it surprising she had never experienced love earlier.

"Rati, do you have feelings for me?" "Yes, I do" "Then say you love me" "How can I? I don't know what that means!" she said, trying to balance honesty with fairness. "Alright then. I have to go now. You go ahead. I'll walk back"

"From here? It's too far away from the *Chaudhary haveli*" she said. "My horse will take you to the *haveli*. I will go walking as my hut is close by" "Don't be silly" he scolded her. "Let's go together"

"Alright" They rode on one horse, with one stride, one movement. From afar, it seemed as if they were not two but one person. Ajju didn't want the ride to end, but the *haveli* was reached sooner than he would have wanted.

He got down gracefully, watching Rati take off, turning back once to look at him, her grin saying what her lips couldn't. Taking in the warmth of the moment, he turned away. Both were so engrossed in their new-found attraction, that they failed to notice the multi-coloured *haveli*'s terrace, where Tara witnessed the horse ride of both Ajju and Rati.

Vengeful annoyance tore through her, as she banged the washed clothes back into the steel bucket. *Chaudhary* Dhanush's son had done it again! Tara had been noticing Viren's attraction towards Rati and had spoken to her *Chachi*, who had agreed.

Tara's family was the richest in all of Bassi. Rati's *Chachi* was thrilled at the proposal, awaiting further instructions from Tara about the ceremonies to be followed. Her convoluted logic tried to justify Ajju's popping up every time she thought about her son, time and again.

It was almost as if Ajju's father *Chaudhary* Dhanush was watching over him, snatching something from her son Viren in the bargain. Ajju got ready for breakfast, smiling at Leenata, when he met her. "Well?" she asked.

"Well, what?" he asked innocently, munching on some delicious *papad*. "Where did you meet her today? You have that smile you get when you see her!" "You're a nosey Parker, aren't you?" Ajju said, pulling her ear.

She was happy Ajju was getting over Aradhana. She was happier his attention had been captured by the likes of Rati, one of the sweetest girls in

Bassi. She wished this time, Ajju *Bhaiya* stays happy, without anyone trying to deprive him of the same.

Little did she know that plotters and schemers were brewing a plan which could very well be the beginning of a raging fire that could divide the entire village of Bassi, into two parts. There was more to lose than to gain in a situation, brewing at that very moment.

Love and war are two passionate emotions with no holds barred anyway. If the signs are not paid heed to, then either of these two emotions take over as a causal force, bringing about drastic changes into the lives of those, who may not even have participated in it.

# CHAPTER THIRTY TWO

The *Chaudhary haveli* located at the centre of the village could be seen clearly from the next big house- Giriraj and Tara's. The sprawling terrace of Tara's, was big enough for Viren to play cricket with his friends in, when he was younger.

Now, it was a great place to hide with his thoughts. His father was too quiet for his own good. But, when he spoke, it was to condone an act of his son he disapproved of. How difficult was it to tend to cattle?

The stupidest cow herder could do it. Giriraj still found faults with how Viren handled them. When his father was away from him, his mother would hunt him down. Tara was over ambitious from the start.

The moment Viren was born, she knew her hopes of being somebody important had been revived. Viren was fair like she was, his thick crop of hair forever demanding to be either chopped up or tied.

Every time he would attempt to crawl to his father, Tara would pull him back. "Don't disturb your *Baasa*. He is very busy working" He heard these words over and over again, through the years.

Finally, one day during his teenage years, he gave up his methods of approaching his father simply because his mother began to poison his mind. "Have you ever seen him come to you? Why do you reach out to him?"

"I will always want what is best for you. Turn your attention towards how to become bigger, better, richer and more powerful than him. The only one who can give you all of that is Vansh, *Chaudhary* Akash's son"

Smoking on the terrace while reminiscing his journey this far, he smiled as he heard his favourite voice off late. "*Khammaosa*, Viren!" "*Khammaosa*, Rati! Where are you off to today?" "Dhara has lost one of the bells of the white cow. If I don't find the brass bell, *Chachi* says she will buy it with the money saved up for my dowry!"

Laughing, he offered to help but she said she was going by the riverside anyway, to let the cattle graze. "If I don't find it, I will let you know" Watching her walk briskly with her long stick to control all the livestock she owned, he sipped his *chai* and took another drag of his *bidi*.

"There you are! Why haven't you finished your meal, Viren?" Tara came up with her son's plate, with half-eaten *dal bati churma* still in it. "I ate as much as I needed to, *Maasa*" he answered. "Do you want some more chai?" she asked, worried he would stop talking to him as compared to earlier.

Turning around to face his mother, Viren handed her the empty *kullad*. "You'd disappear for days while *Taiji* took care of Malika and I. Then you would reappear again. Where did you go to, *Maasa*?"

"*Arre, bawle*! (Oh, you silly boy!) Your father and I always divided the work between us. How do you think we are the richest family in Bassi today? It is purely through hard work and increasing our livestock, one handful at a time"

Feeling as if she had managed to convince him, she turned to leave the terrace. "You left a few days ago again. There is no need for you to tire yourself anymore. If anyone needs to go to the city, it ought to be me"

Viren was still looking at the horizon, when Tara walked up to him. "It's a good change for me, *beta*. I'm stuck either within these four walls, or confined to the boundaries of Bassi" "Fine then. We will go together next time. *Taiji* has been trained well enough by you to take care of the household in your absence"

Cornered, Tara chose to change the topic for now. "I spoke to Rati's *Chachi* about your *rishta*. She has agreed and wants to know when the *pundit* will read out the auspicious dates for the wedding"

She saw his expression mellow a bit, understanding his mind was on Rati now. "You've stopped riding like you used to, Viren" "I used to ride with Vansh. He has no time for me anymore" "Then go yourself. You don't need Vansh anymore"

Surprised by her change of stance he questioned, "You're saying this? After all these years, pestering me to follow him around to make myself indispensable to him?" "Yes, I am. Things have changed quite a bit, Viren"

"Have you not noticed how Vansh rejected your sister's marriage proposal, after claiming he wanted to prove his worth, by bettering the dilapidating condition on one hand; and, given the chance he got to loaf around with the *firangan* Malika saw him with, he forgot all about his promise?"

"Yes, that is true" Viren voiced his double disappointment, both as Malika's brother and as Vansh's friend. "It is also true that he will marry this city girl and move out of Bassi. That is why he left with Leenata and your sister for his trip to Delhi"

"The *Chaudhrain* is sly, Viren. She is trying to settle her children someplace, where they have a scope to prosper. They know our family is getting richer by the day. And with wealth, comes power" Viren sat down, almost done with his second *bidi*, when Tara continued to speak.

"As a parent, I have the right to want what's best for my children. Whether your sister stays here at Bassi or someplace else, I'll ensure she is well taken care of. You've never had it in you to be a follower, my son. You are a born leader!"

"Really? You think I have it in me?" "I'm as sure of it as of the fact that the sun rises every morning. All these years, I sent you behind Vansh for I wanted you to learn the ropes. With Vansh's clear involvement with the city girl, it is evident he may not settle here in the long run"

"That is one, out of the next *Chaudhary* race" "Ajju *Bhaiya* is still there, *Maasa*. The real heir to the throne" Viren said, putting his mother's facts into perspective. "And that was not a problem either. Not until his *firangan Beendni* died"

"How does that change anything? He lives in the city still" Tara ruffled his unruly mop of hair. "So you have been gifted with some of your father's innocence after all! Innocence does lead to being gullible though"

"And, if you are not careful Viren, it could throw you into the pit of vulnerability" Her words made no sense to him, especially since he couldn't understand the context in which she spoke. His expression mimed how he felt.

"Ajju has a new prey now. His eye has rested on none other than the one you are about to marry!" Viren jumped up with a start. "That is a lie! Ajju *Bhaiya* would never do anything like that. Especially knowing his younger brother is marrying, who I was betrothed to earlier"

Viren was quietened down again by the conniving Tara. "Where is Rati now? I saw her walk with her handful of livestock, from the kitchen window" "She has gone to graze them by the riverside" Viren mumbled.

"Go for a ride on Jigar, Viren. See for yourself, what your mind refuses to believe" He brushed past his mother, desperate to prove her wrong. Stomping to the stables, he mounted Jigar, before the stable boy could saddle him up.

At the riverside, he saw Rati pulling the new born foal, an addition to her tiny livestock, laughing merrily. Relieved at not having to believe his mother, he turned Jigar around to race back and put his *Maasa* in her place.

"*Ruko*!" he heard the familiar voice of Ajju, who he saw on the opposite bank of the river, racing towards the bridge. The thick shrubbery Jigar was nibbling on, was the right place for Viren to observe the two meeting.

In that short period, Viren was terribly uncomfortable with the proximity of their forms. He left in a huff, walking back from the stable. "Check the accounts, Viren. I am going to rest awhile" Giriraj instructed his son, while Tara kept silent.

The next morning, Viren dropped his *kullad* from the terrace when he saw Ajju and Rati on the same horse, riding towards the *haveli*. "*Maasa! Idhar aayiye*! (Mother! Come here!)" he yelled for Tara.

Hurriedly, she rushed to his room. "What happened?" "Tell Rati Singh Rana's *Chachi* that I'm no longer keen to marry someone, who walks with other men" he said, in a matter-of-fact manner.

Knowing Viren had seen them together, Tara tried to get on his good side. She was putting clothes on the terrace, when she had seen them as well. "It hurt me when you called me a liar yesterday, Viren"

"I cannot stress enough as to how much I always want what's best for you. The truth was not meant to hurt you. The truth was meant to open your eyes, Viren" "It hurt me all the same, *Maasa*" Viren said, pounding his fist on the terrace wall.

"*Gusse se kaam bigadta hai* (Anger will ruin everything) If you want, I can help you find a way" Tara offered. That evening, Viren woke up early, to hushed tones outside his window. Straining to hear, he recognized his mother hissing at someone over the cell phone.

"It's too risky now. Things are heating up here. Go to the meeting and keep me in the loop. Don't do anything without checking with me first. Oh, I assure you, your reward is anxious for you as well"

Hanging up, Tara almost dropped her cell. "Who're you speaking with, *Maasa*?" Turning to face Viren, seconds after changing her 'caught red-handed' expression, she said, "My contact in the city, Jai Prakash"

"There are some hybrid bovines he wants me to take a look at" "You can go if you want" Viren said resignedly. "You don't want to come along? The change will be good for you" Tara suggested, making it evident she had nothing to hide.

"If I run, I am an escapist, a coward. I won't let what has happened affect me. You're right about one thing though. With money comes power. You and *Baasa* have spent years making us rich"

"It is time for me to get us the power that will make our house the *Chaudhary haveli-Chaudhary* Viren's *haveli*!" Tara patted her son, who was finally beginning to show signs of dancing to her tune.

"I thought I would never hear you say it, *beta*! I have no doubt you are the right candidate for the *Chaudhary*'s throne" "All that is fine, *Maasa*. But how do we go about it? Ajju *Bhaiya* is *Chaudhary* Dhanush, the original *Chaudhary* of the *Raika*'s first born"

"Vansh is the current *Chaudhary*, *Chaudhary* Akash's son. Who am I?" Tara looked at him while she chewed her tobacco. "The richest man in all of Bassi. Someone the *panchayat* will think a million times over the others, as one who can bring Bassi back to what it used to be"

"Vansh may have the ideas, but where will he get the money from? Ajju may choose to marry Rati, as bad as it may sound. Where will they stay? He'll want to take her to the palace he owns at Delhi"

"She has nothing here anyway. Who will Bassi's people look to for a stable future, Viren?" "Yes, I get it now. Our family is about to undertake a huge responsibility. One I am ready to take. There's much to be done. But first, I'll speak to *Baasa*"

"*Baasa* has no ambition like you do. Keep him out of it. He'll pour water over your plans, before you give yourself the chance to realize a dream. Believe me; he has done it to all of us many-a-times"

"Being a simple man, he expects everyone in our family to follow his path. Little does he know that you, my son, are born for nothing short of greatness!" Sufficiently pumped up by the cunning Tara, Viren chose to keep his new-found enthusiasm for an old ambition between him and his mother. Caution was key, as he had begun to realize.

Ajju had to control how he felt about Rati. That girl was taking over his senses, like a fragrant flower numbs one to feel, solely from the heart. He was reminded of Mia or Aradhana though, whenever he saw her.

The same shade of cornflower blue eyes was shared by both. But, their nature was quite different. No, he mustn't compare the two. Mia was his wife, Rati is… Frowning, he got up from his bed and walked to the balcony at the back.

The window jutted out, locally called a *jharokha*, with stained glass depictions of a man and a woman on a white elephant. "Who is she to me?" he said loudly, conscious of having voiced his thoughts out into the open void.

"Some relationships can never be defined" Turning around, he saw Vansh standing at the doorway. "I couldn't sleep. Come in" Vansh walked in confessing, "I couldn't either" Taking the cigarette Ajju offered, he lit it and said, "Smoking kills"

"So does love" "As does hatred, *Bhaiya*" "What's on your mind, Vansh?" Dropping the ash, Vansh perched on the window ledge. "Leenata told me about your interest in Rati Singh Rana. She was who you were thinking of when I came in, isn't it?"

After seeing Ajju nod, he said. "Somehow, Viren's family is continuously being attacked, by both your family and mine" "I still don't understand, Vansh. Speak clearly" Vansh told Ajju about Viren's interest in Rati.

"It is rumoured that Rati's *Chachi* is already consulting a *pundit* for the *shubh muhurat*" Turning away from Vansh to cloak his disappointment, Ajju said, "I didn't know she was spoken for. Leenata told me otherwise"

"Leenata wouldn't know, Ajju *Bhaiya*. Ask Rati yourself when you meet her tomorrow" "And how do you know I'm going to meet her?" "Beera needs some exercise, as I haven't been riding off late. Please take my horse for a spin tomorrow"

Ajju knew Vansh was offering his horse to him with the hope he might meet Rati again. "Why are you helping me go after someone I should steer clear from?" Vansh smiled, walking away from him.

Stopping by the doorway, he turned around to answer. "It's because of you I met Jiya. I didn't know what love meant until I met her. She too has a lot of regard for you and your family" Touched by affection, mending an old enmity based on hollow ambition, Ajju smiled back at the man who gave him an opportunity to see the mesmerizing Rati again.

That night, Ajju slept peacefully in between crossfires of colour-coded thoughts; more questions than answers. Mia was plucking a rose, when her finger got pricked by a thorn. She showed him the drop of stark red blood, that dripped into a palm full of water.

They were Mia's tears. He woke up with a start again, wondering why her memories tormented him so. He remembered he was to take a ride on Beera and hurriedly got dressed. Rati was saddling her horse up, when she saw him walk in.

"An early morning ride on the horse of the *Chaudhary's* son. Lucky you!" "Rati, I want to talk to you" He asked her if she was betrothed to Viren. Seeing her expression was the same, he felt there was hope yet.

"I'm not married to him yet. My *Chachi* approves of the match, but I have yet to give mine. I've never interacted with him, other than daily pleasantries from a distance." "So, what are you doing here with me?" he asked her bluntly.

"With you? I didn't even know you're coming to ride today! I ride mine every day, early morning" Realizing he was being rude, Ajju apologized. Rati was mounted already on her chestnut beauty, waiting for Arjun to mount the black beauty, Beera.

"If you catch up and reach the *tila* before me from the boundary wall route, I will tell you a little secret" She sped off, leaving him to gather his thoughts before he could gather Beera's reins. Try as he might, she kept leading, up until the last turn where Beera caught up, crossed, reached the *tila* before Rati.

"You ride well!" she complimented him. "You should see my cousin. He's an equestrian" He had to explain what an equestrian was to her, something she related to in fairs and festivals when the animal was the focal point.

"So what's this little secret?" "What secret? I was just joking!" she said playfully. He caught her by the arm, pulling her close. The horses were grazing beside the two, while they stood to catch their breath.

Ajju's harsh tug at Rati's forearm made her swerve back into his barrel chest. Her arms were resting on them, her eyes resting on his. Nothing moved around them, as if time had stood still. Eternity had a stop watch, waiting to see who made the first move to a story that was waiting to happen.

"I cannot say yes to Viren because off late…" "Off late?" Ajju coaxed her, wrapping his arms around her waist. She pushed him away and ran to her grazing horse, mounting him elegantly. "Off late, I have realized what it feels like to be in love!"

Ajju didn't even have to ask who she was in love with. Her eyes, her breath, her heartbeat were louder than any word that was man-made. Ajju was in love, grateful for it being reciprocated. He wanted to have her with him at all times and began to plan how to go about just that.

# CHAPTER THIRTY THREE

Vansh left for the city of Delhi, the very next afternoon. He had reached the end of his tether, having to hear Diana cry out of loneliness over the phone. He had to man himself up to confronting his father.

Choosing not to give the real reason though, using Ajju's excuse as more plausibly acceptable one. Luckily for him, Ajju's forewarning paid off as Bindiya, suspicious as ever, made *Chaudhary* Akash call Arjun to confirm the urgency.

Arjun played along for the sake of poor Diana, who was literally left all alone, even though she was a part of his family. The moment Vansh reached Lilavati Hospital, Diana broke down in his arms.

Coping up with all that had happened was becoming difficult for a frail person like herself, to face alone. She always had Mia to bank on, then Vansh. Mia was lost forever, but Vansh planned to stay besides her for that same period of forever.

They drank coffee at the cafeteria before leaving for Elite International. Diana had booked him in the same hotel as he had requested earlier. He chose not to stay at Swarn Niwas, despite Ajju's offer, because he wanted to be closer to Diana.

"How's your mother, Jiya?" he asked her, looking out of the window as she was cuddled up to him, the closeness giving her the reassurance and strength she desperately needed. "She's not my mother. She can barely even stand me" she replied, feeling sorry for herself again.

"Listen Jiya, if you don't care about her…then why don't you come back to Bassi with me?" "That wouldn't be right, Vansh. She could have left me in an orphanage after my parents died. She chose to raise me alongside Mia instead"

"As her toy or a pet" "Whatever. I owe her just this much. When she gets back to the hotel, I plan to walk away from her forever" "And where would you go, my darling?" Vansh asked, holding her closer, afraid she'd say back to the foreign land.

"I was hoping you could solve that puzzle for me" she said, smiling a bit for the first time since the accident. "I'll talk to my parents. In fact, I'm taking you back with me a few days from now!"

Diana was happier being Jiya. She was hopeful as they reached the hotel. Vansh hadn't even unpacked his bags, so they freshened up in their respective rooms, meeting downstairs for dinner at the hotel's posh restaurant.

It was there that Jiya told him about the fact that Ramona was still Arjun Pratap's legally wedded wife. "But that would mean Dhanush is born out of wedlock!" "Yes. That's why I'm telling you. I don't want you to think that I withheld information from you"

"My mother, I mean, Ramona kept information as power within her grasp, willing to use it to her advantage whenever she pleased, not realizing how many were being affected in the process" Vansh thought about what Diana had told him all night.

How could he let Dhanush marry his sister now? The information would shatter the reputation of his family at the village. If he accosted Dhanush, the Prataps would turn against Jiya for trying to sabotage Dhanush and Leenata's wedding.

He felt stuck, having to choose between the devil and the deep sea. Checking his wrist watch, he saw the time was close to midnight. He dialed Jiya's suite, pre-deciding to disconnect a few rings later in case she slept off. She picked his call in the first ring.

"I couldn't sleep either" she said, as soon as the mouthpiece was close enough. "How did you know it was me?" Vansh asked her. "Who'd think of me at such an unearthly hour? The only person who would, was Mia"

"Jiya, can I come over?" "Yes. Please come" "Won't you be scared?" Vansh asked, surprised at the bold encouragement given by her. "I know you've been raised in a village. Even so, you will behave like a thorough gentleman, never crossing the line that could make me feel even the slightest of discomfort"

Touched by her trust, Vansh changed quickly from his night clothes, reaching the suite in less than a minute. The door opened to a richly furnished room with a yellowish glow. Jiya was wearing a beige satin nightgown, slender and sleek, with a slit on one side up to her knees.

The gown she wrapped over her was kimono-style, with humming birds made at the back. Whatever theory Vansh had convinced himself of before he came into the room, was left outside it.

The raging fire of passion and youth poured out of his eyes, searing through Jiya's translucent skin, making her blush as she lowered her eyes. "I didn't have time to change into a suit" she said, pulling the gown closer to herself, suddenly conscious of her state.

"Go then. I'll wait" When she didn't move, he said, "Wear this after we are man and wife so that I can show you how I feel. Until then, do not tempt a man who is desperately in love with you, Jiya!"

They spoke over coffee and tinned chocolate chip cookies. "What was bothering you, Vansh?" she asked, picking a crumb off the floor. Vansh moved the hair that covered her face, pulled her closer, looking into those eyes.

Both their eyes were identical in colour; a brown that had an elusive tinge of bronze. Vansh felt like he was looking into a mirror. He bent over to kiss her on the cheek. She smiled as he moved away, frozen by his move.

He came close again, kissing her other cheek, then the forehead. Resting back on the couch, he lit a smoke. Disappointed he didn't kiss her on the lips, she frowned. He was waiting for that very reaction, hopeful so as not to offend her.

He kissed her gently, the petals of her mouth parting readily for him to move in for a kiss full of passion, promise, love. Jiya reciprocated with equal vigour, alarmed at her own hunger for his touch.

Moving away minutes later, they talked some more. Vansh told her about the questions that refused to let him rest. "Do what you feel is right. I will support your decision, whatever it may be" she said.

"I can't break my sister's heart, Jiya. We must find a way that could mend the situation that'll spiral all of us into an abyss of happiness" "How is that even possible, Vansh? Ramona is Arjun Uncle's wife by law."

Although he has filed for a divorce, till she doesn't give it to him, he can never marry Dhanush's mother" "So, he has filed for a divorce, then?" Vansh asked. "Yes. I thought I'd told you" "Must have slipped my mind."

"Get Arjun *Chachu* to come to the hotel. I think there is a way, but we need to get him on board first" When Jiya agreed, Vansh pulled her closer.

"I'm going to ask you something that only you can do, tomorrow. Would you do it for me, Jiya?"

"I would do anything for you" she said, closing her eyes as his kiss gave her wings to fly away from all of reality. The pain, the hurt, the angst of loneliness became a speck of dust that left her body, leaving her mind clear, crystal clear.

Jiya called Arjun, inviting him to the hotel for the coming day, before he reached his gallery. "He's staying at your hotel?" Arjun enquired. "Yes Uncle" "No wonder he didn't want to stay with us!" he teased her, promising to get there on time for breakfast.

The following morning, Vansh and Diana had just gotten comfortable at the corner most seating in the restaurant, when Arjun walked in. Vansh touched his feet, "*Khammaosa*, Arjun *Chachu!*" Arjun hugged Vansh, who had changed for the better over time.

Curious to know why he was called, Arjun asked, "So, what are you both up to?" "*Chachu*, I have an idea. Your lawyer…does he have the divorce papers ready to be signed?" "Yes, he does. The court date depends on when Ramona is fit enough to appear"

"Right. What if I told you there was a way you could get the papers signed? Would you consider marrying *Chachi* for real?" "Where is the doubt? I'll marry her as many times as I have to! But, if this involves forgery, count me out. I've never done anything illegal, all of my life"

"I assure you *Chachu*, my plan is not only completely legal, but also foolproof. The implementation of the idea though depends solely on Jiya..I mean Diana" Vansh lost the thread of his conversation momentarily with the slip-up of the name he had given her.

"Everyone knows you call her Jiya! Please continue" Arjun said, checking his watch. Over a quick breakfast of eggs, bread rolls and an assorted selection of cold cuts, Vansh spoke slowly. "As we all know, Ramona has temporary blindness, a stay for another week or so at the hospital"

"Now, if you get the divorce papers that need to be signed from your lawyer to us, then Jiya could make Ramona sign on them!" Jiya almost choked on her garlic bread, when she heard his plan. "She would never listen to me"

"You're absolutely right. But, she thinks you're Mia, not Jiya. All you have to do is tell her, as Mia, that you need her signatures to pay for the hospital bills. She doesn't recognize my voice, so I could be the Hospital Administrator"

"Well now! This could actually work. Diana, what do you think?" Earlier, Jiya would have flatly refused. Her loyalties lay with her family, her blood. Not only did she realize Ramona was not her blood, but she had also lost the only person she knew as her family - Mia.

She had to build her future with Vansh. If this is what it took to prove to him that she could do anything in the name of love, then, so be it. "Yes. I will do it" Both Arjun and Vansh heaved a sigh of relief.

Arjun zipped to his lawyer's office, bringing the documents straight over to the hospital where Vansh and Jiya were waiting for him already. Handing over the papers to Jiya silently, he stepped aside.

"Mother, the Hospital Administrator is here. I'm sorry to bother you but I've spent all the ready money paying for our stay at the hotel" "Don't you worry your pretty little head, Mia. Give me the papers and the pen. Show me where to sign" Ramona said, smiling with a blank expression.

The job was done within a few minutes, after which Arjun sped off to Mr. Yadav's office. Technically, everyone would have been ashamed of this deceptive act, were the victim anyone but Ramona.

Mr. Yadav was astonished at the signatures, but assumed Ramona's blindness teamed with the loss of her daughter, may have served as motive for a change of heart. "How soon before I can remarry, Mr. Yadav?" Arjun asked, hardly able to contain himself.

"Next morning!" Mr. Yadav replied, tickled on seeing the usually reserved, composed Mr. Pratap clicking his heels in the air. Arjun called the Anands to give them the good news. Sangharsh enquired how he managed to pull off such a feat.

Arjun told him the truth, to which he replied, "Now the Anaconda will know what it feels like when you take advantage of someone's helplessness. No one is ignored in the cycle of Karma" Arjun agreed with him, albeit partially.

"I'm going to Maya's Reality. Get ready for the marriage ceremony tomorrow. We leave for Bassi the day after that" "Sure thing, *dost*! I'll take care of everything. Just get to court on time. I'll have your outfits sent to you at Swarn Niwas by this evening"

Arjun had to keep reminding himself not to drive fast, but his heart and mind refused to listen. He got off at Maya's Reality and walked straight to Suhani's office. She was admiring Nandish's handiwork, with Abhimanyu seated in front of her.

When she saw Arjun, she turned pale. "*Saheb*! What're you doing here? Is everything alright? My boys?" "Calm down, Braids. Everything is alright. In fact, it is now more than alright! Soon, it will be better than alright!"

Getting the hint that they wanted some privacy, Abhimanyu excused himself. "What is the matter with you?" Suhani asked Arjun, giggling away as he picked her up in his arms. "I'll tell you on one condition"

"And what is that?" "Come home with me right now. Make me a cup of tea" "I'll come home a bit later. I've work to do and so do you" Holding her close, he kissed her for the longest time. "Come" he said, holding her hand as she left with him, just about managing to pick her purse.

The music in the car was on full volume, with Arjun singing along after a long time. Suhani loved to see him happy again. "You used to sing when we were younger" she told him when they reached their room at Swarn Niwas.

"We're still young. Where are you going?" he asked her. "To make *chai* like you asked" "Come here. The *chai* can wait. I on the other hand.." They were exhausted after showering their deep passion on each other.

Shanti served *chai*, always happy to see both Suhani and Arjun together. Sipping her tea, Suhani could contain herself no longer. "At least tell me now. I'm dying to know" Not wishing to test her patience anymore, Arjun said, "The papers are signed!"

Elated, Suhani jumped towards him, toppling them both over. "And you thought we were getting old, *Beendni*?" Arjun commented jokingly. "And now, sit up so that I can discuss another serious matter with you"

"And what is that?" "The house is in your name. The gallery now has a partner. I am not as rich or young as I used to be. Would you still do me the honour of being my wife?" She nodded, gulping hard.

"In that case my darling, you better get moving because we are getting married tomorrow. I've told Sangharsh and Nalini. I'll tell Dhanush and Ajju as well. All this is because of Diana, Braids"

"And Vansh, of course. Originally, the plan was his. God bless them both" Both Ajju and Dhanush were relieved more than anything else, that the marriage at Bassi would still go as per planned.

Ajju expressed his disappointment at not being at their wedding, but assured them more good news awaited, when they joined him at Bassi. The next morning was a blessing, a magical day that both Arjun and Suhani more than anyone else had been waiting for.

Arjun wore the same suit for both the court marriage as well as the *Saptapadi* ceremony. Suhani, keeping pace with him, wore a red *sari* with simple brocade work, the mirror work at the borders giving it that extra ethnic-festive punch.

They reached Swarn Niwas, happy again to be together as husband-wife. Another couple also in love, were discussing the same situation from another angle. "What will happen when she finds out I tricked her into signing on the papers?" Diana asked Vansh, worried as she recalled how vicious Ramona could get, when she was in one of her raging tempers.

"She'll huff and puff, try to blow the house down. But the Prataps are one now. Dhanush and Leenata's marriage is safe from any mud-slinging. "I don't feel proud of what I did though, Vansh"

"Yes, I know. But weigh the good that has come out of this. One signature has changed the life of so many people for the better" "You're right. The doctor says she can keep a maid and a private nurse. If she agrees, I'll come back to Bassi with you. If the offer is still open, that is"

"Jiya you are my heart. If I take you with me, I have all of me together. Why would I never leave it as an open offer?" he said, meaning every word that was pulled out from his core by his deeply-embedded feelings for her.

"Lean on me, my love. I'm here now to protect, take care of you. You'll never have to walk alone. I'll never let you feel anything but loved, wanted, cherished" He began to kiss her as soon as they reached her hotel suite.

Their arduous passion sent them spiraling, into spaces between the surreal and fantasy. She gave herself to him, holding nothing back, He took what he had to, without breaking through the line. It was getting tougher though.

Vansh was determined now more than ever, that Jiya was to be his *Beendni*. He knew it might endanger his position as the next *Chaudhary* of the *Raika*s. He was ready to forfeit his crown, his ambition for the sake of love.

He knew power could never compensate for love. He knew money could never replace companionship. Vansh had chosen his path. So had Ajju. Viren's path was the most destructive of all three.

What remained to be seen was, who managed to walk across the valley where the mettle of a human is tested. Another day passed by uneventfully, till it was time to leave for Bassi, where Leenata waited for Dhanush in anticipation.

# CHAPTER THIRTY FOUR

After leaving the National Highway to reach the village of Bassi, Mrs. And Mr. Arjun Pratap began to speak about Dhanush's upcoming wedding. "It is inconvenient to have the wedding in Bassi instead of at Delhi"

"But, all of *Chaudhary* Akash's relatives can be better catered for at the village, than with us" Dhanush was driving his Humvee behind them with Andy, who needed an excuse to visit Malika.

The excuse presented itself in the form of some shots for their gallery, that needed to be taken again. After his amazing photo shoot with Maya's Reality, everyone who saw the pictures had nothing but praise to shower on him.

He was already looking at chunky offers for freelance photography, from a few well-known magazines and advertising houses. "Aren't you nervous?" he asked Dhanush, taking a shot of what he saw.

A lone, parallel road stretch with a camel cart moved slowly. A heavily-moustached, turban-clad old man played a local instrument, while a lady, perhaps his *lugai*, sang along with the tune he played.

"Not in the least, strangely. One would have assumed a commitment like marriage would have gotten me terrified. But more than that, the thought of not having Leena as my bride terrifies me" "Dude, you're all soppy!"

Andy nudged him, getting nudged back in the process. "Look who's talking! What's the progress in your love life?" "That's why *Baasa* and *Maasa* are following us in their BMW. To secure my future, I hope!"

The convoy of three cars was zipping through Rajasthan, to reach Bassi before the noon meal. Smartly, every one of them forgot to pack any food for the journey. The crate of mineral water that Dhanush thankfully had, was enough for all to sustain, till a hearty meal at Bassi was offered.

"What're you thinking, Sangharsh?" Nalini asked, reducing the air-conditioning. "How are we going to pull this off, Nalini? Malika is Viren's sister. The wronged one, as I'm sure his greedy mother Tara must have taught him by now"

"We'll figure something out. There's no point in worrying about it" "I suggest you start thinking now. We're already on the way, Mrs. Anand!" Nalini was worried too. She knew Tara and Giriraj would never agree to the match.

Even if *Chaudhary* Akash tried to intervene, it just wouldn't work. "Sometimes, when a solution seems impossible, we should have faith in fate, Sangharsh. Remember how we made the impossible happen?"

Turning to glance at her, he said, "Yes, my apple pie. You are absolutely right" "How many times do I have to tell you, stop calling me all these ridiculous names! We have grown-up children now, who would probably pass out laughing if they found out how you address their mother"

Before Sangharsh could tease her some more, the Prataps called them on the phone. "Thanks for calling, before I could have gotten into more trouble!" Sangharsh said, laughing along with Arjun on the other side.

"We're reaching in ten minutes. I've told *Chaudhary* Akash we need to be fed, before we die of starvation" "Are they expecting us? I mean Nalini and I?" "Yes. I told them already. Don't pick up Malika's topic. Let me speak with *Chaudhary* Akash about this first"

Agreeing to Arjun's suggestion, Sangharsh hung up. "I don't understand what all the fuss is about. Malika's parents should be overjoyed that she is being wedded into a family, where she will never face the dearth of any want" Nalini blurted out in exasperation.

"Villagers have extreme emotions. For them, love and hate stem from the same root. I've seen the love of a villager, as well as its flip side. They're the ones that forgive too. But forget is something that doesn't exist in their dictionary"

"You're thinking as Nalini. Think as Tara and you'll get what I'm trying to say" Sangharsh explained. They reached the *Chaudhary haveli*, not expecting the welcome that awaited them. *Chaudhary* Akash was standing with the *Chaudhrain* Bindiya, with a *tikka thaali*.

"*Khammaosa, Chaudhary Saheb*! Why go through all this formality?" Arjun said. "We are to be related soon, Arjun *Saheb*. This is how we greet relatives from our son-in-law's side" Suhani and Bindiya held hands, smiling at each other.

"Our friendship will be strengthened. Who would have thought our children would wed each other and relate us, *Samdhan!*" Agreeing with Bindiya's remark, Suhani said, "It is all *vidhi*. No one can deny the will of the Almighty"

Moving into the cool interiors, the group quickly washed up for the meal. Bindiya wasn't pleased to see the Anands, for she could foresee trouble with them. "Where is Ajju *Bhaiya?*" Dhanush asked, eager to meet his brother.

"He should be back anytime now. Lord knows where he disappears to, the entire day. The only time we get to see him, is during the noon meal or at night. He must have collected a million pictures of my people by now!"

"Hello, everyone!" Ajju walked in, muddy from head to toe, his jeans and *kurta*, once in blue, now more brown. The only thing that shone, were his black eyes. It was evident that wherever he had been, was a successful venture.

Welcoming him by expressing joy on seeing him, Arjun said, "I missed you" "Me too, *Baasa*" "I'll take you out in the evening, to show what I've been up to" Interrupting the father-son reunion, Bindiya said, "The *panditji* is coming in the evening today"

"The dates are closer than we would have expected" The brothers embraced, happy to see each other again. "How've you been, Ajju *Bhaiya?*" "Protecting your property for you, as you can see" he said, just as Leenata came into the courtyard.

Dhanush's heart skipped a beat as he watched her lips quiver into a smile. Soon she was going to belong to him, a thought that made him content every moment, off late. "I'll have a look around and be back" Andy said, garlanding his camera around his neck.

"We'll go with him as well. Come along, Leenata" Ajju said, taking Dhanush and Leenata along. It was pre-planned between them, for the elders would never let Andy meet Malika alone. The fact that Andy was not alone, was in itself a relief for his parents.

The villagers of Bassi still regarded Ajju with a great deal of respect. It was always a bit strange for *Chote Sardar* Arjun to have these two sides within him. One side called A.J. belonged to the city of Delhi.

The other was Ajju of the *Raika*s of Bassi. Sometimes it was tough to balance the two, but off late he realized merging them as one, made a good Arjun Chand. The group of four youngsters went to Gurukul, where Malika was sitting on the Acting Principal's chair.

The way she got up, walked up to Nandish, showed how much in love she was with him as well. "I thought you'd never return" "Where else would I go? You have my heart" "As do you" "Excuse me, Romeo"

"We have to get out of here before her bull dog brother gets a whiff of you in the vicinity" Ajju said, walking towards the gate. "When will I see you again?" Malika asked. "As soon as possible. My parents have come to ask for your hand for me" Malika stepped back.

"What? Where are they?" "At the *Chaudhary haveli*. Why do you ask?" "Because Viren *Bhaisa* has been quite silent, off late. I have heard him talk to *Maasa* about wealth and power. He doesn't approve of us, Andy"

"That's stale news, Malika. Has he mentioned why he doesn't like me? He doesn't even know me!" "When Viren *Bhaisa* doesn't like something, he doesn't need a reason to justify it. You do know, we are the richest in all of Bassi, right?" Malika reasoned.

"Yes, Leenata told me. Well I just wish I had a chance to ask your brother myself what his problem is with me, per se!" Andy said, frustrated. "Here's your chance, buddy boy. Consider your wish fulfilled"

"Viren is walking towards Gurukul with four *lathaits*!" Dhanush reported. "You must go. All of you. Leave from the back" Malika panicked. "*Na*. We are not cowards, neither have we committed a crime"

"I will speak with him, if need be. We will walk through the main gate of Gurukul" Ajju declared. Viren stopped abruptly just outside the gates of the school, stopping the men who were following him with a raised palm.

"So the news was true. The city folk are back. To take away more of what belongs to us. Spread havoc like locusts!" His provocation had no effect on Ajju. "We don't want any trouble. Stop saying things you don't mean" Ajju said, watching Viren closely.

Opening the gate aggressively, Viren stood in front of Ajju. "And who are you to order me around? Are you *Chote Sardar* Arjun Chand of the *Raika*s? Or, are you A.J. the photographer of that gallery in Delhi?"

"Does it matter, Viren? I'm elder to you. *Maryaada rakho*! (Stay within the limits of our traditions!)" "*Maryada*? You talk of *maryada* when you yourself toss it around? You and your brother chase our girls around, disrespecting our women"

"That is untrue!" Leenata came from inside the staffroom. "What do you think you're doing, Viren?" Viren glared at her. "I have no wish to speak with you. Go back to your classrooms, *Maatsa*"

"I have no wish to speak with you, either. This is a temple of Knowledge, not a wrestling arena! Take this elsewhere" Viren couldn't argue with the justification. "We will wait for you all, outside" Viren announced, walking out of the gate with his manpower.

"Quick, Malika. Take the cycle that's in the back, the one that's resting against the wall. Go to the *haveli* and tell the elders what's going on. I will handle things here. *Jaldi karo*! (Hurry up!)" Malika slipped away from the back door, ready to pedal as fast as her legs could manage.

"Just do exactly as I say, if you want to live" Leenata murmured to the city men, opening the gate herself, standing between them and the men from the village. "If there has to be a fight, it has to be fair"

"Thus, there must be rules as well. A neutral person is also required to ensure, no rule is broken" Viren glared at Leenata. "We're not children. This isn't a game, Leenata!" "Who said anything about children or games?"

"I will be the neutral party. Hand me all your weapons. Let this be an old-fashioned fist fight, one-on-one. Unless you and your men are afraid to take on the city folk" A challenge was to be accepted, to avoid a bruised ego.

Both parties agreed to fight one-on-one under the scorching sun, outside the gates of Gurukul. Viren and his two men handed over the *lathi*s. Ajju and his two men handed over their cameras. "Wait. Let me take a picture, for posterity sake. Lord knows how you all will look, after the fight is over"

Leenata was enjoying herself thoroughly, knowing none present would dare disrespect the daughter of *Chaudhary* Akash. The only other who was enjoying was her fiancé, Dhanush Pratap.

He was impressed by her ability to divert the situation, from possibly lethal to ridiculously hilarious. Before the first match between Ajju and Viren could begin, a group of horses rode up with their riders outside the village school.

"What in God's name is going on over here?" *Chaudhary* Akash's roar got everyone up in attention. "*Chaudhary hukam*!" Viren stuttered.

"Viren, what is all this?" "Nothing. It's just a friendly match. Nothing to be concerned about"

"I sent you to watch over our cattle, Viren. Not to spar outside the gates of Gurukul!" Giriraj got his horse ahead of the others to face his son. "This is a shame! Do you know who you were about to fight? That is our great *Chaudhary* Dhanush Chand's eldest-*Chote Sardar* Arjun Chand"

Glaring at how his son embarrassed him, he got down from his horse. "Here, go home. I will escort the city folk back to the *Chaudhary haveli*, myself" Viren had no choice but to obey his father.

He raced back on his father's horse to vent at his house, leaving Giriraj to mend a damaged fence. "I apologize for my son's insolence, *Chote Sardar*" Ajju caught his folded hands. "Please don't"

"Your hands should be on my head to bless me, not folded in front, as I am younger. I am equally to blame. I should be folding my hands, instead of the other way round" Giriraj looked closely at the young man, his squint making Ajju a tad uncomfortable.

"My God! You are the spitting image of your father! Even your nature is just like his! Look everyone, *Chaudhary* Dhanush is back!" A substantial crowd had gathered outside Gurukul, by then.

Passersby going about their daily chores, parents who came to pick their children from school, all looked at Ajju closely, as if he was the *Kohinoor* itself. "Here, let me have a look" The tattoo artist of the village, who was now old, bent out of shape, but sharp as a razor, said.

"Yes! *Chaudhary hukam*'s son has his built, looks, and from what I hear, demeanour as well!" The crowd roared in jubilation, lifting him up on their shoulders. The huge crowd marched him to the *haveli*, seemingly jubilant over having their *Chote Sardar* back.

From afar, Suhani and Arjun witnessed the crowd of villagers shouting cheerful slogans of praise, as they got Ajju back. "Look how happy our Ajju looks, Braids. I think it is time. He belongs to Bassi. If the Lord *Shiva* wants him to be the next *Chaudhary*, I think we should encourage him"

"Yes, *Saheb*. He seems to be at home here. It is not the same at Delhi. I feel he loses himself there, but finds himself here. I feel it too that it is...time" "*Woh dekho! Chaudhrain*! (Look! It's the *Chaudhrain*!)" someone yelled from amongst the crowd, pointing at Suhani.

Arjun nudged her to walk to the doors of the *haveli* to welcome her son. The moment she stepped till the *chaukhat*, the crowd became silent. "*Khammaosa aap sabko*! (Greetings to all!) the last time I addressed you, was to inform that I was leaving with my son"

"I also told you that I will bring him back one day, after having raised him like a *Raika*. Come here, Ajju" Ajju walked up to his mother, facing a divine goddess, full of purpose, power. "Do you wish to be their *Chote Sardar*?"

"*Ji, Maasa*" She turned towards *Chaudhary* Akash who nodded his approval. "I am handing over my son Ajju as *Chote Sardar* Arjun Chand, son of *Chaudhary* Dhanush Chand of the *Raika*s of Bassi and the *Banjara*s of Nagri"

"It will henceforth be his moral duty to raise the bricks of Bassi, to what it used to be. I have kept my promise to my late husband, as I have delivered what belongs to this land. *Har har Mahadev! Jai Ma Bhavani*!"

The crowd roared deafening shouts of the same chants, looking at *Chote Sardar* Arjun Chand as their new ray of hope. He looked different to Suhani now. His smile was confident, his gait was royal, his demeanour was humble.

He was quite comfortable interacting with the village folk. "If you make him wear a *dhoti kurta*, he will look just like *Chaudhary* Dhanush!" someone suggested. And so, he was made to wear the outfit befitting the *Chote Sardar* of the *Raika*s.

It was post siesta when the crowd finally dispersed. "Ajju…" Suhani caught her son's face in her palms. "Where are you going?" "To meet someone I have given my heart to. Her name is Rati Singh Rana. She will be your *bahu* one day, not very far from now"

Suhani was thrilled with the news, but for now, there were other concerns to deal with. "You are a very powerful man now. Never leave the *haveli* without protection. There will be two *lathait*s with you, at all times"

"You will have to travel by horse, never on foot" Ajju nodded, accepting his mother's word, for she knew the ways of the *Raika*s well. "Do not eat anywhere outside. Trust no one because you are not the *Chaudhary* yet. There are enemies that lurk yet in the shadows, sans Vansh. Beware!"

On one hand, Ajju was happy to become the *Chote Sardar* of the people, who were like his extended family. On the other hand, the restrictions imposed, did not permit him to move around freely like he could earlier.

He wanted to see Rati, but couldn't without a horse and two body guards. He wasn't at all happy about the extra caution that came with the position. Suhani had already informed Arjun about Rati, Ajju's love interest.

The *panditji*, among all the chaos had managed to give the dates of the marriage, the most suitable being a month from that day. The city folk decided to leave Bassi early next morning. Ajju wrote a long letter to Rati, entrusting its delivery to her, by Leenata.

When Rati read the letter, something shiny fell down from the envelope. It was a ring with all the nine gems on it. She took the thread she wore, slipping in the ring as a pendant, smiling at Leenata. Theirs was to be a lifetime of close sisterhood and friendship, to be emulated by many.

# CHAPTER THIRTY FIVE

The moment the clean, straight path of the highway was reached by the convoy, everyone began to discuss the happenings at Bassi. "You know Sangharsh is going to ask you why there was no talk about Nandish and Malika, right?" Suhani voiced her concern to Arjun.

Dhanush, driving his Humvee, responded to his mother instead, looking at her from the rearview. "The confrontation outside Gurukul would have escalated to a full-fledged battle with a little more than *lathi*s and cameras, *Maasa*. That's why!"

Suhani still looked towards Arjun for an answer. "You heard the boy, *Beendni*. I couldn't get myself to put pressure on *Chaudhary* Akash, after all that happened. He was indeed graceful to give his consent to Ajju being *Chote Sardar*"

"Consent? Ajju is *Chote Sardar* by right!" Ajju was sitting next to Dhanush, gazing out of the window. "Bassi has changed, not just by modernity touching its outside, but the inside as well" he whispered softly.

"Everything changes with time, Ajju *Bhaiya*. Vansh has always had an issue with you. Look how close you both are today" "Yes. That is true. But what about Viren? I didn't know Rati was.."

"Ajju *beta*, no one doubts you not knowing. You told us yourself she hadn't given her consent, although her *Chachi* had approved" "Yes *Baasa*, I did. I know, as crazy as it may sound, that if I just speak with Viren alone, I could make him understand that there was no intention on my part, to hurt him"

Curbing his softness, Suhani said, "It's not just Rati that is the issue anymore. I know his mother Tara well. She has been ambitious, since the first time I saw her. She wanted to use her beauty to become the *Chaudhrain*"

"With *Chaudhary* Dhanush's untimely death, she chose to live her ambition through her children. Once Malika's proposal was rejected by Vansh and Viren's by Leenata, she must have found a new way"

"From what I see now, mixed with what I know of her…she is poisoning Viren's mind, egging him on to become the next *Chaudhary* of the *Raikas*" Her precise analysis, got everyone in the Humvee thinking.

It was an extremely believable theory, that put pretty much everything into perspective. "What's going to happen now, *Maasa?*" Ajju asked. "You've been declared the *Chote Sardar* of Bassi. You've chosen Rati Singh Rana to be your bride. Both of these were what Viren had his eye on"

"Why do you think we left so soon? We had planned on staying longer but it would have put you at risk" Turning to Arjun, she said, "Your father suggested we should leave, before you are put in a situation of grave danger"

"We know you must have wanted to meet Rati. But, it would have been a foolish move; something your enemies would expect, be prepared for" Ajju agreed with his parents, their concern visible clearly in the way they were looking at him.

The car behind them had Nandish at the wheel. His parents, Sangharsh and Nalini Anand, were discussing the same situation. The only difference was that they saw it from a completely different angle-their own.

"Why did Suhani have to be so selfish?" Nalini blurted out her innermost thoughts. "What does that mean, Nalini?" Sangharsh asked, checking his mobile for any calls from Annie. "Dhanush is almost married to Leenata"

"Ajju is now the *Chote Sardar* of the *Raika*s. As a mother, she has succeeded. As a friend, your *behan* has failed pathetically" "Nalini…" "No, let me speak. We went for Nandish's *rishta*. Arjun said he'll handle it. Where is the progress on that front?"

"At least Nandish got to meet her" Sangharsh said. "And almost started a war in the process!" Andy added, secretly pleased at his determination to see Malika. "There was no way Arjun knew about the situation at Bassi. Blaming the Prataps entirely is unfair on your part, Nalini"

"Is it? I feel like we ruined a visit, not to mention the day. Just touch and go. This could have been done over the phone. Nandish, go to Bassi alone next time. Whenever Malika is ready, bring her to Delhi and we'll get you married"

Sangharsh could have put his foot down to end the conversation for the time being. He conceded because he was concerned about the safety of his son. He wasn't keen to let his son go to Bassi alone though.

"If you must go, then take Ajju and Dhanush along. You're not to go alone at any cost. Give me your word, Nandish" Andy agreed, wondering when he would be able to go to Bassi again. By the time the packed *alu* and *mooli ke paratha*s were over, they had already reached Delhi.

Sangharsh insisted the Prataps stay at their home for a while, but they wanted to get back to their own home too. Agreeing to meet for dinner at the Anand villa, the two cars went their separate ways.

That evening, Annie and Abhi were to have dinner with his father, Dr. Shekhawat. Ajju, Dhanush and Nandish stayed back at DTD till late, to finish up with all the pictures they had taken pains to fix, retake and match, for the new theme Arjun had recommended- **Regressive Progression**.

That left the senior Prataps dining alone at Anand villa. The tensed atmosphere was obvious, the moment the comparatively mono-syllabic dinner was over. "Have dessert, Suhani. There is *mithai*"

"You have things to be happy about. Your sons are going places in their lives, thanks to you both!" Nalini said, offering assorted *laddoo*s to her. "Are you being sarcastic?" Suhani asked, shocked at the way she bluntly put things.

"I speak the truth. Why do you feel guilty?" "Why should I, Nalini? I didn't do anything wrong" "Then, I wasn't being sarcastic!" Sangharsh and Arjun had a few *laddoo*s, looking at each other. Their wives were arguing for the first time since anyone could remember.

Both men had no idea how to deal with the situation, aware that if they as much as attempted to stop the two, it would backfire on them. "Nalini, you're being unfair" "Suhani, you're being unreasonable"

Both women paused their argument as soon as their respective spouses addressed them at the exact same time. "Unfair?" Nalini turned to Sangharsh. "Unreasonable?" Suhani turned to Arjun. "Bad move, Arjun!"

"Ditto, *dost*!" "I was trying to diffuse a situation" Sangharsh confessed. "So was I. Nalini was being mean to Suhani but I still ignored it" Arjun retorted. "Suhani was feigning ignorance but I ignored that!"

Both women were now watching their men squabbling over something, that refused to make sense any more. "Are you trying to distract us by any chance?" Nalini asked them both. "Confuse is more like it"

"But if distraction is the word you like better, then that's cool with us!" Sangharsh said, laughing as Arjun threw a *laddoo* straight on his old friend's nose. "Trust you to spoil the fun, Sangharsh!"

"You should consider joining the theatre, Arjun. Awesome performance!" Sangharsh threw a *laddoo* right back at him. "Hey! Stop behaving like children!" Suhani yelled at them, both Nalini and her getting away from them, just in case they got pelted with sweetmeats by the madmen.

The large *thaali* now stood empty of *laddoo*s, which were strewn around, pieces on their clothes or the table, some on the floor. Nodding at Sangharsh, Arjun spoke, "We'll have coffee at the balcony. Let's talk. Not shout or accuse. Just talk"

The party of four moved to the balcony, the pre-monsoon breeze swaying the beautiful silver oak trees, as if they were dancing to a tune only they could hear. "Did you think throwing *laddoo*s at each other was childish?" Arjun asked Suhani.

"Of course!" she answered. "Then, what you and Nalini were heading towards was an example of maturity?" Sangharsh asked his wife. The intention behind the silliness hit both women, shame taking over the two.

Years of friendship, standing by each other no matter what, would have been strangled in an instant of maternally-wronged fury. "I'm sorry for being so harsh, Suhani. I.." "I'm sorry too, Nalini. You two are the only family we have. I really don't know what came over me"

"It's called maternal instinct. Slightly misplaced, but there it is" Sangharsh explained. Arjun breathed a sigh of relief, but chose to speak on. "Now that we have all consented to stop acting like children, let's put our heads together and come up with solutions as adults"

All four children between the two couples had to be catered to. Their thinking caps put together produced a brilliant solution. "Do you remember Ajju said how things had changed over the years?" Arjun asked Suhani. "Yes. And you said…" "Leave that part, Braids"

"Think about what he said. Thinking changes because people change. But, their basic thinking remains the same" "I don't understand, *Saheb*"

Lighting up a smoke, Arjun said, "We are connected to both the *Chaudhary's* family as well as Giriraj's, through the children"

"If the question is about money and power at Bassi, then both families need to work together to achieve what they desire" "It's not as simple as that, *Saheb*. Why would Tara agree to Ajju or Vansh to become the next *Chaudhary*, and offer her financial strength?"

That's when Sangharsh came up with the answer to untangle the first knot. "Make a deal then. Ask for Malika's hand for Nandish. In return, let Viren be the *Chaudhary* or *Chote Sardar* for a certain time period. If he can prove himself, he can keep the title"

"Not possible, Sangharsh *Bhaisa*. That's not how things work" "Worked, not work. Things change, people change. Remember? I don't know whether Ajju wants to settle in Bassi or not. What we four know is that, he may not want to be the next *Chaudhary*"

Sangharsh did make sense, forcing the Prataps to agree partially with his advice. "Ajju would never agree to a deal that would demean his status. Akash and Bindiya would be up in arms too if they found out Ajju was flaunting his power as *Chote Sardar*" Suhani said, standing at the edge of the balcony, breathing the cool night air.

"Why don't we work with what we have, instead of creating hypothetical situations?" Nalini spoke for the first time in the discussion. "Such as?" Sangharsh enquired. "Such as, use a little bit of all of your ideas and come up with a brand new, doable one"

They now put their minds together, intent on solving an issue that could affect their children adversely. The doorbell rang with footsteps running up to the balcony. The whole lot of youngsters were now standing in front of them.

"We thought your party would be over by now. Shouldn't you be resting more as you near old age?!" Dhanush teased his parents. Nalini threw a napkin at him. "We were just about to find a solution to the Bassi problem, before you all interrupted us!"

"*Chachi*, we have come up with one ourselves. Hear me out first" Ajju described their plan in detail, impressing everyone with his tact, innate sense of planning, and just nature. "Will it work?" Arjun asked.

"It did a long time ago. It is true time changes people, but they are still the same inside. I love Rati as much as I love Bassi. I'm ready to be the *Chaudhary* of the *Raika*s, if Akash *Chachaji* is alright with it"

Suhani had tears in her eyes. She never knew that secretly this is what she wanted for her son too. "You must bring Bassi to its previous glory, *beta*"

"Yes, *Maasa*. I have that as my primary motive"

It was almost early morning when they dispersed for their respective homes. Before they knew it, it was time to wake up to a new day. The previous night's discussions had instilled a new found hope into everyone.

The ones who were doubtful, would have to be brought on board with gentle coaxing, showing how they would benefit personally in the long run. "What's the progress in our gallery? The pictures had to be presented to Dr. Shekhawat today" Arjun asked his sons on the way to work.

"They're ready for you to have a final look, *Baasa*. We've completed all the corrections you had pointed out" Ajju said, looking at Dhanush. Pleased, Ajju reached the gallery, called the doctor after checking his morning mail.

The doctor was eager to see the pictures, mentioning he had to get back to Jaipur. Arjun took the call, of not involving his new partner in their Bassi plan, for now. He doubted if he could help anyway.

By the time the doctor reached DTD, the slides were ready to be viewed by him. "Our theme as you know**, is Regressive Progression**. Over time, everything that could show progress, brought with it its share of both perfections as well as flaws.."

Dhanush was giving an apt description of each shot, impressing not just the doctor, but also his father. When the slide presentation was over, the doctor clapped heartily. "Wow! I've never seen anything like this! This is phenomenal!"

"I've been to a few galleries in the past few days. This..is unique! So, when do we display it?" "We'll need a week at least. As you know, my youngest is about to tie the knot, so our hands are almost full already" Arjun confessed.

"Yes, Abhi told me. I have a suggestion, if you don't mind, Mr. Pratap" the doctor said, checking his watch. "Please go ahead" "Why don't you hold young Dhanush's wedding reception at the gallery? You'll be calling the same guests anyway"

"The gallery could display this theme and host the reception as well. What do you think?" Arjun had been chewing on the very same thought, but was skeptical so far because of the catastrophe that happened the last time, with the showdown between Ajju and Aradhana.

He also believed that this time, if all went well, it could well turn out to be a chance to redeem the prestige of the gallery, not to mention that of the Prataps. He chose to give the entire idea's credit to the generous new financier of DTD.

The doctor left a half hour before lunch, since he had to leave for Jaipur that very day. "I'd like to meet Abhi and Sarvani before I leave. He has changed so much, that it pleases me immensely" Expressing happiness on the change as well, Arjun waved, watching the doctor's cab move out of the gallery's driveway.

"*Baasa*, can we talk?" Ajju said. "Sure. We're all having lunch together in the backroom" "No, *Baasa*. Just you and I. In your office" Over their meal, Ajju said, "There were some other decisions that were taken, between the three of us"

"Since you already know I wish to become the *Chaudhary* at Bassi and will move permanently, Dhanush is ready to learn the ropes of DTD so that any time you're confident enough, he will be ready to take over"

"Nandish wants to be a freelancer, although he will be with us whenever required" "Sounds great! I'll have to run the ideas by the doctor though. The ones pertaining to the gallery, I mean" "Right. There's one thing more that I need to do. It's the only way for me to say goodbye to my past, to Aradhana"

"She wanted to launch **Nara Apparels** and I have all of her sketches. Andy says Annie and Abhi could help with the launch. Abhi has enough experience to jumpstart the brand. We'll get the Anands as financial advisors, on board. What do you think?"

Arjun, for the first time, saw traces of Ajju's biological father in him. "The apple really doesn't fall far from the tree, after all!" he remarked, sipping his ice-cold lemonade. "So, you approve?" "Ajju, you have all the makings of a great man, an honourable leader"

"You've found the solution that will put everyone's wants into the desired perspective. That's a trait your father, your biological father, had. Never think when you're at Bassi that I won't think of you as my first born"

"Wherever you are, whoever you might become, I'll always say 'Ajju is my son'!" Feeling blessed at having a man like Arjun Pratap shower his blessings, affection on him, Ajju began to set the ball rolling.

There was much to be done, within a framework of time where agendas were plentiful. He had to make sure he would do justice to Aradhana's dream; for, not only was that the only way he could wish her soul to rest in peace, but it was also what Abhi wanted as a business to run on his own.

Once **Nara Apparels** would get into the profit-making zone, Abhimanyu would repay the generous funding provided by the Anands. Thinking to create was what Ajju realized he was beginning to enjoy.

Create a new life for himself with Rati, create a better Bassi, create a company for Abhi and Annie. Much had to be done for many. He hoped Lord *Shiva* would guide him all the way through, to their completion.

# CHAPTER THIRTY SIX

Indo-western clothing, is the fusion between South - Asian and western fashion. With an increase in the exposure of the Indian subcontinent to the western world, the merging of clothing styles was an inevitability.

Many Indians settled in both India, as well as abroad, still prefer to wear traditional outfits. However, sometimes the younger generation in particular, has to wear ethnic clothing during celebratory or festive occasions.

That is how the structure of Indo-western clothing, the real fusion was born; to cater to the needs of the new generation, that wants to add its mark on traditional modernity. The clothing of the quintessential Indo-western ensemble is the trouser suit, which is a short *kurta* with straight pants, teamed with a *Jawahar* jacket.

Newer designs often feature slight variations, customizing the outfit to suit the palette of the individual's personality. Regal *sherwani*s and elegant *kurta*s teamed with *dhoti*s, *churidar*s or plain trousers with rich colours, embroidery done in detail at the collars, were the designs Ajju had to show the Anands and Abhimanyu.

"These will take the market by storm! We're in the apparel industry and know a few business houses exclusively for menswear, Ajju. But this…this is a new concept in a new package. Nothing stale about it from any angle!" Sangharsh complimented, momentarily saddened by a waste of talent due to Mia's untimely demise.

"I want to make the average man to be able to afford these. The quality should not be compromised in any way. The designs should be as per the sketches you see before you. Andy here will cover the launch fashion show of **Nara Apparels**, where Abhimanyu Shekhawat will be introduced as the owner, and Sarvani Anand as the Lead Designer"

"Is that alright with all of you?" Ajju looked around the conference room at Anand Creations, getting subtle nods from everyone present. "Mia must get the credit for these designs at least. I couldn't take the credit for them, Ajju *Bhaiya*" Annie confessed.

"She wouldn't like to take the entire credit, Annie. You will be breathing life into lifeless sketches. Think of this as a sort of inspiration for you to design even better in the future" Annie had already chosen to work on the white *sherwani*, teamed with the coffee brown trousers first.

It was filled with regal brocade work in dull gold, the closed collar and sleeves with more intricate work done on it. Abhi loved the quilted front-open, close-collared, long *kurta* in a delicious shade of coffee mocha that was matched exquisitely with a toffee brown, silken *dhoti*, the same fabric draped as a regal stole.

Each design was done with such finesse, that it was tough to move away from the sketches. "How long before you start on them?" Ajju asked Annie anxiously. "My doll line is ready to be launched. Andy has to take pictures and my website ought to be functional shortly as well"

"I have nothing to do as of now, so all of my time will be dedicated to bring **Nara Apparels** to life" she said, smiling back at Ajju. "You'll have to find a replacement once you start at **Nara Apparels**, Abhi" "Yes, I know. Mrs. Pratap has it in her agenda already"

"She wants me to shortlist a few candidates, so that interviewing is easy for her. Then she'll send the chosen candidate to me, before I leave Maya's Reality" "So, when do we expect the fashion show of **Nara Apparels**?" Ajju asked again.

"Not before fall, Ajju *Bhaiya*. Making the designs, setting up shop, production costs, everything has to be built from scratch" Abhi said, giving an honest estimate. "That's too far away. I want it done within the next two months"

"Sixty days is enough to get the work done, with the levels of efficiency you follow. Help Annie so that she can focus solely on a fantastic finished product, Abhi. I'll ask Mr. Guha to look for suitable candidates for Maya's Reality"

A lot of arguments could have broken out at Anand Creations' conference room that day, if this would have been said by anyone other than the changed man who stood before them. No one could do anything but agree with Ajju.

He seemed to have morphed into a surreal superman. He spoke with such intensity and reason, that it was near impossible to question his authority. No one had ever seen this side of him, although Sangharsh had witnessed his birth father's notably similar qualities, many years ago at Bassi.

Dismissing the meeting, Ajju began to leave for the gallery, when Sangharsh confided in him. "Give me your personal assurance that Nandish will not be harmed, Ajju" Ajju turned to respond to the man before sitting in his Eco Sport.

"I've played with him on my lap, promising to watch out for him as my little brother" Watching Sangharsh amazed at his recollection of such an old memory, Ajju nodded, "Yes, *Chachu*. I never forgot"

"You have my word, not just as the future *Chaudhary* of the *Raika*s, but also as his elder brother" Back at DTD, Arjun had started Dhanush's training already, not relying on anyone but himself to teach him the impeccable running of the gallery.

He wasn't confident about Mr. Guha's loyalty yet, but he was sure that his methods were easy enough for Dhanush to understand. The boy had the photographic genius of his father and the keen business acumen of his mother.

The biggest problem everyone had with him was his irresponsible attitude towards everyone and everything. Since his involvement with Leenata, Dhanush had turned a complete 360 degrees, shedding his inhibitions of taking onus for his actions.

Mr. Guha had noticed this training on the job, which he'd informed Ramona when she called in the morning. "How was there a merger? DTD is mine!" she had screamed over the phone. "Not anymore, Madame"

"There is a Dr. Shekhawat from Jaipur who has become Mr. Pratap's business partner at DTD. I'm sorry but my loyalties lie with them now" "Be quiet, you fool! Do you think they would welcome you in their fresh venture with open arms and floral garlands, when they find out you've been working for me?"

"If there is one thing about Arjun Pratap I can bet on, it would be his ability to never forgive or forget" Mr. Guha went pale, his heartburn making him take his prescribed pills for acidity. "What do you want from me now? The merger is complete"

"But you're the only one who will continue to give me a call and any information I need, every day. And the next time you choose to become conscientious, remember what you read in the newspapers. Corporate espionage caught, sentence of ten years in imprisonment given." Ramona threatened.

"You wouldn't! I am a family man. My daughter is near about to be married!" "Good for you. Just do as you're told then, Mr. Guha. I'm not bothered about you and yours. Give me the information asked and you'll be fine"

Hanging up, Ramona's fiercely stern look changed into a ponderingly concerned one. Ringing for the attendant, she asked him where her daughters were. Puzzled by her question, he said, "On their way, I think. The doctor will see you first though, Madame"

Dr. Krishnan was pleased to see the partial recovery in her eyesight. "Your scans show you can see shapes and maybe hazy forms, right?" "Yes, doctor. But, it gives me a headache" "It's just the strain of having to focus. I'll give you something for that as well"

Thanking him, she was about to dial another number, but saw the doctor still standing. "Was there something else, doctor?" "Yes, actually. I'm going through your chart. As you know, our hospital has a strict policy of all bills to be cleared, of the tests that have been conducted on each of our patients"

"Of course I do" Ramona answered, wondering why the number she was calling no longer existed. "Well, you have a long list of unpaid bills that have been brought to my notice, Madame" Dr. Krishnan said apologetically.

Hanging up the phone out of frustration, she frowned, "Well that's just not possible. I've signed on a cheque which your hospital administrator himself received. My daughter Mia got the papers for me. Please, doctor...I don't feel strong enough to have this discussion for the time being"

"You're perfectly fine, Madame. In fact, you're free to leave anytime you wish, providing you come back for regular check-ups. Your wounds are almost healed now. It's just a matter of time, before your eyesight gets back to normal too"

"I'll let you rest now. Your daughter had left a message to say she's stuck in traffic and will reach you soon" When the doctor left, Ramona tried

Mia's number again. She was wondering why she just couldn't get through, when she heard Diana's voice.

"Sorry, Mother. I got caught up in traffic. It has started raining so you can imagine what the condition is outside" Kissing her on the forehead, she said, "The doctor gave me the good news. Soon, we can leave and you can see almost clearly already!"

Ramona gave her half a smile, showing her mobile. "I tried calling Mia. Her phone is dead" Diana bit her lip, knowing the time she dreaded was close. "Mother the accident took her away" "Took her away? To where?"

"Mia has passed on. She didn't make it, Mother" Ramona slapped Diana hard across her face. "How dare you say that! You're lying! Why are you lying to me? She must be angry with me, so she doesn't want to meet"

"That's it, isn't it? Then say it as it is. Don't say something so horrible!" Ramona kept on blabbering, staring at the ceiling, the walls, as if they were Mia. Diana sat down next to her. "Mother, I am sorry but it is true"

"She didn't survive the accident. I have been looking after you all these days" Ramona heard her words from a distance, falling back on her pillow. Diana ran to get Dr. Krishnan who came immediately.

"The shock needs a sleep-off. I've given her a sedative. Go easy on her when she wakes up. Better still, call me as soon as she awakens" Diana sat down on the chair besides the bed where Ramona lay.

Vansh called to check on how things were. He chose to stay at the hotel, to do some research on concepts floated by Diana about bettering Bassi. "I found a large amount of information on Agri- and Ecotourism, Jiya"

"This could be exactly what Bassi needed. You are truly a God sent!" Diana gave him a pre-occupied thank you. "What's wrong?" he asked, sensing the same. "Mother asked about Mia. I had to tell her the truth"

"She fainted after being delirious for a while. The doctor had to sedate her. I am to watch her and call him when she is awake" "I'll be there in an hour" Vansh replied to her unanswered question. "Yes. Thank you"

"You have got to stop thanking me, *chori*! I'm to be your *Beend* soon!" She couldn't put into words what it meant, felt like to have someone to be with her, even when the physical proximity was missing. The feeling of belonging to Vansh, warmed her all over.

The hospital bed moved a bit an hour later, with Ramona groaning as she woke up. Squinting to make out the person standing in front of her, she recognized it as Diana. "Who is that standing next to you, Diana?" she asked, still groggy from the sedation.

"It's Vansh. *Chaudhary* Akash of Bassi's son" "He's here because?" "He's here with me" "With you? Nobody is with you, you silly girl! Everyone is with someone for some reason. Once the aim has been achieved, they are discarded like used napkins"

"Yes, Mother. That is what I thought. And so did Mia. But then, she met Ajju *Bhaiya* and I met Vansh" "You are reasonably good-looking, slim. That boy has probably gone for your looks, the kind he can never have in the village he comes from. You're so naïve, Diana"

"Don't you know men only want one thing from women?" "Mother! Do not undermine what Vansh and I have. He is the most respectful man I have ever met" "You meet this boy and forgot all about what I have taught you? Just like Mia. You're both the same this way"

"Ajju *Bhaiya* and Mia's love was unconditional. Yours Mother, was wrapped in layers and layers of exhaustive conditions" "My Mia..so young, so beautiful. Everyone would stare at her since she was little. Boys would line up at my doorstep when she was a teenager"

"Her dream was to have an apparel line of her own. I tried to get her interested in Photography, hoping to get the gallery back on my name one day. Try as I might, she kept sketching whenever she could"

Looking up at Diana's hazy silhouette, Ramona said, "You hardly had any creativity in you. You couldn't even speak properly, stammering all the time. If it weren't for Mia, you would not even have finished your school"

Diana didn't want Vansh to hear what Ramona said about her childhood. Vansh noticed her embarrassment and couldn't hold back any longer. "There is nothing wrong with Jiya. She is perfect in every which way"

"It is her intelligence in creativity that will move the people of my village to be more enterprising. You wouldn't know anything about my Jiya, because you never tried to get to know her, Ms .Rai!"

Ramona was eerily quiet, even after Vansh had finished speaking. "Now, this is what is going to happen. Either we pay the hospital and take you back to the hotel; or you choose to do all of that yourself"

"Diana is dead. Jiya is born now. She is coming with me to Bassi where I will marry her. Now, which do you choose?" Ramona quietly got dressed, while Diana and Vansh completed all the administrative formalities.

They hired a nurse, an attendant to be stationed at the hotel for Ramona. In the cab, Ramona was silent, looking out of the window. "I'm Mrs. Pratap, not Ms. Rai" she said, her features still as stone.

"You're the ex-wife of Mr. Pratap. That makes you Ms. Rai" Vansh corrected, fed up of the way his Jiya was being treated. "Don't talk nonsense! Arjun has filed for divorce. I'm aware of that. Until it isn't over though, I am still his wife"

"Sorry Ms. Rai, the divorce is over. Mr. Pratap has married Suhani *Chachi* already" Ramona's expression remained the same. She was still quiet, all the way till they reached the suite. "Will you leave me too?" she asked Diana, holding on to the white door of her bedroom.

"I have to go with Vansh, Mother. He is the one I choose to spend my future with" "You mean he is the one who controls you now" Ramona said, still standing with her hand resting on the brass knob.

"Why does everything have to be about control with you?" Diana said. "It is all about control, whether you like it or not, Diana!" "No. Not this time. Love doesn't control you. Love gives you wings to fly"

"Then go! Fly away! Don't come crying back to me because I will not let you in. I took you in once as if you were my own. But, not anymore. You don't deserve my pity" "Yes, I know I'm not your daughter. I found out by accident while you were in hospital"

This was too much for Ramona to take. "Do you think you have done me any favour, by any chance? If nothing else, you owe me your life!" "Again, you're misunderstanding as usual. I stayed back because although you never thought of me as your child, I still considered you to be my mother. If I knew I was such a bother, maybe I could have joined my birth mother…"

Not seeing the point in sheltering an open secret, Ramona screamed, "That's right! Your birth ruined everything. We were happy until you happened. Your being born was a curse on so many. You should've gone with your parents when they were leaving that day. Maybe then, my Mia would have been alive!"

Diana had tucked Ramona in, who was delirious again. She dialed Vansh's number, telling him she was ready to move permanently to Bassi. They were to leave the day after tomorrow when the nurse and attendant could arrive.

Vansh had already informed his parents he was returning in a day's time with Jiya. He didn't give them any information in detail, deeming it best to speak to them face-to-face. Ramona dreamt of Mia that night.

She was sitting in a pretty pink frock with a blue satin sash. "Look Mother, I made a drawing!" "Not now. I'm busy" she heard herself speak in her sleep. Softly crying into her pillow, Ramona began to regret each moment she spent away from Mia. She had no one to call her own now.

Her helplessness quickly tricked down to self-pity. She had to become as hard as a diamond now. She may not have any family left. But, she still had two things everyone was after-money and power. Deciding to begin planning all over again once Diana left with Vansh, she dozed off peacefully.

# CHAPTER THIRTY SEVEN

"What're you reading, Vansh?" Jiya asked him, sitting beside a very engrossed man, the taxicab taking them straight to Bassi. "Studying this graph I picked up while researching about Agritourism on the internet at the hotel. Here, have a look at this" he said, showing her the table.

"The Indian Government had sanctioned a substantial amount of money to enhance tourism at the Ajmer-Pushkar destination, as well as the Desert Circuit" "There is a desert circuit? I thought there was a Golden triangle as a tourist destination!" Jiya exclaimed.

"That's Delhi-Agra-Jaipur. It's called the Golden Triangle. Jodhpur-Bikaner-Jaisalmer is called the Desert Circuit. All in all, there are over twenty projects running, in just the state of Rajasthan alone!" Vansh declared, slapping his thigh merrily.

"What does that mean?" Jiya asked. "That means we don't have to worry about a government sanction, as long as our plan to introduce Agritourism to Bassi is passed by the government of Rajasthan.

Jiya knew the money involved in the project they both intended to start, was far more than a mere bank loan. Pleased at Vansh's enthusiasm, she coaxed him further. "Tell me what else you've learnt. I'm keen to know what how you've been keeping yourself busy, while I was at the hospital"

Taking slices of cut apple from her, Vansh began. "I learnt enough to start off now and end until we reach Bassi. Don't worry, I'll try to shorten it though" "I can hear you all day" Jiya said, pleased at Vansh's eagerness to share what he had learnt.

"Tourism is not only a growth engine, but it is also an employment generator. Agritourism is a part of Rural Tourism, which in itself is multi-faceted and takes place only in the countryside. Also, as against conventional tourism, it has certain typical characteristics" "Such as?"

"It is experience-oriented, the locations are less populated, it is predominantly in natural environments and it is based on the preservation of culture, heritage and traditions" Showing her diagrams and charts he had sketched, Vansh continued.

"My aim won't just be to generate revenue for our community, Jiya. It may well be the key to stop the exodus from Bassi to Jaipur and other cities!" They kept exchanging to and fro, excited about their new venture.

By the time they reached Bassi, it was noon already. Bindiya was waiting outside the *haveli* with her husband, the moment Vansh called to say they were about to reach. Beaming as a mother should, she hugged her son after he touched her feet.

"*Khammaosa, Maasa*" "*Jeete raho, beta*" Bindiya looked inside the cab as another passenger got off. "You're Diana, right?" she asked. "She is Jiya hereon, *Maasa*" Vansh corrected his mother gently.

Akash's look forbade her to question what was really going on, so they all walked into the cool courtyard, slightly wet due to the monsoon showers. "*Bhaiya*, welcome back! How're you, Jiya?" Leenata came out to greet them, dusting her hands with a cloth napkin.

It irritated Bindiya that the siblings shared more between each other than earlier, when she would be included in their discussions too. The three big suitcases were brought in and put in the guest room, where Jiya was to stay.

"How many days has she come for exactly?" Bindiya asked Akash softly. "Shhh! We cannot insult guests at our home. Let's wait till they freshen up. I trust Vansh to have a perfectly good explanation"

The noon meal had a rich *matar paneer* with *roti* and *masoor dal*, followed by *sohan halwa* for dessert. Dabbing his mouth and hands, *Chaudhary* Akash called for Vansh to join him for a *hookah*. "*Baasa*, I would like Jiya to be with me when we speak, with your permission"

His curiousity piqued, the *Chaudhary* agreed, insisting that Bindiya and Leenata join them as well. "Good that all of you are here. Before anything, Leenata knows pretty much everything. I've been speaking with her everyday"

"*Baasa*, I owe you an apology. I lied to you. Arjun *Chachu* never called for me to see Leenata's reception venue. I went to meet Jiya" Vansh narrated how Ramona's accident had hospitalized her, how Mia's loss was tough for her to handle.

"Despite all of this, Jiya kept her emotional loss aside, serving the mother she thought was her own, day in and day out. She was adopted to give Mia company, but never told that she was her step sister"

Now was the tough part. Vansh ploughed through, despite his parents' raised eyebrows. "I've gotten her back with me for more than one reason. *Maasa*, she was Diana earlier. Now, she is Jiya and she is to be your *bahu*, my *lugai*"

"All her luggage is upstairs. I'm not letting her go away from me anymore. As far as her family goes, consider me to be all she's got" "Vansh, you can't just bring an orphan home like you used to get stray animals in to tend to, when you were smaller!" Bindiya remarked, much to everyone's dismay.

Jiya got up to leave because her heart hurt to hear what she just did. "No, Jiya. Sit beside me" When Leenata got her back to sit down, Vansh spoke sternly, "I expect her to be given the respect she has earned in my eyes"

"Eat your words, *Maasa*. What Jiya has brought into the family is something that will make us all indebted to her forever" "And what might that be?" *Chaudhary* Akash asked, puffing at his *hookah*.

"I've been researching her concept and am a hundred per cent confident that a way has been finally found out of our financial misery" The *hookah* stood still, both elders listening to Vansh keenly.

"Jiya, speak freely about your concept" Jiya explained Agritourism to them, simply as 'living the life of a farmer for a stipulated duration'. She explained how she, Vansh and Leenata planned to execute their respective roles.

"I'll contact the Ministry of Tourism and the State government for the loan we require to set up the basic infrastructure, so as to meet the requirement of the state team as and when the loan is sanctioned."

"Leenata will be looking after the business aspect of the Agritourism at Bassi. We aren't the only ones who are en-cashing on this lucrative venture. There are hundreds, maybe even thousands of villages all over India, that are thriving under its umbrella as we speak"

"She speaks the truth, *Baasa*" Leenata added. "I've been researching as well and what she says is perfectly doable. Give us your consent, your blessings" Bindiya was never so ashamed in all of her life.

"I cannot take back the words that have been spoken. I can ask for your forgiveness, Jiya" "Please don't say that. I understand your apprehension, but I assure you that my interests lie purely in the betterment of Bassi and the happiness of your son"

The words she spoke travelled into the hearts of Vansh's family members, who accepted her readily with open arms. Their worry was having both Vansh and Jiya under the same roof. "We must speak with *panditji* tomorrow for a wedding date"

"Until then, let her stay at Neeraj's place. We cannot set a wrong example for our people" Akash suggested to his wife that night. Bindiya decided to call for the priest the next morning, planning her son's wedding with pomp and show, drifting off to sleep.

Tiptoeing to the guest room, Vansh kept his hand on Jiya's soft arm, where the glow of the moonlight illuminated her fair skin. She woke up with a start, but quickly calmed down on seeing who it was.

"Go back to your room, *Chote Thakur*. If they find you here, we're both in trouble!" she teased him. He came closer to her and kissed her tender, parted lips till she was breathless. "I cannot sleep any longer without kissing you goodnight, my love"

"Sleep well, Jiya. Tomorrow, they will probably make you stay someplace else, as it is against *maryada* for the boy and girl to be under one roof before their wedding. Wherever you go, I will come to see you and stay with you from morning till evening"

Feeling blessed once again to have a loving partner, Jiya smiled herself to sleep. The next morning, Bindiya asked Leenata to drop Jiya at Neeraj's place. "No need, *Maasa*. Let Leenata go to Gurukul. I will drop her to Neeraj Chacha's place"

The luggage was taken by a bullock cart to the venue, while both Vansh and Jiya walked. The Chaudhary had already prepared Neeraj to expect a guest, so no questions were asked in that regard.

Bindiya welcomed the *pandit*, who came after his morning prayers at the temple by the River Bhairach was complete. Checking his books, the half-torn Hindu calendar, he finally spoke. "You are lucky parents indeed!

*Chaudhrain*, the date of your son's wedding falls on the same day as your daughter's!"

Bindiya was overjoyed when she heard this, informing her husband as he returned from the fields in the afternoon. "Bindiya, we'll be even poorer after their wedding. We hardly have anything left"

"Maybe that is why *Ma Bhavani* and *Bholenath* sent us Jiya. I have a hunch this plan of theirs will bring prosperity, back to Bassi" Not meaning to curb her enthusiasm, Akash continued, "That's a few months from now before everything is fully functional"

"I'm talking about right now. Their wedding is a month from now. How will we manage not to make a mockery of it all?" "I have a suggestion. Two, actually. You will dislike them both, Akash"

Bindiya spoke while walking to the cool matki, to bring her husband a glass of water to drink after his meal of *rajma chawal* was over. "Let me be the judge of that" Akash said, glugging the water down to wash the *ghee* that coated her throat.

"We can either ask Giriraj, or Arjun *Bhaisa* for the money. Payment with interest can be given as an assurance" "Impossible! Arjun *Saheb* is our *samdhi* now. Our daughter is going into his house as his daughter-in-law"

"As far as Giriraj goes, do you believe for one moment that he would help in any way with the wedding of our offsprings, when we rejected theirs?" "So that's one option that you've dismissed. The other one is taking a small loan from a doctor who sits in Jaipur"

"If you recall, there was a Dr. Shekhawat who had accompanied *Chaudhary* Dhanush, in the helicopter after the accident" Seeing him nod, Bindiya continued, "Tara had taken loans from him time and again to increase her livestock"

"We could take a loan from him to see us through both the weddings and repay him when this concept of Agritourism, begins to yield financially profitable results" Akash gave his consent to the idea of the loan from the doctor at Jaipur, making it clear to his wife not to breathe a word of it to anybody.

"If anyone asks, tell them I've gone for business to see some hybrid varieties of plants at the exhibition" While Akash left for Jaipur the very next morning, Vansh and Jiya were busy explaining to the farmers about the benefits of Agritourism.

The school premise of Gurukul was used to explain the entire concept in detail to each farmer at Bassi. "Tourists will come to stay in your homes, work alongside you in your fields, and pay you generously for the experience"

"You must remember to keep your surroundings clean, have water and food ready for them, explain in detail what they wish to know or learn. Most of all, do your daily work diligently and show them you are hard workers with soft hearts"

Vansh's words had made way for Jiya, when she took over with the amount of money that would be given to them by the state, how much would be their approximate quarterly profit, and other tidbits of information that translated into an upgrade in their standard of living.

The farmers were convinced with the information the two imparted. They went back to their homes to discuss the same with their families, spreading hope that they were about to lose over their living conditions.

Word reached Giriraj and Tara about a girl called Jiya who Vansh brought to Bassi. She was hailed as the messiah for progress and prosperity for the people of Bassi. "Good news at last! I hope their venture is a success" Giriraj blessed them, finishing his last bit of *dum aloo* at dinner.

"Don't you think before you speak? God gave you a brain, Giriraj. Use it once in a while" Snubbed as usual by his wife once again, he asked what the problem was now. "The problem has always been you. God knows what my parents were thinking when they got me married to you"

"You lack ambition, drive, the makings of a real man. Don't you ever wish your son becomes the wealthiest and most powerful man in all of Bassi?" she hurled insults at him mercilessly. "I wish him to be loved and respected as a good man. You are ambitious for the both of us, my dear" he said, walking away from the furious Tara.

She followed him to their room, trying to drive sense into him. "If their plan of this Agritourism business succeeds, we will no longer be the richest at Bassi. We've worked hard all these years to increase our herd, Giriraj"

"All of your efforts will go waste if they succeed" Poor Giriraj fell for the seductive Tara's charms like almost every other victim she would cast her eyes on. After giving herself to him completely, she waited until Giriraj asked her.

"Tell me what to do and I will do it. I'll do anything for you, Tara"
"Go to the *Chaudhary haveli* tomorrow. Ajju has been declared as the *Chote Sardar* of Bassi. Vansh is the *Chote Thakur*"

"You are to ask *Chaudhary* Akash when he will declare the next *Chaudhary* of *the Raika*s. I have come to know that both Vansh as well as Leenata's wedding dates fall on the same day-the end of this month"

"Ask him to declare who the *Chaudhary* is to be before that" Tara whispered. "And what good would that do? What if he refuses and asks me who am I to question his authority?" "My darling husband" Tara looked deep into his eyes again.

"If you do as you are told, I will reward you over and over again" Enticed, Giriraj obliged her demand, as she did his. Ajju called Vansh that evening, telling him what his plan was. He was coming to Bassi in a few days' time and wanted to make sure Rati was alright.

Vansh surprised him by giving Rati's cell number, a gift from Jiya, so the lovebirds could talk to each other. Ajju hurriedly wrote the number down and called her as fast as his fingers allowed him to type her number on his cell.

A sleepy Rati answered her cell. "Hello, Jiya *di*?" "My love!" Rati got off her cot and ran outside to the moonlit night. "*Chote Sardar*!" she whispered, her voice quivering as if she were about to cry.

"How are you, my heart?" "I'm fine. When are you coming here?" "Very soon. If you need anything, speak to Vansh. This is my number. Save it and call me anytime you want." They spoke some more, and filled each other with sweet nothings that travelled into their beings from miles away.

That was the magic of being in love. Distance meant nothing if it were on the outside. But, if on the inside, it could spell disaster for any relationship. Vansh had shifted Rati to Neeraj *Chacha*'s house as well, not just to give Jiya company; but also to keep her away from her *Chachi*, who was still loyal to Tara.

Rati's little sister Dhara, slept peacefully when she returned after Ajju's call. She curled up to the child, smiling as she dreamt about the man she hardly knew anything about…except for the one and only thing that mattered.

Every time he held her, touched her she knew she had reached a place she never knew existed…home. That, for Rati, meant love.

# CHAPTER THIRTY EIGHT

Sarvani Anand had the creative genius of her father from the very beginning. The moment she was in Anand Creations after school, she would sneak into the cloth-cutting room, picking up colourful bits and pieces, *gota*, lace, rick-rack…anything that caught her eye.

Slowly she accumulated a boxful of bits of cloth, buttons of various shapes and sizes. She was a teenager when her parents presented her with a Barbie doll. She used the pieces she had collected to make a plain *ghaghra choli*.

With Nandish's acrylic colours, she gave it an ethnic look. When her parents saw the doll, it was hard for them to believe that it was Annie's handiwork. The cut, style, fine finish made them think they ought to encourage her to design for Anand Creations, one day.

"But I like making dolls with cloth and dress them up!" she told her twin, Nandish. "There's no money in that. Have it as a hobby, if you must. But you will need a proper job. Doll-making is anything but"

Annie collected a handful of dolls with different features, that she had stitched from scratch over the years. She began to make outfits for them, changing their clothes occasionally. Nobody knew what her secret passion was.

When she met Abhi, she was struggling with the idea of whether or not to tell him about her secret passion, when matters between them reached the seriously-committed stage. One fine day, she collected a few of her dolls along with a lot of mustered courage and drove to his office.

Dumping them on his table, she said, "I made them. Does that make me crazy?" Abhi looked at the dolls that were cleverly made, with tender love and care. "It makes you creative. Soft and gentle that you are Annie, these dolls show how affectionate you truly are"

She fell in love with him that day. He gave her the strength she always needed to voice her opinions, her thoughts. From then to now, was almost five years, wherein both had grown to love and respect each other, more and more with each passing day.

Andy was coming to Anand Creations that day, for the sole purpose of taking pictures of Annie's doll collection. The dolls, now finished completely, were ready to be presented for the world to see.

The body was made with cloth, the facial features painted by hand. The hair was wool and their clothes hand-stitched, as well. No machinery was involved in their making, from start to finish. Andy saw dolls in pairs depicting the states of Rajasthan, Bengal, Punjab and several other states.

"They're awesome, Annie!" he complimented her, amazed at the amount of patience that was required to make each and every one of them. "I'm going to take single shots as well as in pairs. Then, we'll launch them on the net right away"

"We should be done in a couple of hours" he informed her. Another creative input from Annie, was the background used for the dolls. The tourist attraction or specialty of that respective state became a board she had made as the doll's exclusive backdrop.

The *Rajasthani* couple had a board behind them that showed the Great Thar desert, with a row of camels walking along with their owners on a dune, just before sunset. Andy had never done any photography like this before.

This was a challenge he was bent on learning from. He took plenty of shots of each of the dolls, from the most flattering of angles. By the time their *chai* was served, the shots were done. They went over to meet their parents, who were coincidentally also on a tea break.

"All done?" Sangharsh asked. "Almost" Andy replied. "I need to take these back to the studio, fix and Photoshop, bring them back here and launch **Annie's Doll Collection** today itself" "But why today of all days? It can be launched tomorrow too"

"No harm done in missing out on one day, to move with caution" "I have to launch it today, *Baasa*. I met Abhi five years ago on this very day. If it weren't for his faith in me, **Annie's Doll Collection** would stay in the boxes within my room!"

"Well now! This I did not know, Annie" Sangharsh said, finishing the last sip of his tea. "Break's over. Get cracking, you two. After the launch, meet us right here and we'll all go out. Dinner's on your mother"

"Hey! I paid the last time. Not fair, Sangharsh!" Nalini protested. "After all these years of giving you the best years of my life, today you squabble with me about paying for a dinner?!" Nalini threw a piece of chalk at him, her giggle giving way to a series of smiles from both her children.

Andy looked at Annie and said, "And all those years ago, you thought you were crazy!" "Maybe I got it from them through the gene pool" she suggested. "It's not a bad thing to have, you know. If you remember to laugh at the end of the day…there's much to say about a life like that!"

It was late afternoon by the time Nandish left for DTD in his champagne-coloured Nissan Sunny. He reached at a time when Arjun was training Dhanush, an act that he had grown to get used to. Obedient Dan, tolerant Dan, responsible Dan.

Now that was one thing he never thought he would hear. "How was the shoot?" Arjun asked his prodigy. "Amazingly insightful to say the least. Before I saw the dolls, I thought I was doing Annie a favour"

"Now my perspective on who did who a favour has changed quite a bit. She even had apt backgrounds to prop her dolls against" "Dude, you're sounding as excited as when she got her first Barbie!"

Reprimanding his son, Arjun said, "Never underestimate the thrill of photography, Dhanush. You used to be the 'Hunter' of DTD. Now, you're the creator of her future. A creator sees the magic, where for others there isn't any"

"Learn from what Nandish says. Go and see what pics he's taken, while I go and check on Mr. Guha" Dan watched Andy while he photoshopped the pics, refining the shots to precise perfection.

"These are indeed truly amazing. I take my words back. If I have a daughter with Leena, I'll probably end up buying the entire collection." "Not if I have one with Malika first!" Andy joked in the same vein.

By the time Nandish reached Anand Creations with the finished pictures of **Annie's Doll Line**, it was almost evening. He was beat, but wanted to do full justice to his sister's diligence. Abhi was sitting with Annie, chatting about the designs of **Nara Apparels**, when Andy walked in.

"Hey, Abhi! What're you doing here?" "Your sister summoned me and I humbly conceded." Noticing the same way Sangharsh spoke, Andy said, "You're like the younger version of my father."

"I called Abhi because I want him to launch my line. It would mean the world to me" Annie said, smiling at Abhi, coy as ever. **Annie's Doll Line** was launched that day, marketed and supported by the parent company Anand Creations. The next time Annie checked the website over dinner, she almost toppled over with delight.

"More than half are already sold out! Did you hear me? *Maasa, Baasa,* Abhi, Andy? Everyone likes my dolls!" They raised a toast to the most shy and the newest entrepreneur of the soft toys industry-Sarvani Anand.

"Soon to be Mrs. Sarvani Shekhawat!" Andy said, raising his glass of white wine. "To you both, Annie and Abhi! May you ever support each other and grow old together!" Sangharsh toasted the couple.

Everyone was intoxicated that night, except Nalini, who drove them home to safety. While the Anands celebrated the launch of the much-awaited **Annie's Doll Collection**, Ramona was pacing up and down her suite at Elite International.

The nurse and attendant kept for her, were beginning to get on her nerves once again. She wasn't used to being bossed around. Neither was she used to, being swept under the carpet. "Mr. Guha, what took you so long to pick my call?"

"I was talking to Mr. Pratap. How could I take your call in front of him, Madame?" "By excusing yourself, you dodo! How else?" "You make it sound so simple" "It is simple. But you're not smart enough to understand that. Anyway, stop wasting my precious time. Tell me what is the latest at DTD?"

Mr. Guha was sick and tired of being Ramona's reporter. He was glad initially when the merger between Mr. Pratap and Dr. Shekhawat took place. But Ramona had injected a deep fear in him, that not only would Mr. Pratap lose his trust on him, but would also ensure him jobless.

What was worse, the fear of going to jail for corporate espionage gave the poor simpleton sleepless nights. "Have you fainted, Mr. Guha? I asked you to brief me on the latest, at the gallery."

"Yes, I heard you. As you know, there has been a merger between the doctor from Jaipur and Mr. Pratap" "Yes, I do. What else?" "Mr. Pratap's son Dhanush is to be married, at the end of this month" "Mr. Guha, stop testing my patience. I asked you for news pertaining to the gallery, not the Prataps."

"I know Dhanush is getting married at Bassi, end of this month" "What you don't know, Madame, is that their wedding reception is to be held at the gallery, with the theme picture launch of **Regressive Progression**"

"The Bassi then and the Bassi now's comparison through photography" Ramona sat down on the chair, taking a few sips of her iced tea. She had regained her vision completely, except the occasional headaches at night.

She chose not to tell Dr. Krishnan about the headaches during her previous check-ups, in case he chose to detain her at the hospital again, to conduct tests as if she were a guinea-pig. "Madame, are you there?" "Yes, yes. I'm thinking" "If that is all, I would like to go now. I have to lock up and leave for the day"

"Do you have the backroom keys?" "Not anymore, Madame. Mr. Pratap has started a new policy, where the last one to lock up hands the keys of the gallery to our main guard, who in turn goes to Swarn Niwas to hand them over to Mr. Pratap"

Seeing a ray of hope, Ramona barked, "Stay there and don't move. Send the guard on some wild goose errand exactly a half hour from now. I don't want to be seen when I enter or exit" Before Mr. Guha could protest, Ramona hung up, hurrying to leave so as to reach on time.

"Well done, Mr. Guha" Arjun said, smiling from the doorway. "Have I redeemed myself?" "Not yet. Do as she says and make sure the security cameras are on with the volumes on high" Obeying Arjun, Mr. Guha got busy, asking the guard to get a few errands done, checking on the CCTV cameras.

Within an hour, Ramona walked in dressed in a black jumpsuit. "Give me the master-key" she ordered. "Madame, I don't have it. I told you the rules around here have changed" "I need to destroy the pictures of the new theme"

"Once that doctor from Jaipur sees DTD as a sinking ship, never able to deliver as promised, he will withdraw his partnership. And then, I will buy the gallery back. The property of the Rais shall belong once again to the Rais!"

The consistent claps she heard were timed with the footsteps of a man. Arjun was standing in front of her, resting at the doorway. "Your little tricks are getting predictably boring, Ramona" Feeling slighted, she turned on Mr. Guha.

"I gave him money as bribe for information. If there is anyone you should point fingers at, it should be him!" "Madame!" Mr. Guha protested, hoping Mr. Pratap wouldn't give her suggestion a serious thought.

"You have a dirty habit of taking advantage of the simple, helpless ones. Situations that you can twist to what suits you the most" Arjun accused her, continuing, "If there is anyone who is to be in trouble with the law today, it would be you"

"You have no proof" "I have all the proof I need. Mr. Guha is clear, but you are not. I'm going to put you behind bars once and for all!" "Arjun, have mercy! I'm not in the right frame of mind. I just lost Mia. Diana has abandoned me for Vansh"

"I have no one who could get me out on bail except my lawyer. I…" "Alright. There is one way you can stay out of jail, for now. I doubt if you will be able to follow through, though" Ramona knew she had been cornered, caught red-handed.

If Arjun reported her to the authorities, she was looking at a minimum of a decade in imprisonment. But, there was more to fear, especially if Interpol found out where she was. No, she had to stay away from the police.

The accident all those years ago had enough police hovering around her already. Luckily no one took her fingerprints yet. If they did, the match would put her behind bars for sure. She had to agree to whatever Arjun had on offer.

"I'll do it. Tell me" she said grudgingly. "Arjun sat down, pulling the chair in front of him for her to sit on. "Write a confession of how you tried to bribe my employees to take over DTD" He pushed another page towards her.

"Write you are divorcing me out of your own free will" The third and last paper he pushed forth, got her goat. "Write if you ever return to India, I will be obligated to hand you over to the police. Mr. Guha, get Ms. Rai a cup of coffee. She looks pale enough to need one"

"I'll be at my office till the paperwork is done. Watch her Mr. Guha, for you and I both know she is a slippery one!" Ramona wrote all three documents as instructed, walking into what once used to be her office.

Handing over the papers to Arjun, she snapped. "Now what more would you like to humiliate me with?" "Look around you, Ramona. All this belonged to you once. The hunger..this bottomless pit you have of power, control has changed you so much, that you fail to recognize the damage you cause yourself"

"You think everyone is giving you a hard time, whereas you've done nothing to gain their trust, make them believe you mean well" Ramona was fidgeting in her seat. "I'm due for my check up tomorrow. If your heart-wrenching sermon is over, I'd like to go"

Arjun had to leave for home too. Suhani was beginning to worry, as it was almost an hour past midnight. He watched Ramona take off in the city cab, calling his *Beendni* on the way home. "I have all the letters handwritten by Ramona"

"She will never be any reason to cause any strife to our family again" Ramona reached the hotel, packed her bags quickly. Arjun had given her until next day, when after her check-up at Lilavati Hospital, she was to leave town, subsequently the country, never to return.

She tried to sleep but couldn't. Pouring some wine in a goblet, she began to worry. She couldn't go back to London because there was a double homicide suspicion against her. She had no relatives elsewhere who would perhaps protect her from harm, or worse, Arjun's wrath.

She thought of giving Diana one last chance, to get on her good side. Mr. Guha had given her enough ammunition to set Bassi on fire. Tara was Dr. Shekhawat's mistress, Dhanush was born out of wedlock. Tara was Ajju's birth father's mistress too.

Yes, she had enough information to feel the rush of power that made her feel alive, important. She booked a cab from a new taxi service this time. She would disappear into a hotel in Rajasthan, perfecting her plot, after which, she would enter the realm of Bassi.

If Ramona wasn't happy, no one else ought to have the right to be happy either. That was the exact attitude Arjun was trying to show her. She chose to follow the same path, that was the root cause of her bitterness.

It was silly on her part to be hopeful for an ending, that would be to her advantage. She finished her wine in a quick swig, sleeping peacefully for a few hours, until the nightmares of the tortures souls she had murdered for her way to be cleared, recurred again.

She yearned for a dream in her sleep, where she could dream of becoming everything she could possibly be. It had now become an impossible reality, as her actions did not corroborate the intentions, that could reflect on contents that were part of an exemplary life. On the contrary, Ramona single-handedly sabotaged her own life, but had still not learnt her lesson.

# CHAPTER THIRTY NINE

*Chaudhary* Akash had always been a dotingly devoted father. He participated in the upbringing of both his children, by being the hands-on parent Bindiya never imagined he would become. His love for his wife increased, the moment she became the mother of Vansh.

Subsequently, Leenata sealed the deal of his devotion as a family man. Tara never even tried to entice him, neither did the thought even cross her mind. Akash knew her true character, as did Bindiya refrain from being overly friendly with her.

*Chaudhary* Akash's children were now grown up, ready to start families of their own. He had gone to Dr. Shekhawat at the clinic he owned at Jaipur, to ask for a loan that would see him through both the weddings.

In return, he was to offer the loan repayment with interest, that was expected as and when the Agritourism project yielded its much-desired results. The clinic was more like a palace, with large columns, white elephants on either side.

The steps were made of white marble, where half a knee lift sufficed to reach the next step. Ramps on either sides of the brass hand-holding pipes, were frequented by patients in wheelchairs. The reception already had a crowd with innumerable demands that were being met.

Akash had to smile his kindness through, as an old lady tried to gain the Receptionist's attention. "*Inhe dekh lo aap pehle* (Please have a look at her first). She is old and looks like in need of help" The lady at the Reception obliged the request, calling for the village man thereafter.

On hearing his query, she said, "My grandfather was from Bassi. Have a seat right here. I will ensure you meet the doctor today, before you leave" Akash sat on the plastic chair attached to a row of several others, full of common folk awaiting their requests to be catered to.

About an hour or so later, a man in a safari suit, bluish-gray in colour, came to escort him to the Doctor's chamber. Akash entered at a point when a husband and wife were about to leave. "Take good care of her. She is the mother of your children"

"Collect her medicines on your way out, but remember there is no compensation for love and affection" Thanking the doctor, the couple left. "*Aawo, padharo*! (Please come in!) What can I do for you, *Chaudhary hukam?*"

Akash felt good in his presence, for his ego was battered when he realized he had insufficient funds for the wedding of his children. A man of such an obvious stature as Dr. Shekhawat spoke to him with a degree of respect that made him forget momentarily why he was in his office in the first place.

"*Khammaosa, Doctor Saheb*! I have heard of your kindness and generosity in helping those in need, sitting at my *haveli*" "Kindness and generosity are big words, *Chaudhary hukam*. I come from a rural background myself, where pursuing an education to become a doctor was tough for my parents"

"The day my father died, his last words to me were that I must help out those like him as much as I can, to let his soul rest in peace" Taking his glasses out, he looked at Akash, smiling. "His name was also Akash, by the way"

They smiled understanding each other perfectly. Men of the land were true to their word. "I've not spoken about my family to anyone in a long time. Maybe your name triggered some memories.." the doctor said, offering water in a clean glass to him.

Sipping the water, Akash apologized if the memories hurt him. "On the contrary, it feels like you have been sent as a reminder that my father watches over me, for I do his bidding as much as I can"

Akash found the educated doctor to be more of a down-to-earth human than a whimsical, eccentric one as he was known to be. Opening a *potli* of *achar*s and *murabba*s, tightly sealed in small jars, Akash handed them over to the doctor.

"I feel silly doing this, but my wife thought your family might like to try these with your meals" Touched by the gesture, the doctor opened the *aamka murabba* and picked on a piece. "Just as my mother used to make it!"

"Delicious, *dost*!" The doctor told him over tea, while they chatted like old friends. They chatted about how his wife passed away when his son was very small. His son left Jaipur to work in Delhi and was about to be married.

"So, you have no one special in your life?" "We men have our needs, as you know. I have enough people to take care of my hospitals, my house is more of a palace with a staff ready to serve whenever I wish"

"There is a lady who visits me as and when she can. We have a special friendship. That is all" said the doctor, suddenly coming forward from his swiveling chair. "Did you say you're the *Chaudhary* of the village of Bassi?"

Akash nodded clarifying, "A lady called Tara came to you for loans that made them rich enough in livestock. You were the doctor who brought *Chaudhary* Dhanush from Pushkar after the camel race accident, all those years ago, in the helicopter"

"Yes, I am! What a small world. Your daughter Leenata is to marry Dhanush Pratap, am I right?" Surprised at how the doctor who sat all the way at Jaipur knew, he nodded. "Dhanush's father Arjun Pratap, is my partner in the gallery at Delhi. Not only that, my son Abhimanyu is to marry Arjun's friend Sangharsh Anand's daughter Sarvani soon!"

Akash stumbled with the amount of information the doctor gave him. "Small world indeed, *Doctor Saheb*!" Now things were highly uncomfortable for *Chaudhary* Akash. How was he to take a loan from a man who knew Leenata's would-be in-laws, so closely?

What if they found out he was not rich enough for their status? What if his own children found out that all the money that was kept for their wedding, was spent in raising them while they made ends meet?

How could he face his son if he came to know his father had taken a loan for his wedding just to keep up appearances, for the sake of saving face in front of the clan? "Well *Doctor Saheb*, it was very nice meeting you. I have to leave for my village. *Khammaosa*!"

*Chaudhary* Akash got up to leave. "*Baitho, Chaudhary hukam*. I know your plight, your condition. You have come for a loan that will be given" "You don't understand, *Doctor Saheb*. I am the *Chaudhary* of Bassi"

"If anyone finds out I don't even have enough money for the marriage of my children, what face will I have left as their leader? What if my children found out?" "You will have to trust me. I want to help you, but you will have to learn to trust me"

"If it makes you feel any better, I will tell you a secret I keep close to myself, that has been weighing heavily upon me off late" Akash sat down on his chair that faced Dr. Shekhawat, across the table.

"A rich man's secrets are not as dangerous as a poor man, who has secrets attached to his self-respect, *Doctor Saheb*" "On the contrary, *Chaudhary hukam*. A rich man's secrets could puncture his wallet, not to mention his reputation"

"Anyway, do you recall I mentioned earlier about a special lady friend, who came to meet me off and on, whenever she could?" "Yes" "It's Tara. Giriraj of Bassi's *lugai*. And, before you say it, she didn't come for a loan!"

Akash was sickened by the behavior of someone, who was of the same community as him. "She says she loves me, but cannot leave Giriraj because of the children" "*Doctor Saheb*, Tara had a clandestine affair with the previous *Chaudhary*, *Chaudhary* Dhanush Chand as well"

"She is known as a wayward woman who will do whatever it takes for money, for power" Seeing the doctor's saddened expression, *Chaudhary* Akash said, "I'm sorry to have to tell you this. You seem to be a good man. So is Giriraj, Tara's husband"

Akash hoped his telling the truth as it stood, would not affect his chances of getting his loan. "I cannot thank you enough for telling me this. So far, I thought…" Laughing at his own gullibility, the doctor shook himself, as if setting his thoughts, feelings for Tara, free.

"It had to come out eventually. They say that love and truth are two such things that can never be hidden" Pulling a file from one of his drawers, he wrote something on the first page. "Take this form to the room opposite to the reception"

"A man called Rakib Chand will help you fill the loan form. Fill in any amount you require, *Chaudhary hukam*. We both have our secrets to protect, so we do not have a choice but to trust each other"

Akash hesitatingly took the surf-blue folder and left the doctor's chamber after thanking him. They exchanged phone numbers before parting ways. At Rakib Chand's room, *Chaudhary* Akash got to know that the loan sanctioned to him was free of any charge of interest.

"Why is that?" Akash asked, not wanting any favours from anyone, however nice they may have been. Rakib Chand showed the scribble that

Dr. Shekhawat had done, before handing over the folder to him at his chamber.

That one word made Akash realize how essential it is to always remember your roots, stay humble no matter how high, or for that matter how low, the journey of life takes you. "Family" Akash said, remembering how the doctor tasted Bindiya's hand-made pickles.

It was time for him to head back, once all of the paperwork was done. The ride back was time for him to reminisce, for a lot had happened in that one day. A complete stranger made him his family, giving him a loan that would sail him through the coming commitments.

He was thankful to the Lord *Shiva* for looking out for him, at a time when he felt all hope was lost. Bassi was the last stop of the air-conditioned Volvo bus he travelled in, to and fro off late. Earlier, he would have hired a taxi.

Times had changed since Akash had to cut his coat according to his cloth, as his finances dwindled. When he reached his *haveli*, he washed up and went straight to bed. Bindiya had packed *gobi ka paratha*s with *lehsun ki chutney* for him in a circular steel box, that he had eaten in the bus itself.

When he woke up to Bindiya nudging him awake to have the evening *chai*, Akash kept his cup on the bedside, pulling her to him. "*Arre*, what are you doing?" "Pulling my wife closer for a kiss, what else?" he said, claiming it from her.

When they were facing each other, she said, "Looks like your meeting with the doctor of Jaipur was a success" "That, *Beendni* isn't even half of what I have to tell you" he said, pulling her close to hold her in his arms, while he spoke about his entire visit in detail.

He described the palatial hospital, the kind Receptionist, Rakib Chand and the peon who escorted him to the doctor's chamber. When he came to the part when the doctor told him that he was a widower for several years, Akash kissed her on the forehead.

"Bindiya, I cannot imagine my life without you" "Me neither" she said, resting her head on his chest again, while he continued. He finally came to the part where he acknowledged, that the lady friend who visited him was none other than Tara.

"Giriraj's wife, Tara?" Bindiya asked, getting up to shut the window. "How many Taras do you know? Of course Giriraj's Tara" "But she used to go to the doctor for loans for her livestock" Bindiya murmured.

"Did you think she would tell you the real reason why she visited him, or what she gave him in return of the loans, which by the way have not been paid till date?" Akash added, making Bindiya feel nauseous.

"How could she? She has two grown children, a man as simple as Giriraj for a husband!" "Having a simple husband like Giriraj didn't stop her the last time with Dhanush *Bhaisa*" Akash murmured.

The couple vowed never to speak of this part of Akash's visit to the doctor again. Akash told her how Abhi and the doctor were related. "Small world" she said, getting up with the empty tea cups.

"Yes. That we all agree on. Come *Bindi*. Let's take a walk together like we used to, when we were younger, of our Bassi. We will go to Neeraj's house and meet Jiya and Rati as well"

Liking the idea of a walk when Bassi was winding up for the day, Bindiya rushed to inform the cook at the *rasoi* what to make for dinner, and left with Akash. They walked to many places that held memories, of when they were younger.

Reminiscing as they walked, both Akash and Bindiya were laughing when they reached the abandoned well. It was where everything had started. The then *Chote Sardar* Dhanush Chand had seen Suhani and Akash had seen Bindiya.

"You *Banjaran*s had us *Raika*s locked in your fists from that very moment!" Akash accused, pulling at her biscuit-coloured *odhni* as she moved away, glaring at him in jest. "So why all this romance all of a sudden, Akash?" Bindiya asked.

She was wondering, as to what did she owe the extra special attention he was giving her. "Because I believe now that being loyal to your spouse is not the only way you can show, you are committed to her. You need to show love as often as possible, as well"

"After meeting the doctor, I realized how loneliness can make a man desperate enough to trust anyone. After hearing about Tara, I also realized how lucky I am, to have a woman like you in my life"

"You have upheld the honour and respect of being my *lugai*, the mother of my children, the *Chaudhrain* of the *Raika*s, well over the years. I am a very lucky man and wanted you to know that I've never taken your presence in my life, as something for granted"

He then went on to present her with a beautiful ring, with an enameled peacock in gold inlay. "It looks expensive, Akash" "It is. But, I haven't given you anything in a long time. After the visit and on my way to the bus stop, I thought of you"

"I saw this at one of the windows on display, in a jewellery shop" They smiled at each other, grey-haired, wrinkled, but together. They walked back all the way to their *haveli*, after paying their respects at the temple of *Ma* Bhavani, that stood by the river Bhairach.

The discussion on the long list of items to buy for both weddings, was on the agenda next. Clothes, flowers, gifts, puja items had to be covered, invites to be sent. Akash called the doctor to thank him in the evening.

The doctor mentioned he had the *achar* Bindiya had made with his dinner. every evening. "It would be an honour if you could come for my childrens' wedding, Doctor *Saheb*" Akash said. "The honour would be all mine. We are family, after all!"

The doctor had just switched off his night lamp to go to bed, when his cell rang again. "Where have you been? I've been calling you all day!" Tara whispered, sounding hassled. "I've been busy. *Bolo kya baat hai* (Tell me what is it)"

"*Kya baat hai?* (What is it?) What is that? Have you found someone else to replace me?" "Tara, I don't have the energy to argue with you. If it's nothing important, we can talk tomorrow" "Oh, I see what this is. You are upset with me because I haven't been able to meet you off late, isn't it?!"

"Oh, if only you knew how much I missed you, your touch…" The doctor smiled over the phone. "I understand why you cannot come, my vixen. In fact, I got an invite today to come to Bassi. Looks like we will be meeting soon after all!"

"No, no. You can't come here. It's too dangerous" "Dangerous? For who, Tara? I'm coming on an invite. Who would want to harm me?" "What if my husband finds out?" "That you spent all the money he gave you to repay my loan on yourself and pleasured me in return of each rupee?" he spat out.

"*Chup karo*! (Be quiet!) How dare you speak to me this way!" "Women like you ought to be spoken to in exactly the same way. You don't have to worry about my coming to Bassi. Even if I do, I have no intentions of meeting a person like you"

"A person who used me by lying, making me believe she is my partner; whereas all she is, is a blood-sucking parasite!" Tara felt like a piece of jelly on the floor, about to melt. What was she to do now?

If Dr. Shekhawat was planning on visiting Bassi, it would prove to be acutely detrimental to her plans. What if Giriraj got an inkling of what had been going on behind his back? What face would she have left in front of her children?

# CHAPTER FORTY

Looking out of his Eco Sport, Ajju saw the desert landscape of Rajasthan whizz past, merging the brown sand with bits of greenery, here and there. From the rear view, he watched the straight road behind-the National Highway.

A thick blackish-grey rope-like road was being released by the very vehicle that carried him, as if he was being released himself from that which held him back, into something that he wanted.

"I'm going to Bassi tomorrow to accept *Chaudhary* Akash's offer, to be the next *Chaudhary* of the *Raikas*" Ajju had announced to his parents over dinner at Swarn Niwas, the previous day. "Alone?" Arjun asked, not comfortable with the idea, especially after witnessing the happenings of the prior visit.

"No, *Baasa*. Vansh is there, as is his family. My Rati awaits my return. She is my Braids, just as *Maasa* is yours" Ajju replied, his tone making it clear he was determined, prepared. Ajju had shopped all day, picking up a backseat full of gifts for Rati.

Saris, jewellery, were stacked in boxes for her alone. He didn't remember ever buying anything for Aradhana. She always had enough of everything. Whatever lacked, she would go out to get. Rati was of the village, not as outgoing or independent.

He wanted to show her the city he lived in, the world, his heart, his soul. Full of hopes and dreams, Ajju reached the *Chaudhary haveli*, happy to see Leenata waiting outside. "*Maasa* and *Baasa* are on their way back from Jaipur too"

"How've you been, Ajju *Bhaiya*?" "Good! You look lovelier by the day. Dhanush sent this for you" Ajju said, handing over a packet full of baubles and what seemed to be a letter in an envelope.

"You have turned my lady-killer Casanova brother into a soppy, lovesick puppy!" he added jokingly on entering the *haveli*. It looked shiny and new, the chipped edges on the sides in places now freshly cemented.

The entire *haveli* had been spruced up, giving it the regal look it rightfully deserved. "The *haveli* looks beautiful. They must have spent a fortune" he said, lighting up a smoke as Leenata offered him *chai*.

"They have been spending with fervor, off late. The wedding shopping is entirely from Jaipur and Chittorgarh" she said, conscious of her blush. Before Ajju could tease her about the change in her colour, the jeep of the *Chaudhary* pulled in the driveway.

"I told you not to buy the brown sari because it makes my Leenata look old!" "Your taste in clothes is neon enough to stop traffic! She needs subtlety in her wardrobe, Bindiya" "Your taste in clothes should be restricted to menswear. You don't even know the difference between chiffon and georgette!"

Quarrelling all the way into the courtyard, they saw Ajju sipping *chai* with their daughter. "Ajju! When did you arrive?" Akash exclaimed, instructing the house-help to keep the brimming boxes and packets upstairs. "I see you've been on a shopping spree! Any plans of slowing down?" Ajju asked, winking at Akash.

"Ask your *Chachi* that. She drags me from one shop to another till the last row, only to return to the first shop to buy, what first caught her eye! I know how I have survived today" "You're such a liar! Don't listen to him, Ajju"

"He went to shops that I had left, picking up what I didn't approve of. You don't see me complaining about any of that, do you?" It was all over by the time the noon meal was served. Hot *kachori* with potatoes, varieties of pickles and chutneys to add to the taste, were devoured.

Bindiya went with Leenata to show her what had been bought for the weddings, leaving Akash and Ajju with their *hookah*s at the verandah. "So, what brings you here? I see you have come alone"

"I do not mean to be blatantly forward, but I have noticed how tense things have become in Bassi. If you permit, I am ready to take over as the *Chaudhary* of the *Raika*s. We can get the *Banjara*s of Nagri to join us once again and build a stronger clan."

Akash agreed, saying the crown was getting too heavy for him. "I held on to it for years, hoping you would take over someday. Vansh began to get ideas in between, egged on by his mother. Viren is another one who has his eye on the crown, Ajju"

"In fact, Giriraj, his father, came to meet me a few days ago, asking to declare the new *Chaudhary* of the *Raika*s before both the weddings" Looking at his cousin, Dhanush Chand's replica, Akash said, "It's miraculous"

"Lord Shiva has sent you back with the wisdom and sagacity of your birth father. I will announce it in the *Panchayat* tomorrow. Are you ready to stay here permanently?" Akash asked the obvious question.

"With permitted visits to Delhi to check up on my parents, yes I am" "You must marry Rati as soon as I give you the *turban* and *lathi* of the *Chaudhary*. Her alliance will show everyone, you plan to stay among your people"

Ajju had been listening carefully to *Chaudhary* Akash so far. The moment he heard the word 'Rati', he became restless. "*Chachu*, I must meet her" "Leenata will bring her to you in the evening. You cannot step out of the *haveli* before tomorrow"

"It is my duty to ensure your safety, both as the future *Chaudhary* of Bassi and Nagri, and as your uncle" Agreeing with him, Ajju waited till Leenata would bring Rati to the *haveli*. It was better to be safe than sorry, which is what Ajju was beginning to learn.

Looking out at the back of his room's balcony, he saw a *Raika* male singing a local tune, walking without a care in the world, his *lathi* resting atop his shoulders horizontally, with his hands slung loosely around it.

A few minutes later, some *Raika* women adorned with chunks of silver around their necks, limbs and ankles, were chattering loudly, laughing as they balanced their collected twigs of firewood for the day on their heads, happy to go home to their families and feed the poor, hungry souls.

"This is my home" Ajju thought, feeling the need to close his eyes, breathe in deep. Bassi had always been a place, where his beating heart beat even faster. Now, the added attraction of Rati, made him altogether set to plant his flag there.

The evening tea was about to begin, when Leenata returned with the one Ajju had been waiting for, with baited breath. "How've you been, my angel?" he asked her, when they were left alone in the courtyard.

*"Khammaosa, Chote Sardar.* I have been good" she answered, looking into his eyes. The blue of her eyes still mesmerized him, as did the black of his. They stared at each other for a while, like long lost souls.

He put his palm forward, inviting to put hers on his. "I am to become the *Chaudhary* of the *Raika*s of Bassi and the *Banjara*s of Nagri soon. Will you do me the honour of being my *Chaudhrain*?"

She looked up at him for a moment, pulling her hand back. Hesitatingly, she said, "It is too much of a responsibility, for a commoner like me to be trusted with. I do not come from a royal bloodline like you do, *Chote Sardar*" she said.

She calmed down, the moment he gently held her in his arms. "Say 'yes' and I will teach you everything you need to know, never to leave you alone, forever by your side. Say 'yes'" he said, feeling her heartbeat as she closed her eyes and breathed a tender 'yes' into his chest.

Their hearts knew oneness from that moment on. He sat her down again, explaining what was required of her, telling her all about the gifts he got for her, that she could take with her if she wished.

Rati refused to take anything along, since she was sure he must have splurged on expensive items of luxurious taste. Charmed by her lack of greed, he asked her about life at Bassi, all these years.

She began to tell him how her family - Dhara and her blind grandmother *Daisa*, came to Bassi when her parents passed away. She loved to read whatever she could get her hands on. Leenata used to teach her how to speak in Hindi and English.

Her *Chachi* was a greedy, old woman who wanted her livestock to increase. She had Rati's studies stopped, sending her to graze the cattle instead. "I will teach you to read and write, Rati. There is never an end to learning, my love"

Affected by his words, she continued, "Viren started to become friendly, but I never saw any ulterior motive in it. He would come with his huge herd by the river Bhairach, sometimes with his friend Vansh, or at times with his father"

"One day, he gave me flowers and I put them in my hair. The next thing I hear is his mother speaking to my *Chachi*, asking for my hand in marriage for her son!" She went on to shock Ajju by saying that her *Chachi* would be gifted a few camels, cattle and goats on the day of her marriage, as per Tara.

"Greed has no end, just like knowledge. The only difference is how much effort one is willing to pursue, to which extent, to what use, to which degree" "Your words are full of wisdom, *Chote Sardar*. I wish I could speak like you"

"And so you shall one day, my dear. And so you shall!" Ajju reiterated her belief, that together, she and Ajju would grow, helping each other learn more as time went by. Time flew by as they spoke too, as Leenata began to light the night lamps that surrounded the courtyard and the corridors of the *haveli*.

"You must leave now" Ajju said, nodding to Leenata to take Rati back safely to Neeraj's. Before she could ask him when they were to meet again, he rested his palm on her cheek. "I will come for you so have faith"

"Do not speak of meeting me here. We cannot trust anyone till I become the *Chaudhary*" She left with Leenata into the still night, the lamp disappearing into the darkness as they moved further and further away from the *haveli*.

Vansh was back the next morning from the village of Nagri where he had gone to spread the awareness of Agritourism, so that the farmers there could participate in the revolution germinated by Jiya and himself.

*Chaudhary* Akash told him Ajju had finally agreed to become the *Chaudhary* of the *Raika*s of Bassi and the *Banjara*s of Nagri, to which Vansh's response was, "It is a legacy that must be passed on into the right hands"

"Ajju *Bhaiya* has always been the rightful heir. It is the greed of those aspiring to be the leader of the two villages, that makes them want what is not theirs" "Forgive me, my son. But at one point you wanted to be *Chaudhary* too" Akash remarked, wondering what made him change his mind.

"Yes, I did. But I am not built like Ajju *Bhaiya* is. He is a born leader. I spread awareness, knowledge. Jiya and I will continue to uplift Bassi through Agritourism, make it our life's work if possible"

"I would rather be the king of the heart of Bassi without the crown, than be the tyrant who tried to snatch it from the rightful heir" Akash patted his son, proud of how he had put his stand into words. Yes, love with the right person does change one for the better.

Vansh's primary ambition of succeeding his father was now no longer a priority. He wanted to help his fellow villagers, teach them how to work towards improving their living standards. His selflessness was a gesture encouraged by the girl who had stolen his heart-Jiya.

Vansh ran off to meet her, not having seen her for one whole day. There was much to talk about and he knew Neeraj *Chachaji* would start coughing loudly if he didn't leave an hour after arriving, since it was against *maryada*.

Ajju called his parents up to ask how things were. "Everything is normal here. How are you? Did you speak to *Chaudhary* Akash? What did he say? How is Rati? Did you meet her?" Arjun's barrage of questions made Ajju regret not having him around.

He barely remembered his birth father, although anyone who saw him claimed that the resemblance was uncanny. Arjun was his soul father, if there is such a term. He raised him with values not far from home, always encouraging him to follow his heart.

"I miss you, *Baasa*" "We miss you too, Ajju" Arjun had a lump in his throat after a long time. Ajju told him all that transpired during the day, including what Akash said was to happen tomorrow.

"If Akash is going to speak to the *Panch* members tomorrow, I suggest you stay indoors until further notice" "Yes, Akash *Chachu* said the same thing. But, I don't see why, although I will do his bidding" "Superstition mostly"

"The evil eye being cast on something good that is about to happen to the villagers, after almost two decades. Don't forget who you are, Ajju. You are the son of the King of the *Raika*s and the Queen of the *Banjaras*"

Pausing, he said, "I love you and have always been proud of you. You have what it takes to change what is happening there, that I believe. Just promise me, you will not risk your safety in any way at any time"

Giving his word on the same, Ajju wished him a good night. He slept a sound sleep that night. So much had to be done, but nothing could get started. Not until he became the *Chaudhary*. He was deeply moved by what Vansh had said to his father, sometime earlier.

The level of passionate commitment he showed, convinced Ajju that their concept of Agritourism was exactly what Bassi needed, to come back to what it used to be. He had a plan in place, but didn't know if it could be pulled off or not.

The first thing he would do after becoming the *Chaudhary*, would be to marry his Rati. The second would be disbanding the *Panchayat*; and the third, would be appointing Vansh as the *Chote Sardar*.

He was convinced it was the right thing to do, so that those who believed in his way of thinking would support him, whereas those who didn't could be convinced otherwise. Ajju did not know how dangerous this decision of his would become, for him.

He was seeing each move from the long-run point of view. Sadly, not everyone shared the power or the insight of his vision. Tara had succeeded in poisoning Viren's mind completely against *Chaudhary* Akash's family.

Rati's *Chachi* had meekly apologized to Tara a few days ago, saying that Rati had rejected Viren's proposal. Viren had been upset for obvious reasons, going off to ride on Jigar for a long time on hearing that Rati too, like Leenata, had fallen for someone else.

In his case, the 'someone else' were brothers of the same family. His ego, self-respect had taken a major hit which saw no respite for him. He could never recover from the villagers, who he thought mocked him behind his back.

His family was the wealthiest in all of Bassi and Nagri. And yet, he felt the poorest at that moment. Money could not buy him the love of a woman, peace of mind, respect, trust of those who mattered at one point.

He missed his old friend Vansh, as loneliness hit him again. The howl of a hyena woke him as he lay in a drunken state. It was early morning when he rode Jigar back to the stable, sleeping off as soon as he reached his multi-coloured home.

# CHAPTER FORTY ONE

There was a welcoming breeze blowing through all of Bassi, the entire morning. The sweetness of hope in the air was followed by the rays of a brighter future, as the day progressed. Akash was ready to hand over the crown he had been entrusted to safeguard to the heir himself, Ajju.

The boy had grown over the years and become the spitting image of his father, the tenacity and mental strength of his mother adding to his list of endearing qualities. Bindiya was pleased Akash had done full justice to his position as a *Chaudhary*, never misusing his position even once.

If anyone's character were to be tested, giving him power was a good measure to judge him by. Everyone respected the *Chaudhary* who tried his level best to maintain peace and harmony in the villages of Bassi and Nagri.

Today was when Akash had sent word to all *Panch* members to assemble for a meeting. He lacked the eloquence *Chaudhary* Dhanush Chand had before him, that was a given. He did earn the respect of all *Panch* members though, gradually over the years, which he was planning to en-cash on that day.

"Bindiya, am I doing the right thing? Does it make me a bad father for depriving my son of what could have been his?" he had asked his *lugai*, the previous night. "You are an honourable man, a trait your son has clearly acquired"

"I don't know what is to happen to Vansh's future, for I hoped he would become the *Chaudhary* one day. But, he has changed now from the Vansh we knew him to be. This man who stands before us as our son, has chosen a path of virtue"

"Be happy for him, for I think he has found what he was looking for" Yes, Akash thought to himself, sipping his *chai*, looking out of his balcony across the sleepy village that was slowly coming to life.

He was prepared to face the *Panchayat* to inform them of his decision, his last decision as their *Chaudhary* was to be. The *Panch* members trickled into the enclosure that held meetings under the banyan tree.

The monsoons had brightened Bassi with splashes of green in places, the season bringing a mood that showed in the jovial faces of all the members, as they sat in front of him. "Many thanks for coming on such short notice"

"What I have to say today is of importance to each one of you. The future of Bassi is now here amongst us. As your *Chaudhary*, I ask for your support in my decision, just as you have supported me through all the years"

"You have to tell us what it is, although if it is your decision, we trust it is for the better" Neeraj, now older than before said, the rest agreeing with him as they shook their heads. "Very well then"

"*Chaudhary* Dhanush Chand entrusted me with the *pagdi* that is now heavy for my old shoulders. As you all know, choosing the new *Chaudhary* has been the sole right of the old one. I still believe the *Panchayat* has the complete right to participate in a decision that will affect each one of us"

"The heir of *Chaudhary* Dhanush Chand is here. *Chote Sardar* Arjun Chand has been gracious to accept the *pagdi* that his father had entrusted to me. I recommend we crown him as the new *Chaudhary* of the *Raika*s of Bassi and the *Banjara*s of Nagri by the light of the morning, tomorrow"

The crowd that had assembled to hear him held all the important village locals, who affected life at Bassi in some way. The richest one was Giriraj, who was also present, as were the ones who owned the largest farmlands, the cluster of craft shops, and so on.

Most of them had put their daily trade on hold, once the summons came from their *Chaudhary*, donning on their garb of a *Panch* member. "Ajju is here? Where is he?" Neeraj enquired, voicing the question of all present.

"He resides at my *haveli*. He arrived yesterday and has been by my side ever since. I have spoken to him if he is willing to make Bassi his home. He said it was always his home, but now he wanted to take responsibility of bringing it back to the home he knew it to be"

Neeraj turned to the village council, talking to them in hushed whispers for a while. A bit later, each one of them broke into smiles that reached their weather-beaten eyes, deepened wrinkles, wizened over the years.

"It is the kismet of Bassi that *Chaudhary* Dhanush Chand has sent his son to us, at a time when we needed him most. We accept your decision whole-heartedly and give our consent for the crowning ceremony tomorrow, *Chaudhary* Akash!"

The wave of relief that washed over him was incomparable to anything he had ever experienced before. He was expecting some of the members, especially Giriraj, to resist his decision. To have a unanimous vote in his favour was something he had not expected in the least, but welcomed it whole-heartedly all the same.

He thanked them, his dismissal making all the members rush to their respective bread-earning professions. Village life is directly linked with daylight. To make hay while the sun shines, is a term that originated from here.

It is apt as every moment counts, from when the sun rises to when it chooses to rest for the night, like all who depend on its light. Akash couldn't wait to tell Bindiya the news, screaming for her the moment he entered the *haveli*.

"Bindiya, you'll never believe what happened!" The expression on his face gave away the information before he spoke. "The *Panchayat* agreed to crown Ajju tomorrow?" "Yes! And no one questioned my decision to hand *Chaudhary* Dhanush's *pagdi* over to his heir apparent either!"

Ajju heard the conversation as he came down the stairs, dressed in a pair of jeans and a long *kurta*. "You should wear our tribe's outfits, complete with the turban" Bindiya suggested, blessing him while he touched their feet as his daily respect.

"Forgive me, *Chachiji*. I do not share the same opinion as yours. How I feel about Bassi ought to reflect through my actions, not what I wear. It is not who I have chosen, to become. It is who I have become, to be chosen"

For a moment, Bindiya thought she saw a flash of Dhanush, Ajju's birth father, in the glittering eyes. "You have the gift of speech of Dhanush, your father. May *Ma Bhavani* watch over you" she said, hoping fate had a happier future in store for him, as compared to his father.

Vansh and Jiya entered after their morning horse ride, laughing merrily over the sights and sounds of Bassi. They too were informed of the successful meeting with the *Panchayat*. Vansh did not waste a moment in congratulating Ajju, declaring that Bassi and Nagri were blessed indeed to have a leader like himself, for glorious days to come.

"I'm hoping you give your consent to my decisions, Vansh. I have a few things on my list I need to do the moment I become the *Chaudhary*. You are point number Two" Ajju said, enjoying Vansh's puzzled look.

"Point number Two? List? What are you talking about?" "You'll get to know soon enough! *Chalo, Chachaji.* Let's take a ride along Bassi" Ajju suggested, fed up of staying confined to the four walls of the *haveli*.

"From tomorrow you are free to go wherever you please. Today, you are under my protection. Bear with me Ajju *beta*, for I wish to keep you safe until then" Akash said, apologetically. Accepting his reasoning once again, Ajju chose to spend the rest of the day in preparation of the ceremony due tomorrow.

Akash had already informed the *pandit* that the new *Chaudhary* would wed Rati at the *Ma Bhavani* temple, making her the *Chaudhrain*. Neeraj's family was on guard, knowing the future *Chaudhrain* of Bassi was resting under their roof peacefully.

The Gods watched over the transition that took place without a glitch the next day. Because the occasion demanded it, Ajju was dressed in the regalia that befit the *Chaudhary* of two of the wealthiest villages, this side of Chittorgarh.

Akash and Bindiya were to be the first of many who would see him and believe in the reincarnation of the spirit. It looked as if Dhanush himself had returned to reclaim, what rightfully belonged to him.

The *Panchayat* watched in awe as he walked up to them. "Dhanush *Bhaisa!*" Neeraj shouted, his old eyes recognizing him instantly. "*Chachaji*, it's me, Ajju" The clarification did not suffice. The rumour spread like wild fire.

Dhanush had returned as his son to claim his right as *Chaudhary* of the *Raika*s of Bassi and the *Banjara*s of Nagri. The priest anointed the new leader, handing him the crown *pagdi* encrusted with rubies, emeralds and pearls, similar to the *Chaudhary lathi* with the brass camel head.

"Your father gave these to me saying you would return one day. I never knew he was talking about himself returning through you" Akash had tears in his eyes as he looked into Dhanush's, smiling through his son.

"People of Bassi and Nagri! I present to you *Chaudhary* Arjun Chand, son of *Chaudhary* Dhanush Chand and *Chaudhrain* Suhani, the new

*Chaudhary* of the *Raika*s of Bassi and the *Banjara*s of Nagri! *Har Har Mahadev! Jai Ma Bhavani!*"

Akash announced loudly, his chants booming all around those who had gathered to see Ajju, to witness history repeating itself. They echoed back cheer and happiness on seeing their rumoured, beloved *Chaudhary* return in the form of his son.

Ajju stood up tall, a bit uncomfortable in all his regalia, and addressed the *Panchayat* for the first time. "It is my priviledge, my honour, to be your leader. I know my father would have wanted me to be your *Chaudhary*, when I was ready"

"I feel his presence with me now, therefore I know I shall never go wrong. As your *Chaudhary*, I give my first gift to my people of Bassi and Nagri. I shall wed Rati Singh Rana, making her my *Chaudhrain* to prove to you, Bassi is now my home"

"A home where I shall raise my family, my children, just like all of you" It was obvious everyone was mesmerized by the similarity Ajju displayed to his birth father, in the way he conducted himself, reminding them of the man who once was God-like for them.

They shouted praises of the new *Chaudhary*, looking forward to his marriage that very day. Rati was waiting with Bindiya, Leenata, Dhara and her *Chachi* at the temple of *Ma Bhavani*, the *lathait* bodyguards of the *Chaudhary* protecting the soon-to-be *Chaudhrain*.

Ajju had to restrain himself when Rati stood before him, dressed as his bride. She emanated the divinity of a goddess, the beauty that glimmers within itself, the glow love gifts every woman, the power a *Chaudhrain* ought to have.

Her eyes were lowered throughout, but her soft lips curved into a smile, the moment he took her in his arms that night.

"My Rati, my *Beendni*. You and I together will grow old, loving each other every day" he said, moving closer to complete his *Gauna* with her.

She gave herself to him willingly, trusting his love for her to show itself, through his tearing hunger as a man. The next morning, he told her about his other two decisions that he was to take as the *Chaudhary*.

"They will not be as supportive, Ajju. I hope you know that" "Yes, I am aware of what you say. But, this is the only way we can steer forward to a more progressive future, of that I am sure" He called for the *Panchayat* and told them what his two decisions were.

"Why do you need to disband the *Panchayat*? Don't you need our advice anymore?" Neeraj asked, hurt at being discarded despite supporting him, thus far. "*Chachaji*, I will always need you. All of you. But, there are others who wish to be heard as well"

"Wealth of advice is one thing I require at this point when Bassi is being rebuilt. The wealth of your experience is as important as the farmer who tills our lands, the cow herder who grazes our livestock, the women who tend to their families. Should we not hear what they think as well?"

"Or must we restrict our thinking to just a handful of representatives, who might not have the opinion of the common man of Bassi?"

This was something no one had thought of. Contrary to what it looked like, *Chaudhary* Arjun was moving ahead, keeping each one of the villagers in mind.

He made them count, showed they mattered. Once he explained his perspective, they all agreed readily, happy to be a part of the generous, accommodating thought process of their new *Chaudhary*.

Vansh was standing beside him, watching the power he exuded affect all those around. "The son of Akash *Chachaji*- Vansh, is to be *Chote Sardar* Vansh henceforth. He will have all the freedom to educate all our farmers, to understand and participate in the revolution called Agritourism"

"No one is to restrict him in any way as a mark of respect to me. His family will stay in the same *haveli* as they have been, all this while. My *Chaudhrain* and I need but one room to stay in, other than your hearts!"

A good leader ensures that he doesn't walk in front of the crowd that he is meant to represent. He follows the crowd, like a shepherd tending to his flock.

*Chaudhary* Arjun was displaying characteristic features of a leader thus.

He would not only be successful in ushering the people of Bassi and Nagri into a better future, but he was also proving time and again how each villager was to participate, in the construction of a dream, that entailed the Bassi of the glorious yesteryears.

He called Delhi, informing both his parents of his crowning as well as his wedding. Both Arjun and Suhani knew that he was no longer just theirs anymore. It was a bitter-sweet moment for all of them.

His duty, his calling, his love, had claimed him in totality. All they could do was bless him and pray for the couples' long, healthy, happy life.

Suhani managed to extract a promise from Ajju. The wedding reception and their honeymoon were to be funded by them.

Ajju agreed, but not immediately. He asked for a few days before he could leave with his bride to meet them.

The mood was celebratory, both in Bassi as well as in the faraway metropolitan city of Delhi. The skies were clear, the storm clouds gone.

Rati proved to be the perfect partner for Ajju, in every which way. She tended to all his needs, showering the love of a dutiful life as she ought to, behind closed doors.

She stood by him as he spoke and passed rulings over trivial squabbles, villagers sometimes had.

Their invigorating horse riding on a regular basis, early in the morning, made *Chaudhary* Arjun present a beautiful *Marwari* specimen of the equidae, Vahini, to his wife, Rati.

She was a mix of brown, black and white, with a touch of grey near its mane. Rati looked a lot like Pocahontas when she rode Vahini for the very first time.

"Who is that?" Rati enquired, while their horses grazed by the riverside.

*Chaudhary* Arjun narrated the story of Pocahontas, walking beside his *Beendni*. "An American Indian who fell in love with a Captain named John Smith. It's essentially a love story"

"Is this our love story, Ajju? What's happening to us? What will be?" she asked. Looking at him, she lost herself once again in his black eyes.

"It started from the moment that I saw you. It will continue even after we are long gone. I want children soon, Rati. We must give the people of Bassi the hope of a secure future"

That night, Rati obliged to his demands as her husband, keeping in mind what he said about having children to secure the future of Bassi.

She began to think if she were second to his love for their village. Or maybe, his third love…after all, he did marry that *firangan* Mia…"

# CHAPTER FORTY TWO

Giriraj was expecting Tara's volcanic anger to erupt, the moment he heard Akash mention while sitting amongst the *Panchayat*, that Ajju was to be the next *Chaudhary* of Bassi and Nagri. He took Viren with him to the city for a day, so that as and when Tara did find out, she couldn't poison his mind any more than she already had.

The happy-go-lucky Viren was not the same anymore. The perpetual frown, stares into oblivion for long periods of time, didn't go unnoticed. Giriraj tried to get to know his son in that one day at the city.

Try hard as he might, he didn't come even an inch closer to know his son any better than when they'd left Bassi. It was too little, too late. Tara had already snipped the bond that could have been, between father and son for the sake of controlling him herself.

He was to be her weapon to realize her ambition, the part that she herself could not. Viren was quiet throughout; the occasional conversation when moments arose that needed him to speak. Giriraj was upset with what Tara had done to him, but refused to accept that all was lost.

When they reached Bassi the next evening, he was in for a browbeat he had been delaying for his own peace of mind. "*Aawo, aawo*! Come, sit, enjoy the air of the new Bassi. With a new *Chaudhary*, a new *Chaudhrain*, all thanks to so many of our *Panch* members, who themselves agreed to be disbanded!"

"You never fail to amaze me, Giriraj. Just when I think you couldn't act any more foolish, something occurs that makes me believe otherwise" Tara took a moment to stop shaking with rage, when Viren asked, "*Maasa*, what are you saying? Who are the new *Chaudhary* and *Chaudhrain*?"

"And the *Panchayat*? What's going on?" He put his bag down, refusing the water Malika offered, "*Maasa*, don't start right away. Let them rest a bit" she said. "*Chup karo*! (Be quiet!) I don't even know whose side you're on anymore, *chori*! Ask your father, Viren"

Tara hissed, turning to her husband who was questioned by their son. "What is all this, *Baasa*? We were together for a whole day. Yet you never breathed a word of all this" Giriraj felt cornered, which Malika detested.

She had been watching her mother overpower her father all these years. The poor man did her bidding purely to let peace prevail in the household, but there were numerous occasions when she wished he would stand up for once to speak his mind.

"Viren *Bhaisa*, you can have this talk with *Baasa* after the noon meal. Do your questions have to be answered right now?" she asked her brother gently. Viren loved his sister dearly and saw her nearing tears.

Guilt made him withdraw his accusations temporarily, letting his father rest. The breathing space ought to have done Giriraj some good, were it not for Tara's continuous grumbling, along with banging steel utensils to express her discontent.

He lit up his *hookah* in the evening and called for his son. "*Aawo, baitho.* Viren, you are a good boy, an obedient son, a caring brother. Remember all of this when I speak to you" Viren softened by the gentleness of his father, as he heard those words.

"*Betaji*, you must know we do not stem from the royal bloodline. It was wrong on your mother's part to show you dreams that were not meant for you. Make your goal to be a good, upright, honourable man"

"I have amassed enough wealth for you already. For you, your sister, your families. All I ask of you in return is that you strive to be a better human being" How different his parents were, Viren thought.

His mother, Tara, wanted power for Viren, while his father, Giriraj wanted his son to be a good person. "A powerful man needn't always be corrupt, *Baasa*. It tests one's character, which differs from one person to another. I was born to be a leader"

"You were born to be who you choose to be, Viren. Choose wisely for your choices will begin to define you" "I have, in fact, already made my choice. Now tell me what you left out, while we were away from Bassi"

Giriraj had no choice but to tell him about the new *Chaudhary*- Arjun Chand, and his *Chaudhrain* - Rati Chand. The disbanding of the *Panchayat* was the next hammer that hurled into Viren's brain.

The third was the making of Vansh into *Chote Sardar*. He got up, walked to the edge of the terrace, where both father and son had wanted to speak to each other, without the confounded interruption of Tara.

"So Ajju *Bhaiya* is now the *Chaudhary* and Vansh is *Chote Sardar*. What does that make me? I could have been made *Chote Thakur*" he said. "*Chaudhary hukam* cannot walk around distributing ranks and designations around Bassi, Viren"

"Attempt to understand that if he did, the whole act of his disbanding the *Panchayat* to give an equal hearing to the common man would have gone waste" "You justify his deeds well, *Baasa*. Pray tell, how do you justify him and his family depriving your son of two prospective brides?"

"I have no face left among these herders who are on your payroll. They respected me once. Now they mock me!" "Respect and fear are two separate things, Viren. They feared you for your temper"

"As far as I know, no one dare mock you. If you hear of such a person, bring him to me" "And what are you going to do about it?" Tara joined them, having heard the conversation from the beginning, hiding behind the wall that separated the terrace and the steps.

"Go downstairs and do not interrupt me when I speak to my son!" Giriraj yelled at her. Tara's eyes turned to stone, slit like a snake about to spread its dreaded venom, that would poison everything that came in her way.

"You are the worst father in Bassi. Not just that, in the whole world! You justify the actions of our enemy and have the audacity to ask your own son to be tolerant in the same breath? My son is not a coward like you"

"You like things as they are. You're a nobody, a non-entity. Viren wants to be somebody; instead of encouraging him you advise him otherwise?" she snapped. "*Maasa*" "No Viren, I cannot stay quiet anymore"

"If he would do his job as a father well, I would not be standing her to remind him of his duties" She turned to leave but spoke before that. "I'm going to Akash and Bindiya. Let the *Chaudhary haveli* echo with the voice of the common man, as our new *Chaudhary* Arjun Chand so desires!"

Before either could stop her, she had stomped all the way to the *haveli* where no one but Akash and Bindiya were, at present. "*Chaudhary Saheb*! Where are you? A common mother has come to see how just you are!" "What is all this, Tara?"

"I'm not referring to you, Akash. You are as common as I am now. I want to speak with *Chaudhary* Arjun Chand" "He isn't here at the moment. Tell me what this is about" Tara smiled at him mockingly.

"You can act simple in front of everyone, but you don't fool me one bit. You've hated me ever since you saw your cousin Dhanush and I together. Now, you've deprived both my son and yours for a stupid promise you made to a dead man!"

"Tara!" Bindiya, eyes glittering with rage, walked up to where they stood. "Do not speak ill of the dead! The man you refer to was your *Chaudhary* too. How dare you question the decision of *Chaudhary* Arjun Chand, the son of our great leader!"

"Have you grown so blind that you cannot see he has returned?" "Dhanush is dead. His son is in Bassi because of Rati. That is the truth. How could he take a simple village girl to a city, where even a house-help knows how to read and write?"

"He was unsure of the *Chaudhary pagdi* earlier. Now, he himself approached Akash to become the *Chaudhary*. Did you not ask him why the change of heart, or was the *pagdi* becoming too heavy for you?"

"I do not owe you an explanation, Tara" Akash said calmly. "Your husband was in the *Panchayat* when I declared my decision. If there was any apprehension, he ought to have voiced it out"

"In fact, if I recall correctly, Giriraj wanted me to announce the next *Chaudhary* to succeed before the wedding of my children. So technically, I did what he asked of me. There should be no reason for him or any of his family members to hold me against keeping my word!"

"Akash, we all know what a simpleton Giriraj is. I will get as many villagers as I can and have them ask Ajju, what made him change his mind of coming back to settle at Bassi!" Tara was out of control like a broken arrow by now.

Akash and Bindiya had to ensure, Tara would not start a war at Bassi. "Dr. Shekhawat" Bindiya uttered, as Tara froze. "What?" "You've been using Dr. Shekhawat of Jaipur, the same way you tried to use Dhanush *Bhaisa*, all those years ago"

"You ought to be very careful who you point out as wayward, Bindiya" Tara said, still not backing down. "We have invited him to our children's wedding. I am sure you have no problem with that, then" Bindiya wasn't backing down either.

Coming a step closer, Bindiya said, "If I hear as much as a word uttered by you against Ajju…I will tell Giriraj and Viren about your escapades with Dhanush *Bhaisa* and the latest Dr. Shekhawat"

"Let them deal with you in their own way" In Rajasthan, infidelity is a crime that spells banishment to those who have committed it. Tara knew she would be walking on broken glass hereon, withdrawing her verbal weaponry, turning to leave.

Ajju, Rati, Vansh, Jiya and Leenata had just returned from the site survey of all the lands that were to be converted into the requirements of Agritourism.

They saw Tara march out, stopping to glare at Ajju, after which she marched away without as much as a word to any of them.

"What was Tara *Chachi* doing here?" Ajju asked, entering the *haveli* courtyard with the rest of the family members. "She came to speak to you as a wronged mother, *Chaudhary hukam*" Akash replied to his query.

"*Chachaji*, please call me Ajju. For you, *Chachi* and all our family members, I will always be Ajju"

"Of course, you are. But now that you are the *Chaudhary* of the *Raika*s of Bassi and the *Banjara*s of Nagri, we must give you the respect you deserve as our leader by voicing it out through your true name. This is a tradition that cannot be broken. Not even behind closed doors"

Accepting his explanation that was coated with conventionality, Ajju moved into his room with Rati, his *Chaudhrain*.

"Why didn't you ask him what Tara came to speak about in detail, Ajju" Rati asked, while he rested his head on her lap.

"If he wanted to tell me in detail, he would have told me then itself. They didn't want to upset me, as I'm sure the visit was highly unpleasant"

"You're smarter than that. Don't forget I know you well" she teased him, tugging at his hair.

"Yes, my little deer. She came as a 'wronged mother' like *Chachaji* said. That could mean she was upset I became *Chaudhary* and made Vansh *Chote Sardar*. She may have felt Viren was left out, coming here to clarify with me"

"Then why did she leave without even uttering a word when she saw you enter?" Rati prodded.

"Come here! You ask too many questions for a beautiful woman who must please her husband, who she is newly-wedded to!"

He couldn't get enough of her, a truth that was making him realize how much he had missed out on.

He never had this companionship, this camaraderie with Mia. With Rati, it was almost as if they were old friends who met after a long time, fell in love, got married.

She felt it too, every time those black eyes of Ajju shone with the love of a man, who was the *Chaudhary* for the world outside.

Behind closed doors, he was the soft, gentle, caring Ajju who wanted to be snuggled into, as if hiding from the cruel, cold world.

He used to say sweet-nothings to her, when they were alone. She wondered if he used to say the same to Mia.

She wanted to ask him how Mia, or Aradhana was, but was afraid to broach her subject.

She had tried once, but he had been curt, cold. "What're you thinking about, my pet?" Ajju asked, covering her from the cold with his blanket as they snuggled closer. Propping herself up on one hand, Rati said, "I have a question to ask"

"Rati, your questions are like the black hole-never ending! One will lead to another, and another and another. I have to sleep. Bassi needs me and I need you to make me sleep"

Rati, sweet and considerate as she was, played with the hair on his chest, made him doze off peacefully.

She dreamt of the *firangan* with the cornflower blue eyes, just like hers as Ajju had once said, sitting on the *baithak* by the bed.

"What you hold in your arms was once mine" Mia said, sadness written all over her face. "The past is the past" she said to the apparition, who now sat next to her.

"He will always hold on to a part of me, Rati. He will never belong to you completely. Don't you see, you silly girl? I was his first love?"

"Then came Bassi because of all the power it gave him. Then you came along, a filler for a man who needs a warm body every night"

"Shut up! You talk filth! Ajju loves me and I, him" "Third love, third love…" Rati woke up with a start, turning to find Ajju still asleep.

She drank some cool water and stood at the balcony of her room. She knew she had to strangulate this feeling of insecurity that was beginning to creep into her.

Sleeping off in her husband's arms, she decided to confide in Leenata about what was bothering her. The next day at Gurukul, Malika apologized to Leenata.

"I know *Maasa* came to the *Chaudhary haveli*. Forgive me Leenata for I could not stop her"

"No one can stop jealousy, envy, the yearning for a hollow ambition, Malika" Leenata replied calmly.

"Viren has become quiet again. He has had my movement restricted. It's for my own protection, he says" Malika churned out more information on her household.

"Protection from whom?" Leenata asked, confused. "Viren and *Maasa* think I am like *Baasa*, which, truth be told, I am. They think I might interact with you or your family" Malika confessed, too embarrassed to look at her friend by now.

"Oh Malika, it must be horrible for you" Leenata said. "Are you keeping in touch with Nandish?" Leenata asked, sympathizing with her situation.

"Yes, he calls me every night. It is he who has kept me sane so far. If it weren't for Andy, I would have run away to an *ashram* by now!"

They laughed and shared their tiffins, exchanging tidbits about Bassi, about Gurukul. "The little boy Nandish gets your special attention, Malika. Any particular reason why?!"

Malika blushed. "You know why!" "Yes, I do. You're such a pair of lovebirds! Look at you blushing away in broad daylight"

It was tough to imagine opposite poles living under the same roof for Leenata. Giriraj and Tara were like chalk and cheese. Viren and Malika were siblings, but very different in terms of their nature.

"Leenata, you must warn *Chaudhary* Arjun. *Maasa* will never back down. She will have the last word. You must ask him to be on guard"

"And what about your brother, Malika? Will he ever come around, or does he plan to sulk forever?"

"I don't really know. He doesn't talk to me the way he used to. The only person who ever gets through to him is *Maasa*. She uses that to poison his mind" That evening, Leenata told Ajju about the forewarning Malika sent for him.

"I leave for Delhi tomorrow with Rati. Vansh will take my place for a few days. Don't pay heed to warnings and fears that are baseless, Leenata"

*Chaudhary* Arjun brushed off the potential threat of Tara, outwardly.

Inwardly, he was quite concerned about the escalating communication gap that was beginning to threaten repercussions, which would affect more than just two people.

# CHAPTER FORTY THREE

The moment Ajju and Rati reached Swarn Niwas, jubilation broke out in the villa. The group that welcomed them took half a day off from their busy schedules, just to show their elation on seeing Ajju after a while, not to mention his bride for the first time.

The Anands, the senior Prataps, Dhanush, Abhi, Dr. Shekhawat, were talking all at once, trying to get Ajju's attention. Annie was the first to whisper to Rati. "They're all mad. Adorable, but mad! Don't be afraid, *Bhabhisa*. Welcome to the family!"

"Whatever she is saying to you is untrue, my dear!" Sangharsh spoke next, Nalini poking his ribs to quieten him down. "Don't scare the poor child! Can't you see she wasn't expecting all of us?"

Rati looked at all of them without making it too obvious. Educated, confident, rich…whereas she had neither of the qualities. Whatever confidence she had as the Chaudhrain, was left back at Bassi.

She moved closer to Ajju, hiding behind his huge physique, petite that she was, and lowered her eyes. Everyone was silent, wondering what was wrong. "*Idhar aawo, beti.* (Come here, daughter)"

Suhani's sweet voice broke through the deafening silence, compelling Rati to look at her. The smile Ajju's mother gave her made the walk towards her easier. Suhani knew how it felt to be intimidated in the city, by city folk.

"I'm your *Sasuma*. But, you may call me *Ma* if you like. My goodness, how beautiful you are! Come, we'll go to my room" She followed Suhani like a magnetized pup, while everyone watched without any movement.

"Don't follow me, *Saheb*. Give us time alone" she said, atop the spiral staircase, aware Arjun was planning to follow her. "Well now! After all these years, she can still read your mind!" Sangharsh teased his friend.

"Where did she take Rati?" Ajju enquired. "I've no idea what's going on upstairs. If I know Suhani correctly, you will have a transformed lady as compared to the meek kitten for sure. Wait and watch!"

"Sounds great! Now, what did I miss?" Everyone began updating what had been going on while Ajju was at Bassi. **Annie's Doll Collection** was a success, the webpage getting more and more liked by the day.

"I never knew there were so many admirers of handcrafted dolls out there, Ajju *Bhaiya*!" "You underestimate yourself, Annie! How is the work for **Nara Apparels** going? Is it as per the schedule we discussed?"

Annie and Abhi looked at each other. "Not exactly" Abhi replied. "Meaning? Don't tell me you'll launch it next year! I am a patient man alright, but pushing the launch to next year will be testing my patience to the limit!"

"Well, A.J" Abhi said, clearing his throat. "I won't say it in that case. But what I will say, is that the estimate launch time changed the moment we hired double the amount of craftsmen; which means, **Nara Apparels** is being launched the day after tomorrow!"

Ajju was impressed with the dedication, the efficiency shown by both Annie and Abhi. "Abhi's father pulled a few favours and imported local craftsmen in need of work. We put them on the job, paid them well"

"They came back with more workers the next time. It was like the 'Elves and the Shoemaker' story!" Annie said, connecting her reality to the stories she heard when she was little. "I cannot believe you guys pulled it off! Abhi, I'm so proud of you!" Ajju declared, meaning every word.

"Wait, there's more. We're getting married tomorrow in court. *Baasa* has agreed to avoid the fanfare and Annie's mom has agreed to host the reception with yours at DTD while your theme of **Regressive Progression** is on"

Ajju turned to his father, Dan and Andy. "We're all set with the theme, then?" "Yes, absolutely!" "Man! I haven't been out for more than a week to ten days and it feels like I've missed out on so much"

"City life is far more fast-paced that village life, Ajju. How are things at Bassi?" Arjun asked. "Well, the…" Ajju couldn't finish his sentence as he got up from the cane chair. Rati was walking down the steps followed by Suhani.

A dull rose chiffon sari with a darker border in velvet of the same colour was complimented by rubies on the ears as studs, a big ring with rubies in the shape of a flower, adorning her manicured hands.

The sari accentuated her hourglass figure, the light makeup highlighting her sharp features. "All yours, Ajju" Suhani said, joining the group back, ordering *chai* for everyone. Rati was normal from then on, speaking when spoken to, joking with everyone.

Her affable temperament made all present, like her instantaneously. The noon meal finished quicker than they would have wanted. The welcoming party left Swarn Niwas, including the senior Prataps and Dhanush, saying they'd be back in the evening.

Suhani had prepared Rati in such a way, that Ajju had to be alone with her soon. The moments they spent in the afternoon while Ajju played with her hair, kept looking at her, touching her lips gently with his, made them feel like no one else existed outside their bubble ball of love and affection.

Ajju was still asleep when Rati woke up. She went walking around to explore the enormous Swarn Niwas. She went up the stairs a bit further and found the attic where old pictures were kept. She found a picture that was framed of Ajju and a girl with blue eyes, just like hers.

Mia! Or, Aradhana as she was renamed. Another frame had Ajju, Mia, Dhanush, Nandish, and...Jiya? What was Jiya doing in the frame with all of them? "She was Mia's sister. Vansh named her Jiya but before that she was known as Diana"

Rati knew who it was but didn't turn back. "She was very beautiful. Mia, I mean" "So are you" "Did you love her?" "If I say 'yes' will you hold it against me for the rest of our lives?" She turned to face him when he looked into her eyes.

"Rati, she is a part of my past. I never knew her as well as I do you, if you must know. I know it's been eating you up from inside to know more about Mia. Ask me and I'll tell you" "Did you want to have children with her?"

"She didn't want any" "Did you say sweet-nothings to her the way you do with me?" "I don't remember. She was more modern and practical. Two traits I thank the Lord you don't have" "Ajju, I cannot be like her. She was a *Memsaheb*"

"And I don't want you to be like anyone else other than yourself, *pagli*. Come on. Let's go downstairs. We have all of tomorrow and I want to show you off, take you to places in Delhi you must have read about in the books Leenata gave you"

She hesitated for a moment but Ajju lifted her up in his arms and brought her to their room. "I was planning to have a reasonable discussion with you, but since you made me work, it's time for my reward!"

He shut the bedroom door with his foot and got ready to shower his affection on Rati, making her feel secure again. They went downstairs an hour later and found Arjun and Suhani discussing their respective launches.

"*Baasa*! *Maasa*! We didn't hear you. When did you get in?" Ajju asked, picking an almond cookie from the table to dip into his *chai*. "It's alright, Ajju. At your age, even I couldn't hear anything when your mother was around!"

Suhani chided him softly, blushing on his remark instantly. Arjun hadn't failed to notice the same shade of cornflower blue eyes that Mia had on Rati. He had discussed the matter with Suhani, wondering if Ajju had gone on the rebound.

"I don't think so. There are many blue-eyed girls he could have picked for himself. He chose Rati not for her eyes, but for her heart" Now that he saw Suhani and Rati chatting in the balcony, he wasn't so sure.

"She has Mia's eyes" he told Ajju, pouring himself another cup of Darjeeling tea. "So she does. This time *Baasa*, it is a mere coincidence. It's not anything you or *Maasa* might think. Even if she had eyes any other colour than blue, I would still be madly in love with her" Ajju confessed.

"Does Rati know?" Arjun asked. "About the eye colour similarity? Yes, I told her when I met her first at Bassi. It did catch my attention at first, but the way she made me feel was something I wanted more and more of, you know"

"Yes, I do know, Ajju. Just ensure she does too. Women need to be told constantly how much they are needed, appreciated, loved" "Agreed. On that same note, I'm taking her out tomorrow for a bit of sight-seeing. Then I'll bring her to DTD for lunch, so she can see where I worked"

"Sounds like a great idea! You can take a look at all the preparations for the theme launch as well. Your mother has been spreading herself thin, since her launch of the new line at Maya's Reality-**Strength of a Woman**, is to be launched shortly too"

"I hope Rati and I have the understanding you and *Maasa* share" "There is only one way to get there. Two words. Consistent communication. If you perpetuate this as a habit, you become an integral part of each other"

"The downside is that in your better half's absence, you tend to malfunction." "Like when Ramona came into the picture" Ajju mentioned. "Don't remind me" "Speaking of the devil, where is she nowadays?"

"Probably left the country" Arjun gave him the gist of the entire fallout at DTD where Ramona was made to sign a document, offering to leave the country, never to return again. "Why would she do that?" "Corporate espionage is a punishable offence, Ajju"

"True. But, there must be more to it than meets the eye, *Baasa*. We ought never to underestimate Ramona. She is not the type to slink into the shadows meekly. In fact, she reminds me of Tara *Chachi* at Bassi quite a bit"

"A sophisticated version of a similar snake variety. Yes!" Arjun was surprised why he had never noticed the similarity between Ramona and Tara before. "Women hold on to so many things. We men are far less complicated"

Suhani had just walked in when she heard the comment. "Oh, really?" she said, looking at her husband. "Yes, Ma'am!" Arjun answered back, winking at her. "Men never grow up, Rati. Outside they are our protectors. Behind closed doors though, they want to be pampered, taken care of like children" "Oh, really?" Rati asked, looking at Ajju. "Yes, really!" Ajju answered, compelling the entire group to laugh at the silliness of it all.

Moments like these leave a happy memory for no reason; a scale to compare other moments when life feels complicated, with troubles piling up with no solution in sight. Each one of the four had their own personal struggles to deal with.

For the moment though, they chose to keep everything aside, to gift each other one of the most treasured of all gifts money could never buy-the gift of happiness. When the senior Prataps were alone, Arjun spoke. "Ajju asked me where Ramona could be, *Beendni*"

"What did you tell him, *Saheb*?" "The truth. She's probably out of the country by now so as to avoid getting arrested for corporate espionage. But, somehow I feel Ajju made sense when he said Ramona is not the sort of person to lay down her weapons so easily"

Suhani turned to him and said, "It's late, *Saheb*. You're thinking too much about something that doesn't matter anymore. The only threat Ramona posed was to us as a couple and the gallery. We're married now and you own the gallery along with Dr. Shekhawat"

Arjun pulled her close, kissing her nose. "You make everything seem so simple, Braids. It's one of the things I love about you" Suhani knew where the conversation was about to lead to. Instead of faking feeling sleepy, she got up facing him.

"Show me how much you still love me, *Saheb*. Come" she said, engulfing Arjun into throes of passion that heightened their heartbeats, until both were satiated, sleeping off blissfully in each other's arms.

The morning saw both couples chatting, when they saw Dhanush's Humvee pull up on the driveway. "Where were you last night?" Ajju asked. "Stayed back at the gallery. *Baasa*, I spoke to Bantu"

"Retaining Mr. Guha after the Ramona fiasco was a bad idea" Folding his newspaper, Arjun looked at his younger son. Dhanush sat down and continued. "Bantu came to me after Mr. Guha left for the day"

"He said he has heard Mr. Guha speaking to Ramona even now. Not only that, your chauffeur Mohan comes in plain clothes and gives envelopes to him occasionally. Bantu happened to open one of them that his uncle forgot to take home one night"

"It contained notes in denominations of 500s and 1000s" You mean Ramona has Mohan, our chauffeur for over ten years as her informant as well?" Suhani said, shocked at how sellable integrity had become off late.

"That's what I believe, *Maasa*" Dhanush said. "I've stayed up all night so I'm off to get some shut eye. What're your plans for the day?" "I'm taking Rati for sight-seeing and then to the gallery. At least that is what the plan was earlier"

"Now, if I take her to the gallery, Mr. Guha will tell Ramona" "Mohan must have told her already" Arjun said, sickened at the thought of his family under surveillance by people on Ramona's payroll.

"I'm calling Mohan right now. I'll tell him to take a month off. Let me see what he says" Arjun declared. "But Sir, who will drive you and Suhani *Memsahib*?" Mohan asked, upon being informed of his paid leave.

"You haven't been to your village in a long time, Mohan. Your family must miss you. Here" Arjun said, giving him a wad of notes. "Give this to your wife to buy clothes for your children. You're like a little brother to me. Give them my regards and…"

Mohan began to shake, his palms joined together in submission as he fell to his knees. "*Maafi! Maafi Sahebji!* I cannot bear the burden anymore. Please throw me in jail. I deserve to be punished for what I've done"

"I got greedy and lost control. Forgive me…" Arjun got up to where Mohan had collapsed, crying on the marble floor. "I will forgive you. But, Lord *Shiva* won't. What you have done is unworthy of second chances, Mohan"

"Leave my sight, this home and never return again" His words sounded harsh even to him, but he knew Ajju was learning that if a crime is forgiven, it must depend on the mature decision that ought to be taken by the one who has the right to forgive.

Arjun made Bantu the Manager of DTD, sacking Mr. Guha without any explanations. It was too close to the gala-cum-reception, but Arjun believed in the blessings of the Lord *Shiva*, choosing to trust himself rather than those who misused the trust he bestowed on them.

Bantu put the placard, Brijesh Kumar on the Manager's table, surprising everyone with his real name for the first time. Brijesh became the right hand of Arjun for days to come, much to everyone's delight.

# CHAPTER FORTY FOUR

Instead of going sightseeing around Delhi, Rati proposed they attend the launch of **Nara Apparels**, where the female models wore Suhani's jewellery from her new collection called the **Strength of a Woman.**

It was quite apt for Mia's designs worn by the male models, to be complimented by their female counterparts adorned in antique *Rajasthani* jewellery in precious stones that depicted a woman showing courage when the need arose.

Andy's shots of the gorgeous jewellery pieces flashed on the big screen under the logo of Maya's Reality. The male models wore each piece of Indo-western wear, with the enthusiasm of one who feels good about looking his best.

The crowd that had assembled at Anand Creations, where the show was being held, had some important clients in the first row, including prominent personalities from well-established media houses.

Cameras were flashing rapidly as the regal models walked, their ethnic traditional attire expressing pride in where they hailed from. Rati had never seen a fashion show before, but was in for the surprise of her life other than witnessing the event.

As a special last moment addition, she was made to wear the exquisite *Maharani* necklace with rubies and emeralds, adorning her swan-like neck, matching earrings and bangles adding to the ensemble of a traditional *ghaghra choli*, in bottle green and wine red.

Ajju was dressed in Abhi's favourite piece from **Nara Apparels**-the quilted brown long *kurta* teamed with a silken *dhoti* and stole.

"Ladies and gentlemen, it gives me great pleasure to introduce the newest member in the Pratap family, who will walk the ramp with my showstopper set"

"She will be walking alongside my eldest son who also happens to be her husband" Pausing to take a breath, checking on her overwhelming moment of pride, Suhani yelled, "Put your hands together for Rati and Arjun!"

The music was a haunting tune sung by Suhani herself. The one Arjun heard her sing in the fields that made him fall in love with her. The same tune she sang to Ajju each night, when he was little.

Ajju turned to look at his mother who was standing behind the curtains, smiling knowingly at him. He smiled back, held Rati's hand and walked into the limelight. The crowd got goose bumps when their eyes fell on the dazzling couple, as they owned the stage together.

The man and wife humbly bowed, before they walked gracefully back to bring the designers Suhani Pratap and Sarvani Anand center stage, to accept the standing ovation given by all assembled.

"Now that was an experience I thought I would never have!" Rati said, removing the jewellery before returning them to Suhani. Her mother-in-law complimented Rati not just as the mother of her husband, but more so as the designer of the pieces she wore.

"You looked like a Queen, *beti*. Will you wear them as a gift I give to you, to wear for your Reception tomorrow?" Until then, Rati had no clue that the entire ensemble-the *ghaghra choli* as well as the matched accessories was a gift for her, put together by Suhani.

"*Ma!*" she choked over her own words, touched by her gesture, her generosity. "Come, come now. Let's change and get back to work. I'm sure Ajju has plans to take you to the gallery"

"Yes, *Ma*. We are to have lunch there and return home. I'll make dinner for all of us, as is customary" "*Jeete raho*! (Live long!) That would be lovely!" Suhani blessed her.

After congratulating Annie and Abhi, Rati and Ajju left for the Dare To Dream gallery to meet Arjun, Dhanush and Nandish. "Who is Brijesh Kumar?"

"That would be me, Sir!" Bantu replied, stepping out of the Manager's office. "Bantu! You look quite smart in a tie" Ajju complimented him, making the new Manager light up like a thousand watt bulb.

"Congratulations on your wedding, Sir!" "Thank you!" Ajju said, walking to the backroom. He never left Rati's hand for a second as they crossed the gallery corridor, where pictures were tastefully hung all the way to where everyone sat.

"There he is! Ajju, come here for a minute" Arjun called for his son, smiling at Rati. He was bent over a table with Andy and Dan, who had been arguing extensively about a shot. "There is something wrong with this shot, although I can't put my finger on it"

"Nandish says the lighting is off, while Dhanush says the contrast is too high" Ajju deftly took out the same picture in the scanned images section on the desktop, changing it to black and white, thereby giving it phenomenal picture quality.

"That's it! God, I do miss you at times like these. Bassi has won a great leader but I have lost my lead photographer" Arjun claimed, sitting to chat the couple up. "So, how was the apparel and jewellery launch?"

"It was out of the world, *Baasa*. In fact, both Rati and I walked the ramp wearing the showstoppers of both the brands in the end!" "Is it?" "You don't look surprised. Did you have a hand in the planning of this sneaky act?!"

"As a matter of fact, I take the full blame for it! I happened to suggest this as an idea to your mother and Annie, when they couldn't figure out how to showcase the most important pieces of their respective collections"

Post lunch, Ajju and Rati were driving back to Swarn Niwas when she asked, "You didn't tell me **Nara Apparels** were designs originally created by Mia" "I didn't see why. It was her wish that was carried out. I hope her souls rests in peace" "Me too, Ajju" He turned to face her.

"Look at me, Rati" she turned to him as he kissed her hand. "I love you with all my heart. Do you love me too?" "Yes, I do. But…" "But what, Aradhana?" She pulled her hand back. Ajju bit his tongue at the folly. "I'm sorry, I…"

What was happening to him? He knew he never loved Mia as much as he loved Rati. The slip up would cost him dearly which he was well aware of.

Rati was stuck on the far corner of the car seat, staring out of the window. They reached the villa, maintaining a superficial mask of cordiality.

Ajju didn't know what to do next so he went by his gut. He walked up to her, held her as tight as he could, wishing he could take away the moment he hurt the pride of his woman.

She ran up to the attic, tears streaming down her face, tearing all of Mia's snaps, one by one. He watched her moments before joining her himself, the pile of torn snaps increasing slowly.

When not a single one was left, he asked her, "Feeling better?" "No" she said, embarrassed at the silly act she just couldn't stop herself from doing.

"Come downstairs. I heard *Baasa* and *Maasa* return with Dhanush" Rati wiped her tears quickly, preparing herself to greet her new family. Ajju was behaving as normal as he could under the circumstances, but Rati was a bit aloof.

Arjun pulled Ajju to one corner, asking what the matter was. "Slight fiasco, *Baasa*" Ajju explained how he accidentally called Rati by Mia's married name. "That is not a slight fiasco, Ajju. That is an apocalyptic catastrophe!"

"If you were still into Mia, you shouldn't have married this poor girl" "Don't get me wrong, *Baasa*. I cared deeply for Mia. But the love I have for Rati is far stronger than anything I have ever known"

"Trust it then, Ajju. Go to her, belong to her and for God's sake think before you speak!" Arjun told Suhani about the strain between Ajju and Rati. "Initial teething problems are always to test the commitment of a relationship in its initial stages"

"Rati is a sensible girl and we both know Ajju could not have done better. Let them iron out their creases" Arjun hoped Suhani was right about what she said. At least Ajju had him and Suhani to talk to. Rati had no one who she could confide in, about how she felt.

He felt sorry for her, in the same breath asking Lord *Shiva* to protect Ajju's married life. He slept off praying in Suhani's arms, while she stayed awake, intending to chat with Rati the next day. She didn't want Rati to feel alienated, unable to express herself freely.

Choosing to wake up earlier than usual, she found Rati walking near the rose bushes. "Do you like roses, too?" she asked the beautiful girl with the sun-kissed cheeks. "I love them. I've never seen them at Bassi although there seem to be plenty in Delhi"

"Now that is an idea! Why don't you take a few saplings and graftings when you go back? You can have your own rose garden if you have green fingers"

Shanti got their *chai* in the garden, where they walked around talking about roses, the men who mattered to them-their husbands.

"*Saheb* is always mixing and muddling things. If it weren't for me, he would end up spending half his day trying to locate everything he's misplaced!" "Ajju has the same habit!" "*Saheb* starts an argument, making it look like I'm the cause for it"

"True. Ajju does that at times as well!" Going for the kill, Suhani said, "Once *Saheb* called me by a name I would never expect to hear from him!" This time, there was no enthusiastic agreement by Rati.

How could she tell Ajju's mother what had happened between them? If Ajju got to know, he would feel let down. "Looks like you are lucky in this one aspect" Suhani said, getting up from the soft grass of the lawn.

"Rati, I know what happened. Ajju was afraid he had hurt you badly and confided in his father at a weak moment. His father told me and that is why I am here" Seeing she was about to cry, Suhani held her hand.

"*Na*, they are precious for all of us. You can talk to me about anything you wish. I promise not to tell anyone. Men will always be men. They do not understand the tender heart of a woman" Rati somehow believed Suhani would be the confidante she always wanted, needed in a life where even good friends were scarce.

It was the much-awaited day of Annie and Abhi's court marriage. They were dressed in a simple, yet striking attire. **Nara Apparels**' tailored suit in pin-striped charcoal- grey, looked smashing on Abhimanyu Shekhawat.

He stood next to his new bride Mrs. Sarvani Shekhawat, dressed in a virgin-pink sari with *mukkaish* work done all over it. The couple took their blessings from Abhi's father, who was elated at the new addition to his growing family.

The Anands were dressed in shades of lime-green and turquoise-blue, carrying the same shades through, to the wedding Reception at DTD in another attire.

The theme of **Regressive Progression** depicted village scenes of the bygone era, alongside the same frame as it stood today.

Some of the pictures could be superimposed and the difference not known, courtesy the precision of shot taken.

The guests trickled in to wish the two newly married couples, with gifts galore. Mrs. and Mr. Shekhawat were now dressed in a traditional Indian costume: a navy-blue *sherwani* for Abhi, a fuchsia-pink *sharara* outfit for Annie.

Mrs. and Mr. Chand wore the same outfits that they displayed, while walking the ramp during the fashion show.

Guests walked around the gallery at leisure, sipping their exotic cocktails, nibbling on tasty canapés. By the time the evening was over, each one of the pictures displayed were sold out.

It was a record of sorts for the gallery. Toasts to the couples, to the success of the evening, were made. Sangharsh and Nalini had made themselves at home with most of the guests, who they knew through their business.

They were the ones who gave Arjun the feedback he yearned for so long to hear. "They want to be amongst the first few to know, when the next theme pictures are put. Now this is what is called a runaway success, *dost*!"

Sangharsh was happy for his childhood friend, who finally got the break he truly deserved. "I see there are a few boards against some pictures that say 'Sold to Anand Creations'" Arjun pointed out. "Nandish's handiwork as he showed us"

"This is the first time his effort has been publicly acknowledged. How can we let it hang on someone else's wall?" Nalini said, looking at Nandish lovingly. It was time to give the aching bodies of the Prataps and Anands some rest, as they called it a day.

Dr. Shekhawat had to go back to Jaipur the next day, so he chose to go with Ajju and Rati, who decided to leave for Bassi after dropping Andy's father-in-law to his residence.

Arjun was exhausted coping up with the previous day's toil to speculate the situation that could, eventually would, arise.

Dr. Shekhawat was having an affair with Tara in his own words. Technically, if Andy was to marry Malika, then Tara would be his mother-in-law, the mistress to Annie's father-in-law!

The mind dulls when the body rests. Attempting to control matters that are destined though, is a waste of precious time.

Sitting in the SUV behind the *Chaudhary* and *Chaudhrain* of Bassi, the same village as Tara's, something was bound to spill out.

Arjun woke up to the thought, jumping out of bed to forewarn Ajju. Unfortunately, the signal to his cell was not within the coverage area.

"If you're trying to call Ajju *Bhaiya*, he's left already. You were sleeping soundly, so he didn't want to disturb you" Dhanush spoke with his mouth full of a half-eaten apple. He looked at Suhani who was cutting his fruit, for it was a Monday.

Monday was the day Arjun showed his belief in Lord *Shiva* by fasting in his name. Suhani pointed to the sky, smiling at her husband, indicating that *Bholenath* would protect their son. Arjun nodded at her and got back to getting ready for the day.

Meanwhile, Ajju's SUV had a very chatty Rati, excited to get back to her domain. She had shopped like crazy for Dhara, remembering to pick up some jewellery pieces for Leenata and Jiya as wedding gifts for them.

"They are beautiful! You have great taste, *Chaudhrain hukam*!" Dr. Shekhawat complimented when she showed him the red and blue boxes full of expensive baubles set in precious stones.

"One is for Jiya, Akash *Chacha*'s son's soon-to-be bride. The other one is for *Chacha*'s daughter, Leenata. They are both getting married on the same day as per the *muhurat* taken out by our village *pandit*" she continued to chatter.

"Yes, I know. I've been invited to their wedding" Ajju looked at him through the rearview mirror.

"If you don't mind Doctor *Saheb*, may I know how you got acquainted to Akash *Chachaji*?" Ajju enquired, inquisitive to find out the connection between the two, now family members by marriage.

"Tara told me about him and how honourable and upright he was. I've given her several loans for her livestock, which are yet to be paid"

"Doctor *Saheb*, do you know who I am?" "Of course I do! You are the *Chaudhary* of the *Raika*s of Bassi and the *Banjara*s of Nagri"

"Then you also know Tara *Chachi* would never speak highly of Akash *Chachaji*. Trust me with the truth, Doctor *Saheb*. I will not misuse it. You have my word on that" Ajju's magnetic charm worked its magic on the doctor.

The doctor told him not only about his illicit relations with Tara, but also the loan he had given Akash for the elaborate marriage of both his children.

Upon having given his word, Ajju could do nothing but retain the information. If he spoke about it to anyone, he would lose face in front of Dr. Shekhawat.

The only person he could speak to, other than Rati, was his soul father, Arjun. "You should have woken me up! Never leave without meeting me again"

"*Baasa...*" Ajju poured his heart out, emptying all information the doctor had given him.

"I have an uncanny feeling Ramona and Tara have either joined forces already, or are about to very soon. They have a common enemy after all"

Ajju knew before Arjun specified. "You, Ajju!" It was true as the blue sky. He knew his work was cut out for him, before he reached his beloved birthplace.

# CHAPTER FORTY FIVE

"Why have you called me here? How did you get my number?" Standing in the room that overlooked the pool of the Lake Palace Hotel, Tara asked the lady who stood by the window. She wore plain grey slacks and a loose peasant top with moccasins.

When she turned to face Tara, the striking resemblance between her and Mia, was what struck her most. "My name is Ramona Rai, mother of Mia who you probably knew as Aradhana Chand, Ajju's first wife"

"That's right. I know who you are now. How did you get my number and what am I doing here?" Tara reiterated her unanswered query. "It doesn't matter how I got your number, Tara. What matters is whether your being here, is going to be lucrative to either, or us both"

"Lucrative? What could you do for me? From what I hear, you have no family and have been practically declared as an outlaw!" Watching Ramona's surprised expression, Tara smirked, "You are not the only one who has eyes and ears everywhere, *Memsahib*!"

"I may be a village woman, but I keep track of things that interest me"
"Well now! I'm impressed you have both beauty and brains. Just like me!" Vanity became Ramona, for she wasn't entirely wrong.

Both Tara and she had no shortage of physical attributes, the appeal that disappears as youth fades, still stayed on within them both. But their minds were darker than the darkest of nights. It wasn't like this since the beginning.

Over time, when one keeps feeding on what they have been unable to acquire, they tend to become negative by nature. A negative person is prone to more acts of destruction than creation, as both cannot co-exist in one mind.

"My daughter Mia, married Ajju because she fell in love with him. Knowing she was the only family I had, the Prataps began by changing her name to Aradhana. I was tricked into not attending their wedding ceremony as well"

"That's horrible! Why would they do something like that? Why didn't your daughter say anything?" Tara interrupted. Breathing in deeply, Ramona stood near the tall window with the Venetian curtains.

"Mia was all about trying to appease the person she loved. First I thought it was me, but Ajju began to gain control over her rapidly. She thought they were trying to include her in the family, by alienating her from me"

"In reality, the reason why they took her away, was to take their revenge from me" "Revenge for what?" "When I came back to India, I was still Arjun's legally wedded wife, which made Suhani the 'other woman'"

"That also meant Dhanush was the child who was born out of wedlock" "Oh my God! This is quite interesting! Please go on" Tara coaxed Ramona, sitting on the sofa near where she stood. "The gallery Arjun now owns, belonged to my father and is rightfully mine"

"He tricked my father into willing it on his name, leaving me penniless. Here in India, he told everyone I was dead. There in U.K., I was poor with two girls to raise. You tell me Tara, what was I supposed to do?"

The warped explanation Ramona concocted compelled Tara to feel sorry for her. "You poor thing" "I came back to India, saw Arjun was happily married to Suhani. So, I went back and agreed to marry my childhood friend who was a good husband, a provider for me and my two daughters"

"Then, he died in a car accident and I was left stranded again. I came back with two grown-up girls, the moment I found out that the marriage I had with Gerard Cotton wasn't registered. So technically, it meant Arjun Pratap was still my husband"

"I always loved him, but he never reciprocated. The first chance he got, he got rid of me and went into the arms of that *Banjaran*, Suhani. In fact, they were having an affair even before, when she was still married to *Chaudhary* Dhanush"

"I wouldn't be surprised, if a DNA test proves Arjun is Ajju's biological father!" "Really?" Tara gaped at her. "I never knew that" "How could you, Tara? I found out about it myself recently" "No wonder *Chaudhary* Dhanush used to come to me at nights. He must have known about Suhani's infidelity, thus naming her new born baby Arjun Chand!"

Ramona knew Tara was almost under her control. "Yes, maybe. Anyway Tara, there is no use of delving in the past. I have been deprived of a life I could have had as Arjun Pratap's wife, the owner of a gallery, maybe my daughter would have still been alive"

"All of that was taken away by the Prataps. I want to take away what is most precious to them. That is where I need your help" "What's that? How?" "Once Ajju is out of the picture, the house of the Prataps will collapse. That is what will avenge all that I have lost"

"You mean kill him? Are you crazy, Ramona? Do you know who he is? He is the most powerful man in Bassi and Nagri. I'd rather send him back to the city, than have him killed. This is too much for me to handle"

Watching Tara backtrack quickly, Ramona asked her to calm down, offering her tea to drink. "Your son Viren I hear, could have become the *Chaudhary*. Is that true?" That set Tara venting out her frustrations as well.

"My story is no better than yours, Ramona. I was to be *Chaudhrain* of Bassi once. Dhanush Chand and I were childhood sweethearts, but his parents had already arranged his marriage to the daughter of the *Chaudhary* of the *Banjara*s, Suhani"

"I accepted it as my fate, as I too was married off to Giriraj. As fate would have it, I was blessed with a son, who was born to be a leader. All I did was encourage his ambition, much to my husband's disapproval"

"Viren fell in love with Akash's daughter, Leenata" "Leenata? That is who Dan, Arjun's younger son is to marry soon, isn't it?" Ramona interrupted, lighting her filter cigarette. "Yes, the same one. Dhanush came into the picture from nowhere and swept that girl off her feet"

"She refused to marry my Viren, leaving him broken-hearted. Not only that, my daughter Malika was supposed to be married to Akash and Bindiya's son, Vansh. He refused to marry her too, claiming he had to prove Bassi was important to him, thus taking precedence over his private life"

"He convinced his parents that much was to be done to improve on the condition of the village. I remember holding my Malika while she cried when she saw Vansh with Diana, who he calls Jiya now" The memory made Tara stand up, flash a dirty look towards Ramona.

"Your second daughter!" "Sit down, Tara. Diana was adopted to give Mia company. She was and never will be my daughter" Convinced, Tara continued, "Viren fell in love with Rati Singh Rana, but Ajju stole her away too"

"The only thing my poor boy was left with, was an ambition of being the *Chaudhary* one day. Not only did Ajju become the *Chaudhary*, but to add salt to Viren's open wound, he made Vansh the *Chote Sardar*"

"My son was left out in the cold, without any hope or dream for the future to look forward to, work towards" Tara checked her watch, getting up to leave. "I have to go now. My bus leaves in half an hour"

"You are with me now, Tara. My friends don't travel by public transportation. We are friends, I assume?" Tara had poured her heart out to Ramona. She knew she was joining hands with the Devil himself, but didn't see much of a choice for herself.

Seeing her nod her head in agreement, Ramona smiled. "Good! I'll have my car drop you to your village outskirts if that is alright by you" "Perfectly fine" Tara answered. They ate lunch together by the side of the clear, blue-tiled swimming pool.

Ramona was pleasantly surprised at Tara's table manners. "I have a rich boyfriend from the city who taught me how to handle cutlery" "You've cheated on your husband?" Ramona acted shocked.

"I made Giriraj rich by giving myself to a man I never loved. My children are now the richest in Bassi because of this sacrifice I made" Tara justified, pricking her broccoli salad. "You are the ideal mother, just like I am"

"I wonder why we are misunderstood" Ramona thought out loud, sipping her bubbly. "That's easy. They're jealous because of our looks. Being good-looking is both a blessing as well as a curse. One ought to learn with time how to use it, that's all!"

They laughed together like old friends, which made Tara feel comfortable. The act of friendship was exactly that from Ramona's end though- an act. She was a one-man army who was used to operating solo.

But since the man whose family she was soon about to annihilate, had not only tied her hands with the letter that she signed at the gallery, but also removed both her snoops Mr. Guha and Mohan the chauffeur, she needed a new foot soldier.

Money didn't seem to make the cut after a while. Hatred, vendetta, were strong emotions that could drive one into doing almost about anything, bordering insane. Love and hate are blinding and uncontrollable.

Now, a wronged mother is even more lethal because all the hatred becomes that much more personal. Tara was the perfect candidate to set Ramona's wheels in motion. She had the motive, the drive, the common enemy.

She was a solo operator like Ramona as well, so she offered her hand in friendship and a chance to take her revenge from their common enemy. "What can you tell me about Ajju's new bride, Tara?" Ramona asked her.

Sipping her *kesar thandai*, Tara gave her all the history there was to know about Rati. "She has the same shade of blue eyes as Mia had" Seeing the change in Ramona's expression, Tara raised her palm to apologize, "I didn't mean to open a fresh wound"

"On the contrary my friend. What you have just said may well be the key to solving all of our problems! In the words of the great Arjun Pratap- there are no coincidences in life, after all!" "I don't understand how Rati's eye colour will help our plan, Ramona"

"You are a woman, as am I. Now tell me, if you found out your husband's first wife had some feature of yours that was a striking resemblance, what would you do?" "I would hate it. No one wants to play second fiddle to anyone else"

"Right. You would perhaps hate your husband based on that one feature, right?" "Yes! I get what you're trying to say, Ramona. Rati needs to be brainwashed into believing that Ajju married her to replace Mia's void, just because of how she looks and nothing else"

"You are smarter than I thought, Tara. We will get along just fine. I do loathe explaining myself in detail to people. It is mentally taxing" "I know how you feel, Ramona. My husband Giriraj falls in that category, where everything has to have a time-consuming explanation!"

Walking back into the hotel room, Tara asked, "Now that we have found a weak link in that family, how do we approach it?" "Not we. You. I cannot enter Bassi at any cost. If Ajju finds out I'm still in India, he will catch his father"

"I have no wish to stay in jail till I'm old" Ramona didn't tell her that the Indian police would eventually hand her over to Interpol, where she was wanted for the murder of Diana's mother and Gerard Cotton.

If Tara got to know she was wanted not just for corporate espionage, but also for murder, she may back out of the entire plan, leaving Ramona without any pawn to fight her self-created, chess-game battleground.

"It's getting late. We'll keep in touch over the phone. As far as approaching Rati goes, I'm sure you will figure out a way" Ramona said, calling for a hotel taxi to drop her to the outskirts of Bassi, as promised earlier.

Tara was Ramona's last ray of hope. She would see the Prataps crumble down to the ground and leave the country, never to be seen again. She wondered if Tara would be able to pull off the plan, all by herself.

She did mention something about a rich boyfriend in the city. Picking her Blackberry, Ramona dialed Tara's number, who was still in the cab. "Hi! Is everything alright? Are you comfortable, Tara?"

"Yes. Thanks for calling. Rajasthan looks so much more beautiful, when you are sitting inside an air-conditioned car!" "Yes, it sure does. Listen Tara, I was thinking about our conversation. You mentioned a rich boyfriend in the city. Are you still with him?"

"No, not anymore. Why?" "Well, as friends that we now are, I'll give you the financial assistance you require, to maintain the status you've been enjoying at Bassi" "Ramona, I don't need to be paid to do your work. It is demeaning, especially when I'm doing it for my personal satisfaction, as well"

Ramona tried as hard as she could, but failed to extract the name of this boyfriend of Tara's. Her concern was only one-no one should know she was at the Lake Palace, at any cost. "No one will, Ramona. I assure you of that. At least not from me"

They hung up after their goodbyes, pleased to have found someone who truly understood what it felt like, to be deprived over and over again of what they thought was rightfully theirs. Tara reached the village outskirts, where she was dropped as requested.

The moment she was out of the cab, the driver of the hotel taxi dialed a number. "Brijesh Kumar, Manager of the Dare To Dream gallery. How may I help you?" "Bantu *Bhai*?" "I'm sorry. This is Brijesh Kumar!"

"Sorry, may I speak to Bantu *Bhai* then?" "Depends on who is calling" "It's Mohan. Mrs. and Mr. Pratap's chauffeur" "What do you want, Mohan? This is Bantu" "Then why did you say you're Brijesh Kumar?"

"Because that's my real name, you moron! I have no wish to speak with a back stabber" "I understand, Bantu *Bhai*. But I need to speak to Mr. Pratap urgently" "I'm sure you do, Mohan. Maybe because all the money that you took to spy on him, must have finished by now"

"The fact that Arjun Sir never gave you any reference, mustn't have helped either" "As a matter of fact, I do have a job. At Lake Palace Hotel. Bantu *Bhai*, for old times' sake, I need to speak with Mr. Pratap as soon as possible"

"You have a job? Ha! I don't believe you. I wish them luck once they find out what a sell-out you truly are! I'm not interested in speaking to you anymore. Goodbye!" Bantu banged the phone down, getting back to his work.

Since he had taken over as Manager at the DTD, he had rectified the discrepancies Mr. Guha had conveniently overlooked. He also made it a point to send daily reports to Arjun and Dhanush by email, so as to maintain transparency at all times.

After what his uncle had done to the Prataps, he felt it was his bounden duty to win over their trust, by sheer hard work and an open door. "Sorry, I'm late. Reschedule the client's meeting for tomorrow"

"This meeting I just came from will get us a chunky business, Bantu!" Arjun walked into the gallery, moving to his office with Bantu trailing behind. "Tell Dhanush, I'm here. He wanted to show me some designs"

"Any messages for me?" "Sir, Mrs. Pratap called to say that A.J Sir's marriage certificate has been picked up by Mr. Anand, when he had gone to get his daughter's certificate as well, from the Registrar's office" Bantu reported.

"That's great! What else?" "The Koreans who wanted their construction sites to be photographed, have asked you to meet them tomorrow to discuss the terms and conditions of their contract with DTD"

"Wow! At this rate, you will have to keep an assistant, Bantu! Well done!" Pleased, Bantu went back to his chair, not giving him the message from Mohan the chauffeur. He debated whether he should or shouldn't for a very long time, up until he chose to finally get it off his chest.

"Sorry to disturb you, Sir" "Yes, Bantu. What is it?" Arjun asked, sitting with Dhanush to take a look at some new designs of the display section of the gallery. "Sir, Mohan called" "Who?" "Mohan the chauffeur. He wanted to speak with you" "What did he want?" "Sir, he wanted to speak with you" Bantu replied.

"Bantu, I meant why did he want to speak with me?" "I don't know, Sir. I never asked him" Assuming it was either money trouble or the lack of finding a job, Arjun dismissed Bantu along with the thought of Mohan's phone call.

Yes, Ramona's secret was safe for now. Luck favoured her at the moment. The question now was what would run out first for her and Tara- luck or time? Bassi was to quake under the fury of two women, presumably wronged, who had chosen to destroy their enemies at any cost.

# CHAPTER FORTY SIX

Rows of *kikar* and acacia trees guarded the serpentine road, leading to Bassi on either of its sides. The beckoning desert yonder was still, with not a grain of sand that moved from hillocks to dunes, at its horizon.

The only noise that broke the silence, other than the motor vehicles on the tar road, were the strings of sheep, goats and cattle that were being grazed around the greenery, alongside the road.

It was an ordinary scene to the locals, but to those who visited, it was picturesque, par extraordinaire.

The *Raika*s took great care of their livestock, since wealth of a villager was measured in two ways alone: either a reasonable livestock or a substantial stretch of farmable land.

Someone who owned a bit of both, eventually became the local money lender or *Chaudhary*. Most of this specimen of *Chaudhary*s further exploited the poor, to increase his own coffers of wealth.

Bassi had a unique history in this aspect. The villagers of Bassi were the keepers of the then *Maharaja*'s camels. They unanimously chose their leader among themselves, who was the great grandfather of Dhanush Chand, the greatly-admired Bhairav Chand.

He passed on the scepter and *pagdi* of a *Chaudhary* all the way to the last of the royal bloodline, *Chaudhary* Arjun Chand.

*Chaudhary* Arjun Chand was the present leader of the *Raika*s of Bassi, the addition to his title as *Chaudhary* of the *Banjara*s of Nagri, courtesy his father *Chaudhary* Dhanush Chand, who was wedded to the princess of the *Banjara* tribe at Nagri, his mother Suhani.

*Chaudhary* Arjun Chand had wedded a local girl from Bassi, a commoner who tied him to the land even more, *Chaudhrain* Rati Chand.

Ajju and Rati were on their way back to Bassi, the land they would see prosper and grow, right before their very own eyes.

"Make me some *khichdi* when we reach home, *Beendni*. City food doesn't suit me as well as it used to. Or better yet, some *kadhi chawal* would be divine"

"As you wish" Rati answered, fixing the *pallu* of her *sari*.

The citrus-orange *sari* was one of many, gifted by Suhani in chiffon and georgette that made her look more like a beautiful and powerful woman, than an attractive village belle.

Suhani had advised her elder daughter-in-law thus.

"If you want to be a *Chaudhrain* deserving to be looked up to, you must look as well as act the part. No more *ghaghra cholis* or *salwars* in Bassi. Wear *saris* when you are in the village. When you come to Delhi, you can wear anything you want"

"Anything at all?" Rati had asked. "Yes! Do you have something in your mind already?" "*Ma*, I have never worn jeans. Do you think it would be too forward if I tried one?"

"Tried one? My dear child, we're leaving right now to get you your first pair!" Suhani said, pulling her along.

Before Rati could either retract or protest, Suhani was walking down the steps to cross the living room floor. "Where are you ladies off to?" Arjun asked Suhani, watching Rati close behind her.

"To the mall. Call for the driver, *Saheb*" "The mall?" Ajju enquired. "Yes. Rati is to be given jeans to wear while she is here"

"Jeans? *Maasa* she has never worn a pair earlier!" Ajju said, taken aback at what was happening. "All the more of a reason why she must be gotten one then, isn't it? *Saheb*..the car" And that was that.

When both women returned a couple of hours later, Rati was the proud owner of six pairs of Levis jeans of various shades of blue. Suhani went ahead and got loose lady-like tops for her, to mix and match with them.

Peep toes, Grecian sandals, pumps were also bought for her as appropriate footwear. When she walked in with her floral top, blue jeans and fawn peep toes, Ajju almost fell off his chair!

Rati loved the reaction, appropriately termed as jaw-dropping by Suhani, her mother-in-law, on seeing her sport the entire ensemble. "What are you thinking, my love?" Ajju asked his *Beendni*.

"I'm thinking of *Ma*. If only she could stay with us, Ajju. I see my mother in her" "She does spoil you. I have never seen her dote on anyone other than Dhanush and I, the way she does, you" Ajju replied, surprising himself with this deduction.

"Really?" "Yes" "Not even…" "Not even who?" Ajju asked, knowing she meant Mia. "You know who" Rati answered softly. "I'm a man. Men are stupid. Now tell me, who you are referring to?"

"Mia" "Ha! I knew it!" "If you knew, then why did you ask?" "Because my sweet simple wife, I wanted to tease you!" he said, pulling her cheeks as she began to smile.

"Hand me the papaya pieces, Rati. I'm hungry" Ajju said next, avoiding the pothole, the size of a Martian crater, at the center of the road.

Eating the frozen pieces with a cocktail fork, he offered her a bite which she refused to accept. "Still mad at me?"

"Nothing like that. I'm not mad at you" "Then? You must be hungry" "Yes, I am. I'll have an apple" "Later. Share the papaya with me. It's too much for one person"

"I can't" "Why? You're so stubborn, Rati. Learn to be flexible at times" "Say whatever you want. I cannot have it"

"You don't like papaya? I thought we both loved eating it once" "Yes, once. Now, *Ma* has said I cannot have papayas anymore. Well, at least for a while"

Ajju slowed down the SUV, swerving it to the side of the road. "*Maasa* asked you to stop eating papayas with me?"

"Oh God! Not just with you, with anyone else! Ajju, don't you get it?" she asked him, frustrated. He moved closer to kiss her over and over again.

"You carry my child, my love. Yes I know that papayas are natural aborters" "Ajju, we must not speak of this to anyone until the first few months. *Ma* has said it is best to keep the evil eye away from our child"

Ajju agreed happily with whatever she desired. He was to be a father, start a family of his own at Bassi.

When they reached the *haveli*, Vansh and Jiya greeted the couple with *bel ka sherbet* and a good meal of *alu matar* and *jeera pulao*.

"I wanted *kadhi chawal*. Too much of rich city food" Ajju cribbed, looking at Rati. "I'll make it tomorrow afternoon" Rati promised, going in to rest.

Jiya left to call Dhara who was playing with her friends, for Rati wanted to see how her sister fared now.

Since Rati became the *Chaudhrain* of Bassi, her sister Dhara had been groomed to look far better than her scraggly old self. She wore well-stitched *ghaghra cholis* that were miles away from the tattered, torn clothing she used to wear earlier.

Her hair was beginning to brown because it would stay unkempt. Now it was well-oiled, combed tightly into ponytails. *Chaudhary* Arjun and *Chote Sardar* Vansh began discussing their common interest at length-the betterment of Bassi.

Other than educating the farmers of Bassi and Nagri to get them to join us in Agritourism, we need to focus on occupation training, handicraft promotion, improvement of the landscape, the basic infrastructure"

"The State government of Rajasthan has agreed to sanction us a loan for our rural tourism project as well" Vansh reported. "That is great, Vansh! All your hard work is about to pay off!" "Mine and Jiya's"

"She speaks *Marwari* almost as good as me now, Ajju *Bhaiya*. But we still have the expectations tourists will have, with regard to Agritourism at Bassi" "What are those?" Ajju asked, fascinated by how a concept revolutionized could help realize the dreams of his people.

"Well, the location has to be convenient, attractive in the ethnic sense, there has to be peace and quiet, we have to have Internet and mobile connectivity, clean surroundings, healthy food and safe water to drink"

"It sounds easy, but when you spend an hour trying to explain to a farmer, that mooing cows behind their homes in a shed is not what the average tourist would like to wake up to, you realize what a back-breaking task it really is!"

"Sure sounds like it. What news of Giriraj and his family? Have they been behaving themselves?" "Ajju *Bhaiya*, to be honest with you, Jiya and I have been neck deep in trying to coordinate between groups of farmers, all the way from dawn to dusk"

"Leenata had been going to Gurukul on a daily basis, but Malika has not been coming to school off late. From what I hear, Giriraj is trying to gain control over his family. Other than that, no news at times could also imply good news!"

"Agreed. I'll go see him after lunch, chat him up a bit. I'll see you later" Rati was waiting for him, knowing he could not sleep until he was totally satiated. The hunger for Rati was a never-ending appetite that Ajju knew he would have to curb, now that she was with child.

Gentle moments passed till she pleasured him all the way to an explosive climax. The sweet satisfaction of sleeping in each other's arms again wrapped them in a soft blanket, like romance does.

Ajju left in the evening for Giriraj's multi-coloured bungalow. He saw the old man trying to get one of his buffaloes to keep steady, so as to tie it in the cool shed. Ajju left his *lathi* in a corner and helped wrestle the bovine, getting the job done faster than Giriraj would have, alone.

"Many thanks, *Chaudhary hukam*. It is nice to see that the power of a *Chaudhary* has not gone to your head" he complimented Ajju. "My power lies not in me, *Chachaji*. It lies in my people such as yourself. I aim to serve those who come under my wing"

Pleased by his outlook, Giriraj invited him in for a cup of tea. When the house-help served them *masala chai* with *nankhatai*s, Ajju asked the obvious question. "Where is everyone?" "Malika is under house arrest, imposed by Viren"

"She refuses to stop talking to Nandish over the phone, which has enraged her brother. Viren is in the fields grazing the oxen and our cows with the other workers. Their mother has gone to Jaipur, to get a loan for new livestock"

"We have been taking loans for so many years now. The good doctor's generosity is the reason we are considered wealthy at Bassi. I save up over time and return the loan with interest, which Tara goes to give to the doctor"

He felt bad for Giriraj and detested Tara's misusing his simplicity. For years, Tara had taken the money Giriraj had given her as loan repayment, putting it rupee by rupee into a bank account she had opened for herself.

What she did in fact, was pay the doctor in kind. Ajju could not find himself to hurt the gentle, simple soul standing in front of him. "I'll take your leave, *Chachaji*. Give my regards to *Chachi* and love to the children"

Wishing him well, Ajju left for the *haveli*, meeting village folk on the way who greeted him with grinning yellow teeth, happy to see him back at Bassi. When he called Annie and Abhi at night to ask how **Nara Apparels** was doing, they informed him they had begun to get orders from international clientele.

"That is great news! Keep at it. Well done!" "Thanks, Ajju *Bhaiya*. In fact, when Abhi's Dad came today, he even offered to have my doll line displayed in the biggest mall in Jaipur!" Ajju should have congratulated her once again, but he frowned instead.

"You mean Dr. Shekhawat?" "Of course that's who I mean! Abhimanyu has only one father!" "Yes, I know" "What's wrong? You seem pre-occupied Ajju *Bhaiya*" Annie asked, concerned. "Not pre-occupied *behan*, just tired"

Hanging up, Ajju began to pace up and down his room. If Dr. Shekhawat was not in Jaipur, why did Giriraj tell him Tara had gone to get another loan from him? Someone was not telling the truth.

The only person who could clear his doubt now, was the doctor himself. He called him immediately. "*Chaudhary hukam*, nice to hear from you again! I just came from Delhi and was told you had left in the morning"

"Yes, that is true. I wanted to be in Bassi by noon. *Khammaosa*, Doctor *Saheb*. Forgive me for disturbing you this late in the night" "Not at all. Tell me what can I do for you?" "Doctor *Saheb*, I just came from Tara *Chachi's* house"

"Her husband Giriraj told me that she had gone to you, to get a fresh loan for their livestock" "To me? But I was in Delhi with Abhi and Annie" "Yes, I just spoke with them. I know you were in Delhi. Then why did Giriraj lie to me?"

"He must have heard her wrong. Wait, I have Jai Prakash, the livestock seller's number. Why don't you try calling him? Maybe she has gone there" Ajju took the number from the doctor, thanked and wished him a good night.

He called Jai Prakash's residence and spoke to him directly. "No, Tara *Bhabhi* did not come today. Why do you ask? Is she alright?" "Yes, she is fine. She must be on her way back. We were just concerned, that's all. *Namaste*"

Ajju hung up before Jai Prakash could ask who he was. So, now it was ascertained that neither did Tara go to Dr. Shekhawat to ask for a loan, nor did she go to Jai Prakash to increase her livestock.

Ajju would have let the mystery be, were it for a tiny detail. Tara lied to Giriraj as to her whereabouts. Not only that, the fact that Malika was being kept at home by Viren, disturbed him all the more.

Feeling restless, he lay down to sleep next to Rati who was already snoring gently. The cell vibrated with the light on the screen, showing who it was. "*Baasa*, I'm so glad you called" "Ajju, *kya hua*? (Ajju, what happened?)"

"I just called to ask if you reached and if everything is okay" "*Baasa*, I have a feeling 'everything' is anything but okay!" "What do you mean?" Ajju told him about his meeting with Giriraj and his attempt at trying to find out where Tara really went.

"Now that is really strange! Where do you think she could be?" "I don't know, *Baasa*. But the *lathait* I had sent to hover around their house said, that Tara returned at dusk, an hour after Viren came back from grazing cattle"

"Where could she have been all day?" Arjun thought out loud. "Your guess could be as good as mine" Ajju replied, watching a pigeon try to steal a scrap of *roti* from another pigeon at his bedroom window sill.

"*Baasa*, where is Ramona?" "Ramona? She must be back in London, or out of India at least. Why do you ask?" "No reason. Nothing substantial for now, at least. I'm really tired, *Baasa*. May I call you in the morning?"

"I'll call you on the way to DTD tomorrow. Rest now. You have a lot of people who depend on your knowledgeable leadership" That night was one of the most restless nights Ajju had in a long time.

He was used to a peaceful life since Rati came along. He came to Bassi hoping to have left the mad rush of the city behind. The surroundings tend to grow on a person, which is why people go to the mountains to de-stress, relax.

But when the person is restless from the inside, the tranquil atmosphere will not matter much. *Chaudhary* Arjun Chand of the *Raika*s of Bassi and the *Banjara*s of Nagri had a dream, in the wee hours of the early morning.

His birth father came to him while he threw pebbles in the river Bhairach. "What are you doing?" he asked Ajju. "Thinking" "While you think, the pebble you just threw, is already far ahead half way down the river"

Ruffling his already unruly mop of hair, Dhanush Chand looked into his son's eyes, black boring into black. The words he heard next reverberated even when he woke up. "Think less. Do more. The pebble is already half way across the river"

Ajju woke up to Rati's shy smile and a piping hot cup of *adrak chai*. He sipped it while staring aimlessly out of the window. What pebble? What was he not supposed to think? What was he supposed to do?

From all of the questions that were already floating inside his head, there was one that seemed the most important- where was he supposed to start from? Before the sea of questions could drown his sanity, Ajju dressed up befitting *Chaudhary* Arjun Chand, stepping out to take a walk around Bassi with his *Chaudhrain*, Rati.

# CHAPTER FORTY SEVEN

*Chaudhary* Arjun Chand had a fan following among the villagers of Bassi, similar to what his birth father enjoyed.

From the old man in charge of all the camels in their enclosure, to the senior most stable boy who was more of an elderly man, the term 'mesmerized' began to be replaced by 'enamoured', when it came to their new *Chaudhary*.

They all saw the commonalities that Ajju displayed in his stature, behavior, mannerisms, mirroring the image his birth father *Chaudhary* Dhanush Chand had created for himself.

Rati had added to the charm of the *Chaudhary* because she knew the people of the land well. He still called her Pocahontas during private moments of affection.

It was the closest he could get to describe her magnificence, since the first day he set eyes on the village beauty who was to become his *Beendni*.

The couple's daily walk through their village was a reminder, of how a hard life can yet be fruitfully rewarding. They saw a *Raika* woman in a teal-blue *odhni* with orange and pink flowers all over, that looked fresh on her haggard face.

She was wearing a pair of thick *lac* bangles on each of her wrists, with coloured mirrors that reflected the sunlight on them. Thin pieces of dried *kikar* twigs with thorns were strewn all around her.

She was meticulously collecting a handful together, using an axe to chop them to about an arm's length, putting them on a pile of already chopped twigs. "*Khammaosa Chaudhary hukam! Khammaosa Chaudhrain hukam!*" she wished them.

They reciprocated the greeting before gliding past. *Rajasthani*s are proud by nature. They are also shy, reserved and don't appreciate being stared at. Ajju had been taught this since childhood, by his mother and practiced it to this day.

A young *chori* was chattering with her fellow mates, a steel pot tucked under her waist wearing jewellery made of beads and thread, that looked pretty on her printed stripes *ghaghra choli*, popularly called the *leheriya*.

"Things look so much nicer since you came into my life" Ajju told Rati, holding her hand gently. Seeing the *Chaudhary* and *Chaudhrain* holding hands, the group of girls broke into loud giggles.

The couple smiled back and continued to walk, watching their Bassi come to life to another day.

"I dreamt of *Baasa* yesterday for the first time" he told Rati, while they sat down to rest near the *peepal* tree. "Arjun *Baasa?*"

"No" Understanding he meant his birth father, Rati said, "It's a sign, Ajju. What did he say?" "It was more like a riddle. I woke up to a bagful of questions, *Beendni*. The funny thing is, I just couldn't find the answers to any of them"

"Can I help, Ajju?" "Be my guest" he said, narrating the entire dream to Rati, adding the questions he woke up to, in the end. "I think I can decipher it for you. It's a known fact that women are more intuitive than men. Ask what you want to"

"Alright. Let's start with the pebble" "The pebble denotes an event that is happening, even as you were dreaming your dream"

"The pebble was in motion, which meant time was passing by. Next question" "What am I not supposed to think?"

"The question in itself is incorrect. You are not supposed to overthink" "Alright, *Maatsa*! What am I not supposed to overthink?"

"Your next move. If you overthink what your next move is to be, you will not only lose the moment it was to happen, but you will also lose the courage you had mustered earlier to make the move. Next question"

"Where am I supposed to start from?" "From now. Start from now. Next question" "What do I have to do to make you kiss me?" Turning to Ajju, Rati asked, "What?" Coming closer, Ajju whispered each breath on her angelic face.

"I said 'what do I have to do to make you kiss me'?!" She couldn't help but feel warm all over at the way he looked at her.

Moving to a side, she gently pecked him on his cheek. "There you go!" Frowning Ajju said, "I wasn't really gunning for that, but it'll have to do for now"

"Rati, your answers were exquisite. How did you know what the dream meant and what the answers to my questions were?"

"I am not as educated as you, Ajju. But, I am of the land. We know more than any book can ever teach, because of the life we lead"

Proud of marrying a woman with such hidden traits, he got up to walk back home with her. "Don't forget your promise to feed me *kadhi chawal* today" Ajju reminded her, to which she replied, "I haven't forgotten"

Arjun's call came when Ajju had just finished his bath and *puja*. "Sorry I got late. Your *Maasa* made such delicious food last night that we ate like hogs, slept like logs and woke up with a hangover!"

"It's alright, *Baasa*. *Maasa* does make some lovely dishes I hope she teaches Rati too, someday" "How is Rati, by the way?"

"She's fine, *Baasa*" "Alright then. Now tell me what's on your mind, Ajju" "Yes. Tara was neither at the doctor's, nor was she at Jai Prakash's"

"If she had to go someplace else, my hunch would be that she had no reason to lie to Giriraj" "Go on, *beta*"

"Is it possible Ramona sent someone to contact Tara, since both seemingly have a common enemy, that is, myself?" "Yes, it's quite possible"

"Then we have to find Ramona. *Baasa*, figure out a way to find her" "How, Ajju? Even if I hire a detective…"

"No, *Baasa*. We don't have sufficient time for that. Ask Dhanush. He is smarter than you think. I've to go, but call me if there's anything at all"

Arjun reached the gallery and waited for Dhanush to finish his morning work before calling him to the office. "I have a question for you"

"Shoot" "If you need to find out where a person is as soon as possible, but do not have the time to hire a detective, what do you do?"

"Do you have her number?" "Who 'her', Dhanush?" "Ramona. Who else?" "How did you know I was talking about her?" "*Baasa*, I'm smarter than you think!" Dhanush grinned at his father. Shaking his head and laughing, Arjun gave Ramona's cell number to him.

Dan went online and said, "This is a GPS tracker. You punch in the number and voila! You know the exact location of the person" Both father and son froze like ice sculptures, when they zoomed in to where the tracker showed the cell location.

"Track this number too while you're at it" Arjun said, rattling out Mohan the chauffeur's number. It was exactly the same point where Ramona's number showed on the screen.

He called Mohan immediately, collecting all the necessary details in depth. Arjun called Ajju without any delay, tapping his foot till he picked up.

"Ajju, brace yourself. I just spoke with Mohan, the chauffeur we used to have. Ramona herself is in Rajasthan. Which means Tara had gone to meet none other than Ramona!" Ajju quietly soaked in the information.

He was folding his sleeves in front of the mirror, watching Rati comb her hair. "I'm going for a walk towards the field, my love. I should be back for my *kadhi chawal* by noon" He kissed her forehead and walked out of the *haveli*.

Ajju had blanked himself out completely from thinking as to how he should begin the conversation. He was hoping against hope though that he would find Tara alone. Malika had called Leenata in the morning, informing her that her cell got confiscated by her brother Viren.

Since there was no other means of getting in touch with Andy, Viren permitted her to go to teach at Gurukul. It was understood between Leenata and Malika that Nandish would speak with her sometime during the day, on Leenata's mobile.

Giriraj and Viren had gone towards the river to supervise the bathing of the buffaloes. It was a tedious task that sometimes had their workers cut corners. This was Ajju's chance to get the truth out of Tara, who he saw was pulling on her husband's hookah, whilst staring into space.

Anyone would have found her strikingly attractive with the sharp features she had genetically passed on to her children. She saw him after a few minutes and jumped up. "*Khammaosa, Chaudhary hukam!* What brings you to a poor man's hut?"

"*Khammaosa*, Tara *Chachi*. Your bungalow is about ten huts put together, in my estimate. Wealth is not just measured in how many coins hold the purse pouch down!" "You have learnt to speak just like your father" "I am my father's son. Why should it surprise you then?"

She left him standing near the footsteps of the verandah, still sitting on the *jhoola* with her *hookah*. He didn't plan on staying long, so asking her if he could come in was practically pointless.

"Your livestock seems to have increased in leaps and bounds, *Chachi*. Your husband and son must be working hard to tend to them" "Yes, they do" "But, buying all these cattle must be costing a pretty penny. Do you have bank investments, or…"

Tara now knew what *Chaudhary* Arjun was zeroing in on. "*Seedhe baat kijiye, Chaudhary hukam* (Speak clearly, *Chaudhary* Sir)! Talking in circles does not suit one as highly regarded as yourself"

Ajju walked up to Tara, looking straight into her eyes. "I know your liaison with Dr. Shekhawat of Jaipur" Watching her go pale, he continued, "I came to your home the other day, met your husband"

"He informed me that you had gone to meet the doctor at Jaipur, for another loan to buy new livestock. It's a pity what happens, when you have to lie repeatedly to hide your crimes. Imagine if Giriraj *Chacha* found out, or worse..it could be Viren"

"*Chup kijiye aap*! (Be quiet!) How dare you come to my home and insult me this way! I'm as old as your mother" "Do not bring my mother into this, *Chachi*. She is pure as the holy water that flows in the Ganges"

"If she were that holy, then she would never allow you to marry your own step-sister, Mia!" Moments of silence dragged between the two. Tara had spoken more than she should have. Ajju's suspicion was now a firm conviction.

"How did you know that, *Chachi*?" "Everyone knows it, but nobody speaks about this openly" "Everyone, such as? Name one person who will say it exactly the way you just did" "I don't have time to play your silly games"

"All I know is, what I have said is the sole truth" "Maybe so. But, if you are finding it difficult to come up with a name who would say the same thing in the exact tone and words, allow me to help you"

Tara looked at him, standing up to leave when Ajju said the one word that left her rooted to the spot. "Ramona" She was afraid to turn, knowing Ajju would sense fear in her eyes, with guilt not falling far behind.

"She is wanted by the police, *Chachi*. If she is caught, she will pull you down along with herself. She probably even knows your connection with the doctor and will not hesitate from using it to her advantage"

"Will your family survive the shame your actions will eventually make them endure, for no fault of theirs?" Tara turned to negate his accusation vehemently, but he stopped her with the way he looked.

"I know you went to meet her at the Lake Palace hotel, *Chachi*. The man who drove you back to Bassi, was the chauffeur who worked for my parents at Delhi. He was thrown out when they realized he was spying for Ramona and was being paid handsomely for it"

Tara walked back with her limp arms swinging loosely, sat on the steps of her home, a blank expression clouding her face. Ajju walked out of her home, went down the steps, but turned again.

"There is always hope. For you. For your family. Ramona has no hope left. She has exhausted all of her options and is a fugitive as far as the law is concerned. From what I hear, your liaison with Dr. Shekhawat is already a matter of the past"

"If you plan to turn into a new leaf, now is your chance. Set an example for Viren. He needs you not as someone who feeds the fire inside him that burns for the wrong reasons; but a mother who will love him unconditionally, like mine does"

"It's still not too late, *Chachi*. Think about what I have said" Ajju left Tara still sitting on the steps of her mutli-coloured bungalow, staring at the world go by. The heavy confrontational discussion was something Ajju was not used to, so he went for a ride on Akash's horse that he himself gifted to the new *Chaudhary*.

Badal was black and white, like evil and good, who could gallop to the speed of the wind, trot to the magical tune of its hooves. Ajju crossed fields of farmers who were being taught the new method of Agritourism that Vansh and Jiya had started.

Vansh waved out at him from afar, as did Ajju. Jiya was going from hut to hut, teaching them how essential hygiene, sanitation was to be for them, not only to get more tourists to stay at their homes, but also for their own health.

Ajju didn't like to be rude to elders. He wasn't raised that way. But, if bad blood entered his village because of Tara aiding and abetting a criminal, it would dampen all the efforts being put in bringing Bassi up to a standard it once used to enjoy.

While *Chaudhary* Arjun was exercising his horse, Rati had gone close to Tara's house to pick curry leaves herself. She could have asked one of the helpers, but didn't want to deprive herself of making something for her beloved from scratch.

"*Khammaosa, Chaudhrain hukam*! How nice to see you again" Tara had seen her unguarded, ready to pounce on her prey with immediate effect. "*Khammaosa, Chachi*! How've you been?" "Oh, the usual. Looking after home and hearth can take a toll on a woman's beauty" Tara said, looking for a branch of curry leaves herself.

"You are still as beautiful as the first day I saw you, *Chachi*" Rati complimented her, going deeper into the thicket. Following her, Tara said, "You are such a sweet girl. When Viren told me he wanted to marry you, I couldn't be happier"

"But you were to become the *Chaudhrain* after all. Only Ajju could give you that honour" Frowning at Tara, detesting the underlying implication, Rati said, "I didn't marry Ajju to become the *Chaudhrain*, if that is what you're suggesting"

"Not in the least, Rati. I'm just saying that you were a gift. A gift from him to Bassi, to show he plans to stay, by marrying a local girl. You were a gift for him too. After all, your eyes and his first wife's, are the same shade of blue"

Rati brushed past her to leave, when Tara caught her hand. "Serves you right for aiming so high, *chori*. You will never be his first love! Ajju loved Mia. Ajju loves Bassi. And you are his third priority"

"You will be used as an incubator, to procreate. When you give him children, you will slip even lower, to priority number four!" Shaking her hand away, Rati glared at Tara. "Your beauty is only skin deep, *Chachi*. Beware of when the axe of fate falls. I'll be watching then"

Her words were so profound that they shook Tara to the core. But, the deed was already done. Rati held on to her tears till she reached home, made the *kadhi chawal* with the curry leaves for Ajju and cried herself to sleep.

Upon Ajju's return for the noon meal, he saw a curled up Rati resting on a tear-stained pillow. He woke her up and fed her from his own plate with his own hands, a morsel at a time. He wanted to ask her what the matter was, but loved her instead.

There is nothing in the world true love cannot fix. He had seen it between Arjun *Baasa* and his *Maasa*, time and again. He wanted that same understanding, that same bond with Rati.

"Talk to me, my heart" he gently asked her, while she told him everything Tara had spewed, while plucking curry leaves that day. He held her close, anger seeping in at Tara for hurting his Rati.

It was evident that she would not pay heed to the warning he had given her. She was bent on destroying herself along with her family.

If it weren't for Malika, who Nandish was in love with, he would have gone and burnt the multi-coloured house down to the ground. Fate though was to throw another curveball at him.

And soon.

# CHAPTER FORTY EIGHT

One of the lesser known wildlife sanctuaries around the state of Rajasthan, the Bassi wildlife Sanctuary, has a mysterious charm partly due to the animals it houses like the panther, the wild boar, the crocodile, the hyena and the *Cheetal*.

Fringed by the rugged *Vindhyachal* mountains, this sanctuary also included the Orasi and Bassi dams that make the tour all the more appealing. Having polished off a heavy breakfast of stuffed *kachori*s, *Chaudhary* Arjun and *Chaudhrain* Rati had left for a tour to report the tourist attraction of the Bassi wildlife Sanctuary to Vansh.

Ajju took his camera with him after a long time, hoping he would be able to spot some animals in their natural surroundings. The park ranger was gracious enough to give a jeep for the couple to travel in, with the driver who told them tales of the park that very few were aware of.

The two *lathait* bodyguards of the couple followed them in another jeep, as it was considered disrespectful to sit in the presence of the *Chaudhary*. Ajju preferred the privacy as well, finally managing to convince Rati she mattered the most to him in the world.

The driver, Suraj, took them to where animals would be spotted, since Ajju wished to click their pictures. The spotted deer was the first one they saw, nibbling on the tall grass, its ears pricking up the moment they reached.

Ajju clicked a few shots of the animal and before he knew it, a handsome stag with an elaborate set of horns walked up to it as if trying to ensure its safety. "This is how I will always protect you" Ajju said softly to Rati.

"You do resemble the stag a bit, including the frown!" Ajju loved her sense of humour, enjoying every bit of her company as they moved along. "*Woh dekhiye, Chaudhary hukam*! (Look there, *Chaudhary* Sir!)

Suraj stopped the jeep, handing over his issued binoculars to Ajju. Trusting it was something worthy of a capture, Ajju passed the powerful binoculars to Rati, zooming in with his camera at a panther, resting lazily on a thick tree branch, its tail swishing from side to side to ward off flies.

The lush greenery, courtesy the recent monsoon showers made the background of the panther glisten with exquisite shades of green. Excitement showed in the way Ajju clicked picture after picture, making their trip a successful one.

Any sanctuary's crowning glory was their jungle cats. If they could be spotted, the tourists would flock in to have a glimpse in hoards as well. Ajju asked Suraj to take them back, but through another route as the ride was bumpy and he was cautious of Rati's condition.

They crossed several animals; some grazing alone while others lazed around in small herds. A shallow stream had to be crossed, before they could join back with the main track of the sanctuary.

"Take a picture of me over here, Ajju. I want to show Dhara and *Ma* where I've been" Although the park rules didn't allow anyone to get down from their vehicles, Suraj had been given instructions to let the *Chaudhary* have the last word.

Giving in to her whim just this once, he walked her towards four short trees with reddish leaves that stood in a broad square, the stream flowing right through it, making a welcoming, gurgling sound.

"Hurry up, *Chaudhary hukam*. This is a watering hole for the animals" Suraj whispered. Ajju clicked a few shots of Rati standing near the trees. She waded to the tree with a swing-like branch jutting out low, its bright pink flowers making Rati look like a celestial being.

Ajju was trying to adjust the lens in his camera, when he heard a splash. Looking up, he saw something that moved in the marshes behind where Rati stood. He could have shouted at Rati to run to the jeep.

Instead, he ran to her, scooped his wife in his arms and planted her safely in the vehicle that sped off. "The crocodile must have laid her eggs somewhere in the vicinity. Seeing us, she must have felt threatened" Suraj justified, thanking *Ma Bhavani* for an averted disaster.

"Why didn't you ask me to run to the jeep, Ajju? What if that animal would have attacked you?" "I'm your stag, remember? My job is to protect you from any harm. Besides, if I would have asked you to run, what if you fell and hurt yourself?"

Rati knew now that Ajju belonged to him alone. He risked his life to save her, which proved how much she meant to him. Thanking Suraj and apologizing to the park ranger for the needless risk taken, Ajju and Rati headed home to their *haveli*.

They had to maintain decorum since their bodyguards followed them at a respectful distance. The moment they reached their room, Ajju's fear of almost losing Rati and their unborn child took over him as he began to show how much she meant to him.

Rati reciprocated, for she finally understood that love understands no reasoning and is a blind emotion built on hope, faith. They sat in their balcony, looking at the pictures Ajju had clicked at the Sanctuary.

They promised each other never to mention the crocodile incident to anyone, lest they get severely reprimanded. Rati seemed interested in photography, so Ajju decided to keep everything aside, spend the day teaching her, much to his wife's delight.

Meanwhile, Viren had been noticing his mother since morning. She had been quiet and demure ever since the rooster announced the beginning of a new day. Normally, she was snapping orders to everyone including his father; but today there was something different about her.

She was sipping tea on the terrace after seeing Malika and Giriraj off, when Viren joined her with his *kullad*. "*Maasa*, are you feeling alright?" "Why do you ask?" "You've been quiet since morning. It's unlike your usual self. Tell me if there is something you wish to share"

Viren coaxed, letting the hot *masala chai* revive his sleepy system. Turning to her son, Tara said, "And what will you do for this old woman, *beta*? You'll give me a patient hearing, turn your back on me"

"You'll get busy with your chores thereafter, Viren. Just like your father. Just like your sister" "They know what is wrong with you?" "They live under the same roof, Viren. But, not once have they asked if I'm feeling alright" she replied.

This answer of Tara's made her son even more anxious about what was bothering her. "*Maasa*, I have to sit with our accounts. I do not have all day. Say what you have to so I can get back to work after that"

Tara kept her empty *kullad* aside, walked up to the corner of the terrace and began to cry quietly. "See what I mean? You're just like all of them. Go back to your work. Leave your poor, old mother to her misery"

Viren felt guilty on alienating his mother, walking up to her to apologize. "Forgive me, *Maasa*. I will wait till you are ready to speak" Wiping her face, Tara spoke, "Ajju came yesterday to our home while none of you were there"

"Really?" "Yes. He came to forewarn me to keep you away from all that is happening at Bassi. The changes Vansh and that *chori* plan to make in our village, do not need disruption from cow herders like ourselves"

"He wants us to graze our livestock away from the village, closer to the forest" "But, that is impossible. It is endangering the lives of the workers we have hired as well as our livestock, *Maasa*"

"The panther, the wild boar, the hyena all await for a chance thus" "I know that, Viren. It is Ajju who doesn't, for he has not been raised in these parts, the way you have. I told him so, which made him lash back at me"

"He said that if I don't control you, he will tell your father that I was having an affair with the kind Doctor *saheb* who sits at Jaipur, from where we get loans for our livestock!" "That rascal! How dare he point a finger at you, when his own brother is born out of wedlock!"

"Exactly, *beta*. Being a Rajputni, I tried my best to defend what I hold dear, but he told me that his friend Nandish was still in touch with your sister, so if we have any plans of getting her married to someone else, we should drop the idea..or else.."

Tara turned clapping her mouth, the extra punch of drama working on Viren, as he walked up to face her. "Or else what?" "Or else he would tell the family we choose for Malika, about her affair and defame all of us"

Viren had heard enough from his mother. He walked away to his room, picked his *lathi*, marched out of the house. "Viren! Where are you going?" Tara asked in a broken voice from the terrace. "Where do you think I'm going, *Maasa*? I am not a coward"

"I'm going to the *haveli* to settle matters with *Chaudhary* Arjun, once and for all!" He walked away, rage, years of feeling wronged, carrying him on its shoulders; fuelling his need to vent out at the one he felt was the root cause of it all.

"*Chaudhary* Arjun Chand! Come out to face me, right now!" he yelled at the *chaukhat* of the *haveli*. He had already entered the courtyard, banging his *lathi* hard on the cement flooring, when Ajju walked down the stairs to him.

"Viren, what brings you here?" "Surprised to see me, are you? Especially after you asked *Maasa* to keep me away" "I never told her anything of the sort" "Of course you haven't, *Chaudhary hukam*!"

"Just like you didn't tell her that if she disobeyed her orders, she would lose face in front of all of us, once you spread rumours of an affair between the Jaipur doctor and herself. Am I right?" "Well not exactly"

"She has twisted it all around, Viren" "No, she hasn't. She told me exactly what happened, exactly the way it happened" "Your facts are all misplaced, my brother. Now that you have come, sit down and let's talk like grown men over *chai* and a *hookah*"

"Brother? I am not your brother! If you were my brother you would have made me *Chote Thakur* once Vansh was made *Chote Sardar*. If you were my brother, you would not threaten to defame my sister to her future in-laws, with an alleged affair with Nandish!"

Continuing with his verbal battering as Ajju calmly seated himself on the large cane chair at the centre of the courtyard under the *gulmohar* tree, Viren delivered the death blow. "Your brother is born out of wedlock. I can have the wedding stopped if I want to"

"But, I'm not as low as you are. Throwing mud on my mother's pure character, when yours had a child with someone else's husband!" "*Bas karo, badtameez*! (Enough, you insolent creature!)" Both men looked up to see, Rati glaring down.

She marched straight to the courtyard, walking up to face Viren. "Your mother is a snake. Ajju's mother is pure as holy water. I am the *Chaudhrain* of the *Raika*s of Bassi and the *Banjara*s of Nagri"

"Viren, you are forbidden from crossing the line of respect for your *Chaudhary*. If you are not happy here, then leave the village!" Viren had seen a happy-go-lucky Rati when he fell for her. This version of Rati, where she defended Ajju like a tigress, was praiseworthy, but it enraged him even more.

"You forbid me? Ajju picked you, a common *chori* and made you *Chaudhrain*, so you consider yourself of royal blood, all of a sudden? Which world are you living in, Rati?" "*Chaudhrain hukam*! Address her as that!" Ajju's voice boomed so loudly that Viren almost dropped his *lathi*.

When Ajju walked to Viren, Rati moved aside. He looked like a tiger who was about to tear his prey to merciless bits. Viren got to see the lethal side of Ajju who had had enough of Tara and her son's rantings and ravings.

"What have you come here for? Have you come here to tell me I am wrong, or have you come here to convince yourself your mother is right?" "They both mean the same thing, *Chaudhary hukam*"

"Not if you really think about it. Once you regain your sense of reasoning, think about what I said" Ajju said, his black eyes boring into Viren's bloodshot ones. "My reasoning will return when my respect is redeemed. That will happen after blood has been shed, as is the custom of us *Rajputs*"

"You want to fight me, Viren?" "Yes. With a sword that will defeat you in front of the entire village representatives, who were part of the old *Panchayat*. Meet me at *Chand Baori*, tomorrow at noon"

Viren left, taking his air of defiance with him. "Ajju.." "I have to" "You don't have to. Viren is an expert swordsman. I have seen him practice. You on the other hand haven't held one in your life!"

"Thank you for putting things into perspective, my love! Now bring me some tea. Speak of this to no one. Akash *Chachaji* and Bindiya *Chachiji* will return late at night from Jaipur, with the last of the wedding shopping"

"I will leave for *Chand Baori* in my SUV tomorrow morning, Keep your mobile on you at all times and wait for my call" Rati was afraid Ajju could get hurt. But, the confidence he emanated made it difficult for her to doubt his return.

If Ajju did not know how to fight with a sword, he would still use his presence of mind to gain over Viren. Although he had banned Rati from telling anyone about the fight, he made up his mind to call his parents on his way to *Chand Baori*, the next day.

He had the *Chaudhary's talwar* brandished and put in the backseat of his SUV that night. As luck would have it, Viren almost forgot about the sword fight the next day at *Chand Baori*, were it not for Tara wailing on top of her lungs.

"What happened, *Maasa*? What is it?" "Viren, Malika has been speaking to Nandish while she went to Gurukul, despite your forbidding her. He would call her on Leenata's cell. Yesterday, our house-help overheard Nandish asking her to meet him at Jaipur, from where they would elope to Delhi and get married!"

"Give me the sword you brandish, Viren. Give it to me so I can die without bearing any more shame!" Tara wasn't ashamed, for a person like her could never register such an emotion. She felt cheated by her own daughter, under the circumstances.

Tara now understood how Ramona had felt when Mia walked off with Ajju, ignoring her completely. "Bless me, *Maasa*. I am going to redeem the honour of our clan today. I will fight *Chaudhary* Arjun to the death at *Chand Baori*"

"Bless you, my son. Beware though, their family always has tricks up their sleeves" "You needn't worry about that, *Maasa*. The old *Panch* members have agreed to come along so as to rule out foul play"

Tara watched Viren go in the Mahindra Jeep that was followed by another jeep, full of old *Panch* members. Neeraj and Giriraj were the only ones not present. Neeraj condoned the fight, but Giriraj had no idea there was a fight in the first place.

Tara called Ramona, who picked up on the first ring. When she was informed of the sword fight, Ramona said, "So you did decide to have Ajju killed after all, Tara!" "He asked for it. Once he came home to threaten me, I knew there was no point being nice to a person like him"

"Your son is a good swordsman?" "One of the best around these parts, Ramona. Ajju doesn't know anything about swords. I'm expecting good news by the evening. Once I get to know, you'll be the first that I shall call"

Hanging up, Tara began to prepare herself for Giriraj. She had to keep him occupied all afternoon so that he wouldn't get to hear about the sword fight. Stupid that he was, he would go to try and stop it.

She waited for a while till one of the workers of their herd came running to tell her that someone mentioned a sword fight at noon in *Chand Baori*, between Viren and *Chaudhary* Arjun. Giriraj had gone to the *Chaudhary haveli*, riding off with Akash to *Chand Baori*, in their respective horses at top speed.

By the time they reached, it was already too late to stop the fight which had already started. While Tara and Ramona hoped against hope that Viren would plant a mortal wound on Ajju, Akash and Giriraj prayed that Viren should let good sense prevail.

The old ways of fighting to reclaim respect were long gone. They wished matters could be resolves through deliberations, but the heat of young blood had to cool down first. Saying a silent prayer in the hearts, Akash and Giriraj tied their horses under the shade of a tree and walked to where the fight was taking place.

# CHAPTER FORTY NINE

Abhaneri is a village, in the Dausa district of Rajasthan. This village is about 90 kms from Jaipur, on the Jaipur-Agra Road. Located opposite the temple of a highly regarded local deity, constructed in around 800 A.D, the *Chand Baori* has been acknowledged as the oldest, deepest step well in the world.

3,500 narrow steps over 13 stories, 100 feet into the ground; it resembles an upside down pyramid from the top. Centuries ago, step wells or *baori*s as they are locally referred to, were built in the arid zones of Rajasthan.

The main purpose of these *baori*s was to provide water all year round. This step well derived its name from the King who had it built- King Chand Raja from the Gujara Pratihara clan. Although it has lost its earlier significance, the geometric pattern precision attracts tourists from all over the world.

The steps form a magical maze with light and shadow, that constantly play hide and seek on its structure, giving it an other worldly aura. Once it is entered, the windows or *jharokha* reached, the enclosed, rectangular courtyard-kind of structure, is prominent.

Descending the stairs on the left, the *baori* seemingly begins to narrow as it reaches the bottom, criss-crossed with flights of steps in the shape of a 'V' on three sides, to reach the water at the centre below.

The stairs encircle the water on all three sides, while the fourth side prides in its three-storeyed pavilion with elaborately-carved *jharokha*s, galleries supported on pillars and two projecting balconies enshrining beautiful sculptures.

Some legends say that a Djinn appears at night floating around the step well, while other legends claim that ghosts built *Chand baori* in one night. Whatever the legend believed, it stands to this day as a landmark with an entity of its own.

*Chaudhary* Arjun, Viren, the old *Panch* members, hadn't gathered at the step well for its historical significance, or its potential for tourist attraction. They had assembled to redeem honour, an intrinsically-embedded jewel treasured by every *Rajput*.

The platform strip that overlooked the steps of the *baori*, sufficed for the space needed for the sword fight. *Chaudhary* Arjun was dressed in a traditional *dhoti kurta* minus the turban, as was Viren.

The eerie silence of the crowd that had gathered was in awe of something that happened hundreds of years ago, when the kings and queens had reigned. Sword fighting was banned now, but logic is left behind when the mind is clouded, by thoughts that need justification from somewhere.

A lone eagle screeched, soaring the sky above the two men, circling round and round, a celestial sign for the fight to begin. Laying their scabbards aside, both pulled their swords out at the same time, with a loud swishing sound.

The collective gasp of the assembled audience made it evident, that they were not prepared to see two young men bleed to death, in front of their eyes. But, it is said in Rajasthan that a sword needs to be honoured by the blood of the enemy, before it is to be returned to its resting place, its scabbard.

Ajju loved watching martial arts movies, especially the ones where samurais would showcase their swordfights. He remembered how important it was to circle the opponent, maintaining eye contact at all times.

Viren looked calm, relaxed, expecting Ajju to tense up in combat. "If you are tight, your muscles not loose, then you will not be able to act with speed, which can be fatal" Viren advised, watching Ajju circle him still.

"Did you come here to fight or to conduct a class, Viren?" Ajju asked, taking a step towards him, his sword pointed menacingly towards him. Mockingly, Viren said, "You look like you could use a class or two, *Chaudhary hukam*! I came here to defend my clan"

"Which I honour as much as mine" Ajju cut him short, surprising him with his words. "You play with my mind with your words, Ajju. Smooth talking befits a politician, not a *yodha*! Balance! Keep your body balanced so you can strike or parry, without being hit"

Blow after blow from Viren's sword came from the left, from the right, the deft block of Ajju with his sword more of a muscle reflex than anything else. Ajju was a foot taller than Viren, an advantage that the latter took with immediate effect.

He swooped low, ducking Ajju's blade that swished, cutting his skin with the tip of his sharpened sword. *Chaudhary* Arjun's flesh wound hardly bled, but hurt him to the point of fury. Viren waited for Ajju to charge at him.

Ajju was blinded with fury, planning to do just that, but halted midway. "This is what you want, isn't it? To impale me with your sword, while I charge at you with anger?" "No, Ajju. I came here to teach you a lesson"

"I have no intention of killing you" Viren said, blocking another blow from Ajju. The crowd was beginning to murmur, admiring Viren's swordsmanship and questioning Ajju's. "They're talking about you, Ajju"

"About how inferior you are to me as a swordsman, although you are blue-blooded and I, a mere cow herder" "So was the *Lord Krishna*. Look what he achieved in the *Mahabharata*. I do not believe in rich or poor, powerful or helpless"

"I believe in the truth, which after all of us have left this earth, shall still prevail" Frowning at Ajju's words, Viren stopped circling him, although his sword was still pointed towards him, in the middle position.

"Attempting to get on my soft side will get you nowhere, *Chaudhary*!" "Again..the truth is what is, Viren, Not what we want to believe. But yes, you are right. It is too late" Ajju's blow came from nowhere, as Viren had become overconfident of his swordsmanship.

The deep gash in his stomach made him stumble backwards, but regain his stepping and stronghold of the sword. "Ajju! Viren! Stop this nonsense right now!"

Akash and Giriraj shouted from the *jharokha* overlooking the platform strip that was beginning to change colour with drops of their children's blood. "*Baasa*, what're you doing here?" Viren said, cringing at the pain that shot through the open wound. "*Chup karo*! (Be quiet!)"

"You are shaming me right now by questioning my authority as your father, as the old *Panch* member of Bassi. Akash *Bhaisa* took our consent, before making Ajju the *Chaudhary* of the *Raikas*"

"Whose honour were you trying to defend, when your own is being crushed by the sword in your hand?" Giriraj and Akash had walked down the steps to the platform, taking the swords away from the two, fighting men.

"Blood has been spilled. Put your swords back in your scabbards. Do not utter a word to each other or us, till you reach the hospital. If we take you home in this condition, your mothers will die of shock!"

Akash looked up at the crowd of onlookers. "Would you have consented to your children shedding blood, while others watched? They aren't gladiators fighting for entertainment. If, God forbid, a life would have been lost, each of you would be behind bars!"

"May *Lord Shiva* and *Ma Bhavani* have mercy on your souls, for the crime you committed today. You all are required to be someplace else, so make yourselves useful. Go back to the village and get to work. Leave!"

The city of Jaipur was luckily closer to *Chand Baori* than Bassi. Akash called Dr. Shekhawat to inform him that he was bringing in two young men, who needed his personal attention. He also mentioned that it ought to be kept quiet, as the prestige of Bassi was at stake.

Dr. Shekhawat returned the favour of Akash upholding his honour, his reputation once, considering his old debt now paid. When Ajju and Viren were admitted, they were kept in a double room with single cots, so that the level of secrecy could be maintained.

Dr. Shekhawat recognized Ajju as *Chaudhary* Arjun, who dropped him to Jaipur. When he got to know who the other man was, what his reason of the swordfight originated as, he found himself in double minds.

The doctor had to choose between either being a bystander who watches everything indifferently, or, someone who breaks his silence to clarify a matter between two warring factions. Dr. Shekhawat chose to break his silence that day.

He sent Ajju to walk around the corridor with a stick, while he told Viren everything there was to tell about Tara and himself. Viren turned his face away, tears of shame falling into the pillow. "What have I done, Doctor *Saheb!*"

"You played into her hands, Viren. That is the biggest mistake you made. You father is a good man. Living a simple life with honour is far more admirable, than living a life that has been over-shadowed by corrupted power"

The doctor left the hospital, letting his patients and their guardians rest for the night. Akash had called the *haveli* to inform Bindiya that Ajju was fine. They were to return the next day. They didn't want Rati to get anxious, as by now it was understood she was expecting.

Giriraj on the other hand, chose not to call Tara. He called Malika instead, asking her to inform every one of the Anands and Prataps to come to the *haveli*, the coming day. "Tell them, Giriraj has requested it. They will come"

When Ajju reached the *haveli* the next day, he was given a hero's welcome. Viren was kept in the guest room, sedated heavily, leaving him groggy and disoriented. Giriraj left Malika at the *haveli* to take care of her brother, who came as soon as she heard he was wounded.

She was accompanied by the senior Prataps, the senior Anands, Dhanush, and her new husband Nandish. The moment Malika had eloped with Andy, Sangharsh and Nalini thought it would be best to get them married immediately, which they did in Delhi.

"*Aawo*, Giriraj. Where have you been all night? Should I not worry about you? Viren is nowhere to be seen either. What is this family coming to?" "Come here, my pet" Giriraj said affectionately.

When she went closer to him, his soft expression crystallized to ice. "The biggest mistake I made was marry a down-trodden, wayward, selfish woman like you. I almost paid the price of my sin yesterday, when I watched Viren as he was about to bleed to death!"

Tara's eyes opened wide as she clasped his hands. "My boy! My boy! Take me to him! How badly is he hurt? Where is he? Say something please!" "Tara, Viren is fine. But, we do not need you to poison our lives anymore"

"I have spoken to Dr. Shekhawat. I will file for a divorce on the grounds of adultery. The doctor will testify to prove, that you are the reason why this marriage is over" She fell on his knees, begging for a second chance.

"Go lead your life the way you want to. Do not come anywhere near Bassi, or my children. If I find out otherwise, you will be arrested for aiding and abetting a fugitive. Yes Tara, I know all that you have been up to!"

"Pack your bags, take whatever money you want. Leave!" Giriraj left the house she had had multi-coloured, to get extra attention from the villagers. He should have put his foot down from the start.

But he always gave in to appease Tara, who never shied away from using her beauty, whenever the need arose. Tara prepared to leave for her sister's place at Jodhpur, after packing her bags. She didn't attempt to meet her children or Giriraj, who she knew was stationed at the *haveli*, awaiting her departure.

She looked around the house she once called her home, the stained glass windows, the coloured walls, the curios of gods and goddesses in terracotta, all looking at her with shame. She had finally conceded to the battle of the conscience.

Her hunger for power, craving for ambition, made her daughter elope, made her son enter a sword fight that could've taken his life, made her meek husband threaten her with a divorce. She never lost her self-respect. What she did, was strangle it with her bare hands.

"Giriraj *Chachaji*, I must go to meet Tara *Chachi* before she leaves" Ajju said, still limping on his stick. Giriraj had declared his plans for Tara, sitting in front of everyone at the courtyard. "Viren is like a brother to me"

"In his absence, while he rests to let his wounds heal, this is the least I can do. Come *Chaudhrain*, we need to wish someone luck to start afresh" Watching the couple leave, tears welled into the eyes of all who stood there under the *Gulmohar* tree.

"You have chosen well, Akash *Bhaisa*. You have chosen well" Giriraj said, wiping his tears. Tara was bolting the front door, when the *Chaudhary* and *Chaudhrain* reached the doorstep. "Gloat all you want. I have no fight left in me, Ajju"

"There was never any fight. At least not from my side. I must tell you a few things. Use them to start afresh" Tara kept her bags down to face him. The words of *Chaudhary* Arjun Chand began thus.

"If you stand tall, are true to yourself, you will rest well at nights when the universe is conspiring to either get what you're striving towards, or to teach you a lesson you truly deserve. Choose with caution what you say and do"

"If the past hasn't taught you anything, then you haven't learnt the lesson yet. Walk to where you want to be. Walk right into your destiny. There is no age to start again…and again. Never give up on yourself to take the first step"

"Never underestimate the potent power of an individual, *Chachiji*. Those who have travelled to the other side of fear, will know that no one is indispensable, possibly because life doesn't always give you second chances"

"Those who feel they are at the giving end, must know that nothing lasts forever. Be mindful of what others do to you, in reciprocation of actions propelled by yourself. It would be foolish not to be aware, that the Receiver will one day be in your place"

"Be ready to thereby be judged, of whether you are worthy of the compassion you will seek, as is the balance of nature. The perspective of any human other than yourself may seem skewed at first, but it should never be undermined"

"To agree to disagree, is as important as to live and let live. Stop focusing on what you have been deprived of. Start questioning what you have been depriving yourself of. The most honourable often get the most criticized, but that's just part of what makes them strong"

"The rudder to your boat will move the way your hand holds its lever. When there is no way out, create one. When you create, you overlap what is destroyed. Change needs courage. Move on, or move over"

"Time stops for no one, so do not expect it to stand still for you. Growing from the inside will begin to reflect on the outside. Be the tree that shades others from the glare, or the bonsai that is incapable of helping even itself"

Tara stood still listening to *Chaudhary* Arjun Chand give his sage advice, before she began her new journey towards a new life. "I'm scared of being alone" she whispered, afraid of not being wanted by anyone.

"We all are born alone and die alone as well. The journey of life hasn't ended for you yet. Be your own friend and you'll never be alone again" Ajju said, folding his hands into a *Namaste* and walking back with Rati.

"Ajju!" They turned back to watch the beautiful Tara, clutching on to her bags. "Is it too late to apologize?" "It is never too late for anything till we are breathing, *Chachi*. Let me speak with *Chachaji*"

"Sit on your favourite *jhula* a bit. I will send for you soon" Ajju went back to the *haveli* and spoke to Giriraj. He requested him to give her one more chance. "An idle mind is a devil's workshop"

"If I show you a way by which we could keep her busy throughout the day, would you let her stay?" Giriraj nodded, taken aback by Ajju's brilliant suggestion.

Tara could stay under the condition of being the Vice-Principal of Gurukul, with *Chaudhary* Arjun as its Principal. Contrary to what everyone thought, Tara accepted the generous offer, putting in her heart and soul at her new workplace.

# CHAPTER FIFTY

Ramona was watching the ice cubes swirl, as they dissolved in her large whiskey. Where did her life go? She had money to afford anything she wanted. She could buy anyone she wanted too. Ramona sat in her room, surrounded by luxury, dressed in designer wear, sipping one of the most expensive brands of whiskey. Alone.

All alone. She missed Mia. She even missed Diana. At least there was someone at the hospital, even if it was Diana. She watched the ice melt into water, tiny crystals settling on the outside that wet her fingers.

A drop of tear fell into the glass, as she kept it aside. Someone had rung the bell, to shake her out of her misery, her padded cell of forced loneliness. "Who is it?" she asked, looking through the peephole, before she opened the door.

"It's the Duty Manager, Madame" Opening the locks to enquire why she was being disturbed at such an unearthly hour, she froze when Arjun smiled at her, flanked by two serious looking men standing behind him.

"You!" "Who else were you expecting? Tara? She is in truckloads of trouble as well. Unlike you though, she has been given another chance. Can we come in?" Ramona stepped aside, letting Arjun enter.

He asked the policemen to wait outside, The Duty Manager was used to make Ramona open the door. Now that the job was done, the Manager hastily left the discomfort zone. "You've come to mock me while I'm getting arrested?"

Looking at the glass kept at the side table, Arjun turned to her, "Drinking alone without anyone to celebrate with? Not much of a victory celebration, Ramona!" "I never liked your sense of humour, Arjun"

"Who told you I was joking? I am serious. Dead serious. And you know what they say- Dead men tell no tales, right?" Ramona felt the icy feeling of entrapment climbing like a creeper through her feet, rooting her to where she stood.

"I've often wondered where these people have disappeared to. Let's start with Tanisha, shall we? She was spying for you. One fine day, she poofs into thin air. Then there was poor Gerard Cotton and Diana's mother, the nurse"

"What was her name again? Ah, yes. Isabella. My, my! You have been busy covering your tracks, haven't you?" "I don't know what you're talking about. Get out of my room" "I will. But first, I want you to hear this"

"Mia felt used by you. She never loved you either. She pitied you, because you always wanted more than she, or anyone else could give. She loathed the way you used to treat Diana and took special care of her, as her way of covering up for your meanness"

"No one stooped her from calling you, when you assumed we were brainwashing her, Ramona. She opted for it all by herself. We all tried to convince her to keep in touch with you, but she refused. She said, she had had enough of dancing to your tune"

"How do you know about Tara?" Ramona asked, managing to shift her body weight from one slim leg to another. "The chauffeur you had bribed to spy on me called Mohan, now works for the hotel you stand in, as we speak"

"He is the one who dropped Tara, to the outskirts of Bassi. He told on you, Ramona. Do you know why? Because, you may have the money to buy anyone, but you'll never have enough to buy everyone"

"I'll be back. Wait and watch, Arjun Pratap" "Oh no, you won't! This time, I've made sure you rot in prison till the end of your days, so forget about your coming back. Do you see the two men standing outside?"

"They are not the state police. They are not even the local police. They're CBI and you will be handed over as a fugitive to Interpol, who have been searching for you for quite a while" It was over. Ramona knew it.

"Please, Arjun. For old times' sake" she said, walking up to him, her eyes pleading for mercy. "Yes, Ramona. This is what I owed you. So consider a debt paid..for old times' sake" Arjun walked off, leaving the sinister Ramona to the plain-clothed policemen.

He reached Swarn Niwas finally, resting his head on Suhani's lap. "Tomorrow we go to Bassi for Rati, our daughter-in-law's *godbharai*. But today, I want you all to myself. Only to myself" he said, their needs removing the gaps between them, making them one, as they were always meant to be.

The Anands were back from work, calling over the Prataps for dinner, Dhanush was clicking pictures of the two couples who were walking in the moonlit lawn, that smelt of all the fragrant flowers that were in bloom, the colours ranging from the softest of whites to the starkest of marsala-reds.

Annie and Abhi just couldn't cease from conversing about anything, everything under the sun. Andy and Malika were quieter, the occasional talk as couples do, making any third person see they were much in love.

"Dhanush, quit torturing them with your flashbulb and get over here!" Suhani called her younger son to the living room. He stood in the centre and began clicking pictures of the four friends sitting together.

"Hey! What do you think you're doing, kiddo?" Sangharsh enquired. "The flash just hit my eye. Now all I can see is my beautiful wife without a nose!" "I'm taking pictures of everything to show Leenata what she could have seen too, were she here with me"

"Besides, during one of our talks, she asked me to show her pictures of the four of you together. I noticed that in all these years, you don't even have one to show! So this is my project as per her instructions"

When children begin to notice their parents while other things take up their time, their energy, it is overwhelming when a child shows attention to those who raised him, keeping everything aside.

"Leenata is a special girl, indeed" Arjun said, noticing a visible change in his son since she entered his life. "I'm special too!" Dhanush protested. Andy slapped his head jokingly, saying, "You are an idiot!"

"You should have eloped with Leena while you had the chance! If you did, then we'd be saved from your crazy flashbulb torture moments!" Laughter echoed across the mansion, promising many more moments, like the one they all were merrily a part of. The Prataps and Anands were happy once again.

News of Rati's *godbharai* had made them all feel like their family was bestowed by the generosity of the Gods up there. "I want to be a grandmother too!" Nalini cribbed, pouting at Sangharsh. "Don't look at me. I can't help you with that!"

"As far as I go, I don't want to be a grandfather ever!" A rain of slaps came down on Sangharsh from Arjun and Nalini. "What an awful thing to say!" Nalini said. "What's the matter with you, *dost*? Don't you think before you speak anymore?" Arjun yelled.

"Stop, stop! Hear me out" When they finally stopped, the explanation he gave made them start to slap him all over again. He said, "I don't want to ever get old. Grandparents are older than parents. I have reached the end of my tether!"

It was late at night when the Prataps reached Swarn Niwas. Nalini had given gifts and jewellery for Rati's *godbharai*. They couldn't tear themselves from their business this time, but they did promise to make it to Bassi, when the baby arrived.

"I hope the gifts for the baby are all in pink? Ajju is certain he will have a daughter" Suhani said. "Even if it is a boy, only a real man can wear pink!" Sangharsh told her, ending the evening with a hearty dose of good humour.

Malika had given a letter for her parents as well as one for Viren, her brother. "To tell them I am safe and happy here" she added shyly. Loaded with all the gifts and good wishes, Arjun and Suhani left for Swarn Niwas, to rest for the day.

Dhanush couldn't sleep that night, for his wedding was only a few days away from Rati's *godbharai* ceremony. He called Leenata who was equally excited to be with him, never to be apart again.

At Bassi, Ajju and Rati were eagerly awaiting for their arrival as well. Jiya, Leenata and Rati had become thick as thieves, inseparable, whenever they were together. Rati was full of ideas, which Jiya could use.

Leenata was, as her name always suggested, full of humility which Rati could use. Jiya had a strong command over English as a language, both written and spoken, which both Leenata and Rati could use.

Good friends grow together, allowing each to flap their wings, prodding them to fly. It's almost like watching fledglings attempt to learn to take flight, for the first time. Viren could now walk straight, since his wound had healed completely.

He was made the *Chote Thakur* of Bassi who controlled all the livestock, even of the farmers. He taught them new methods to improve their chances of raising healthier cattle. Other livestock owners began to look up to *Chote Thakur* Viren, for advice related to their livestock.

He got a set of herders to breed herd of camels which would be a definite attraction for tourists, who associated the animal with a desert state. Vansh, Ajju and Viren had become close, eating at least one meal a day together, to discuss matters.

*Chote Sardar* Vansh became *Chaudhary* Arjun Chand's right hand. *Chote Thakur* Viren became his left. As a team, the trio recovered almost any written off situation, with regard to the village, by working with each other for their common aim-the betterment of Bassi.

*Chote Thakur* Viren's mother Tara, had begun to show interest in Gurukul, telling children stories, teaching them her favourite subject-History. She spent her evenings with Giriraj. Somewhere between morning *chai* and evening walks, they became compatible companions.

It was a relief for a lot of people, to see things smoothen out between the two. It was an even greater relief to see their son Viren laughing more, enjoying his work, without the perpetual cloudy frown hanging over him.

Yes. Life at Bassi was looking up, since the storm clouds of dismay were lifted from it. "How can you be sure we'll have a daughter, Ajju?" Rati asked him, while he was checking the net on his tablet.

The problem of the internet and mobile connectivity was solved, the moment the government sanctioned Bassi's loan for Agritourism. "Because I have magical powers!" he said, looking at her.

"Oh, really?" "Yes, really!" "And what else do you know through your magic?" "That after our daughter is born, you will give me a son exactly a year later!" "A year? Not two?" "No, Rati. One year" "After that?" "After that we'll raise them till they grow up" "And after that?"

"After that we'll grow old together and may even live to see our grandchildren" "I like this magical story" Rati said, smiling at him while combing her long hair. "Then, let's live this story and it will become magically real!"

Ajju held her in his arms, eagerly awaiting the enigma wrapped in a riddle, the next *Chaudhary* or *Chaudhrain* of Bassi. He liked the phrase 'enigma wrapped in a riddle', choosing to suggest it as the next theme to Dhanush, for the Dare To Dream gallery.

He made a mental note of it as it had to be mentioned to his father, who was bringing his *Maasa* to Bassi for the *godbharai* the coming day. Pitch black darkness enveloped the skies in Ajju's dream that night.

The light drizzle of rain made him smell the wet earth, no longer parched, no longer yearning. "It is a good feeling, isn't it?" Dhanush Chand looked at his son, Arjun, who was sitting alongside him, watching the shine of the raindrops through the darkness.

"There is no light, but I can still see the rain, *Baasa*" "Yes. You can feel it more than see it. The land will prosper and flourish under your reign, Arjun.

You have proven your true leadership by depriving neither Vansh nor Viren of ranks they have always wanted"

"Now they will help you raise Bassi to what it used to be, when I was the *Chaudhary*" The rain stopped as suddenly as it had started, leaving behind clear night skies with stars that dazzled as if they had been newly washed.

The full moon shone on the glistening leaves of a rose, a rose like none other. It had a child's face on it, with cornflower blue eyes and everything else from the forehead to the lips just like Ajju's Rati.

"Is that my daughter, *Baasa*?" "Yes, *betaji*. This is my granddaughter Raksha. You must never anger her, for she is the incarnate of *Ma Bhavani* herself. She will excel at being the *Chaudhrain*. You must help her grow, in any way you can"

Ajju woke up well-rested, his smile giving away his having dreamt a beautiful dream. "You look like you've dreamt of mermaids all night!" Rati joked. "Better" Ajju replied, taking his cup of tea from her.

"I dreamt of my birth father, Dhanush *Baasa*. He showed me our daughter, Rati. She is going to be as beautiful as you. We will name her Raksha. Do you like it?" "Raksha…" Rati said, walking around the room, her *odhni* elegantly covering her seven-month old baby bump.

"The baby just kicked, Ajju! Look!" Rati said 'Raksha' and the foetus kicked Rati from within. "If she likes it, I like it!" Rati said, putting an end to the matter there and then. "She? How do you know it's a she?!" Ajju asked, as he pulled her leg.

"Well *Chaudhary hukam*, I thought you had magical powers! You do know I will always believe whatever you say, don't you?" "And why is that?" he asked, letting her rest her head on his shoulder, while she sat on the *baithak* beside him.

"Because I love you" This was the first time Rati had said the three magical words, that if truly meant, could intertwine the destinies of two souls together. "Say it again" he asked, greedily. "I love you, Ajju" He kissed her on the lips, looking into her eyes.

"I love you, Rati" At one time, Ajju would have thought it was not manly to be mushy, like women were. But ever since he met Rati, he realized his life, the kind of life that he had always envisioned for himself, had only just begun.

Looking out of the Mercedes, Suhani asked Dhanush to drop Arjun and herself at the boundary of Bassi and continue to drive himself to the *haveli.* Dhanush knew his parents to be a whimsical, eccentric couple who were also in love.

He left them as they desired and sped away to the destiny that eagerly awaited him-Leenata. Walking into the reddish boundary that is called *gerua* colloquially, Suhani began to talk as freely as the breeze that blew through them.

She spoke to Arjun about the changes Ajju, Vansh, Viren and all their better halves had contributed to, to improve on Bassi. "Where does Rati want to have the baby? Have you asked her?" Arjun asked, waving at Viren who waved back while riding his horse miles away.

"She said Ajju wants her to have the baby right here at the *haveli.* Dr. Shekhawat is in constant touch with Ajju and from Rati's ninth month, there will be a nurse on call stationed at the *haveli* itself"

Sighing, Arjun remarked, "How things change, *Beendni.* First there used to be midwives, now there are nurses on call!" Giggling at his observation, she picked a twig of *kikar,* saying, "Will we ever change, Arjun?"

"On the outside- yes. But on the inside…never" "But we must grow on the inside as well, shouldn't we?" "We love each other since the beginning. We will continue to love each other till the end"

"We understand each other better now..but love..that just remains. When I think of love, I think of you. Not the mother of my children, not the woman I married..just you" Suhani turned to him a few feet away from the *Chaudhary haveli,* stretching her private moment with Arjun.

Arjun rested his palm on her cheek, an action of her *Saheb* she loved. "Our new generation has found their partners to shower love on, Braids. People come. People go. The feelings are the ones that remain. Love is after all..Sempiternal"

Seeing her smile, glow as if his love had touched hers again, he tugged her hand, "Come on, they haven't seen us yet. Let's go for another round. Sing me that song you were singing Braids, when I saw you for the first time"

They went to the same field where Arjun saw her first. He went and sat on the boulder he once hid behind, to take pictures of Suhani. She walked near him, swaying with the song she sang, all the way up to the finish.

"Sempiternal?" she asked him, putting her hand out. Grabbing his Braids' palm and pulling her close, he breathed life into her face in one breath..with one word.. "Sempiternal!"

# ETHNIC TERMS

## RELATIONS

- *Baasa:* father
- *Maasa*: mother
- *Bhaisa, bhai, Bhaiya*: brother
- *Behan*: sister
- *Bhabhisa, Bhabhi*: sister-in-law
- *Choti bahu*: younger daughter-in-law
- *Badi bahu*: elder daughter-in-law
- *Khandaan*: dynasty
- *Beta, Betaji*: son
- *Beti, Bitiya*: daughter
- *Chachiji/ Chachi:* paternal uncle
- *Chachaji/ Chacha/ Chachu*: paternal aunt
- *Dost / Yaar:* friend
- *Jaaneman*: sweetheart
- *Saheb*: sir
- *Memsahib*: madam
- *Beendni/ Lugai/ Ardhangini:* wife
- *Beend*: husband
- *Chaudhary:* village head (male)
- *Chaudhrain*: wife of the village head, or village head (female)
- *Bhaylian*: lady friends
- *Maatsa*: teacher
- *Rishta*: liaison, alliance
- *Samdhan*: parent of son-in-law or daughter-in-law
- *Saasuma*: mother-in-law
- *Saheli*: friend (female)
- *Chote Sardar*: next in line for being a *Chaudhary*
- *Chote Thakur*: one rank below *Chote Sardar* in the village hierarchy

- *Taiji*: paternal Aunt
- *Daisa*: village nurse or someone of similar capacity
- *Maharani*: queen
- *Maharaja*: king
- *Chori*: girl

# ETHNIC APPAREL

- *Anarkali*: *salwar* suit for women with long gathers
- *Pallu*: part of a sari that is hung around the shoulder
- *Mukkaish*: studded mirror-like pattern, similar to metallic polka dots on cloth
- *Sharara*: lose pants in silk, satin or cotton
- *Churidar*: cotton or lycra leggings as part of lower ethnic apparel
- *Jawahar* jacket: a sleeveless jacket made mostly of *khadi* or cotton, for men
- *Sherwani*: an ethnic overcoat for men
- *Khadi*: a material made exclusively by spinning cotton
- *Angarkha*: a short top tied on the side with strings, for men
- *Sari*: a nine-yard drape, worn by Indian women
- *Salwar*: lose lowers worn by both genders
- *Ghaghra choli*: long skirt with gathers and well-embellished tops for women
- *Dhoti-kurta*: loose cloth draped as lowers and a long, full shirt, for men
- *Pagdi*: turban; ethnic headgear made with bright cloth (usually cotton)
- *Zari*: metallic thread used for embroidery, usually on silken cloth
- *Patiala salwar*: very loose trousers worn by both genders
- *Chunni / Odhni / Ghoonghat:* head cover for women
- *Leheriya:* rainbow print typical of Rajasthan
- *Mojri:* footwear made of camel leather
- *Gota:* a shiny, metallic thread made to add glimmer to any fabric
- *Bandhni*: print typical of Rajasthan

# ETHNIC JEWELLERY

> *Mang tikka*: a piece hung by a chain atop the centre of a woman's forehead

> *Jhumka*: metallic earrings that hang with an upside down cone, of various shapes and sizes

> *Hasli*: thick neck piece

> *Bindi*: a coloured adornment stuck at the centre of the forehead, also associated with the third eye

> *Payal*: anklet

> *Ghunghroo*: bell to adorn any accessory

> *Navratnas*: nine gems

> *Lac*: coloured work with clay, on accessories

> *Meenakari*: coloured work on metal, for accessories

> *Kadha*: thick metal bangle

> *Kundan*: uncut diamonds, set usually in gold

# ETHNIC CUSTOMS AND DIETIES

➢ *Bholenath/ Shiva*: the God of Destruction, revered in India
➢ *Ma Bhavani/ Goddess Durga*: the Goddess of strength, revered in India
➢ *Om*: the symbol of Hindus
➢ *Mahabharata*: an epic tale of Indian history
➢ *Lord Krishna*: one of the Gods of Indian mythology
➢ *Muh dikhayee*: seeing the face of the newly-wedded bride or soon-to-be bride for the first time, when usually gifts are bestowed to the lady
➢ *Tikka:* anointing the forehead with vermillion paste and *chandan* (sandalwood paste) as a sign of prayer and celebration
➢ *Pranaam*: touching the feet of elders as a sign of respect
➢ *Saptapadi*: the seven circles of oath taken around the holy fire, as a part of the marriage ceremony in Hindus
➢ *Sindoor*: vermillion or red powder put by women in India, as a symbol of being married
➢ *Muhurat / Shubh muhurat*: astrologically favourable time for an important function such as marriage or a child's first ceremony, etc
➢ *Namaste*: joining hands together as a sign of respect
➢ *Thaali*: a big, metallic plate
➢ *Puja*: prayer
➢ *Rasam:* custom
➢ *Gauna:* wedding night
➢ *Godbharai:* similar to a baby shower
➢ *Kundali:* birth chart's planetary configuration
➢ *Gun Milap:* a couple's birth chart comparison, to check compatibility
➢ *Manglik:* an inauspicious condition that can be rectified through certain practices
➢ *Maryaada*: tradition
➢ *Phera*: circles taken by the bride and groom; seven *phera*s make the *Saptapadi* ceremony
➢ *Byaav:* marriage
➢ *Sagai:* engagement
➢ *Patri:* birth chart
➢ *Rakhi*: silken thread tied by a sister to her brother, pledging his immortal protection
➢ *Ashirwad*: blessings

# VILLAGE DELECTABLES

➢ *Parathas* (*Gobi, Mooli* and *Aloo*): indian flour pancakes stuffed with boiled vegetables, laced with delicious spices (stuffing varieties: cauliflower, white radish, potato)

➢ *Thandai* (*Kesar*): a cooling drink made with saffron and cold milk

➢ *Bel sherbet*: a cooling drink said to bring down the body temperature, on a hot day

➢ *Khichdi*: wet rice and lentil concoction

➢ *Kadhi chawal*: rice and curd curry with curry leaves

➢ *Pulao* (*Jeera/ Peas*): fried rice with (aniseed/green peas)

➢ *Alu matar/ Alu Gosht /Aloo pyaaz ki sabzi /alu ki sabzi*: peas and potato/ spiced potato / potato and onion/ plain potato vegetable dishes

➢ *Nankhatai*: crumbly biscuit usually flavoured with cardamom

➢ *Matar paneer*: cottage cheese and green peas curry

➢ *Kachori*: fried flour pancake with various stuffings

➢ *Masoor dal*: lentil soup

➢ *Ghee*: clarified butter

➢ *Achar*: pickle

➢ *Murabba/ Aamka murabba*: chutney/ mango chutney

➢ *Papad*: crunchy, spiced chips similar to nachos in taste

➢ *Haldi*: turmeric

➢ *Dal makhni*: a thick gravy dish with a variety of dark lentils

➢ *Rumali roti*: an indian pancake made essentially through layering

➢ *Chaat*: a spicy snack usually sold on the streets in India

➢ *Chole bhature*: chick peas curry, with yeast-induced flour tortillas on the side

➢ *Raita*: thinned curd

➢ *Rasgulla*: a sweetmeat

➢ *Sohan halwa*: a sticky sweetmeat

➢ *Mithai*: sweetmeats

➢ *Laddoo* (*Boondi*): circular sweetmeat made with small pieces of *besan*, dipped in sugar syrup

➢ *Jalebi*: spiral sweetmeat coated in sugar syrup

➢ *Rasamalai*: another sweetmeat made with flavoured milk

➢ *Phirni*: a dessert made with milk, boiled white rice and sugar

- *Gulab jamun*: dark sweetmeat balls
- *Gajrela*: sweet dessert pudding, made with finely grated carrots
- *Moong dal ka halwa*: a dessert made with lentil, popular in north India
- *Chai (Adrak* and *Masala)*: tea flavoured with (ginger and spices)
- *Churan*: a digestive, tasty sweet
- *Ram laddoo*: a variety of *churan*
- *Laal maans:* meat cooked with spicy gravy
- *Paan supari*: betel leaf with tiny broken nuts
- *Samosa*: a triangular fillet, stuffed usually with spicy mashed potatoes
- *Bajra*: a crop prevalent in the north of India
- *Dal baati*: a popular dish in Rajasthan
- *Lal mirch ka achar*: red chillies pickle
- *Boondi raita*: thinned curd with little balls of friend *besan* floating in it
- *Mirch ki tipore*: stuffed chillies pickle
- *Amla*: a dried digestive
- *Lehsun ki Chutney*: garlic chutney

# COLLOQUIAL DIALECT

- *Haan*: yes
- *Na*: no
- *Bas:* stop, enough
- *Baitho*: sit
- *Firangan*: foreigner
- *Pagli*: mad, silly, crazy (usually said affectionately)
- *Matlab*: meaning
- *Kain*: why
- *Khammaosa*: similar to *Namaste*
- *Padhaku*: someone who is always with a book (teasing usage)
- *Ladhaku*: someone who is always about to pick an argument (teasing usage)
- *Ankhon ka sharam*: minding the elders while attempting any act in their presence
- *Arre*: an expression of irritation, restlessness or urgency
- *Chanda*: donation
- *Amaanat*: treasure
- *Bawle*: crazy (said jokingly)
- *Jaao*: go

# <u>MISCELLANEOUS</u>

- ➤ *Chaukhat*: entrance to a room or house
- ➤ *Rasoi*: kitchen
- ➤ *Ashram*: a place of penance or religious significance
- ➤ *Baithak*: sitting area
- ➤ *Chatai*: cane mat used to cover windows, or simply to sit on
- ➤ *Palang*: coir bed
- ➤ *Chaudhary haveli*: the mansion of the village head
- ➤ *Angan*: courtyard
- ➤ *Jhoola*: swing usually made of cane or metal
- ➤ *Talwar*: sword
- ➤ *Yodha*: warrior
- ➤ *Cheetal*: type of deer
- ➤ *Matki*: clay, earthenware pot
- ➤ *Kullad*: clay cup
- ➤ *Katori*: a bowl usually made of steel
- ➤ *Kohinoor*: the famous diamond originally from India
- ➤ *Har har Mahadev! Jai Ma Bhavani*: Religious slogans in honour of the local dieties
- ➤ *Bidi*: local cigarette
- ➤ *Lathait*: bodyguard
- ➤ *Vidhi*: religious or scripture-based procedure
- ➤ *Gerua*: reddish-brown boundary design prevalent all over Rajasthan
- ➤ *Gulmohar*: tree that gives cardinal-red flowers
- ➤ *Peepal*: the only tree in the world that gives oxygen both in the day and night; revered as a religious symbol to be prayed in India
- ➤ *Kikar*: a prickly tree usually seen in desert or arid lands
- ➤ *Pithoo*: a game played with stones and sponge balls
- ➤ *Dhaba*: village restaurant
- ➤ *Kul pundit / pundit/ panditji*: priest
- ➤ *Hookah*: smoking pipe
- ➤ *Diya*: clay candle holder
- ➤ *Raika*: camel-breeding tribe of Rajasthan
- ➤ *Banjara/ Banjaran*: nomadic tribe/tribal of Rajasthan
- ➤ *Marwari*: local dialect of Rajasthan/ variety/ regional

- ➤ *Kathiawari*: variety/ region of Rajasthan
- ➤ *Hindi*: language spoken in India
- ➤ *Rajasthani*: of/from Rajasthan
- ➤ *Maike*: bride's home
- ➤ *Rajput*: royal house of Rajasthan
- ➤ *Mandir*: temple
- ➤ *Panchayat*: village council
- ➤ *Lathi*: long stick/ sceptre
- ➤ *Potli / Jhola:* large cloth pouch made to carry food, clothes, etc
- ➤ *Tila*: hillock
- ➤ *Bharoont*: cattle fodder
- ➤ *Bharauti*: headload of grass for feeding cattle
- ➤ *Palang ka paer*: wooden leg of a coir bed
- ➤ *Mandap*: the place where those participating in a religious ceremony sit together with the priest, conducting a puja

# MITSY PLAYMATES

# PHOTOGRAPHY BY NAVTEJ SINGH

# STUDIO ONE

# TIMELESS INDIAN BEAUTIES

Printed in the United States
By Bookmasters